Amphibious

Amphibious

Naomi M. Wong

PAPERBACK ISBN: 978-1-7377275-1-4
HARDCOVER ISBN: 978-1-7377275-0-7
EBOOK ISBN: 978-1-7377275-2-1

Cover art by: fiverr.com/jannatulnisa

Credits for cover photo from Creative Commons:
"Panamanian Golden Frog female Atelopus zeteki" by brian.gratwicke
is licensed under CC BY 2.0. This image was altered for the creation
of the book cover.
https://www.flickr.com/photos/19731486@N07/5009622139

https://creativecommons.org/licenses/by/2.0/legalcode

Author headshot by Claire Garner Photography

Published by Naomi M. Wong
naomimwong.com

To my family, who encouraged my creative spirit
To my Writers 'Ohana, who journeyed with me on this road
To the Lover of My Soul, who is the Giver and Restorer of All Life

Author's Note

Dear Reader,

As an artist, I am comfortable with a fair amount of ambiguity surrounding my work—my fiction particularly. I write stories about things that I like and things that I don't like, things which I admire and things which I find morally reprehensible, and I don't always directly label what is what. I take this approach because I know that my worldview has blind spots. It is also dynamic. It changes as I learn, empathize with others, and learn some more. In the same vein, I submit my art to you, not for blind acceptance but for the provocation of thought and discussion as well as to contribute to that process of learning and empathizing. However, there are some things I must address before releasing you to observe, mull over, and interpret my work.

First of all, the pacing of *Amphibious* may seem odd to you. It starts with action, then slows down, then speeds up again. Issues of great significance will seem to take the back burner for a time as a new reality comes to the fore. I assure you that this is intentional. It portrays, in the very structure of the narrative, the effects of dissociation. Dissociation is a coping mechanism that can slow down the impact of trauma from the survivor's perspective, but this coping mechanism often ends up looking a lot like denial until the truth wreaks so much havoc that it is unable to be ignored. It is a way to survive, but it is no way to live.

Amphibious was so much fun to write! I was really in my element, working with biracial main characters and including glorious nuggets of mixed-race humor throughout. However, I must clarify my representation of Neo-Eugenic law, which is the undergirding of society in *Amphibious*. Neo-Eugenic law is not in any way ideal. Its presence in this text should bring attention to patterns of oppressive, prejudiced thought and behavior that are alive and well in American society today. These patterns have proven to be harmful time and again, so it is worth making every effort to resist their further development. And they definitely should never be implemented in an official capacity.

Writing from a minority-minority biracial perspective, I unapologetically point out some of the harmful ways people—generally uniracial people, but not always—construct identity and society. I do this to highlight the potential consequences of establishing group identity by solidifying and policing the boundaries of racial categories that were given to us by white supremacy in the first place. As one who exists in and between a few different lines, I am painfully aware of the ways white supremacy divides and conquers people groups, pitting them against each other and even against themselves. Fear can easily become the primary motivator for every action individuals as well as communities take to survive. This process is understandable, but it is harmful.

Lastly, I do not see it as unquestionably terrible if any part of this book happens to anger you or unsettle you. We will all be better off if you voice your opinion respectfully and in a way that attempts to build bridges. None of us exists in this world alone, even if trauma, rejection, and oppression make us feel marginalized. We will not find our way back from the edge by acting as one person armies or by demanding that everyone see the world as we do. We will find our way back by learning to *be* together in all of our differences, which is admittedly easier said than done. But that's what much of life is about, anyway, isn't it?

Learning.

On this road with you,

Naomi M. Wong

Table of Contents

Chapter 1

SURVIVAL IS THE NAME OF THE GAME. After all, the world only consists of agents and patients, and survival is most often granted to those who act. Remembering that made it easy for the Agent to forget why her clothes had caught fire. At present, she was more concerned with climbing out of reach of the Doberman pinschers that had chased her across the yard. Flames crackled over her tactical suit as she scrambled up the side of the Buchanans' old mansion.

There were only two things in the whole world that the Agent feared. One was a person who was inside the mansion, but the other currently manifested in the four-legged, muscled masses of fur that were barking at her from the ground. One of the dogs jumped exceptionally high. It snapped at her foot and missed, then landed barking louder than before.

"Good grief," she grumbled as she pulled herself up and into the open window of one of the second-story guest rooms.

Once inside, the Agent beat the fire off of the front of her suit and removed it. Underneath, she wore a lacy, black bra and matching panties, which were completely impractical for the type of work she had just been doing. But such was the life of a female in her field.

Her fingers were undoubtedly burned by the suit's hot metal zipper, but she had been trained not to give much thought to such things. She didn't bother extinguishing the rest of the flames before tossing the suit out of the window. The enamel would wear off in a minute or so, and the whole thing would be a pile of ashes by the time anyone came across it.

The dogs were still barking when she slammed the window shut. There was only so much that compartmentalization could do for a person. In any case, the pesky phobia of dogs only persisted because it was carried over from—well, it had carried over.

As the adrenaline from the chase wore off, the Agent became aware that something was lodged in her bra. It was a memory drive, the old kind that no one ever used anymore. She didn't have the time to think about how she had come to possess it. David would be expecting her back at the party any second now.

She smelled smoky. Myrrh oil could overpower that scent. There was a bottle of it waiting for her on the dressing table across from the bed. She usually used myrrh oil during physical therapy, but tonight it would convey an important message, the details of which eluded her for the time being.

The Agent sat on the bed and massaged the oil into her skin. She took care with the jagged scars that ran like cream-colored fishnets along the length of her large, muscular legs. She imagined that they were still tender. In reality, however, neither the creamy scars nor even the coppery brown skin around them ever registered any pain. The Agent emptied the bottle and worked the remainder of its contents through her long, curly, black hair.

Underneath the table was a bundle she had stashed. It was a long, teal gown, and rolled up inside was her tiny, nearly functionless clutch. David had given her that purse as a reminder not to rely on bulky equipment or high-tech weapons. As he liked to say, she *was* the weapon. She generally only carried the clutch to store things that she didn't want to use, like her stockings. She stuffed the memory drive under the stockings. It would be safe there until she could remember its purpose.

The Agent put on her dress, smoothed the fabric over her hips, and took one last look in the mirror.

"It doesn't matter what you are or who you are," she told the face that stared back at her. "It's all about what people see when they look at you, which is usually fear. Theirs—or yours, if you let them."

The face in the mirror winked at her.

Showtime. She strode out into the antique-filled corridor, walking confidently but with care so that the long side-slits in her gown would not end up twisted diagonally across her thighs.

Chamber music and laughter floated up from the banquet hall. The two burly, tuxedo-wearing security guards posted by the staircase entry did not seem to notice her aroma as she approached. She knew from their hungry stares what they noticed. It was just as well. The message was not for them, anyway.

Pretending not to see them, she peered into the tiny mirror on the inside flap of her clutch to touch up her lipstick. Only after that did she choose to acknowledge the guards' presence. She simpered to give them the impression that she was embarrassed at having been caught maintaining her feminine appearance.

The guards smiled sleazily at her.

All clear. She put the lipstick away and glided between them.

"Hey!" the one on the right whispered loudly. "How much for an hour?"

He would not have spoken to her like that if she had been Class 1 like everyone else at the party. She would have liked to jab her stilettoed foot into the guard's chest, but David hated it when she caused a scene over petty issues. He had also forbidden her to flaunt the grotesque scars on her legs. The scars were—to her—proof of her strength and resourcefulness, but David did not like her to show off. That, and the scars were definitely memorable, which was not an advantage for someone in their profession. She should have worn the stockings.

Pretending that she had not heard the guard, she tried to move past without escalation.

"Hey, I'm *talking* to you, brownie!" the guard sneered, catching her by the forearm.

She fixed her icy gaze upon him. "I'll thank you to release me, sir."

He burst into laughter. "You hear that uppity accent, Morris? The Class 3 whore talks like a Class 1 from the motherland!"

The Agent decided that she would call Morris' coworker "Horiss" since he liked to talk about whores so much. Plus, it rhymed.

"Whores'll play any role for cash," Morris chuckled, "or gunk."

The Agent's eyes flashed. "I'm not for sale. Now, for the last time, *release* me!"

The guards laughed even harder.

Horiss, who was as ugly as he was rude, was probably a foot or so taller than the Agent and about one and a half times her weight. She jiggled her captive arm gently to test his grip. The tendons in his elbow were slightly loose, probably due to an old injury.

3

Horiss drew her closer. "Come now, brownie! You must have been friendly with *someone* to get into this party. Why not be friends with me?"

He grabbed at her behind, but she took advantage of his weak, stretchy tendons and spun away from his grip. She swept his legs and twisted his arm behind his back. Morris seized her shoulder, so she flipped him into Horiss. She then stuck her foot into Morris' chest and pushed him and Horiss into the wall.

"Still feeling friendly, friends?" she asked.

Both men, flushed with shame, shook their heads. The Agent recognized that they were not ashamed of their rude behavior but rather of having been overpowered by a female.

A small crowd had amassed during their confrontation. Some older guests, who had probably come upstairs to use the restroom, were staring at them. Despite her best efforts, she had caused a scene. Here she was, a Class 3 female having scuffled with two Class 1 men in the upstairs foyer of a high society dinner party. And her scars were showing through her slit. She definitely should have worn the stockings.

It was then, and only then, that the Agent's bravado gave way to the impulse to run for her life. But before she could leap into action, she felt a firm grip on her shoulder. A sickening dread spread through her, right down to her bones. That was the grip of her husband, David. While he was known by many names, he was most commonly called 'the Killer.'

The Agent released the guards who rose gingerly to their feet.

Her husband stared coldly at the men as he addressed her, "Already hard at work embarrassing me, I see, even though I only let you out of my sight for one moment."

An interesting choice of words for a man with only one functional eye—the Agent noted—since it took little more than a turn of his head for her to be out of his sight. But she did not dare to say that aloud.

Although his pale, stern face was devoid of emotion, the Killer's reputation preceded him. Morris and Horiss needed no further prompting to make themselves scarce. They tripped down the hall to the men's restroom. All of the other onlookers also dispersed quietly and quickly. When everyone was gone, David released the Agent.

"Did you get it, Sheebs?" he asked.

"Yes, Father," she responded slowly, trying to remember what she might have gotten.

Her memory of anything before the confrontation with the security guards was surprisingly blank.

As David stared at her, he whipped his head up and to the side. His face contorted into a grotesque grimace. Though ugly and menacing, it was a common tic of his, which he used to make up for his lack of depth perception. He was trying to read her the same way that she could read him and most other people.

"Show me," he said.

She opened her clutch slowly, allowing muscle memory to guide her to the portable memory drive that was nestled under her stockings. She held it up for him to see.

"Good."

He grabbed her roughly by neck and thrust his mouth upon hers.

She held her breath briefly, then stepped back, saying, "Someone will see."

Although David's prosthetic eye remained eerily listless, angry sparks snapped in his seeing eye. However, his fury subsided as he realized that she was not rebelling against his authority but simply being her gentle, modest self. The self he had made her to be. Through his facial expressions, she could practically hear him thinking it through, reassuring himself and even relishing the fact that she always presented as so self-conscious in public while, at home, she was ostensibly given as much to passion as he was.

"Your little fingers are twitching again," he said, at last. "I told you to stop with those ridiculous replicas. Come on."

She liked the replicas because they reminded her that she was not all she appeared to be. She did not want to stop, but she did anyway.

As they descended the stairs into the banquet hall, the Agent put on her most brilliant smile and pretended not to notice that all eyes had turned toward them. They were all Class 1 eyes—green, blue, brown, or black, but Class 1 just the same—and they were judgmental. No one was even close enough to see their matching wedding bands, but word would spread soon enough. This was the awkward spectacle that she and the Killer had avoided at the beginning of the evening by being the first guests to arrive. There was no avoiding it now. Thankfully, no one would dare to question the Killer's judgment—not to his face, in any case.

The chatter in the room resumed when David pulled out the Agent's chair at their table. He sat down again in front of his half-finished plate and began to eat. Her place setting had been partially cleared so that only the cutlery remained. She was still hungry, but that was neither here nor there. David had been talking with some rugged arms dealers before she left for her errand, but now the table was full of old, rich, comfortable people.

The billionaire host of the party scooted his chair closer to the Agent's and smiled broadly.

"*Holla, senioreeda!*" he said in the most terrible Spanish she had ever heard. "*Yo soy Errol.*"

She humored him with a tiny nod but said nothing.

"She smells as nice as she looks!" Errol declared to the rest of the table.

The first half of her message had been received. The second half would only be understood at a later time. Two women on the other side of the table, one of whom was the hostess of the party, laughed politely at Errol's attempt at wit.

After the customary half of a second of chuckling, the hostess exclaimed, "Why, David! What an attractive companion you've brought tonight!"

"Greet Faye, Bathsheba," he said as he chewed.

The Agent put her hand over her heart, flicked her eyes up at the hostess, and nodded politely.

Faye looked her up and down. "What is she? A 3.7?"

"3.5 pureblood. She's spent some time outside is all."

The hostess primly pursed her lips, and the woman next to her picked up where she had left off.

"But what a lovely complexion she has! Why, would you *look* at that gorgeous, dark skin? Just like an ermine pelt, only much smoother, of course!"

As the women burst into a good-humored series of chortles, the Agent looked down at the steak knife on her placemat and thought that she might very much like to use it. She was not the only one at the table who could be reduced to a pelt.

"Well, as one so far from well born, she certainly has an exotic allure, doesn't she?" Faye said. "Although David, as one of your longtime benefactors, I *must* ask: aren't you worried at all how she'll affect your image?"

I'll make you worried about image, you eugenist witch! Just as the Agent's hand tightened around the steak knife, she felt David's grip on her thigh, reassuring but commanding. Keeping her gaze downward, she reluctantly released the knife.

"My work is my image," the Killer said casually, "and my work speaks for itself."

6

"Well, can't argue with that," Faye the Eugenist Witch responded.

Everyone else at the table nodded in agreement.

The Agent inwardly smiled. As David's protégé, she was included in his work. It wasn't much, but in his understated way, he had been standing up for her. She touched the gold band around her finger for comfort.

The conversation at the table changed direction as the ladies began to discuss their new tablecloth suppliers. Fine Syrian textiles were the new 'in' thing, and Faye had heard from Tatiana who had heard from Susan that gold, floral embroideries were next to be *en vogue*.

Errol leaned across the Agent to speak to David.

"So, a Class 3.5 pureblood. Hindi, or perhaps something Polynesian—not Spanish, then?"

"English, actually," the Agent replied.

Errol's mouth dropped open. He seemed surprised both that she could speak English and that she dared to speak to him directly. David's expression was some mix of embarrassed and proud. He wore that expression a lot.

"I was raised in England," she told Errol. "Unaffiliated England, that is. But I do speak Hindi and Spanish."

Among other languages—and places, for that matter. Depending on the situation, she could have had a childhood in as many as five different countries.

"That's very impressive!" Errol remarked. But he looked troubled.

"Is something the matter?" the Agent asked.

"No, no," he said. "It's just some gossip going around among my domestics."

She leaned toward him to avoid the appearance of defensiveness. "Gossip of what sort?"

"News of a very beautiful female in town," he replied.

The Agent glanced downward in a sign of modesty.

"A Class 3 female," he continued, "who speaks English fit for a royal court."

"Well, that's hardly something to be anxious about," the Agent said. "As David is fond of saying, I am a female of 'surprising capability.'"

"No doubt," he said, casting a nervous glance at the Killer, who was watching him intently. "But they saw this female at the clinic in Arica this afternoon. I hope you're not sick, Miss Bathsheba?"

The Agent's heart skipped a beat. If she had been in Arica, she could no longer remember why. David's gaze shifted to her. He was already thinking up some terrible, sadistic punishment for her disobedience.

She turned her dazzling smile upon Errol the Tattler.

"There must be some mistake, sir," she said. "You see, we have orders only to seek medical attention from WCE agency medics."

"Of course," Errol the Tattler backpedaled. "My domestics must have been speaking of a different, equally attractive, English-speaking, Class 3 female in Arica."

"Must have been," David repeated.

"So, David," Errol the Tattler said hurriedly, "I'm hoping you can give me an update on the antipersonnel weapon testing for the Cull. You said you'd found a solution for the Poison Arrow holdup?"

"I have, in fact," David replied. "I've made the ultimate weapon."

"I've seen a lot of weapons."

"Ever seen a weapon that becomes its target?"

"Interesting." Errol the Tattler seemed impressed. "I've heard only rumors of such things. Are you saying you've finally perfected your method?"

The Killer smirked silently in response, and their conversation turned to politics and technology. The Agent had never much cared for either of those topics since both always seemed to promise what was just out of reach and they rarely lived up to their promises. In some fashion, David shared this view, particularly with respect to technology. He insisted that she refrain from using of any of the latest gadgets lest she become dependent in the way that others had. This had been to her advantage, at least until that afternoon, when she had perhaps gone to the clinic in Arica in search of a specific kind of technology, the function of which could not be approximated by any other means.

She frantically wracked her memory, trying to will the information about the clinic back into her conscious mind. But she could not. She had been trained to store information so that it was useful only in the right circumstances and otherwise nonexistent. A pit formed in her stomach as she pondered what circumstances could possibly have compelled her to go to the clinic and forget so promptly. Whatever punishment David was dreaming up for her disobedience was the least of her problems.

At the late hour of 23:04, David bade his well-to-do hosts and their guests goodbye. Bathsheba stood poised and lovely by his side as he did so, then she glided with him to the coatcheck. They were the picture of civility and charm, but the Agent knew better than to trust in that façade. Errol's comments about the clinic had stuck with David, and David would make it his personal mission to uncover the truth.

"Miss?" A hand closed around hers.

She started and turned to find one of the coatcheck attendants holding out her dress coat. He had radiant, olive-colored skin and chestnut brown hair, and he was probably the only other non-Class 1 person at the party. She could recognize a member of the Subclass when she saw one, even if no one else could on account of his strongly European bone structure. But his secret was safe with her.

He smiled warmly. "That fragrance—it must be myrrh, am I right?"

He had strong fingers and smooth skin, charming hands for a coatcheck attendant. The Agent returned his smile and thanked him sweetly for helping her into her coat.

"My pleasure," he said, nodding respectfully.

For a moment, she thought that she might recognize him from somewhere. But the moment passed when David took hold of her arm once again. He already had his coat. It seemed that he hadn't noticed her interaction with the attendant, but his agitated expression alerted her to the fact that something had gone awry. The reception area was filled with security personnel and flustered guests.

"I'm sorry, ma'am," a security guard was saying to an angry Class 1.2 woman, "but, we're dealing with a breach of sensitive information. Until we find out who fried the drives, everyone must be searched before exiting."

"But *I* am Maureen Weatherly!" she exclaimed. "My father is Westman Weatherly who eradicated the Subclass from the American quarter of the Chinese Cooperates of Subsaharan Africa! There are three members of the World Council of Eugenics in my immediate family!"

"It's just the rules, ma'am."

"Well, this is a *fine* way to treat well-born guests! I will give Faye an earful about this!" She was practically spitting fire but nevertheless turned her coat pockets inside out and opened her purse for the officer to search.

"You fried their drives?" David hissed.

The Agent shook her head. There had been a fire, but *she* hadn't started it. Someone had set her up. But who?

It was too late to return to the banquet hall. Another member of the security staff was approaching them.

9

"Mr. Miller, Miss Bathsheba." He nodded to both of them and put his hand over his heart.

The Agent reciprocated.

"What can we do for you, sir?" she asked.

"Tom Gavins. Head of security." He glanced nervously at the Killer, then continued, "I'll need to scan you. Would you both kindly empty your pockets and, Miss, may I look in your purse?"

"This is outrageous!" David exclaimed.

"It's okay," the Agent whispered. She turned her pockets inside out and opened her purse, saying, "This old thing isn't big enough to hold anything very useful, anyway."

David looked at her quizzically. Then, as if snapping into his role, he gave permission for the search to proceed. Gavins worked quickly and did not linger around Bathsheba's pockets. He took a quick look in her purse and found nothing but her lipstick and the thick, cable-knit stockings. After that, he scanned her and David with a small device that had a blinking blue light, metal detecting, not a bioscanner.

He nodded at them. "You folks have a good night."

"Thank you, sir," the Agent said as David led her away.

***

The air was tense. It always was when David was thinking. But the Agent dared not pry into his thoughts. She stared out at the darkness. Outside the car, the arid Chilean countryside was flying past at an alarming rate. Although it was difficult to perceive the speed without any roadside lamps, she could feel it in her body, especially at the turns.

"You're in too deep with this study on Agent Thomas," David said, at last. "You need to improve your emotional regulation."

Maybe you'll take your own advice when we get home.

"I think some of what she believed actually makes sense," she replied stiffly.

"But you can't get flustered every time someone mentions classes or Neo-Eugenic law," he said. "You're a registered Class 3 female; you know your place. That's it."

"No, that's *not* it," the Agent countered. "That Faye thinks that she's 'well born' because she's got gray, translucent skin and that she's important because she married into money. And she wants to act like *I'm* some kind of animal!"

"You can only be what you are, Sheebs." He shrugged. "What you are made to be."

Yes, what I am made to be: animal, slave, weapon. To you, that is all I will ever be.

"But in a different time, in a different space, she and I could have been measured on a different scale. Maybe our roles would have been reversed, even."

"Maybe." David chuckled dismissively. "Speaking of your role, where did you stash that memory drive?"

Smiling mischievously, she said, "I planted it on one of the coatcheck attendants as he was admiring me."

The car lurched as David reacted to this news. "You *what*? We can't go back for it now!"

"Relax, Father. It was empty."

He side-glanced her through the darkness. "No trail. Clever."

"I am the weapon," she replied.

"That's what I made you to be."

"The best of the best," she grinned.

"Don't brag. You're in enough trouble as it is."

Don't brag. Don't swear. Don't touch that scanner. Don't eat away from the table. Don't chew with your mouth full—or maybe that was talk. It made her not want to eat, whatever the case. David had his rules. He got upset if they were broken. And *no one* in her right mind would want to upset the Killer.

So, she must have been very desperate to even set foot in the clinic that afternoon. Very, very desperate. David drove past the cliffside house with the red and blue paneling. And it was then that the Agent realized they were not heading home but straight to the dock.

"It's cold." She took out her stockings and pulled them on.

David said nothing for the whole, long, winding road down to the ocean. And whether *he* knew it or not, the Agent knew that this was most likely going to be a one-way trip for her.

Chapter 2

BEAMS FROM A FOREBODING MOON shot like stalactites out of the black
sky, casting a ghastly glow over the distant coastline. About two kilometers from shore, the Killer's bay boat floated calmly on the waveless sea.
The Agent known as Bathsheba sat on the built-in bench towards the
aft of the boat, watching silently as David's large, wiry frame tore back
and forth, overturning every unbolted object and piece of furniture in
his path.

The Agent had a temper to match his, but she knew better than to
interrupt him without good reason. He was a man of particular tastes
and short of patience, a man of a singular view. David hardly ever
raised his voice, but he had a sadistic streak that reared its ugly head
whenever he identified the object of his displeasure.

When he had run out of things to throw and kick, he turned his
seeing eye toward her. His salt-and-pepper, shoulder-length hair had
begun to stick to his forehead. He wiped his face and grimaced, trying
to get a read on whether he'd frightened her into remembering the
information about her alleged trip to the clinic.

The Agent's gaze vacillated between him and the two large millstones on the far side of the boat. The fact that there were two stones
was disconcerting. She had only ever trained with one. Resisting every
temptation to jump out of the boat right then and there, she remained
seated and studied the ropes that were threaded through the center of
each of the stones. One of the ropes was about ten centimeters longer
than the other.

"You want to tell me what you were doing at the clinic in Arica?" David asked in a deceptively calm voice.

She sighed. "I told you I don't remember."

"I don't believe you."

"Well, it's true," she said. "Please, Father, if we just ask them to look up the record—"

"Out of the question!" he snapped, his pale face flushed with rage. "Bourghin and Gomez are watching all medical records for anyone matching *your* description. They've probably already flagged the record at the clinic."

The night breeze blew between them with a decisive chill, mussing her long, curly hair. She smoothed it, much to his amusement. She had always been terribly self-conscious about her hair. He pretended not to like that about her, but she knew that he did. He was struggling to keep from smiling.

He continued, "Everyone was skeptical of allowing a Class 3 female to play such a pivotal role in the Cull, but *I* petitioned the Vice to approve your involvement. Damn it, you're undermining everything I've worked for!"

"Well, let's get on with it, then!" the Agent said.

Getting the stones would be better than having to listen to his lecturing all night. She turned her back to him and shed the turquoise gown, willfully ignoring the feeling of his ravenous gaze crawling up and down her curves.

"Stockings, too," he said.

"I need them for insulation," she replied, adjusting the elastic waistband and turning to face him. "Even with my—extra help—the water's too cold this time of year."

Both statements were untrue. The stockings wouldn't have been anywhere near enough insulation for the average person, and the Agent would have been fine without them. Her body generally adjusted to generate the heat she needed. She simply didn't want to give David any more of a show than she already had.

He likely saw through her excuse since, for the past few months, he had been keeping track of her accelerated rate of recovery from ordinary illnesses and wounds. He knew her body was not that of the average person—not anymore—but they never spoke about that directly.

His gaze was fixed on the shoulder strap of her bra as she tightened it. It would have been practical for her to remove the bra, but she had a feeling that she would be needing it later.

"Whore," he muttered, walking to the other side of the boat.

The word awakened such an anger in her that she leapt forward with the intention of snapping his neck. She had bested many men, groups of them, even. Incapacitating David, who was nearing the end of his physical prime, would have been easy enough. He was, however, unworried.

Throwing her a contemptuous glance, he switched on a recording of her Song and picked up the coils of rope that she had been dreading since they put out from the dock.

"Bow," he said.

She winced and fell to her knees. Still, she crawled toward him, determined not to let the music affect her. But after about a meter and half, the Song really began to take its toll, and by the time she reached David, she crumbled with her cheek to the floor at his feet. He placed the heel of his boot on her temple, a demonstration of his dominance. All she could do was wonder why she had to take this treatment as the lyrics flowed quietly in the background.

There, below, I see her
So lonely in her pool
I can hear her
Her silky bareness
Crying out

The Song's melody was something familiar—possibly a popular nursery tune—comforting like a blanket of fog rolling down over the hills by their house. And even though the Agent abhorred the idea of needing a soothing device, she knew that this fog blanket was for her benefit. It would help her to be a good solider. It would help her to complete the mission. She unclenched her fists.

I'm the king
And I'll have her if I want her
But with a smile she shatters me
Bathsheba

As she relaxed, David removed his foot from her head. She sat up and regarded him calmly.

"You disappointed me," he said, taking on his most fatherly tone as he tied the ropes around her wrists, one each.

Although her mind was clouded, she managed to note that the longer of the two ropes was tied around her right wrist.

He continued, "I can't allow this kind of rebellion, least of all from my protégé. Tonight, you'll be at twice the distance and with twice the weight. Maybe *that* will help you to understand your place."

"Twice the oxygen, too?" She did a poor job of masking the fear in her voice.

"Same amount," he said, turning his head so that his seeing eye was out of her line of vision. "I'll comb the area in the morning. *If* you survive the night, I will retrieve you."

Bathsheba

If she survived? It was probable that the Agent's pride alone would be enough to fuel her drive to survive. Pride was the weakest of her weak points, and David routinely exploited it with merciless efficiency. The Agent had proven that two could play that game, although Bathsheba's technique had naturally developed to be more fluid and less overt—for survival's sake.

I rule everything
But her beauty is untamed
Her curly locks are lawless, free
Her curves as wild as they come
Her evasive gaze is merciless
And with a smile, she shatters me

She stared at him with eyes ice-cold, unfeeling. She had inherited that from him. After all, he had taught her nothing less than to become her opponent. And while neither of them had yet chosen to acknowledge it, they were rapidly approaching a time when they would find themselves at odds. She dared not allow that thought to linger since she had been beaten nearly to a pulp for lesser transgressions.

Yes, she knows, her smile she shatters me

He added without looking her way, "Hey, how about one for the road?"

She didn't smile. As far as she was concerned, he'd get no response but the sloshing of the water against the boat's underside.

"There's my girl," he said.

With that, he heaved the millstones, one after the other, into the water. Then, he tossed her a full-face oxygen mask. She had been waiting for the mask and hurriedly strapped it on before diving out of the boat to catch up with the sinking stones.

The chilly waters closed over her with the finality of a shovelful of soil flowing down over a coffin. She wrapped herself around the stone with the shorter rope. As it carried her down to the ocean floor, she barely heard the swishing and swooshing of the currents. All that rang in her ears was the final verse of the Song.

Now, see, your king
He beckons you
To be over you is his privilege
Or his right
But you're his one obsession
Just only for tonight
He rules you and protects you

Come on, Bathsheba!
Come on, come on and
Give a little something too

She sank into the depths, the cold sinking into her bones, into her soul, and straight through her. She was the cold now; she was the dark. There was no differentiation. The pressure blocked her ears sooner than expected because of the weight of the additional stone. She swallowed over and over to rid herself of the feeling that her head was about to explode.

Bathsheba
Come, Bathsheba

Just as she felt the customary popping in her ears, she became aware of the rocky floor beneath her knees. Immediately, she shed her golden ring, suspecting that it would only be troublesome to keep it.

The feeble moonlight cast shadows over everything in her line of vision. After feeling the rocks around her and finding no holdfasts, the Agent confirmed that David had taken her out beyond the kelp forests, further than he'd ever taken her before. At least he hadn't dropped her in the trench.

Silver lining. She laughed wryly, causing her mask to fog up. Then, she set about winding the ropes around her arms, her torso, and the tops of her legs.

The sharp edges of the rocks were already irritating her calloused palms as she groped about in the darkness to feel the way ahead. This journey would be made like any other: one step at a time, even if on all fours. She breathed evenly and slowly, her bulky legs straining to adjust to the extra weight. Soon, she adapted and pulled herself onward—arm after arm, leg after leg—over the uneven underwater terrain.

Despite the fact that David had never taken her this far out, the Agent had indeed been this far out on her own. Having been punished a sufficient number of times, the Agent had learned the bay. She knew the water's caresses, its habits, its leadings. And she had discovered a way out. This was a triumphant thought, although she brushed away the invasive image of a salty bed to entertain it.

For the moment, no achievement, punishment, or cunning mattered either to her or to the cargo she suspected she carried. Nothing mattered, she told herself. Just the mission at hand.

Come, Bathsheba

In addition to being quite slick, the surfaces that the Agent climbed up and wriggled across were rugged and sharp. She did not stop to examine the scratches on her torso or the bruising on her knees. Her only thought was to get away from where she had been. The currents, some warm and some cool, showed her the way. She climbed onward—arm after arm, leg after leg, rock after rock—heading northward, a safe choice with regard to avoiding the edge of the trench.

When the tentative fingers of first light reached down from above, the Agent's knees were too bruised to bear much of her weight anymore. She felt no pain, but she could tell from her body's jerking movements that she was beyond fatigued. She gave her knees a rest by propping herself up on her hands and feet. Her stockings were worn through at the soles.

As she gripped the rocks in front of her, she felt a slimy, familiar sensation. Although the Agent would have known them by touch, the dim light revealed to her the outline of hundreds of light green, hand-like holdfasts on the rocks around her. She looked up at the great, dense body of kelp in her path. A kelp forest meant that there remained approximately one kilometer to dry ground. It was time to head east.

She plunged into the mess of stipes and holdfasts and fought her way toward the shore. Behind her, the millstones snagged on every mass of kelp and every boulder they could find.

Bathsheba

Her hands were scraped and cramping, and her skin was yielding to rope burns. Still, she forged ahead—arm after arm, leg after leg—through the kelp-infested shallows and up the steep incline onto the rocky beach.

Come, Bathsheba

Ripping the oxygen mask from her face, she unwound the ropes and collapsed onto her back. Her body slipped sideways across the slick, jagged rocks as the undertow drew the millstone attached to her right wrist back down into the surf. She hadn't pulled it quite far enough out of the water's reach.

Bathsheba

She had no strength to drag the stones any further. So, in one final desperate act, she dislocated her right thumb, slipped her wrist from the rope's loop, and released the stone to its fate. Whether she had completed the mission or only just begun it, she hardly knew. She was a new woman, bare-skinned and swaddled in kelp, born again into a bright morning that did not know her and to a self that was equally unwitting.

Then, with the outgoing tide flowing around her, she lost consciousness. She lay supine and limp, disjointed like her right thumb. And for all the songs of the seabirds circling above and the water swishing in her ears, her only lullaby rang out on the hills of her mind, an endless and comforting fog: *Come, Bathsheba. Come!*

Chapter 3

How many hours did she lie there on the rocks with the saltwater lapping at her? Too many, though truly, not enough. While she slept, she also waited, exposed, yet oddly secure in the murky depths of the not-yet-future. The sun grew warmer and, little by little, the Agent was drawn back from the depths.

Somewhere on the brink of wakefulness, she became aware of a sturdy surface beneath her. However, she still sensed the deep, gentle rolling of the ocean and could hear the waves crashing on the shore nearby. She had emerged from the water, but she had not left the ocean. She was both dead and alive, both lost and found, both seeking and sought after.

"See if you can get those stockings off her," a man's voice said. "They're sucking the heat out of her."

A hand gripped the waist of her stockings.

She sprang into motion. Her arms had been pressed to her sides by a cloth-like restraint, but she freed them in a split second. The restraint crumbled off of her like a piece of tissue.

Code black! Fading to red, five assailants, all armed, limited area. Make that four assailants. She had taken it down to two before the words they were shouting at her registered at all.

"Easy, Kiddo! Easy!" A scruffy-faced man dressed completely in black approached her with his hands up.

"Put that away!" he barked at the only man who remained with him in the boat, a Class 1 of bright pink, sunburned skin who had drawn an electroshock weapon with the intent to end their passenger's rampage.

"You'll only aggravate her," the man in black said.

He spoke an American dialect of English, an interesting find in that part of the world. The Agent looked at the weapon-holding man to gauge his response. He was just an underling, a roach, no one important in the grand scheme of things. Yes, that was all he was: a roach. He had to do what he was told, and he could be squashed like a bug. However, his anxious posture and quivering lip informed her that his rational mind was pondering neither the importance of the chain of command nor his ephemeral nature.

"Those don't work on me," she said, motioning with her head to the weapon that he gripped so tightly.

The American accent felt weird in her mouth.

"Put it *away*, Collins!" the man in black ordered.

Pink Collins was shaking, clearly flustered by this counterintuitive command.

The Agent shrugged and stepped back onto something crinkly. It was an emergency blanket, the "restraint" that she had torn off earlier. She bent to retrieve it from the floor of the boat. Pink Collins pulled the trigger. His target caught the probes in her bare hand and tugged on the wire, ripping the weapon from his grip.

"Didn't you hear, mister? I *said* they don't work on me," she growled through a tight jaw.

She resisted the temptation to strangle the roach with the wire from his own irritating weapon. The only reason he was still alive was because she *did* have respect for the chain of command and the man in black had expressed a desire for non-violence. There was no other immediate threat and, therefore, no need for escalation. She clenched and unclenched her hand, which seemed to have seized up momentarily, and hummed a little under her breath.

Bathsheba

Suddenly aware of how little clothing she wore, she pulled the waist of her stockings up to the underwires of her bra and sat cross-legged on the bench seat. She picked up the emergency blanket and wrapped it around her shoulders.

For the first time, she noticed all of the disassembled guns on the floor of the boat. Had she done that? She rarely came out so strongly at the beginning of a mission.

Batting her eyelashes, she addressed the man in black with a smile.

"Now," she said, "who do I need to butter up to get some information around here? I'd like to know who sent you and what you want with me."

The man in black did not seem drawn in by her coyness. In fact, he seemed disturbed by it. Whoever this man thought he was to her, he was not someone that she might be able to manipulate in the way to which she had grown accustomed. She eyed him cautiously.

"We just want to get you home, Kiddo," he reassured her.

They were in a small motorboat, not too far from land but apparently quite far from where she had crawled ashore that morning. She did not recognize her surroundings and only hoped that these men had taken her further north. Yes, she still remembered that her mission should take her northward.

The three roaches she had thrown overboard were treading water in tense anticipation. Even though they remained outside of the boat, she kept track of their every movement. She watched from the corners of her eyes to see how often each of them needed to give a stroke of the arm or leg to stay above water. She listened to their breathing, each man having a different rhythm and cadence. She was learning them how one might learn a score of music, and she would know them by heart if ever the need arose.

For now, it was probable that her focus should be on the two in the boat. The roach recently relieved of his electroshock weapon was potentially hostile but subordinate to the driver—the man in black—who seemed more levelheaded. The man in black was a middle-aged fellow, fit, reasonably tall, tan-skinned and gray-eyed, probably Class 3.1 pureblood. She estimated this class designation simply by virtue of his skin color, prominent brow, and aquiline nose, although she had seen subclasses with similar features.

She found it curious that he led such a diverse team. That was surely out of line with Neo-Eugenic law and, therefore, with the WCE tenets. His roaches were nearly all of different skin tones. It was then that the Agent realized that there was a very real possibility that these were not WCE roaches at all. Was she disappointed or—dare she even think it—*scared* that they were not?

Squinting in the sunlight, she took a breath of fresh, salty air. Her throat was tight from dehydration, and her breath rattled in her ribcage. She felt disoriented and irritated, having just been awakened or born or whatever had happened. In fact, she felt sick.

The man in black was watching her from the bow of the boat. His eyes were the type that honest men have, eyes that droop down slightly at the corners from years of living in dogged defiance of dishonesty's true power.

"Are you okay, Lenci?" he asked, cautiously approaching her.

Lenci. The name disturbed her momentarily, then drew her into a tranquil blankness. The past melted away and then she only *was*. She reached frantically for some explanation, some cover story that she had been given long ago. She had trained for this moment, but now that it was happening, her memory was sabotaging her.

"Valencia?"

A flood of fear overwhelmed her. This was not the way it was supposed to happen.

"No, no! There's been some mistake!" she cried.

The man in black anxiously studied her face.

"No, I'm sure there hasn't," he said.

Yes, yes, there had. She was not supposed to be there—not yet, anyway. Something had gone terribly wrong. Her head spun as the initial panic spiraled downward into a deep anguish.

"Lenci?"

She gripped her head. "No, please, don't call me that. I can't remember."

"Come on, agent. Buck up," the man in black said. "Where is he?"

Yes, she was an agent. If there was anything certain, it was that.

"Where is who? I don't know. I can't remember."

The American accent felt so lazy and nasally. It felt wrong.

A training exercise. She had probably gone off course during a training exercise.

The man in black would not release her from his gaze. "The Killer. Where is he?"

She regarded him cautiously but with an enthusiastically inquisitive mask.

"You know my husband?" she asked.

"Your *husband*?" Pink Collins echoed indignantly. He fell silent at one glance from his superior.

"Well enough," the man in black answered the Agent. "Listen, you've got to come with us."

"Well," she said hesitantly, "I should get home as soon as possible. David doesn't like me to be out without him for too long."

"Lenci!" He grabbed her face in his hands. "Do you *hear* yourself? You're in too deep. Come out of it!"

His mistake was making unannounced contact. The use of *that* name had delayed her reaction, which was the only reason his hands made it so close to her neck. Upon contact, she head-butted him, throwing him off-balance, and she followed up with a combination of strikes to his trunk.

The man in black didn't even block her first few strikes. He seemed to expect her to have some crisis of conscience. The Agent found, after a while, that he had quite an effective outside block. It was his strictly defensive response that caught her attention. And, for some reason, she was only striking him from the outside. Perhaps she didn't really want to harm him after all. She stopped swinging, but her muscles remained tense and ready to react.

"Oh, for crying out loud! I am too old for this," he muttered. "Agent Valencia Thomas of the SSI Phoenix Subdivision! Handler summons is firebird1419. State your ID number, and report your status." His tone fluctuated, swelling and dipping like the ocean's waves.

The Agent stood erect and calmly recited with the same rising and falling tones, "Agent ID number is 14115139102329921. Status: active and engaged."

She brought a hand to her mouth and stared at him in horror. He sighed with relief, a relief that she could not share. This man whom she had thought to be honest, this man in black, was not merely the leader of an agency tactical unit. No, he was potentially something far more dangerous.

"Welcome back, Agent 14115139102329921," he grinned. "Now, please, you need to come with me."

It was very possible that that long, dark night with the millstones had actually been her commissioning. The timetable for the mission had apparently been moved up, and the Agent was suddenly quite aware of how ill-prepared she was. All of the strength drained from her limbs, and she sat down wordlessly, wishing that she was mistaken in this conclusion.

The men in the water looked to the man in black for further instruction. His facial expression told them to stay put.

"Can we get an extraction at these coordinates?" he shouted into the air.

He shielded his earpiece from the wind.

After a brief silence, he continued, "Nearer to Peru's border. Hold on. I'll read them to you. And can you get someone to return the car?"

"Wait!" the Agent interrupted before he could read the coordinates to the dispatcher. "Please, since you have a car, take me inland before airlifting."

She didn't know why she had said that.

"Actually," the man in black grinned, scratching his scruffy chin, "send it inland."

He listened to the brief response. Then, "Just send me the coordinates to an abandoned airstrip anywhere in Northern Chile when you get a chance. We'll meet them there."

He looked kindly at his passenger. "Do you mind if the men reembark? Might be a rough ride for them out there."

She glanced at the roaches solely for his benefit. She had never lost track of any of their positions. Judging from his deep, gasping gulps of breath, one of them seemed to be a weaker swimmer than the rest.

"Fine," she smiled. "But if anyone so much as reaches for a weapon, I'll break all of his fingers—and his pinky toes."

Pink Collins shuddered.

The Agent looked him directly in the eye and whispered, "Avid pinky-toe lover, hm? Well, just behave, then."

"You heard the woman!" The man in black started up the boat's engine as his roaches climbed aboard, cold and soggy.

While the Agent could tell that he was on edge, his tight shoulders and locked knees informed her that he was doing his best to hold it together. She thought that she might remember that feeling of holding it together. Now that she had committed herself to this man's custody, she sensed an imminent reordering of her life. Whether everything was coming together or falling apart she did not know.

Within minutes, the boat was sloshing just behind the shore break.

"This is it," the man in black called. "You all swim to shore while I cover our tracks."

"Don't leave *her* with us!" the weak swimmer protested with a wheeze. "Dear goodness, I will sink the boat by myself if I have to!"

The man in black sighed. "Take someone with you. No sense in you drowning to avoid broken bones."

Pink Collins stayed with the weak swimmer while the rest of the team swam to shore. The Agent noticed that the roaches formed a loose circle around her, but they kept a respectful distance. The man in black was behind her. And strangely, that did not worry her in the least.

After fighting her way out of the break, the Agent struggled the last few meters to dry land. She still felt no pain, but her body moved stiffly up the rocky incline. She picked a piece of kelp off of her arm and rewrapped herself in the emergency blanket, which she intended to keep until such a time as she could obtain regular clothing. Even when wet, the blanket provided decent protection against the strong marine breeze.

Turning to the man in black, she said, "Better that you didn't leave me alone with your men. I might have bolted."

He said nothing, calmly and quietly studying her. Not too far away, she could hear the pounding of the waves on the shore, but that was nothing compared to the pounding of her heart. She averted her gaze. There was something about this honest man's kind, gray eyes that made her ashamed. She could no longer look directly at him.

"For some reason, I trust *you* not to take me back," she said.

"To where?"

There was a small commotion as Pink Collins and the weak swimmer came ashore. Pink Collins was calling for assistance as it seemed that the weak swimmer had hyperextended his knee fairly badly. They were struggling to make their way up the steep, rocky beach.

The Agent watched the team rally to their aid, then shifted uncomfortably and looked down at her scratched up, scabbing hands. It was only then that she remembered her dislocated thumb. Gritting her teeth, she popped the thumb back into its socket. The man in black watched her do this. She knew that he did. Sensing her awkwardness but ignorant of its source, he turned his attention to a nearby bend in the coastal highway.

"My car is over there." He pointed to a silver, two-door sedan that was parked in the shoulder. "We'll drive to the airstrip where the agency has a jet waiting for us. The men will take separate commercial flights."

She desperately wanted to ask this honest man exactly which agency was sending a jet for them. But she did not.

Upon reaching the silver sedan, the Agent lay flat with her stomach to the ground and gave the bottom of the car a once-over. The man in black opened the door for her on the passenger's side but paused with an amused expression to observe her behavior.

"So, this is what he's taught you? Paranoia?"

Her time with the Killer was rapidly fading from her memory. It was succumbing to the blankness of a new mission. Her face was expressionless as she climbed into the passenger's seat and watched the man in black walk toward the trunk.

"Judging from the heat inside the car, I'd say you parked it four hours ago," she said. "A lot can happen in four hours. I can assemble a functioning bomb from common beach trash in two."

He chuckled and opened the trunk. "You're lapsing. When you left us, you could assemble an improvised explosive in thirty minutes."

"Hm." She crossed her arms in ardent disbelief, but the look on his face actually caused her to wonder.

Pulling a bag out of the trunk, he said, "I brought you these."

She gave him a scrutinizing glance before picking through the contents of the bag. He had brought her clothes, brightly colored and baggy, probably from some foreign run, tourist-trap kiosk, and a large, woven satchel of bold colors to use as a purse.

Still, clothes were clothes. She stood up and gave him an appreciative nod before turning her back to don the gaudy tourist outfit over her bra and stockings. From the sound of his shuffling feet, she could tell that he turned his back as she let her emergency blanket cover fall to the ground. This caused a huge smile, a genuine smile, to spread across her face and throughout her entire body, although she was not entirely sure why. The smile was gone before she sat down again, but its warmth lingered inwardly.

He still had his back to her. Apparently, his observation was not all that keen. She knocked on the side of the car and coughed softly to get his attention. He turned around slowly, his expression pensive.

"I'm ready to go home," she said, allowing her gaze to meet his only to convey a brief flicker of hopefulness.

He went around to the driver's side of the car and sat down, regarding her calmly.

"Where's home?" he asked.

She hesitated for a moment, only a moment, with a blur of a million, billion, trillion facts that she had memorized running through her mind. Where *was* home?

"Diablo," she said, proud to have passed the test. "Please."

Although he was slightly taken aback at this request, the man in black cleared his throat and recovered quickly.

"Diablo it is, then," he replied.

The Agent took note of his astonishment, but she did not confront him about it. From what she could understand, situational tides were taking her in a different direction than she would have chosen. However, currently, all she wanted was to get out of the country, and the man in black appeared to be her ticket to do so.

He closed the door and buckled his seat belt. Then, as if remembering something disappointingly hilarious, he chuckled wryly.

"The Killer knew we were coming for you after your medical record ping, hey? So, he dumped you in the ocean and fled. So much for the oath to guide, teach, fortify, and help!"

Outwardly, the Agent appeared calm, but her mind was racing, trying to figure out who "we" could be and, again, what agency could possibly be sending a jet.

After no response, the man in black shrugged and turned the key in the ignition.

"My name is *Chandler* Bourghin," he told her.

He looked expectant. Another test. She fiddled with the air conditioning knobs to stall for time.

"Chandler," she mumbled, "Chandler, rambler, Sandler, no, pan-handler, handler. You—You're my handler?"

"Good, Lenci," he said, pulling out onto the road. He seemed relieved that she had remembered that much, although his tone suggested that there was more she could have remembered. "We got your distress signal months ago, but we couldn't decipher it all. And it took us this long to find you because you stopped communication until that final fax—which was extremely imprudent, by the way."

She looked out the window silently.

"So, what gives?"

Still unsure of what she could say that would not get her killed, she did not respond.

"Look," Chandler said, "I am *for* you. But I need to know what happened, so we can fix this together."

Again, no response. Rather than meet his probing gaze, she turned her attention to the floor of the car.

He pulled over and parked.

"Okay, just tell me this much: is the mission compromised?"

Reality was coming down in smithereens around the Agent, and all that was left was the mission. But, perhaps that, too, had been taken away from her. She no longer knew what it meant for the mission to be compromised. Lenci's handler had come for her, and he was holding her accountable.

She raised her gaze to his and maintained it as she shakily replied, "I don't know."

Chapter 4

THE AGENT DID NOT SLEEP ON THE JET. Instead, through closed eyes, she kept track of every movement, every breath, of the man in black. It was early afternoon the next day when they landed at the airport in Forsythe, the capital district of the Western States. When the door of the jet opened, a blast of hot, dry air accosted the Agent. She shielded her face as she descended onto the tarmac.

Forsythe was the most modernized district of the Western States, equipped with some of the latest technology and infrastructure. The cloudy skies were alive with holographic screens and lights and the buzz of commercial delivery drones. The airport was bustling with people and machines going this way and that, whirring, bumping, yelling.

For the Agent, the transition from the stillness of the ocean night to this hubbub was overwhelming. From the very instant that she exited the jet, she struggled to keep track of every breathing, moving individual, every buzz and thrum of machinery, every potential threat in the swarm around her.

On a less crowded walkway, a woman appeared in front of the Agent with a body scanner.

"Would you like a free scan to see if you're a match for Adrenabalm sweat gland swapping? You can be a drier, healthier you!" She held the scanner up to the Agent's face.

"No scans!" the Agent yelled, striking the woman on the neck.

The woman disappeared in a pixelated burst of harmless white energy.

"Thank you for your time," a mechanized voice droned.

The Agent stared incredulously at the spot where the woman had disappeared.

"Just an ad," Chandler said softly. "You don't have to kill them to make them leave. Just swipe them away like this."

He waved his hands one after the other in front of his face to demonstrate. The Agent mimicked his movement.

"You got it." He nodded and motioned her forward.

The pop-up ads grew more numerous as they passed by the gates, but after a couple of successes at dismissing them, the Agent became less skittish.

Heads turned as she and Chandler made their way toward the curbside pickup area. Bystanders started nudging each other, pointing, and whispering. When the Agent thought about it, she figured that Bourghin—to the inexperienced eye—might resemble a tan Class 1 man. And that was a problem since he was traveling with her: a registered Class 3.5.

The States, Lenci's home country, was one unfortunate place in which the World Council of Eugenics continued to gain influence. Eugenism was assumed in the States, and most district governments—with the exception of those that were exempt or unaffiliated—were beholden to the WCE for its substantial financial support. In this way, district governments were slowly transitioning to private ownership and acceptance of Neo-Eugenic law.

The Agent had not visited the States since the Divisive Round, the event which had formalized the rigid, heavily-regulated borders of the Eastern and Western States and their districts. Even before the Divisive Round, the Western States had been obsessed with class stratification. But now that the societal structure was reinforced by law, inhabitants of most Western districts, including Forsythe, had taken to using the threat of social and physical danger to pressure everyone to stay within class boundaries.

The formalization of distinct, hierarchical classes was said to have validated the identity of pureblood groups, giving them a better chance at survival through the right to assert their identity and police their social boundaries. All it really accomplished was a heightened prejudice among the classes and especially toward those of 'impure' blood and association: the Subclass.

It was a strange answer to the issue of racism back in the 2020s—the Agent thought—as it seemed to cause more conflict than it resolved.

"Distinct but valid" didn't cut it in a system that was unapologetically hierarchical. The majority group in the States claimed to be Class 1, and all of the other pureblood groups grudgingly accepted the hierarchy because validation seemed to be the next best thing to equality.

Since the oglers at the airport thought that Bourghin was a Class 1 man and that the Agent was a Class 3 female, they did not approve of their association. Here was a reminder that eugenists could come in many different hues. They had a similar look, though. Their squinty eyes and wrinkled rat-noses, even in silence, practically jeered the ugly motto taught in all of the State-sponsored schools:

Four is lower than three, than two, than one, since adding is subtraction
So, we keep the peace with our division, dividing without fractions
Everything divided by one is the same, and same divided by same is whole
Keep the average, keep the peace, keep control!

The Agent stared defiantly back at the oglers, daring them to express their thoughts aloud. One college-aged Class 3 spat at her, and his saliva landed on her arm. She stopped abruptly. As the warm ooze trickled down to her hand, she began to calculate how many eugenist faces were within literal striking distance. Bourghin placed a gentle hand on her arm and wordlessly encouraged her to take no heed of the spitter, or the other onlookers for that matter. She acquiesced, and Bourghin fell in just behind her as an inconspicuous but intentional shield from prying gazes and any additional spittle. She marveled at this gesture on his part, noting the compassion that seemed to manifest in his every action toward her.

His shoulder was touching hers, so she could feel the shifting weight of his body and sense which direction he intended to walk. It was in this way that he led her to the row of cars waiting to pick up new arrivals.

They came to a small stretch limo with tinted windows. There was no driver in the front seat. The Agent peered curiously through the partition into the empty space where a driver would have been. There was nothing but machinery, blinking lights, and a steering wheel to placate the wandering eye of an anxious traveler.

"I have to warn you," Bourghin said, buckling himself in across from her. "There's a marked disparity among the Western States, most notably between Diablo and Forsythe."

She turned to face him and drew up her legs to sit cross-legged. "I'm not afraid of rough neighborhoods, Chandler. I'm not afraid of anything or anyone."

"You never have been, you little knucklehead. That's what made you a great protégé." Bourghin grinned, nudging her chin fondly with his fist.

His action was slow and tender enough that the Agent understood it to be non-threatening. She nudged back with her chin and impishly mirrored his grin.

"That and the fact that I'm the smartest and best-looking agent in the West."

"Ergh," he winced playfully. "How did you find out?"

"I have a feeling you used to tell me that frequently."

He didn't respond. Perhaps someone else had told her that.

She shrugged. "You should hear what they're saying out there in that big, wide world, Chandler. Rumor has it my combat skills are nearly unparalleled."

"Is that what makes you great?"

"Couldn't hurt."

"Don't be bigheaded, Kiddo."

She cast him a mischievous glance, then leaned against the window and pretended to sleep.

Forsythe, with all of its screens and lights and glitz and glam, faded into a lonely country road. Lenci Thomas had traveled this road many times as a child because her parents had worked to get her into a fancy school in Forsythe. Despite pressure from her peers as well as the administration, Lenci had made the three-hour commute every day with other children from Diablo who showed potential. Too bad she never lived up to that potential.

Despite skipping through the grades at Forsythe's School for the Gifted, Lenci dropped out of high school at the age of fifteen, only months before her graduation. The reason for this sudden abandonment of her academic pursuits was shrouded in mystery, but seeing as how she joined SSI shortly thereafter, the Agent had reason to believe that the agency was involved in some way. SSI—that was where Bourghin was taking her, she was now sure.

At the district border between Forsythe and Diablo, Chandler held up his badge so that the border agent would fast-track them to an area where they could switch to a different car.

This car had a human driver, a large, silent figure that did not turn his face away from the road ahead. He didn't even respond when the Agent greeted him.

"Might as well be an auto-car," she muttered.

31

"HQ is only half an hour away from here," Chandler said kindly. "We just had to change cars because—"

"I know; I heard," the Agent interrupted. "Diablo's an exempt district. I did watch the news while I was away, Agent Bourghin."

Diablo, a social island in the districts of the Western States, was affiliated with the WCE as all Western districts were. However, it was exempt from the implementation of Neo-Eugenic law. That made its citizens exempt from anti-miscegenation laws and class exclusion in employment, but they were also exempt from most Western federal funding and reliable law enforcement. Because Diablo had refused to opt into the WCE-funded federal programs that mandated social stratification, the district had been condemned to high crime rates, rampant gunk addiction, poor infrastructure, and the simple technology of decades past.

When they drove further in, though, the Agent's jaw dropped. She had not anticipated the trash-filled streets and the rows upon rows of run-down buildings, which posed a stark contrast to the sturdy architecture and immaculately kept roads of Forsythe. This, however, the Agent would use to her advantage. In such an environment, it would be easy to blend in and, in fact, to disappear almost entirely. GPS tracking, facial recognition, drone charging stations, and biometric scanning elevators would be few and far between, if at all present.

People from the outside world would not be able to rely upon technology to hunt her. So, if they really wanted her, they'd have to come in and find her the old-fashioned way.

The car stopped in front of a glass skyscraper, which sported a professional sign that read: **Sopient Solutions, Inc.** Although the Agent did not recognize this building, she marveled at the irony of its simultaneously physical transparency and its functional opaqueness. It seemed to her a monument to betrayal, but she could not, for the life of her, remember why.

***

In a dark room with a reflective window that was probably meant to intimidate her, the Agent sat across from the man in black with a scrutinizing look on her face. They had been there for forty-five minutes, at least. And they weren't getting anywhere in their conversation.

She placed her elbows on the cool, hard table, rested her chin on her hands, and studied Bourghin intently in hopes of finding a soft entry point, a gateway to his desires and self-image, a way to maneuver him into cooperation.

He had asked about her training with the Killer. Although he had truly seemed to be asking because he cared, the Agent could give him nothing. Her time with the Killer was over, and all that she had learned was nothing in light of her recent change in circumstance. Bourghin became increasingly anxious to the point of wringing his hands and scratching his scruffy chin.

Now he was sitting, leaning toward her, with his broad shoulders somewhat hunched. There was something that he wanted from her. Or was it *for* her? His eyes were honest, still, and sadder than before. She thought that she might remember what it was like to be honest and sad. She gave him a practiced smile, shy and sympathetic.

"Okay," Agent Bourghin said, at last. "Why don't you tell me about yourself? What makes you tick?"

She crossed her arms. "Seriously? We're going to do some kind of weird speed dating exercise right now?"

Her handler said nothing.

Realizing that this must be another test, she straightened up and spoke in a calm, even tone. "Well, where to start? My name is Valencia Thomas. I'm a Class 3.5 pureblood, female as they come, born and raised in Diablo, but I went to school mostly in Forsythe. I guess, if there's anything that makes me tick—gosh, I almost said *music*, but I'd have to say it's my brother."

"Interesting," he said coolly. "Can you tell me more about that?"

All of a sudden, she laughed a bright, charming laugh, and responded with a glowing face, "Oh, what can I say about my brother? He inspires me every day. I guess, he just—he helps me to be better."

The brilliant smile lingered for a moment before fading to her question, "That enough?"

Agent Bourghin remained in a pensive silence. His hands were folded, a posture she was sure he used to hide the fact that his hands were shaking. Something about her safe and generic summary had rattled him, and now he was thinking furiously about what direction this interrogation should take. She waited while he thought.

At length, he pushed a sheet of paper across the table at her. Sitting back in her chair, she took the sheet, studied the string of words printed thereupon, and handed it back to him.

"Well?" he said. "What does it mean?"

"How should I know?"

"You sent this message—along with the coordinates where we found you—encoded into a fax from the clinic in Arica, did you not?"

She said, "I have no recollection of that," which was true.

He cast her an incredulous glance, then read the message as if that might jog her memory, "Amphibious takedown operation mirra brother tether."

She waited for him to explain this nonsensical phrase, but he instead asked, "Did David Miller ever train you to carry out water-based land assaults, Lenci?"

How could she know?

Unfazed, he continued, "What is Operation Mirra, and why are you taking it down?"

The Agent shrugged.

"What is your brother's name?"

"Stupid question."

"Is it?"

"Yes." An indignant flame flashed in her eyes as she met his gaze, but it was gone just as soon as it had come.

Bourghin fell silent, probably reasoning that they would have plenty of time to discuss the fax later.

He finally asked, "Why did Miller let you go?"

Thinking about what he might want to hear, the Agent replied, "I escaped."

"How?"

"Good timing, I guess," she said.

Finding out that her escape attempt had been intentional seemed to break the dam holding back Chandler's gushing relief.

"Sending this fax was gutsy, Kiddo!" he remarked, waving the crinkled paper at her. "You are a rambunctious young lady and a *knucklehead*, you know that? But you sent it just in time. You know your mother was on my case about finding you..."

The Agent mirrored his smile, pleased that she had given him the answer he'd been looking for, but as he bumbled on, her smile slowly disappeared. She listened to his heartfelt statement of relief more as one might listen to a bedtime story. Her attention moved to his five o'clock shadow, a mix of gray, apricot, and honey-colored stubble. She decided that she didn't like it.

Chandler cleared his throat. "Lenci, did he—hurt you?"

She couldn't tell from his questions what he wanted from her, and in any case, she didn't remember much from the time before she had awakened in the boat.

She remembered the great urgency and determination of her night on the ocean floor. She remembered the swishing of the currents. She remembered her skin raw from chafing and her legs twitching and stiff. She remembered the Song and that the mission was above all else. She remembered Pink Collins trying to electrify her. Besides these things, she had no past. And every time the man in black asked about it, she was afflicted by a mind-clouding headache.

"But why cut off communication?" Bourghin asked exasperatedly. "Lenci, you've got to give me *something*!"

The blank slate name was his device for distraction, but the Agent knew that she needed to focus on the mission. Doing her best to ignore her aching, throbbing head, she took a deep breath.

Come, Bathsheba

She sat up straight and made eye contact with the man in black.

"A doctor," she said. "I want to see a doctor—and not some agency medic. I want to see a family practice doctor. Someone that knows me under an older alias that is harder to track."

Taken aback by this sudden and direct request after hours of silence and vague answers, Bourghin stumbled over his response, "Of course! Um, yes. We—we'll arrange a transport for you, immediately."

He looked toward the reflective glass and brought a hand to his ear like an old-style telephone for the benefit of whoever was watching.

"I'm sorry for bringing you straight to debriefing rather than having you examined first," he told the Agent. "I was just so concerned. I'll— yes, of course. Right away. Debriefing can wait."

She watched the man in black with an ice-cold stare as he fumbled his papers together and stood up. He was sweating profusely, and for the first time since they had landed, she noticed that his face was twisted with fatigue. He had not slept on the way over either.

"Finished so soon, Agent Bourghin?" A tall, ivory-skinned woman of high cheekbones and a pointed chin leaned through the open door, her exquisitely manicured hand still on the knob.

Bourghin started at the sound of her voice. "Director!"

He rose hurriedly and followed her out of the room, closing the door behind them both.

The Agent was quite pleased that the interrogation had gone so well. She had succeeded in forgetting the much sought-after details of her life with the Killer, although admittedly, a general feeling of unease overcame her whenever they said his name.

That aside, she had scored a trip to a doctor to safely assess her condition. Once the necessary tests were run, she would know how to proceed to the next step of the mission.

Chapter 5

Director Gomez and the assistant director, Blair Lee-Smith, received Agent Bourghin expectantly. Blair stood uncomfortably close to him, but she seemed to believe that backing up would betray a lack of confidence. Bourghin took a small step away from her and began digging through his pockets for a handkerchief, which he found at length, and used to wipe his sweaty brow.

The director cleared her throat and said, "Agent Bourghin, from the way you're perspiring, I can't tell whether you've got good or bad news for us."

"He's just nervous," Blair said. "Look at her body language. She's quite obviously preening for him."

The three of them turned to look at the young woman in the interrogation room. She sat with her arm draped over the back of her chair in a casual-looking half-stretch that accentuated all the right curves tastefully but noticeably. Although they observed her through one-way glass, she seemed to stare back at them with her odd, calculating stare.

"Well," Gomez said, "if she is preening, it's only what she learned from the Killer. You've heard the reports of how he breaks his agents. It's no wonder all of them are versed in enticement."

Blair shrugged. "She seems *well* versed in it."

As if—by some impossibility—she had heard Blair's comment, the woman in the interrogation room smiled. It was not the wide, brilliant smile of the girl who had gone missing three years before but an almost imperceptible upturn of the corners of her mouth. One might not have noticed it at all but for the fleeting warmth that glimmered in her eyes before dimming to cold calculation once more.

"She feels threatened by me, by us, by all this," Agent Bourghin whispered, more to himself than to his interlocutors. "But why?"

Blair chuckled. "If your claims about what you were training her to be are true, then she might not even remember who you are."

"But she should *always* remember me!" Bourghin said perplexedly. "She was primed to respond to me. When I used the handler summons, it should have brought her back from wherever or *whoever* she thought she was."

Three armed officers brushed past to retrieve Bourghin's trainee from the interrogation room. She appeared in the doorway and gazed intently at the director and her assistant. A hint of sadness crept into her face.

"Did you really allow him to take me?" she asked Gomez in a trembling voice.

The director's eyes widened. "What do you mean?"

"The Killer said you authorized the mission," the young woman said, her voice evening out.

"The Killer said—" the director echoed incredulously. "How could you believe that I would *ever*—"

"She absolutely did *not*!" Agent Bourghin said. "How could you ever think that we'd do something like that to you?"

"Just wondering." His agent motioned to the abnormally high collar of the director's blazer. "Nice collar. Is that the fashion nowadays?"

"I've always worn this style." Director Gomez fidgeted with her collar. "I feel exposed otherwise."

A puzzled look from the Agent.

Blair stepped in front of the director.

"I'm Blair Lee-Smith," she said, smoothing her mousy brown hair. "I transferred from the Eastern FBI a couple years ago to be the assistant director here."

The Agent took on an inquisitive expression. "They do that now? Transfers from the FBI? I thought once you're in, especially in the East, you're in for life."

"Well, I was one of the first transfers." The assistant director smiled. "And I *had* to come here when I heard about the hypnotics department. I wanted to learn only from the best."

She shot a furtive glance at the director. The Agent looked between the two of them in a moment of peculiar silence. Then, she met Agent

Bourghin's gaze briefly before following her escorts into the elevator that led to the parking garage.

When the elevator doors had closed and the number display over them began to count down, Agent Bourghin, the director, and her assistant moved into the conference room across the hall.

Director Gomez regarded Bourghin pointedly. "So, you think the handler summons was unsuccessful?"

"Well, it was at least partially successful."

"What does that mean?" asked Blair.

"It—well, um, it means—" Bourghin's forehead wrinkled as he searched for the right words. "I'll just show you."

He pulled out a small, portable holodevice, one of the older models that had been phased out in the Eastern States, and flung it into the middle of the table. It brought up a 3D image of Valencia Thomas sitting in the interrogation room.

"This is a little over five years ago," he said, "a few weeks after she signed on with us. I recorded this interaction to establish a baseline. Take a look."

The teenager in the recording sat on the edge of her chair, grinning from ear to ear. Beneath her bob of curly ringlets, her regard was bright—gleeful, even. She fidgeted, drumming on the table and tapping her feet in an elaborate rhythm.

Okay. Bourghin's voice came through the speakers slightly muffled since, in the original recording, he had been behind the camera. *Why don't you tell me about yourself? What makes you tick?*

The girl in the recording raised an impish eyebrow. *Seriously? We're going to do some kind of weird speed dating exercise right now?*

She paused to think, then began to drum on the table again. *Well, where to start? My name is Valencia Thomas. I'm a Class 3.5 pureblood, female as they come...*

"It's exactly the same!" Blair exclaimed over the recording. "She's saying the same exact words!"

Bourghin motioned for her to keep watching.

I guess, if there's anything that makes me tick, I'd have to say it's my brother.

The director gasped and sat down in the nearest chair.

Interesting. Can you tell me more about that?

Then, much like in the recent interview, the girl's face lit up. *Oh, what can I say about my brother? He inspires me every day. I guess, he just—he helps me to be better.* She smiled bashfully. *That enough?* Bourghin answered in the affirmative, and her smile widened.

The image flickered out, and the director and her assistant stared dumbfounded at the holodevice.

"So, the words were the same," Blair said slowly. "But the delivery was astronomically different. She spoke nearly at a monotone today, but she had almost no modulation in the original recording."

"Did you catch the part about the music?" the director asked. "*That* was different from the recording. Today, she said she 'would have said music.'"

"The music thing's not a huge deal," Bourghin told her. "She's probably pushing some of Miller's interference out of the way, so she can retrieve the memories."

The director suddenly looked very disturbed. "You mean, the Killer used music to interfere with your bond as handler?"

"Possibly, so that gives us a little insight into her life with him," Bourghin said. "But here's the meat of the issue, director: the information in this recording—well, not all of it is completely factual."

Blair frowned. "Is that ethical? Baseline recordings serve to establish what truth looks like on a person. How can you call it a baseline recording if she wasn't telling the truth?"

"Ms. Lee-Smith, you ought to know by now that covert agencies absolutely must protect their agents," Bourghin said. "I did this in Lenci's best interest."

All of the color drained from the director's face. "This is *not* good."

"I'll say," Blair exclaimed. "At the FBI, we never would have—"

"No," Bourghin interjected, "you probably wouldn't have. But you're missing the point. I'm trying to tell you that, in the absence of facts about her time with Miller and in the regurgitation of this false information from her intro, Lenci is *sending* us a message!"

"Explain," Director Gomez said, her voice deepening as she tried to regain her composure.

"Lenci's reverted back to the fictional Agent Thomas from her intro recording, so she must have been under considerable pressure during her time with Miller," he replied. "But maybe she *can't* tell us what happened because the situation here is so serious that we can't just talk about it plainly."

Blair's eyes narrowed. "Simply put: you think Miller has people here at SSI?"

"We've thought so for years, now," Gomez said glumly. "That was actually the reason we were priming Agent Thomas. We intended for her to infiltrate the WCE and, among other things, to figure out where the leaks were on our side."

"Well, that backfired on you, didn't it?" Blair said matter-of-factly.

"I wouldn't say so," Bourghin said, "not irreparably, anyway. Lenci is still primed to respond to me. She may have forgotten everything to ensure that she doesn't reveal something she shouldn't. But with the trigger-prompt approach that the director approved, we'll have her rehabilitated in no time, and we'll get the information we need."

The director and her assistant did not look nearly as convinced.

Bourghin turned toward Gomez and said in a hushed voice, "She specifically requested a family practice doctor. Can we keep any updates off her record for now? She thinks her older aliases may be protected, but I'm not so sure. Miller can find a needle in a haystack, and I know he won't give her up easily after spending so much time training her."

"You are the only person at this agency who knows her identity of origin," the director replied. "So, just send her to a physician who saw her in her childhood and use her existing records."

"But how can we keep her identity of origin safe if—"

Side-glancing him, the director continued, "That way, if the Killer is looking for her under her agency name, he'll have a harder time of it."

Ms. Lee-Smith nodded in approval. "I know a great tech specialist who can develop a virus to encrypt the medical records remotely. She can encrypt or decrypt anything, pretty much."

"You don't mean that *delinquent?*" Gomez's eyebrows nearly met her hairline. "Do you really think it's a good idea to involve Agent Thomas' pre-teammates in this?"

"Rackelle Wernicke is a genius," Ms. Lee-Smith insisted, "and loyal as an agent can be. She's very excited at the prospect of working with Agent Thomas. Theresa, on the other hand, may need to be persuaded."

"Or ordered," the director said bluntly. "Your call, though."

Blair nodded. "Noted. And with your permission, I'd like to request that all the information Agent Bourghin has on Agent Thomas be released to me, so I can properly brief her pre-teammates."

"Now, wait a second," Bourghin said. "There's a reason that info's confidential. Revealing too many aspects of Lenci's personal life is dangerous, not just for her but for those closest to her!"

"Alright, okay," Director Gomez interjected. "Let's compromise. Rackelle and Theresa will need, at least, to know Agent Thomas' name of origin in order to work with her. And I will only approve the release of any other information at your discretion, Bourghin."

"Fine, but only one of them can gain proximity to her family," he said. "That'll be more than enough."

"Why don't we make Racky the main liaison to the family since she already has to know the name of Agent Thomas' doctor in order to encrypt the records?" Blair suggested. "Theresa can be around as an extra pair of eyes without knowing all of Agent Thomas' info. Agreed?"

Bourghin sighed. "Just be careful. Lenci's sensitive enough that she could pick up on the smallest deception. I'm worried what would happen if we broke the already fragile trust we have."

"That's part of the risk of doing a trigger-prompt," the director told him. "Remember, this was your idea, Agent Bourghin. It had better work. We *need* it to work."

Chapter 6

THE NURSES AT DR. WILLIAMS' OFFICE called the Agent by the name of Valencia Chang. She was surprised by this name of origin but figured that a Class 3 female might well have the name 'Chang' if she were from, say, one of the northeastern states of India. In any case, the uncommon name-class pairing worked in her favor. The Killer would have a time of it trying to find her under that name, and that was the way she liked it—because if the Killer couldn't find her, no one could.

Despite the Agent's excuse that she had fallen while rock climbing, the nurses made a fuss over the bruising, the scratches, and the mild ankle sprain that she hadn't really noticed before. They insisted upon running multiple tests, and it was in the ensuing argument that the possibility of an X-ray was established as an impossibility. Other equipment was necessary for the examination that needed to take place, and from there the post-mission checkup took on a completely different tone.

"We're not like the fancy medical offices of the Eastern States, Ms. Chang," one nurse said. "We don't have those no-contact scanners, so we'll be doing a blood test to best—"

"No blood tests," the Agent said, staring at the floor.

"But—"

"I said *no!*" Her gaze snapped upward.

Then, becoming aware of the tension among the nurses, she said more softly, "I think I'm far enough along that you could use ultra-sound—please."

"Alright, Ms. Chang," the nurse said soothingly. "I'm sure Dr. Williams will be willing to accommodate. We'll ask her about it."

The Agent watched as the nurses exited together. They looked over their shoulders at her like she was some kind of monster. It was not the first time anyone had looked at her like that. Although she had no particular memory of such an instance, she felt a familiar indecision about whether to cry or laugh in response.

When the door closed, she turned her attention to the medical supplies that were sprawled across the counter in front of her. She took a blood pressure cuff and slipped it into her satchel.

***

Dr. Williams was supposedly driving in from Forsythe when she gave her approval for an ultrasound. The nurses conducted the procedure with the screen turned away from their patient. Then, they sent her out of the room in the most unprofessional and gleeful anticipation. They apparently did not understand that, sometimes, directness was what a patient might need most—especially with this kind of news.

In the waiting room, a thin, old man plunked down in the seat next to the Agent named Lenci and beheld her with wide, appreciative eyes. She nodded at him but suddenly felt as though she were entertaining unexpected company. After all, she had not been in this life long, so she did not yet feel comfortable striking up a casual conversation. There was little she could say about a self that she was still learning.

She snagged a fashion magazine from the table in front of them.

"Good grief," she muttered, staring at the cover model decked out in metallic lingerie.

It seemed that faux chain mail intimates were now considered *haute couture*. Having been on tour with the Killer was like having been outside of time for decades. Technology, fashion, arts, and music had all been advancing while she was gone. She tossed open the magazine and flipped through the pages to see what else she had missed.

She could not, however, escape the feeling that the man next to her most likely had not blinked since he first laid eyes on her. She met his gaze expectantly. He continued to stare without shame. Because she was feeling polite, she cleared her throat and scooted a few centimeters away from him.

"Miss," he said, at last, "you're very beautiful."

"Thank you."

44

She looked down at the article that she had been reading, but the words were blurry.

"Ms. Chang?"

The Agent started. That was her.

The nurse smiled warmly from the doorway. "Dr. Williams will see you now."

The Agent stood.

"Bye, Miss!" the old man called after her.

She nodded at him, then followed the nurse back into the examination room. She watched mutely as Dr. Williams, a short, Class 4.14 woman in her fifties, pointed to the ultrasound images on the computer screen. She seemed so happy.

The Agent allowed her tiny, dazed grin the ten seconds of fame it was due. The smile felt like a rip in her face.

"So, that's that!" Dr. Williams beamed. "Looks like it'll be prenatal vitamins and virgin margaritas for you, at least for the next seven months or so! Oh, you're *all* grown up, Lenci!"

The Agent hated that name. She threw the doctor a dour glance, then quickly masked it with a wide, brilliant smile.

Bathsheba

Her shoulders, which had been tense and drawn up, began to relax.

"What wonderful news, Doctor," she said, varying her tones so as to not sound numb. "My father will be thrilled."

She swallowed hard.

"And your mother and brother, I imagine." The older woman smiled sympathetically at her patient.

Lenci considered the idea of her brother being thrilled, just for a moment, but her head began to ache before she could even bring her mind to conjure the image of his face. She was sinking, sinking right through her chair into the depths.

Come, Bathsheba

"I understand if you're nervous," Dr. Williams said. "Look, I know an OB in Forsythe whose unit just got their hands on a hand-me-down surrogate device from the East. I could refer you, if you like."

The Agent cocked her head at the doctor. "A surrogate device?"

"It's nothing like what they've got in the Eastern States currently," Dr. Williams said, "but it may save your body the trouble. They'll

45

monitor you just after the transfer, but they'll send you home within a week or so."

"What's the survival rate?" the Agent asked.

"For you? At this stage, ninety-two percent," the doctor replied. "But I imagine you're asking about the baby. If they transfer the baby in the next couple of weeks, the device will deliver sixty percent successfully, which is better than many of the earlier models."

Sixty percent was not great, but it was better than nothing. The problem was that Forsythe was full of technology that could be used to track the Agent. It had been dangerous enough to pass through once, but to stay there for a week was a bad idea. Facial recognition from a drone or a saleswoman giving samples or, more likely, a security camera in the OB unit could give away her position.

The WCE, which had influence everywhere, would have operatives infiltrating the place within an hour of her arrival. They would, of course, wait to act until she was incapacitated for the procedure or during her recovery. Then neither the cargo nor she herself would have much of a chance of survival at all.

The Agent shook her head. "Sixty's not good enough. What's the rate if I stick with you?"

Dr. Williams smiled proudly. "We've got an eighty-five percent survival rate for both mothers and children. That's the highest in the district."

"Then, I'm staying here," the Agent said resolutely.

She had, after all, beaten the odds in less likely cases.

"Very well," Dr. Williams said. "You were always such a strong girl. You can do this."

A wry laugh from the Agent. "Just going to miss my favorite whiskey on the rocks."

The doctor chortled gaily. "Your baby and your liver will thank you, Lenci. Diablo hasn't gotten funding for any of those synthetic organs like they have in other districts. And a healthy child—"

The Agent looked up abruptly, fixing her cool, determined gaze on the doctor. "Next visit is in four weeks, you said?"

The doctor nodded, encouraged that her patient seemed to be engaging this process at last.

"I exercise a lot. Do I have to change my exercise routine at all?"

"Goodness, no!" The doctor chuckled. "Do you know how many patients I have to badger into staying fit during pregnancy? Honey, if you want to exercise, be my guest!"

"Hm." The Agent relaxed a little. "Well, thank you, doctor. I greatly appreciate your advice."

"Don't mention it, Lenci. Listen, now, I remember how much you hated needles when you were little, but for the sake of your pregnancy, I hope that you'll reconsider your decision about the blood tests and amniocentesis. We just simply don't have the technology of other districts, but if you'll cooperate—"

The Agent wordlessly fled from the room. Despite Dr. Williams' entreaties for her to come back, she sprinted as fast as she could down the hallway.

The waiting room and the lobby were surprisingly empty, which caused her to wonder if SSI had planted an ambush out at the street exit. Turning sharply at the edge of the lobby, she made for the parking garage. She would hot-wire a car there and find some place to lie low until she could dump the cargo and reinitiate contact with the WCE.

On the top floor of the garage, she approached a gray jalopy. The car was practical for a low-profile getaway as long as she stayed in the poorer districts. It had no alarm, was too old for GPS tracking, and had easily replaceable parts. She stuffed the blood pressure cuff she'd stolen into the crevice between the driver's side door and the body of the car and pumped as fast as she could. A small space began to grow between the frame of the car and the door. As she was feeding the car antenna through the space she'd made, she realized that her respiration had kept pace with her pumping.

All at once, she found herself lightheaded and weak in the limbs. Her throat was constricting and no air could pass. Or maybe she was hyperventilating. Retching—that's what she was doing, doubled over, vomiting beside some stranger's car.

Wretched—that's what she was. David would have given her the stones with triple the weight for making a scene like this. Anyway, he would probably kill her when he found out about the cargo. And, if he didn't, the Vice would probably order it done. The mission had become complicated beyond belief.

Wiping nonexistent tears from her cheeks, the Agent rose gingerly to her feet. Just then, she heard a cough, which was actually the clearing of someone's throat. Sliding into code orange, she turned to face her observer.

"This is where you used to hide when it was vaccination time. So, when Dr. Williams told me one of her patients was making a getaway, I figured I'd find you here." The older lady with curly hair and skin the color of milk chocolate smiled at her knowingly. "You forgetting something?"

Instinctively, the Agent lent herself to the woman's open arms. For the first time since she had arrived in the States, she dared to indulge in a tiny giggle. This woman, who was almost assuredly a Class 4.14 pureblood, was supposed to be Lenci's mother.

"Pureblood" was an imprecise descriptor for any human being, given that it assumed biological causes for differentiation among groups that had differentiated due to social factors. The term essentially referred to a group's recognized status within the Neo-Eugenic hierarchy.

For instance, the designation of 4.14 was given to Americans whose ancestry included slaves, slaveowners, and oftentimes indigenous people as well. Neo-Eugenic law distinguished them from other Class 4s who were understood to be distant genetic relations of the 4.14s but spoke different languages and came from other areas of the world. The slave ancestors of 4.14s had been brought from one such area, Africa, but most of their now-free descendants called the States their home. Despite the diversity of phenotypes within the class, its members maintained a designation of 4.14 unless they became subclass by association in a domestic partnership with someone of a different class.

The Agent wondered if it really could be that Valencia Thomas, now Chang, was subclass. And if her mother was Class 4.14, what on earth could her father be?

The mother held the Agent at arm's length.

"Our baby's having a baby," she said with sparkling eyes.

She smiled broadly as she unlocked a green sedan next to the gray jalopy.

"Come on! Let's get you home."

The whole situation felt wrong. The Agent briefly considered hopping into the gray car and driving until she lost this woman who had come to claim her. However, the thought of spending the next few months running from place to place with no papers, barely sleeping, stealing food to get by, and trying to find good medical care for the cargo kept her rooted where she stood.

The Agent studied the mother's face. She must have been involved with SSI since she knew exactly where to be at the right time to make contact with her.

"Get in the car, silly girl," the mother coaxed with an empty laugh.

The Agent took a mental note of the mother's empty laugh and made a move for the driver's side door.

"Don't even try it," the mother said. "I don't know if you had any driving training wherever you were, but until you pass a real and true Western States license exam, you will not be driving *my* car."

Sighing, the Agent trudged back around the car to sit on the passenger's side. The older woman's tactics were more roundabout than those of the man in black, but she also seemed to be biding her time, awaiting a convenient moment to extract the information that she wanted.

As they rolled out of the parking complex, the mother said, "Your dad arrived earlier this afternoon, and he and your brother are spending some time together at the bowling alley. Guy time, you know? They should be with us in time for dessert."

Then, she tossed out what seemed to the Agent to be a baited line. "But you know, the *Wilsons* were excited to hear you were back. And they invited you and me to dinner at their apartment this evening."

After a moment's confused silence on the Agent's part, she clarified, "To welcome you."

"Oh," the Agent smiled. "How kind!"

The mother glanced at her sidewise, not necessarily in suspicion but not necessarily trustingly either. "I told them you might be too tired, but—"

"No, no," the Agent said, shaking her head enthusiastically. "I'm tired, but I've missed the Wilsons dearly. It would be a joy to have dinner at their apartment tonight."

Her response had been too enthusiastic, perhaps. The mother's facial expression informed her that there might be a reason why Lenci would not have been so quick to accept a dinner invitation from the Wilsons.

"Their boy, Karthik, has really connected well with Lorenzo," the mother said, looking into her blindspot before changing lanes. "Well, Karthik's hardly a boy anymore. You remember Ethan, don't you, Lenci? He goes by his first name nowadays. Anyway, he moved back in to take care of Preeti while James is away. Took a desk job to do it, even though he loved patrolling. It'll be nice for you two to catch up."

The Agent did not respond because she was searching for something. In her fuzzy tangle of facts about Lenci, there was no Karthik. In fact, she was fairly sure that a boy named K. Ethan-James Wilson might not be so amenable to the idea of being called 'Karthik.' She glanced suspiciously at the driver of the car. The mother was staring straight ahead, but the Agent knew that she was watching her out of the corner of her eye.

Chapter 7

THEY WERE NOT FOLLOWED—the agent was sure. She had been watching the rearview mirror for most of the ride over from the doctor's office, but no one had been tailing them. It seemed strange that SSI was not keeping a closer eye on her. She concluded that there must be trouble brewing under the surface of this tranquil reunion.

The mother parked in the multilevel garage of an apartment building in Central Diablo. It was not a glamorous building. In fact, it was quite run-down. This should not have come as a surprise to the Agent seeing as how Central Diablo was one of the poorest boroughs in the district.

The ride up the elevator was silent but for the creaking of the elevator cables. They rode up to the sixth floor, which made the Agent very uncomfortable.

"I don't like sixes," she rationalized aloud.

The mother simply responded, "I hope you haven't picked up that superstitious nonsense your Aunt Adenia is into."

Aunt Adenia, of course, for whom Lenci had been named, which made her Valencia Adenia Chang. Other than that, all that came to the Agent's mind was bananas. They stopped in front of an apartment with a faded blue and pink doormat. To the Agent's horror, the mother did not knock. She simply pushed open the door and stepped in.

"We're here, Preeti!" she called out from the Wilsons' living room.

"I need to pee," the Agent said, fleeing down the hall of the apartment in search of the bathroom.

She found it with no trouble. Once inside, she wearily closed the door and leaned against it. This was her first moment of real privacy since she had awakened in the boat. She splashed some water on her face, ran her hands through her hair, and inhaled deeply.

The air was damp and warm, reminding her of the humid nights she had spent in a house somewhere in Chile. The smell of soap dredged up an echo of the dread that she used to experience at the opening of the bathroom door after David's post-training shower. She refused to think about that, though. The nightmare of training and night training and David and Bathsheba was over.

Suddenly, she was filled with a different dread, a dread stemming from the fact that she had run straight into the arms of a family that expected her to be Lenci Chang, their daughter and sister whom she did not know any better than they knew Bathsheba. She fingered the colorful fabric of her tourist-trap shirt and groaned.

Gripping the sides of the sink, she stared into the mirror and sighed, "What did you get us into this time?"

"I find myself asking that question when—never you're around," a male voice responded.

The Agent whipped around to find a young man peering out at her from behind the shower curtain. His skin was like the bark of a manzanita tree glistening after a rainstorm. On his head, there was a curly, black crop of tight springs from which water beads dripped onto his broad shoulders. She stood aghast at the realization that she must have walked in on the end of this man's shower. He grinned sheepishly.

"Can you hand me that?" he asked, motioning to the bath towel beside her.

She mutely handed it over, too embarrassed to say anything at all.

"Thanks," he said. The curtain concealed him briefly and then he stepped out of the shower with the towel around his waist. "Uh, welcome back?"

He inched around her, shielding his bare torso as he did. His movements were slow, yet choppy, as he seemed to be trying to decide whether or not to hug her.

Probably thinking better of that, he said, "Well, I guess I should get some clothes on."

"Yeah, me too," she said. "I mean, you should. I should—"

They both tried to exit at the same time.

"Oh, sorry," she said.

"N—no, after you," he replied, motioning for her to go first.

51

"Thanks," she mumbled, rushing down the hallway.

She paused at the edge of the living room, struck by an incomprehensible reverence for the space. It was a comfortable living room and dining room combination, open and spacious—inviting, even. The furniture was well maintained, though faded with age. A chair and two couches with floral prints, a loveseat and a sectional, were congregated around a mahogany coffee table in the living room. A blanket delicately embroidered with sprays of blue and pink flowers was draped over the back of the loveseat. And beyond the loveseat was the dining table.

Lenci's mother sat at the table, facing away from her. She was placing forks and spoons on paper napkins at each place setting.

"Have a seat, Lenci," the mother said, without turning around.

The Agent came to the table and slid into the chair closest to her. Down the hall, she could hear a door closing and footfalls thumping toward them. The young man had finished dressing.

"Eat the salad for now!" a lively voice called out from the kitchen.

The mother smiled knowingly. "Preeti always brings out all of the main dishes at the same time."

"And somehow, they are *all* still hot when she d—does," the young man added, sitting down across from Lenci.

She stared at him silently, wondering why he seemed so at ease during what had promised to be a shocking reunion. Lenci Chang had returned after five years away, three of them dark, and there were no tears or hysterical hugs. It was as if she were picking up right where she had left off.

"Lenci, you remember Preeti and James' son, don't you?" the mother prompted her.

The Agent said nothing but continued to study him unabashedly. She had been reluctant to do so when he was naked and sopping wet. She liked his earnest, long-lashed eyes more than Bourghin's, because there was a playful gleam in them. This man's regard prodded her toward gaiety rather than sorrow.

"Sure, you remember me," he grinned. "We met in the, uh—" He motioned toward the hall.

What he left unsaid proved the absurdity of the whole situation. They were all performing roles like actors in a play. He was aware of the falseness of the whole setup, and he was goading her with it.

With a pained smile, she replied, "You're having fun at my expense, Ethan."

"I go by Karthik n—now." He said it as if choosing to go by his first name were some praiseworthy feat.

It wasn't. At least, not in the Agent's book. She stared at her empty plate.

As Preeti had suggested, Monica served salad to the two young people and then sat down next to her daughter with a plate of her own. The salad was a mix of fruits and vegetables tossed together in what smelled like a sweet vinaigrette. The Agent had eaten something like it during her travels through Kerala. Grateful for familiar food in an unfamiliar setting, she stabbed at a pomegranate seed with her fork. It flew off of her plate and landed in the middle of the table.

"Oops," she mumbled, grabbing the juicy seed and placing it back on her plate.

She moved on to something more stabbable: a piece of apple. It landed on the floor underneath the table. One would hardly believe the amount of well-aimed stabbing she had actually done in her lifetime, even in the past couple of years alone.

"Oops," she mumbled again.

From the tense silence, she gathered that both her mother and Karthik were watching. She resisted the temptation to crawl under the table to retrieve the apple but seriously considered feigning illness just to be excused.

She looked up and hesitantly met the amused gaze of the young man.

"You n—nervous, Lenci?" he asked rather mischievously.

It bothered her that she was so unsettled by him. She never had that problem with anyone. Misdirection was her tactic of choice in the survival game, and yet there was something about Karthik's gaze that was entirely too fixed. She had nowhere to hide. So, she resorted to her practiced deadpan look.

"Welcome back, Lenci," Mrs. Wilson said, coming out of the kitchen with a serving bowl full of a delicious-smelling stew. She nodded her head contentedly as she sat down. "We are glad to have you back from all of your wanderings across the world."

Although her voice sounded robust and strong, she was physically quite a frail woman. From the thin tufts of hair that had only just grown back, it was not difficult to deduce that Mrs. Wilson had recently undergone an aggressive cancer treatment. Neo-Eugenic law had never been kind to those understood to have a predisposition to terminal illness, but the Agent found herself strangely affected upon observing the consequences of its influence on Western Federal healthcare.

She smiled politely. "Thank you for having me, Mrs. Wilson."

The older woman's laugh was iridescent, shooting like beams of light from her fragile frame. "Please, call me 'Auntie Preeti,' still. The past few years are no obstacle to me."

"Oh, Preeti," Lenci's mother jumped in, speaking mechanically as if she were repeating information solely for the Agent's benefit. "The doctor said Lenci was having some trouble remembering aspects of her childhood—all due to a rock climbing accident, you see."

Auntie Preeti nodded understandingly. "Don't worry, Monica. Our memories are not what they used to be either. Come. Help me get the rest of the food from the kitchen. We'll leave these two to reminisce. Perhaps something will come back."

The Agent heard her chuckle as they walked away, "They're a long way from running through the sprinklers in diapers, hey, Monica? But they are just as handsome together as they ever were."

She frowned. This charade was going to prove even more difficult than anticipated.

"So," Karthik began, "d–didn't think you'd t–turn up here ever again. What's new?"

If the Wilsons were truly as close to the Changs as they seemed to be, then it would only be a matter of time before they found out, "I'm pregnant?"

Karthik's angular jaw shifted ever so slightly, but he said nothing. He seemed less surprised than she had expected him to be. Maybe he was just searching for the right words. She waited. He tapped his long, slender fingers on the table in sequence from pinky to thumb and thumb to pinky—both hands, back and forth—like he was playing two partial scales simultaneously on the piano, two octaves apart. A nervous tic, perhaps.

She had known someone with a tic, not a nervous one, though. Well, it had actually been more like a grimace. But he was of no consequence at the moment—she hoped.

At last, Karthik stopped tapping his fingers and asked, "What made you come back?"

She huffed. "I can't visit my family without people asking questions?"

His eyes began to laugh, but his mouth very seriously responded, "I d–don't think it's strange th–that you'd want to visit us. I just thought—"

"I said my '*family*,'" she interrupted.

54

The laughter in his eyes faded, and an incredulous half-grin melted onto his face. "I thought you were joking with all th—that 'Mrs. Wilson' st–tuff. But even after our blowup, you wouldn't d–disown mom. You really d——don't remember us, d–do you?"

It had taken the Agent a while to notice this peculiarity in his speech. Some sounds apparently snagged his tongue and wouldn't let go. His stutter had become more pronounced presumably because he was getting upset. Although the Agent found this unique trait rather endearing, her countenance remained defiantly expressionless.

Karthik began to rattle off a list of activities. "Board games and pillow forts? Outsmarting th–the Rump Bumpers? Run–ning from the d–dogs after curfew? Camping at Eucalyptus State Park? Our semesterl–ly finals parties? Skinny d–dipping at Fairw—"

She threw him such a scandalized look that he dropped off. The impact of Karthik's assumption of intimacy colliding with her ignorance of it seemed to stun him into silence.

After a moment, he ventured to ask, "What have you been d—doing th–that made you forget our ent–tire childhood?"

"I don't know," she said truthfully. "I remember nothing."

She could tell from his face that the statement stung. The table vibrated lightly underneath her fingers as he began his tapping again. And although she found his gaze overly probing, she decided it was believable that this Karthik, who had known Lenci since her childhood, cared about her deeply.

It's a shame that my only memory of you, Ethan or Karthik or whoever you are, is that you were just the neighbor boy.

There was no love or care in her memory, only fact, fact that had been drilled into her for the sake of a mission that she could not remember. And even fact, it seemed, was not entirely reliable as she had learned it. The neighbor boy, then, would prove a useful asset through which to glean updated and correct information.

The mothers returned to the table and, after the food was blessed, the conversation turned to other matters. Among the many dishes that Auntie Preeti had set out, the smoked pork in axone caught the Agent's attention. This must have been food that Lenci grew up eating, a dish from Nagaland where Auntie Preeti's mother had been raised. Lenci, the Agent imagined, had probably had the most terrible cravings for the smoked pork with axone, especially during her transition to the Academy. As it happened, the Agent was quite fond of the rich, smoky taste of the fermented soybean base, and it was no trouble at all for her to show Mrs. Wilson that she enjoyed her cooking.

Auntie Preeti began to fill Lenci in on major events that had taken place during her absence. Among some of the more interesting news was that Karthik had joined Diablo's most upstanding police department. Out of the district's four police departments, Canon was the most reputable. It was known to hire qualified members of the Subclass, and it had a zero-tolerance policy on corruption. Half as much could not be said for the other three departments.

"You know he's moved up in the department, Lenci?" Her mother said it less as a question and more as a statement that expected a comment.

The Agent named Lenci responded through a full mouth. "Oh, has he?"

"Yes," Auntie Preeti chuckled. "And he's at a desk job now. But he still stays in shape for patrolling, in case you couldn't tell from his toned physique."

"Mom!" Karthik stared at her in mortification.

She winked at Monica as Lenci began to stuff her face with renewed resolve.

Auntie Preeti tried to cram her raucous laugh into a more manageable giggle. "Oh, my Karthik. He doesn't like me to brag, maybe least of all about his looks, although the girls have always been chasing him. But, you know, he's also won multiple awards for his commitment to the community."

"Your dad and I were able to make it to his most recent ceremony," Monica told Lenci. "Karthik was awarded an eight-point star for his exceptional judgment and strategy in that hostage situation. You probably remember seeing something about that in the news maybe a month or so ago."

"I'm afraid not," Lenci said. "Last few months are pretty fuzzy for me."

Auntie Preeti mercifully changed the subject. "Monica, my cousin Constance's fourth son is getting married here in Diablo tomorrow. They only gave us two tickets to the reception, though."

"Again?" Lenci's mom frowned. "Preeti, they always do this to you. Have you talked to them—"

"Nothing to talk about." Auntie Preeti coughed a rumbling, body-wracking cough and waved her hand dismissively. "When my uncle joined the WCE, they started to treat my family differently.

Besides, they have limited tickets because they always want to host the reception at that expensive Palm Tree Veranda place, just across from the canal in Niebla Beach. We're just a convenient place to cut the costs."

Monica looked at her apprehensively.

"Kingston's family has been no different concerning you all," Auntie Preeti shrugged. "It is a mark of life in the Subclass, especially when our families of origin receive incentives from the WCE to 'keep the average.' Don't you agree?"

Monica inclined her head deferentially.

Auntie Preeti continued, "Anyway, James and I are seeing a concert for our anniversary that night. We've already got the tickets, and it would be a pain to change. It would be a shame, though, not to have a representative from our family at the reception. Do you think that Karthik and Lenci might go together?"

"Well, why don't we let them work it out?" Monica smiled.

Karthik's mom elbowed him in the side, prompting him to ask, "Would you like t—to go, Lenci?"

"Okay, but I'm not going to pretend I'm Class 3 or anything." It popped out of her mouth before she knew what she was saying.

"L—like I asked you t—to when you came with us t—to my cousin Shawna's wedding? In sixth grade?"

She rambled, trying to make sense of her strange outburst. "I don't remember that. But the classification system is completely unreliable. Why should we perpetuate the fallacy that skin color and bone structure are the main determiners of class when we more often categorize people groups based on language, geography, whether or not they have a military, or the social opinion of a generation? I will not stoop so low as to *pretend*—"

"*N—now* you're sounding more like yourself," Karthik said, a playful grin spreading across his face. "I bet you remember a l—lot more than you're l–letting on."

"Um, no," she said.

She could sense another round of Remember When approaching. So, she reiterated, "I remember nothing."

"Now, Karthik," Auntie Preeti entreated, "don't pester the girl."

"I bet she d–does remember, though," he insisted. "Lenci, d–don't you remember when we went t—to Ms. Gretchen's family ranch in kindergarten and the l–llamas peed on us through the fence?"

"Nope." She said it with some satisfaction and thought about adding "Go fish" but resisted the opportunity. She didn't want him to think that she was becoming friendly with him.

"What about the t–time when the Rump-Bumpers cornered us, and we tricked them int–to running through Professor Reymund–do's yard?"

His shoulders began to shake.

Then, after taking a deep breath, he continued, "She had th–those flesh-hungry d–dogs—"

His voice started trembling again and then he began to laugh so hard that the story dissolved into hiccups, stutters, and fake growls. Lenci was certainly amused by his story, even though it had not conjured up any memories of flesh-hungry Pomeranians—or whatever type of dogs they had been. Karthik's contagious laughter struck a chord in her much in the way that an oldie but goodie playing on the radio might feed a homesick soul. Despite this strange sensation, she refused to join in the laugh fest.

Taking a couple of deep, shuddering breaths, Karthik folded his slender fingers and leaned toward her. "Okay. You're going t–to play stone-face with me, Lenci? Well, I got a good one for you. D—does the word *'Buttface'* mean anything to you?"

"Karthik!" the mothers exclaimed in unison.

"What a word to bring up at the table," Auntie Preeti said, shaking her head.

"Sounds like a personal problem to me." Lenci glowered at Karthik.

Her haughty attitude was interrupted by his smirk. Karthik had discomposed her, and he knew that he had. And now, he was leaned back in his chair with the smuggest and most unbearable face that basically told her to eat dirt.

Noticing the mothers' confused expression, she stammered, "I—I'm sorry. I don't know why I said that."

"Don't be sorry, girl," Auntie Preeti said in her sensible way. She popped Karthik upside the head with her open hand. "Shame on you!"

He rubbed his head gingerly but did not dare to talk back. Meanwhile, the Agent sifted through her cache of learned memories. The term "Buttface" was nowhere to be found.

"Oh, Preeti, it's okay," Lenci's mom said. "It must be difficult for him to see her this way. There will be plenty of time for them to catch up in the coming days. Perhaps we should get home now."

Auntie Preeti rose and gave both Monica and her daughter a firm hug.

"You come by anytime," she commanded. "It is just like old times: standing invitation."

"Thank you, Auntie Preeti," Lenci said. "Goodbye, Karthik."

"N–nice to have you back," he replied.

The Agent watched mutely as he reached across the table and extended his right hand, pinky outstretched. Without thinking much about it, she mirrored his gesture, and he hooked her little finger in his own.

The mothers smiled at each other knowingly. The Agent felt her face grow hot. Without another word, she unlinked her hand from Karthik's and hurried out the door.

Monica stepped into the hallway after her. "See you tomorrow, Preeti. Come on over after your shift, Karthik."

He shouted his goodbye as Monica swung open the door to the Chang apartment.

Chapter 8

IF FOOD WERE EQUIVALENT TO LOVE—as it seemed to be in the Chang family—then Lenci's parents could not have loved her more. The feast of desserts that the Changs had prepared for her would have been enough for ten dessert times every day for ten days. However, the reason that the Agent stopped dumbstruck in the doorway was not the endless potential for sugar rush.

At the dining room table, there sat a man with golden beige skin and short, straight, black hair, whom she presumed to be Mr. Chang. Due to his asiatic bone structure, he was most likely some sort of Class 2. If he were Class 2.0 exactly, then the family's lowest possible designation would be a whopping Subclass 6.14.

It was a ridiculous system, but that was how it worked. Mathematics had been used to calculate class designation for a couple of generations. The rules were simple: those who procreated within their own class averaged their designations to calculate the designation of their child, and those who procreated across classes added their designations to calculate their family's subclass designation. Neo-Eugenic law made it known that it was preferable to keep the numbers as low as possible.

Therefore, it appeared that Agent Thomas, who was registered as 3.5 pureblood, was a woman with scandalous secrets. However, this strange surprise would work to the Agent's advantage. Being subclass would make her much harder to track since members of the Subclass were not registered at all. Plus, the Killer would not initially think to look for her outside of Class 3 communities.

"Come in, Lenci," the mother said.

Mr. Chang sprang to his feet and smiled broadly.

"Hey!" he boomed with an authentic southern twang. "There's my girl!"

She rather hated that phrase, but she gave him a tiny smile and allowed him to hug her. She pondered the familiarity of that feeling with her ear pressed to his sternum and the vibrations of his voice coursing through her. Perhaps that sensation reminded Lenci of security, of a life before her world had turned upside down.

"How was your trip?" she asked politely, wondering where Mr. Chang could have arrived from.

Lenci's dad was a traveling businessman of some kind. He could have been coming from anywhere.

"Oh, that Windsailing to Forsythe flight *never* gets old. I love that view out the plane window, especially when crossing over the Meridian. Now, don't get too comfortable. Come this way!"

She followed him as he flitted away to show her how they had kept her room just the same as she had left it "except cleaner, of course." Lenci's old pillows and stuffed animals were on her desk, and her sheets sat washed and folded at the foot of her bed.

"Mom and I made *all* your favorites," her dad chattered excitedly. "And Mom really outdid herself this time. You know how she is. She couldn't just bake a tray of chocolate chip cookies and leave it at that. Oh no, she had to make the chocolate chip, the coconut macaroons, the snickerdoodles, the fruit pies, *and* a chocolate cake. But that's your Mom for you. I love her for it. I made everything else: the pecan pie, the *don tot*, the ice cream, and the strawberries. Well, I bought the ice cream, and God made the strawberries, but you get what I mean."

"Kingston!" Lenci's mother called down the hallway. "Your son needs you to talk to him."

"Coming, Boss!" Her dad sighed, shaking his head.

Then, grinning, he continued, "How do you like it? He's *my* son whenever he does something bad, but at all the honor student club celebrations he's *her* son."

He closed the door and, shortly thereafter, his heavy footsteps thudded away down the hall. The Agent named Lenci sat on the edge of the bed, taking a deep whiff of the musky air, and stared at the corner nearest the door.

When she was young, Lenci had stored her box of special trinkets in that corner, and the box had never obstructed the door's mobility.

The doorframe to this room was only about thirty centimeters from the corner, leaving a space much too small for a box that contained a childhoods' worth of special treasures.

"I don't care that you did it! If you didn't turn it in, it doesn't *count!*"

There was a muffled response, then Kingston shouted, "Yes, even if all of the answers were right!"

Lenci smiled. Her brother was being reprimanded for not having turned in his homework. She could hear her dad from behind the two closed doors between her room and the common room. Kingston Chang was living disproof of the quiet, unassertive Class 2 stereotype. And of all the loud, assertive Class 2s in the world, he was one of the loudest and most assertive. Of that, she was entirely certain.

She turned her attention back to the corner by the door. Squatting down, she sniffed the wall and then touched it with one finger. It came away a little stickier and beiger than before. *New paint.*

Someone had gone to great lengths to make her believe that this was the room where Lenci had slept for the majority of her childhood. But perhaps it was a mistake to credit mere civilians with such an elaborate plan. Force of habit, she reasoned. She hadn't survived this long by trusting everyone that came across her path.

The congregation of stuffed animals on Lenci's desk beckoned to her with their open arms and stitched-on smiles. The small, purple, plush sheep at the edge of the group had most likely been her favorite. Well, it was her favorite now, in any case. She took the sheep in her hands and turned it over. In faded ink, the name "Eugenia" was scrawled sloppily onto the tag on its rear end.

Eugenia the Ewe—that was a cute story. Lenci had first met Eugenia when Monica and Kingston first brought her infant brother home from the hospital. The stuffed sheep was Lorenzo's gift to her. Being the newcomer, he was expected to bring some sort of tribute to persuade her to grant him a space in her kingdom. Or, that's how she had explained it to her parents, who graciously obliged. And somehow the generous, wrinkly bundle that they had brought home eventually evolved into a witty pudge-ball of annoying little brother.

Her brother! She hadn't even had a chance to greet him yet. Quickly stepping out of the gaudy tourist outfit, but leaving on the stockings, she searched through the closet for something more comfortable. She found some old pajama pants, which were quite snug on her muscular thighs, and a fuzzy bathrobe.

Tying the bathrobe shut, she hurried down the hall and threw open the door to the common room. She was shocked to find her parents sitting at the table with a lanky young man whom she didn't recognize.

"Oh." She hesitated, looking around for the little boy who had just gotten a talking-to from their parents.

Her mom chuckled. "Lorenzo, greet your sister, please. It has been five years, after all. This isn't the time for a 'hey, what's up' kind of salutation."

The young man at the table stood up and begrudgingly approached Lenci. She regarded him half in awe, half in horror as he came near. Where had that chubby little jokester gone? This was an adolescent with a hint of facial hair framing his jaw line! The mess of curly hair, which their mother had so often threatened to cut off if he did not wash it, was neatly buzzed. His solemn eyes reflected the light from the overhead lamp, giving them the appearance of two golden orbs planted shallowly in his thin face.

"Lolo?" Lenci was unable to contain her surprise.

"I go by Renzo now," he informed her testily.

She put her arms around him, mentally fumbling around to find something that could make sense of this mess.

"Weren't you, like, six the last time I saw you?"

"I was nine," he replied, pulling back. "You know, back when you abandoned us all?"

He returned to the table and angrily piled more desserts onto the already sizable mound on his plate.

"Lorenzo!" their father and mother exclaimed.

"No," Lenci mumbled, taking her seat at the table, "it's okay. I just wish I had an explanation for you all."

Her head was reeling, and her heart was pounding. Memorizing facts had not prepared her for the magnitude of emotions that she would encounter. She had not trained for this.

"James Wilson and your dad are working on a project out in the Windsailing District," Mrs. Chang said. "If you're feeling up to it in a few months, we'll spend the holidays with them out there in the Eastern States. It could be nice to spend some time in the only unaffiliated district in the country, don't you think?"

The Agent looked at her blankly.

Kingston cleared his throat. "You see—I'm only visiting right now, honeybunch. I'll go back to Windsailing tomorrow morning. James wanted to be here to greet you, too, but we were notified on such short notice—"

"I called him as soon as the doctor's office called me about your visit," the mother added hurriedly. "Dr. Williams thought it would be better for me to come and get you after the tests instead of the police showing up to process you on the details of your disappearance or something crazy like that."

The hours didn't add up. Windsailing was on the far eastern coast, and Diablo was on the far western coast. Even in a supersonic, that trip would have taken at least three hours with the drive from Forsythe and the border crossing. Suppressing the urge to demand how exactly Mr. Chang had arrived in Diablo so quickly after that phone call, the Agent simply nodded.

"Kingston," Monica said, serving herself a piece of cherry pie. "Wouldn't you know it, Karthik and Lenci are getting along just like old times?"

"Really?" Lenci's dad grinned at her somewhat incredulously. "I definitely didn't expect it to be all that easy after the last conversation y'all two had. I mean, I thought there'd be at least a little groveling on his part. Let him off easy, did you?"

"Was our last conversation that remarkable?" She mirrored her dad's grin. "I can't imagine what we could have talked about that you'd still remember five years later."

"Pretty hard to forget," Kingston said.

He scraped the last bit of lemon meringue off of his plate and prepared to slice the pecan pie. "Well, we don't know what it was all about. Probably another of your typical arguments about class identity, complete with yelling, fist-shaking, and door-slamming. Just, after that one, you—well, the way you described it was that y'all's 'paths diverged.'"

Lenci thought she would have remembered a discussion like that, especially one that had resulted in her losing contact with her family, but she didn't. She remembered nothing.

"Well," her mother said, "that's all behind us now. Lenci's back, and she and Karthik are friends again. In fact, he'll be coming by tomorrow to take her to his cousin's wedding reception."

"I hope you told him you're not going through any more of that pretending-to-be-Class-3 crap," Kingston said. "You're a Chang and proud of it!"

Lenci smiled at her dad. She didn't tell him that there are people groups of different classes from many places in the world, even Class 3 people, who actually do have the name "Chang."

"Don't worry about that, Lenci," Monica said. "I'm sure you two will have a lovely time."

"Karthik doesn't have a night shift tomorrow?" Lorenzo perked up in his chair. "Maybe after the reception, we'll get through the next level of *Zombies With Protruding Umbrellas*!"

Perplexed, and maybe slightly intrigued, Lenci repeated, "*Zombies With Protruding Umbrellas*?"

"Yeah," her brother said, smiling for the first time since she had been home. "It's where the Z-virus can be passed through the typical biting method but also through injector umbrella sticks that protrude from the butt cheeks of the *undead*. And the *only* way to stop a zombie is to cut off the umbrella *and* stick it through the host's cranium!"

The mental image was nearly as fascinating as any mind that would habitually choose to dwell on it.

Lenci turned to her parents and asked, "When did Ethan start going by his first name?"

"The year you, ahem, disappeared," her mother replied quietly.

It was a conveniently emotionally charged answer but entirely plausible. Lenci fell silent, and her parents' empty chatter about Kingston's project in Windsailing took over the conversation. Their discussion turned to some important paperwork for Lorenzo's charter school, then quickly jumped back to Kingston's life in Windsailing.

As the Agent compared the scene before her to descriptions of Lenci's home life as she had learned them, she found the two to be quite similar indeed—maybe too similar.

Perhaps that was a silly thought.

The reunion passed slowly for Lenci. She was glad to see her parents so happy. Her younger brother was even allowing his chilly attitude to thaw, just a bit. But there was a pit in her stomach, a dull ache that became a weight as the evening progressed, and she could find no relief from it.

At long last, her mother stood up and began collecting dishes.

"You must be tired after all that travel," she said.

Lenci smiled at her gratefully. "I never sleep well in the air."

She had nebulous memories of having been in the water before she'd been in the air, but those were fading fast.

"Well, in that case, why don't you head to bed? For tonight, we can manage cleanup without you."

Yawning, Lenci hugged her mom and her brother.

"Welcome home, baby," her dad said, kissing her on the forehead.

"Thanks," she replied before making her way down the hall.

"*I'm* the baby of the family," she heard Lorenzo declare as she shut the door to her room.

"I was the first baby," she whispered.

The words felt strange in her mouth, but she rather liked the sound of them. She glanced at Eugenia the Ewe, who was still sitting on the desk. She had half-expected the stuffed animal to develop a scary one-eyed grimace in her absence.

Now, that *was* a silly thought.

Turning her attention to the sheets that had been set out for her, Lenci grit her teeth and began her attempt at making the bed. Her absolute least favorite part of that process was wrangling the fitted sheet. After giving it her best effort, which was no small feat on account of her bruised knees, the stretchy corners finally stayed on the mattress, and Lenci skipped to the bathroom in triumph. She brushed her teeth and splashed water on her face, which felt cleansing in more than one way.

Hearing laughter down the hall, she rushed back to her room. Her mother was doubled over with tears streaming from her face.

"You put it on sideways!" Her dad snickered, motioning to the wrinkled sheet that was stretched lopsided across the mattress.

A hint of pink appeared in Lenci's cheeks since, being brown-skinned, she never turned such a color as red.

"It's okay, baby," her mom said.

Then, nudging Kingston in the side, she whispered, "See? She still needs us, after all!"

With a little more joy than Lenci thought they should have had in the process, her parents made her bed, tucked her in, and turned out the light.

"Good night, sweetie."

As soon as the tiny sliver of light under the door vanished, the Agent found herself accosted by darkness. With slithering hands, it groped her, grabbing at her from all directions and stealing her breath away. It had her by the neck, and it had begun to squeeze. Then, like a lustful tongue parting her lips, it wormed its way in, abruptly and angrily. She was not Lenci now. She was just herself. And there was no light, not even from the moon, to keep the darkness at bay.

Flailing her arms to beat the darkness from her body, the Agent leapt from the bed and frantically felt around for the light switch by the door. The darkness retreated, at least for the time being. Sighing with relief, she left the light on and returned to bed.

Lenci listened to the family washing the dessert dishes and putting them away, and her heartbeat slowed to normal. Later, her dad turned on the TV, and her mom was on the phone, most likely talking to one of her relatives in Windsailing. She always got louder when she talked to her family of origin. Hopefully, Lolo was doing his homework as he yammered away about *Zombies With Protruding Umbrellas*. Somewhere far away, below them maybe, she heard piano music. These were the sounds of life.

If the Agent had not suspected that these sounds were meant to compel her to abandon her mission, she would have allowed herself to be comforted.

Chapter 9

THE NEXT MORNING, THE AGENT awoke well rested. As the haze of sleep wore off, however, she remembered that she was in a fake room in a fake apartment with a family who did not know her, although they were embarrassingly easy to deceive. They truly believed that she was Valencia. As did SSI—it seemed—since they had not yet ordered her imprisonment or execution. Maybe that was still to come. In the meantime, she had a role to play.

Deception was never the Agent's favorite part of her work. She preferred the straightforward hits, no emotions, no personal histories to complicate matters. Her line of work was simpler in many ways than life in a family. Still, she reminded herself that *her* life was not the only one to take into consideration at this point.

Eugenia the Ewe was still smiling at her from the desk. The Agent named Lenci smiled back begrudgingly and crawled out of the bed. She was lucky that she didn't feel pain or else she would most likely have been too sore to complete her objective for the day. She planned to find a job and, in so doing, create credibility for her alias by plugging into the community. She would make sure that her new workplace was somewhere that played the news constantly. David had taught her to always watch the news.

She pulled off her pajama pants and the stockings that she had worn underneath them. Examining her scarred legs in the mirror, she touched the shiny cream-colored skin.

How could such scars have come from a rock climbing accident?

She'd have to find a way to keep them covered. She was in hiding, after all.

The clothes in Lenci's dresser were stale-smelling and too small in more than one way. Nevertheless, the Agent examined everything and set aside the items that she wanted to keep. Nothing in the dresser was acceptable interview attire, except for some gray, itchy tights, which she pulled on immediately. There were also some black stockings, but they looked too nice to wear in a gym.

In Lenci's closet, there seemed to be nothing but cocktail dresses, stilettos, and one-shouldered smock shirts. After a nearly fruitless search, the Agent noticed a bit of blue fabric on the top shelf. A pair of gym shorts was peeking out from underneath a large cardboard box labeled "Specials."

Unable to find a tank top, the Agent donned a magenta, ruffled smock shirt, the tourist-trap shoes, and the gym shorts. Her muscular thighs swallowed the shorts so that they were just a small band of blue stretched to capacity around her pelvis. Shuddering, she turned away from the mirror and promised herself that she would buy more sensible clothing once she had a job.

Among other personal effects, such as house keys and emergency sanitary napkins, an old, clunky cell phone sat on the dresser. It very well could have been Lenci's phone from before she signed on with SSI. All of the photos, messages, and apps were erased, though.

No information to be gleaned there. She smiled wryly as she stuffed the phone and the keys into her tourist-trap satchel.

To her relief, no one was in the living room or the kitchen. There was a message somehow projected onto the front door in red light.

It read: **Didn't want to wake you, sweetie. Took brother to school, dad to airport. Will be back from work around 1700 today. Little cash on table. Food in fridge.**

Lenci was slightly taken aback by her mother's mention of going to work. Last thing she recalled, Monica Chang had been staying at home to homeschool Lorenzo in order to accommodate his learning disabilities. A lot could change in five years, though.

Instead of rushing out the door, Lenci poured herself a bowl of cereal and milk and sat at the table like a civilized person. During her time away, she had been forced to break unrefined habits like sitting on the couch while balancing a bowl in her lap, although she still considered that the most comfortable way to eat anything in a bowl.

The cash that the mother had mentioned was sticking out from underneath a couple of papers. The Agent stuffed the money into her purse. The papers that had been on top of it were copies of registration forms for a charter school in Central Diablo—right around the corner, in fact. Lorenzo had just enrolled a couple of days before.

That struck the Agent as odd, seeing as how school was just about finished for the year. Perhaps it was summer school enrollment. Anyhow, it was none of her business when Lenci's parents enrolled her brother in school. She finished the rest of her cereal, washed the bowl right away, and rushed out of the apartment.

***

When the Agent named Lenci hopped off the bus at the mall in the most recently gentrified Diablan borough, Resplendent Oaks, she knew she was in the right place. A gut feeling told her that the gym in this mall would be her new employer. She imagined that mall gyms tended to have high staff turnover. And for her, that would be an advantage.

She turned some heads when she walked into the gym, probably because of her strange outfit, but she didn't let that bother her. She marched right up to the sign-in desk, put her elbows on the counter, and flashed the receptionist a huge smile.

"Hello," she said. "I'm new here, and I'm looking for a job. Any chance you're looking for a personal trainer?"

The receptionist was tall and toned as one would expect a guy working at a gym to be. He wore a tight puce T-shirt and black slacks. Pinned conspicuously to the side of his belt was a name tag that read: **Hi! My name is Rory**.

Rory the Receptionist looked the Agent up and down scornfully. She could tell that he was judging her by her outfit and possibly by the fact that she was a woman. She decided that she did not like him.

"Don't waste your time," he said, folding his hands over what looked like a stack of blank application forms. "We only have a few openings, and our hiring process is very selective."

She stared at the pile of applications, then at his hands for a moment.

Playing a hunch, she said, "I hate to do things this way, but may I speak with your manager?"

"I'll call him, but don't get your hopes up. He'll tell you the same thing."

Rory gave her one last disdainful glance before picking up the phone and paging for the manager.

The Agent leaned casually against the counter, occasionally shooting dagger eyes at Rory, who had taken to staring at her bare shoulders with a disturbing ravenousness. She turned her attention again to his hands, and most specifically his fingernails, which she had noticed were slightly blue at the lunulae.

Most of the exercisers politely only glanced her way for a second, even if multiple times. However, their glances became full-fledged stares when they passed on her side of the desk and caught sight of her outfit or her humongous legs. She couldn't tell which of the two was more distracting to them. One guy even ran into a pillar because he was looking back at her after he had already passed.

After a few minutes, a grumpy man who looked as if he had not had time to exercise in a while, came out to the reception area.

"This is the female I was telling you about," Rory the Receptionist whispered to him.

"Woman," the Agent corrected him with a smile. "I was just telling this *gunk-sniffer* that I'd like to apply for a job as a personal trainer in your gym."

Rory's eyes grew wide. "What makes you think I'm a gunk-sniffer?"

The Agent shrugged. "The wheeziness of your breath and your blue lunulae. I'd say you've been using for about six months?"

"*Again*, Rory?" The manager glared at him. "I told you that we wouldn't send you to rehab another time!"

Rory's face became bright red. "I'm sorry, boss! I swear I'll stop today."

"Oh, give the guy another chance," the Agent said. "Whenever a gunk-sniffer tells me they'll stop, they *never* start again."

The manager's mouth melted into an upside down *U* as Rory looked at him imploringly.

"Oh, alright! But you'd better stop for real this time, you hear?"

Rory nodded and scampered off to somewhere that the Agent would not be able to uncover any more of his deep dark secrets.

The manager sighed deeply. "My name is Bread. How can I help you, Miss?"

His name tag read: **Brad**. However, because of the way he had pronounced his name, the Agent decided right then and there that he would forever be 'Bread' to her.

"Lenci." She smoothed her frilly shirt and smiled once more. "Like I said before, I'm hoping to apply for a job as a personal trainer—"

"We don't have any openings," the manager said decidedly. "Sorry."

He didn't seem too sorry to her, and the fact that the receptionist had previously told her that there *were* some openings led the Agent to suspect that Bread was lying about more than just his sorriness. He opened his mouth to ask her to leave before he called security, but he stopped short when a gentle hand fell on his arm.

"Hey, Brad!"

The Agent's heart skipped a beat. There, standing before her, was none other than Chandler Bourghin, the man in black. Well, he wasn't wearing black at the moment. He was wearing a loose, gray T-shirt and darker gray basketball shorts. He looked oddly casual, too casual.

He glanced back and forth between her and the manager. "What seems to be the problem?"

"Eh, nothing, Sam," Bread said, grasping Chandler's hand in a firm handshake. "This female, excuse me, '*woman*' wants to apply for a job as a personal trainer here. I told her we don't have any openings."

"Sam?" The Agent shot Bourghin an inquisitive look.

He ignored her.

"Well, now, Brad," he said, "Maybe you should just give her a little tryout. She might surprise you."

"You kidding me?"

Chandler's gray eyes were sparkling mischievously as he looked at Lenci, but he said nothing.

"Look, just give me a chance to show you what I can do," she said to Bread. "And, after that, if you can't see how I can add to your gym, I'll leave and never come back."

That last part seemed to be all Bread wanted to hear.

"Okay, come on." He motioned for her to meet him on the other side of the desk, and his eyes widened upon seeing her enormous legs.

Chandler the Handler followed them. The Agent could hear his shuffling footsteps about five meters behind.

"Alright," the manager said, bringing her to the Ladder Bars, the most challenging piece of equipment in the whole gym. "Might as well start here."

"Oh," the Agent breathed.

She looked up at the tall column of bars. They were kind of like a ladder, but the rungs were more than a body-length apart.

"Aren't these the kind of bars they often use to train elite secret agents?" she asked.

"Yup," Bread replied proudly. "We actually got this set in near-new condition from the Warbuck training center directly. Cost us a pretty penny. We also set up this extension to the side for the *most advanced* athletes who want to move laterally and not just up and down—a little extra challenge."

The Ladder Bars towered over her. Even with a good jump, it seemed unlikely that a person of her height, which was on the short side of average, could reach the bar closest to the ground.

Bread continued smugly. "At our gym, we have all the best equipment for only the *best* athletes. The Ladder Bars are made for males who are in their physical prime. So, there's no shame in not being able to—"

"Hold this, please," she said, passing him her satchel and slipping out of her shoes.

Bread seemed to know a lot about the type of people who came into his gym. He did not know, however, that Lenci had practiced on this very set of Ladder Bars a few years before, while she was seconded to Warbuck. It had been her favorite piece of equipment in the Warbuck training center.

So, with Chandler the Handler as a kindly spectator and Bread the Manager gawking like a fish, Lenci bent as far down as she could to get a powerful jump. Then, she sprang upward, flipping in the air, and caught the first bar in the crook of her knees. She swung back and forth to get the momentum for another flip, then flung herself upwards to catch the next bar with her hands. Soon, she was looping up and down the vertical frame of the Ladder Bars like a human pinwheel. When that bored her, she free-fell from the top bar and caught the first bar of the lateral set.

By the end of her third lap on the lateral set, a small crowd had formed. Weightlifters and other gym members who were there strictly for the aerobics classes all cheered as she made her way back to the vertical set. She would have done that all day if that is what it took, but Bread finally called out to her.

"Okay, okay," he said. "That was alright."

The Agent triple-twisted during her dismount to the cheers of all the onlookers.

"So, I have the job?" she asked, smoothing her frilly shirt.

The manager shifted uncomfortably. "Well, you're a little *too* gifted. I mean, we don't need acrobats here. We need regular old weightlifters, people everyone can relate to. I need people that can teach my guys—"

"And women," Chandler said, clapping him on the back. "Brad, may I have a word?"

"Punishing excellence only breeds mediocrity!" Lenci called after them.

The men looked back at her, one with a disgusted glance, the other with an amused one.

She winked at neither one of them in particular and fiddled with the nearby leg press machine to give them the illusion of privacy. After linking up three-hundred kilos to press, she sifted through the hum of the busy gym to focus on the voices she wanted to hear.

Bourghin whispered to the manager, "Listen, Brad, how long have we been friends?"

"A long time, Sam," Bread replied. "But this female'll ruin business for me, showing all the guys up like that! If you think that you can convince me to give her a job, then you'd better just walk away now."

The Agent huffed indignantly, pushing out her legs. Leg pressing three hundred was little more difficult than squatting without weight. Her audience began to move in behind her, but she pretended not to notice.

Bourghin was laughing. "Ruin your business? She'd be a great trainer for anyone who actually wants to be trained and a great spectacle for anyone who wants to buy a membership just so they can watch her."

"What's it to you, Sam?"

"I just see potential in her. That's all."

Bread turned to look at her, and she waved from the midst of the crowd.

"Is this seriously all the weight this machine can take?" she asked just loud enough for everyone to hear.

Her new fan club roared with excitement.

"Oh, alright," the manager said, turning back to Bourghin. "But she's got to get some different clothes, and leg pressing without shoes is against the rules."

"You're the best, Brad," Bourghin said, thumping his back.

Bread grunted in response and trudged back to his office.

Bourghin sent the crowd away and knelt down next to his agent. "You heard everything, didn't you?"

"I didn't need you to handle that for me," she said.

"Well, I am a *handler*; it's kind of what I do." He snickered at his own joke.

"Are you allowed to talk like that out in the open?"

He shrugged. "The general public is stupider than you'd think."

She gave him a scrutinizing glance. "Why are you following me?"

"It would appear that *you* are following *me*."

"And who's to say we should go with your version of the story?"

Chandler scratched his scruffy cheek and grinned. "Well, for starters, *I* introduced you to this gym. I trained you here before you were seconded to Warbuck. That was before Brad became manager, of course."

"Hm." Lenci examined his face for any sign of deception, but she found none.

"Alright, well, riddle me this, Chandler the Handler," she said, crossing her arms, "*Brad* called you Sam. Why did you tell me your name is Chandler?"

"Because it's my name."

"Is it?"

"As names happen to be at times," he replied, smiling at her as if she should detect humor in his statement.

"Hm."

They sat in silence for a moment.

Then, Lenci asked, "So, if I'm following you, why did I come *here*?"

"I guess we'll find out, eventually." Chandler stood up. "Well, I've got to get home. Dr. Bourghin is returning from a tour in the Sovereign Nation of Hawai'i, and I told her I'd make her favorite dinner tonight."

"*Doctor Bourghin?*"

"Our loved ones are our best kept secrets, hey, Lenci?" He paused, then addressed her in American English. "You may see other folks you recognize around here, but don't be alarmed if you do."

It was only when he spoke to her in Lenci Chang's mother tongue that she realized they had previously been conversing in a mix of Hindi and English.

"Goodbye, Chandler." Nasally American dialect.

He nodded and headed toward the treadmills. The Agent headed for the door. There were four hours until she had to be ready for Karthik's cousin's wedding reception, and given the state of Diablo's bus system two of those hours would be spent in transit.

Bread had left the tourist-trap shoes and satchel on top of a trashcan outside of his office. Luckily, maintenance had not been by there yet.

The Agent poked her head into the manager's office and sang, "See you on Monday, *Bread*!"

"Now, look, everyone here has to work at least one Saturday per—"

"I'll make sure to have plans. See you Monday!"

She was about to bolt when she noticed Tanzanian drum music pulsing from one of the multipurpose rooms. The teacher of the aerobics class squawked instructions over the loudspeaker, but even the squawking couldn't distract from the beauty of the music. The Agent leaned through the doorway to get a glimpse of the class in session. Just as she did so, however, the music stopped.

"Well, that is all for today, my beauties!" the teacher squawked. "Remember to eat well, hydrate, and stay wonderful. I will see you on Wednesday!"

She was a lean young woman of average height with skin like a delicate, creamy rose and an abundance of honey-colored ringlets that were stretched into something that rebelled fiercely against the idea of a ponytail. She wore a bright orange, sequined camisole and violet yoga pants under which—the Agent happened to notice—she was not wearing any underwear. On her thin wrist, she wore an old analog watch. It was almost certainly an antique, given that women's timepieces had not been in fashion for as long as either of them had been alive.

"Ey, girl!" the teacher said, smiling broadly. Her headset was still transmitting her voice over the loudspeaker. "Well, don't just stand there. Get in here!"

The Agent stepped into the room, fascinated by the boisterous young woman.

"My name is Racky," the teacher declared, her voice still booming through the speaker. "Actually, my name is Rackelle, which is why you have to say it like 'Rocky' not 'rack-ee'. 'Rack-ee' is my pet peeve, especially since I am *not* well endowed."

She glumly looked down at her flat chest and then back up at the Agent with a shrug.

The Agent smiled, extending her hand. "Lenci. I just signed on as a personal trainer."

Racky took her hand, yanked her forward, and clapped her on the back.

"Ey!" she exclaimed happily. "Alright, Circus! All my students were jabbering about your stunt tricks out there. 'Downright acrobatic' these seditty women called you. You are making waves already, new kid."

Lenci shrugged. "Well, I had to put on that show to even be considered. That manager of yours—"

"Ah, *Bread*." Racky shook her head. "Good thing you put him in his place. He needs someone around who won't butter him up too much."

"Is *that* why he's called 'Bread?'" Lenci asked. "I thought it was because he was so crusty."

The sound that came out of the aerobics teacher was something akin to the sound that a drunk llama might make after inhaling helium.

She did a couple of jumping jacks and proclaimed over the loudspeaker for all the world to know, "New girl's got jokes! Alright, Circus. You are okay with me!"

Lenci's brow furrowed slightly.

She thought she might have misheard before, but since Racky had repeated it, she asked, "I'm sorry. Are you calling me *'Circus?'*"

"Yes, she is," a cool, sharp voice cut in. "No doubt because of your little, ahem, performance for the musclemen out there. Drew quite a crowd, I hear."

The speaker was a sour-faced woman who approached them like a raincloud advancing across a sunny plain. She was mocha-colored and shapely, though certainly athletic, and her wavy, black hair was pulled into a low, sensible ponytail at the nape of her neck. Her face would have been prettier with a smile on it—Lenci imagined—but she was a fine-looking woman all the same.

"Theresa, my girl!" Racky's voice resounded all over the room until Theresa snatched the headset from her head and turned it off.

"We can hear you *without* the microphone," she glowered.

"Killjoy," Racky muttered.

The Agent extended her hand to the newcomer as well.

"I'm Lenci."

"Yes, the *amazing* one and only." Theresa crossed her arms, looking Lenci up and down. She explained, "I heard about you from Bread. You match his description almost exactly."

"But he neglected to mention my effervescent charm?"

The Agent did not like the smugness of Theresa's smile. She occasionally ran into women that, for one reason or another, had it out for her. This woman was one of *those*.

"Pity," she said aloud.

Racky shifted uncomfortably. "Don't pay her any mind, Circus. She could freeze hellfire with that attitude, but it won't matter if you just ignore her frostiness like I do."

"Can we go, Racky?" Theresa asked.

Sighing, Racky put a hand on Lenci's shoulder. "We carpool. Can we drop you somewhere?"

Judging from Theresa's alarmed expression, Lenci gathered that Theresa had hoped that she and Racky would ride home without her. So, she politely declined.

"I've got a bus to catch," she smiled. "It was nice to meet you, though."

As Lenci walked through the door, Theresa called after her, "Oh, Lenci! Aren't you forgetting something?"

Racky was holding out Lenci's phone with a goofy grin. The Agent couldn't even think of a moment when Racky could have reached into her satchel.

"Thank you," she said, eyeing the aerobics teacher as she took the phone. "I must have dropped it on my way in."

"Oh, no," Theresa said. "Racky lifted it from you because she's a klepto."

"No!" Racky protested. "I'm the—"

"Right, right, right," Theresa said monotonously. "You're the great equalizer, the one who brings equilibrium to the universe by shifting matter from area to area with or without the consent of those who own it, as if anything in reality can actually be owned."

Racky, who had been mouthing the words of this verbose recitation with a slight delay, nodded in satisfaction at its conclusion.

"I almost never keep the stuff I steal, anyway," she shrugged. "I do it mostly for the challenge of taking it. And the thrill. Then, the equilibrium."

"I'll have to keep that in mind," the Agent replied warily. "See you around."

"Back at you, Circus!" Racky called. "Working together's going to be a riot!"

"Indeed," Theresa purred. "Now, let's go before we're late."

***

"Did you complete the clone on Agent Thomas' phone?" Blair's voice came in with a slight echo over the speaker in Racky's junky, champagne-colored sedan.

Racky did not dignify that with a response.

"Of course she did," Theresa answered hurriedly, "but your outdated equipment took so long that she couldn't return the phone undetected. We had to improvise."

"And now Lenci thinks I'm a klepto," Racky said with no small amount of indignation. "I haven't stolen in years!"

"That's covert life in the Western States for you," Blair responded. "Once upon a time, people actually did function without mid-range cloning devices, and you can too."

Racky sucked her teeth and focused on the road ahead.

Theresa cleared her throat. "What are our orders?"

"Get in close. Win the family's trust. Win *her* trust. Report when you can. And Racky?"

"Yes, Blair?"

"Let me know if there's any call activity that is not to a family member. I don't care if she's ordering takeout; I want to know about it."

"Yes, Blair."

"I also need you to make an updated version of her record in the public system. Since she was a minor when she was assigned her agency alias, she won't have an official public record under her identity of origin. Import her childhood record, update the age, and arrange her new papers."

"Want the world on a silver platter, too?"

"The director says this is top priority."

"It will take time to work out the papers. My contacts are in Australia for the summer."

"Fine. Just get it done ASAP."

"Yes, Blair."

"Good work, ladies. Keep your phones on. Good night."

"Good night," Theresa and Racky said in unison.

Blair hung up, and Racky finally exploded. "This is backwards and trashy! We should have just told Lenci the truth about who we are."

"Those weren't the orders," Theresa said calmly. "Besides, what does it matter to you whether we tell her the truth?"

"All these lies—it's not at all decent, especially toward one of our own!"

Theresa scoffed. "You know what David Miller is capable of, so just imagine what he got out of her. She's probably betrayed us all. And if she did, she's about as far from deserving of decency as any human being can be."

"Theresa, you are just unbelievable."

"Me?"

"Yeah, you," Racky said. "You still can't let it go that Lenci made you second-ranked in our subdivision."

Theresa threw her a venomous glare. "And *you* need to lay off the hero worship of that traitor!"

Racky slammed on the brakes in front of Theresa's house.

"It's not hero worship to refuse to condemn a person without any kind of real evidence!" she said.

"Evidence," Theresa repeated, collecting her stuff. "Well, I guess that's what this mission is all about, isn't it?"

"I guess so," Racky replied curtly.

Chapter 10

IN THE CONFERENCE ROOM AT Sopient Solutions, Incorporated, Agent Bourghin told Director Gomez and Blair Lee-Smith about how Lenci had shown up at the gym and asked for a job according to protocol. And while she seemed familiar with the physical routine of the Ladder Bars, she did not appear to have regained her lost memories.

"So, I think it's a good start," he said, in conclusion. "She's following protocol, and her implicit memory seems to be intact. The trick will be getting her explicit memory retrieval to kick in."

Gomez shot him a skeptical glance.

"From the visual files of her Academy training, it seems pretty obvious that Agent Thomas has always had a flare for the dramatic," Blair said. "I think she betrayed agency secrets to David Miller, and now she's giving us the memory loss runaround to cover it all up."

"She's got better character than that," Bourghin said.

"No one who encounters the Killer escapes unscathed," Gomez reminded him. "Now, Lenci is probably the most gifted hypnotic we have, and as such she is extremely suggestible. After three years with the Killer, we don't know *what* character she has."

Bourghin forewent the opportunity to remind her that he had objected to borrowing David Miller from the ghost prison to train their up-and-coming sopients. It was true that Miller was a gifted tracker with unparalleled insight into hand-to-hand combat. Moreover, the man was second to none when it came to enhancing the natural abilities of his trainees. He could transform a lump of coal into a diamond in a matter of months. However, David Miller's excellence was always consistently overshadowed by the specter of his cruelty.

The man had been locked up where he belonged, where he wouldn't hurt anybody, and Gomez just had to insist on letting him out. She knew prison hadn't reformed Miller, but she invited him to train her agents under the mistaken belief that she would be able to keep him on a tighter leash. The project was doomed from the start.

Exhaling deeply, Bourghin said, "I'll concede that we've got to assume Miller was grooming her while they were away. But Lenci was primed to respond only to me, so whatever he did can't have been too successful."

"I once saw her learn three men simultaneously in sixty seconds," the director said. "She essentially *became* them, took on their mannerisms down to their very breaths. Now, if the Killer used control tactics on her *uninterrupted* for three years, don't you think he could have completely overhauled even her trust in you? For a mind like hers, one could liken it to having been raised from birth with him!"

"Lenci legitimately believes the cover Miller gave her," Bourghin admitted. "But it's a defense mechanism, like a locked box. The information we need is still in there. I just need a few months to find the key."

"We may not have a few months," said Blair. "Depending on what the Killer did to her, we may have a double agent on our hands."

Bourghin's words were carefully chosen and calmly articulated, although his body was beginning to shake as he said, "Assuming Lenci is a double agent is premature. She still believes her status is 'active and engaged,' which is hindering her from accessing the info she'd need to give a full mission report."

"Which begs the question of *which* mission she thinks she's on, Bourghin," Gomez said. "Has it occurred to you that the Killer may have corrupted her, and now she's just buying time until the WCE's next big strike? If she's flipped, we'll have no choice but to—"

"Don't!" he exclaimed. "Please, don't."

He paused to collect himself, taking a deep breath. "We can cross that bridge, *if* we come to it. For now, can we—can we—I'm just worried about her."

His interlocutors exchanged a glance.

The director sighed. "What do *you* believe is the priority here, Bourghin?"

"Lenci's health. I understand that the fax requesting medical records was a way to get back on our radar, but I can't get why she was so fixed on going to the doctor once we got her home."

"Well, she had that cute little fake limp," Blair offered sarcastically. "Maybe the family practice doctor told her how to treat her stubbed toe."

"She was favoring her left side when I found her. Her ankle's sprained," Bourghin said. "She's got rope burns all over her body, too. Also, her thumb was dangling from her hand. She and Miller must have had an altercation just before we found her."

Gomez scoffed. "She's had worse from training at the Academy."

He looked at her patiently, but his voice was insistent. "I know my agent, Director. Lenci wouldn't have asked for a doctor if she didn't need one."

"I don't think she was fighting with Miller," Blair said matter-of-factly. "They were most likely romantically involved. So, she probably sprained her ankle doing something else."

"I don't like what you're insinuating," Bourghin growled. "Lenci was only *fifteen* when we started her training with him, and we did everything we could to ensure an appropriate learning environment for her."

Blair seemed pleased to get a reaction out of him. "But you couldn't be with her every waking moment of every day. Have you *seen* those recordings of them sparring at the Academy? Even I could tell it was only a matter of time before she would end up in his bed!"

"Enough, Blair!" the director said. "Your tone is less than professional. And unprofessional is unproductive. Now, if you have any insights into the staggering lack of information we have gleaned, please share them now. Otherwise"—she motioned to the door—"I believe you've got some research to do regarding my missing agents!"

Ms. Lee-Smith nodded at her and Agent Bourghin before slipping out of the room. When she was gone, Bourghin sighed with relief.

"Assistant director or not, that young lady is the same age as my *niece*," he said, "and her fixation with using suggestive statements to get under my skin is disturbing."

"Relax, Samir," Gomez replied, calling him by his name of origin as a reminder of the trust they shared. "Perhaps you've forgotten what it's like to be young and impetuous. This is a perfect time for Ms. Lee-Smith to get some useful on-the-job experience."

He replied only with a glum glance.

She continued, "Anyway, my primary concern right now is the national crisis of missing agents. Your long-lost hypnotic is of particular interest in that respect, as is her possible connection to the World Council of Eugenics through one of the most dangerous ex-assets SSI has ever engaged."

"Miller's a mastermind," Bourghin said. "He probably found a way to fake authorization for the mission from Warbuck. Whatever happened, Lenci didn't know that you weren't the one sending her."

"I know." Gomez sighed, rubbing her powdered forehead. Her lavender eye shadow was beginning to smudge. "But haven't you heard what happens when a missing agent suddenly turns up these days? There've been two just recently at those Eastern agencies: Winehill and the Hive."

"I attended Ms. Lee-Smith's presentations on the internal crumbling of both agencies," Bourghin replied grudgingly. "But Winehill and the Hive had spotty management, at best. It doesn't have to be the agents' resurfacing that caused their collapse."

Gomez pounded the table in front of her. "Forty hypnotics from around the country have gone dark in the past three years! Twenty of them were from *our* agency! And now our hypnotic ops poster child, who was last seen with the WCE's most notorious contract killer, just happens to reappear without explanation? Samir, *tell* me you don't smell fish on this!"

"I *do*, Director! I just—"

"I know this is difficult for you as her handler. But you've got to get some emotional distance on this."

"My emotions haven't got the better of me," he said, casting a weary glance in her direction. "And I don't need you to understand why I believe in Lenci's loyalty and capability as an agent. However, I would expect some empathy from your side since you know what it's like to be in too deep, respectfully, Director."

She glared at him, but he thought that the absence of a verbal response could mean that she was taking his words to heart.

Emboldened, he continued, "Besides, you've seen what Lenci can do. Do you really want to be so trigger happy with that kind of talent? She survived her time with Miller and has potentially *learned* him. There is no one else on God's green earth who could make that boast."

Gomez looked pensive. After a minute of silence, though, Bourghin began to wonder if his spirited defense had fallen on deaf ears.

"It's a stroke of luck that she wanted to come here instead of to Windsailing," the director responded, at length. "We're a few steps ahead because the Killer doesn't know where she's gotten to. I guess that has bought us *some* time. Have you spoken with the family recently?"

Bourghin sighed with relief. "The relocation was successful. Thank you, Director. We had a few bumps along the way, of course. The apartment is actually on the floor directly above where Lenci lived as a child—same basic layout, though, with minor differences."

She side-glanced him as she opened the door to the conference room. "I'm sending a surveillance team of sopients who have already graduated from our Academy and proven their loyalty. Males."

"She's not going to go easy on them just because they're male," he muttered.

Gomez had been strangely on edge since Lenci's resurfacing. Given the director's own past with David Miller, Bourghin did not begrudge her the need to process the feelings that this situation was likely triggering. He just hoped that those feelings would not interfere with her ability to make sound judgments where his agent was concerned.

Chapter 11

THE AGENT HAD THE ENTIRE BUS RIDE to think about why the aerobics teacher had taken her phone. While she did not doubt that Racky could be a kleptomaniac, it was actually Theresa's smugness that made her wonder about an ulterior motive. So, as soon as she disembarked, the Agent tossed her phone into the trash compactor by the bus stop.

Her mother and brother were already in the apartment when she entered.

"I got a job today, mother," she said while Mrs. Chang bustled about in the kitchen.

"That's nice, sweetie. Want to give me a hand while you tell me about it?"

"Sure. What are we making?"

"Nothing fancy. Can you start shredding the chicken for the tacos?"

Lenci washed her hands and took her place at the counter in front of the rotisserie chicken. Her brother was doing his homework at the dining room table. Things had not seemed so normal to her in years. She thought she might actually have missed all this.

She cut off the string that tied the chicken's legs and took hold of one of the drumsticks. But when she ripped the leg out of its socket, the Agent was overpowered by a loud scream, anguished and shrill. Her hands were dripping with blood, and darkness descended so that she no longer knew where she was. The sound of breaking bones and that terrible scream swam chaotically in the air around her. And all through it, the darkness stroked her and whispered a horrible reminder.

Relief!

She gasped, dropped the drumstick into the dish, and rubbed her hands together frantically as if that action alone could wash off the blood.

"What's wrong, Lenci?"

Lenci regarded her mother with wide eyes. She couldn't remember what had been so upsetting to her. Looking around the kitchen for something to cue her memory and seeing only ordinary household items, she looked at the floor and said nothing.

"It's okay," Mrs. Chang said, eyeing her warily. "I'll finish that. Why don't you take a seat in the living room and tell me about this job you got?"

"Oh, it's, um, *nothing fancy*," Lenci said, grasping for a phrase she'd heard recently in order to make sure it was appropriate for this context.

She plopped down on the couch. "I just thought it'd be good for me to have a job. You know, contribute something around here. It's at the gym in the Resplendent Oaks mall."

"How nice," her mother replied.

"How was your day?"

Her mother described her day signing a lease on a property in the Sandland district where she would be recording training clips for the Sandland Zoo's camel vets, then silence settled between them. Lorenzo was still working on his homework, and Mrs. Chang was frying corn tortillas. Lenci took a fashion magazine off of the coffee table and began to leaf through it. She wasn't really reading it, though. She was secretly observing her brother.

Lorenzo was staring intently at his calculus homework. He scribbled away in his notebook, occasionally checking his work on the calculator beside it.

The memory that Lenci had of a spastic pudge-ball named Lolo, if it could be called a memory, floated on the surface of her consciousness like a vibrant reflection in a murky puddle. But here Lorenzo was in the flesh, a teenager, working with a quiet diligence that was becoming of his budding adulthood. In addition, she marveled at what a handsome young man he was growing up to be. She could hardly believe that he was the same child but for his unrelenting, razor-sharp gaze.

It was only then that she realized she had been staring. And now, he was staring back, his eyes prodding at her in the way he often used a stick to poke at poison ivy in their backyard.

"When did you start reading fashion mags?" he asked.

She hadn't. She didn't—or, she didn't know, actually. And there wasn't any poison ivy in Diablo.

There was a knock at the door. Soon after the knock, keys jingled and the door swung open. There, in a traditional Indian suit with a contemporary twist, was Karthik.

"Apparently, he has a key," Lenci said, surprised.

"Hi guys!" he grinned. "Mom's coming, too, but she sent me first."

"I gave him a key," Mrs. Chang told Lenci. "He just knocks to be polite. Come in, boy."

He handed the older woman a package and whispered something that Lenci didn't bother trying to overhear. Mrs. Chang took the package with a knowing smile.

"*Karthik!*" Lorenzo blurred past his mom and sister and caught Karthik in a sloppy single underhook.

His element of surprise was a short-lived advantage, if any at all. As soon as Karthik got a hold of one of Lorenzo's legs, he placed a hand on the back of his neck and leaned him into a gentle takedown.

"If you break any of my furniture, I'll break you." Mrs. Chang nudged them out of the way with her foot and closed the door behind them as they grappled on the floor.

"Here, Lenci," she said, handing her the package from Karthik. "Get dressed."

"What is it?"

"It's a gift from the Wilsons," her mom replied. "You should wear it to the reception."

Lenci had already been reluctant to go to this event, but now there were costumes involved.

"It'll be fun," her mom coaxed, holding out the gift.

Lenci sighed and took the package into the bathroom. It was wrapped in newspaper, but she knew better than to harbor expectations based on the wrapping. She lost her breath upon peeling back the first corner of the paper.

Peeking out from its periodical cocoon was a cream-colored piece of fabric with gold stitching. She hurriedly opened the rest of the package to reveal a *kasavu saree*, a traditional petticoat, and a blue *saree* blouse. The stitching was fine and sturdy, and the golden borders were decorated with the most intricate and beautiful pattern that Lenci had ever seen.

The petticoat did stretch, but it was quite tight around her thighs, so tight that she was afraid it would rip at her slightest movement. So, she decided to go without it. She fumbled through the bathroom drawers to find a safety pin to secure the end of the *saree* to the shoulder of her blouse. She was not about to take any chances while representing the Wilson family at the reception.

Likewise, she chose to wear the nice pair of sleek, black stockings that she had found in her room earlier that day and her gym shorts. While these served as extra layers of protection in case of an unraveling emergency, as the petticoat would have, they also kept her gargantuan thighs from chafing.

She wrapped the *saree* in such a way that the fabric flowed down to the floor in a cascade of folds, probably the way she had seen Auntie Preeti do it before every special event.

No, on second thought, no pleats. She took another look in the mirror. Maybe it didn't matter.

When Lenci came out into the living room, her mother and Auntie Preeti were sitting at the dining room table. Auntie Preeti gasped aloud when she saw her.

"Oh, Monica, look!"

Karthik's curly head popped up over the side of the sofa. His face lit up when he saw Lenci, and his eyes quickly became mush. In fact, he was so busy relishing the feeling of her image burning into his memory that he didn't notice Lorenzo's rather betrayed gaze boring through his temple. Lorenzo sighed and pulled himself up onto the couch, recognizing that their grappling match had come to an end.

Monica gave her daughter a quick once-over. "Yes, Preeti, she's beautiful and incredibly intelligent, per usual."

"Please, Mom," Lenci said, sitting down beside her to put on a pair of stiletto sandals.

Monica shook her head, possibly at her daughter's embarrassment and definitely at her bold taste in shoes.

"A little affirmation is not a bad thing, girl," Auntie Preeti said.

She stood up and held Lenci at arm's length to get a better look at her. Then, she took a small piece of wax paper out of her purse. Affixed to the wax paper was a blue-jeweled, ornamental *bindi* with gold trim.

She placed the bindi on Lenci's forehead and smiled broadly. "My goodness, Monica, she looks like a pureblood 3.3!"

Lenci thanked her to be polite, but she felt uncomfortable. It was a complicated matter to be taken for a member of a class with which one had no heritage link, even if unintentionally.

Her mother smiled at her sympathetically.

"Well, it's about that t–time," Karthik said, walking over to take Lenci's arm. "How d–do we look?"

As if on cue, they simultaneously struck a pose for their mothers' benefit.

"Wonderful, as always," Monica replied, chuckling. "Have a good time, you two!"

Suddenly feeling self-conscious on account of her familiarity with the neighbor boy, the Agent unwove her arm from his.

"Yes, have fun and be safe," Auntie Preeti added.

"Safety first," Monica agreed. "Karthik, don't let her drive."

"I'll try," Karthik laughed as he opened the door. "You know how persuasive she can be when she puts her mind to it."

Lenci rolled her eyes and stepped into the hall. "I won't drive tonight, mother. Don't worry."

"Yes, *mothers,*" Karthik echoed teasingly as he followed her. "Mother and mother, your children will be perfect little angels tonight to uphold the family honor."

"Get out of here!" Monica said good-naturedly.

In the elevator, Lenci asked Karthik about the concert that his parents were going to attend for their anniversary.

"I thought your dad was still in Windsailing for that project?"

"Oh, yeah," he responded. "The concert's just one of those online streaming things. Mom hasn't really been well enough to go out anyway, and dad couldn't come here for their anniversary. So, I set her up with one screen to chat with my dad and another to watch the Windsailing Symphony online streaming concert. Dad's going to be watching from their house."

"Whose house?"

She noticed that Karthik was not stuttering at all. Maybe he didn't stutter when it was just the two of them talking.

"I mean," Karthik seemed flustered. "My d——dad's house in Windsail–ling. D–dad's house."

She took it back. He didn't stutter when they were alone as long as he wasn't flustered. Her question had flustered him. It seemed that she was not supposed to know that Mrs. Wilson may have, until recently, lived in Windsailing. The elevator doors opened, and they walked through the lobby to the parking garage.

She changed the subject. "The *saree* is beautiful, but I thought you said I wouldn't have to do this."

"You d–don't have to pretend," he said, opening the door of his jeep for her. "It's just a gift—that also will make it so we don't stick out like a pair of sore thumbs."

"I don't believe this," Lenci muttered.

"It'll be fun," Karthik replied as he scooted into the driver's seat. "Just like when we went to the ninth grade dance. Remember that?"

"Don't mess with me," she said. "I know you didn't take me to that dance."

"I thought you didn't remember, Lenci." He flashed her a playful smile before pushing in the clutch and letting the engine roar to life. "And I only didn't take you because you t–told me to ask Maude Jackson. Remember *that*?"

"I remember nothing."

The Agent folded her arms across her chest and looked out the window. This situation made no sense. Only a couple of days before, she had had no family. She had lived with her husband in Chile, and he had protected her so that she could be trained. She certainly didn't belong here in the States.

And yet, she had a history here in Diablo, a mother and a father and a brother, and Ethan's family. It was true that she had been sent home to her family, to live in her room, to a place where she belonged and was loved. There were two truths, two realities, which she did not know how to reconcile.

"You know, *you* changed your name too, Ethan!" she said accusingly. "So, you don't need to get so high and mighty with me."

"I didn't know you'd changed *yours*," he replied, slightly taken aback at her outburst. "And it's not being high and mighty to be called by my first name."

"You used to hate it when people discovered your name. What's with the sudden spurt of exoticism?"

He frowned at her. "I thought you'd be glad to hear that I stopped trying to pass as a pureblood 4.14. Maybe all those lectures you gave me about claiming my whole heritage and associating with *all* my people finally started to sink in."

Lenci paused, then said, "You mean, you don't keep your heritage a secret anymore?"

"You remember a time when I did?"

She said nothing because, of course, she remembered nothing.

Karthik shrugged. "I saw how you struggled on the border of your two worlds, and I considered myself lucky to be able to pass. But I just lived with this terror of having to explain myself to people when they discovered I was subclass, which they inevitably did whenever they met my mom."

"Hm."

He smiled. "That's all you've got to say? I just told you 'you were right and I was wrong,' and you're just going to snort at me? Girl, I've never seen you pass up an opportunity to rub my face in the dirt!"

Side-glancing him, she asked, "Who does the *saree* belong to?"

"It's yours, of course." He shifted uneasily, keeping his eyes on the road. "It's a gift."

"It's not your *mom's*, is it?"

The jeep turned onto the highway. Karthik remained silent as he crossed the five lanes to the express lane.

"No," he said, at last. "I picked it out for you when I went to visit my mom's people last summer."

"Hm." She looked down at her exquisitely embroidered outfit with fresh eyes. It fit perfectly. "How did you know my measurements after all this time apart?"

This time, it was Karthik's turn to seek refuge in awkward silence. But the Agent had seen the many shallow scabs the size of needle pricks on his fingertips before they had even gotten into the car. They were the battle scars of a hurried tailor with an accurate, however slightly invasive, eye. He must have estimated her size when buying the petticoat and been unable to alter its stretchy material after seeing her in person. Nevertheless, his work on the *saree* and *saree* blouse was impressive.

Lenci was about to jokingly give him a hard time about how good of a look at her he must have gotten the previous evening to be able to tailor her an outfit for her, but her attention was drawn to the rearview mirror. A curious group of vehicles crowded the lane directly behind them. A large SUV with a motorcycle humming on each side was following them at distance of about three meters. That was too close for the Agent.

The cluster of vehicles continued to tailgate Karthik's car, even after he rolled down his window to wave them on.

"I've been meticulous about my speed, especially since I joined Canon," he explained. "Doesn't matter if I'm at a desk job right now. It's the principle of the thing that matters. These guys can tailgate me all they want. Speed limit's ninety, and ninety I will go."

The Agent's heart was pounding. Maybe it was silly to be afraid. No, *of course*, it was silly to be afraid. What did she have to be afraid of?

Lenci didn't rightly know.

The SUV and the two motorcycles followed them to the Palm Tree Veranda. However, when Karthik pulled into the valet station, the vehicles behind them drove into self-parking. It was only then that Lenci began to breathe more easily. She was even able to laugh at herself for having been so silly. After all, what did she have to be afraid of?

She didn't rightly know.

Chapter 12

THE RECEPTION HALL WAS ABUZZ with people dancing, eating, laughing, and talking. Well-dressed servers wove through the crowd with large, silver platters of appetizers. Lenci and Karthik took the first half hour or so to greet Karthik's relatives, all of whom were kind and welcoming. Some of them even remembered Lenci from previous family events, but they were very understanding when she explained that her memory was "not what it used to be" due to a rock climbing accident.

After Lenci and Karthik had congratulated the bride and groom, an extremely danceable song began to play. The music coursed through Lenci's body, awakening something that had long been dormant. She tugged on Karthik's arm excitedly. He didn't need any verbal prompting to know that it was time to dance, and although there was very little space on the dance floor, he graciously allowed Lenci to drag him into the crowd of celebrating relatives.

Lenci thought that she might remember a time when combat had been the only dance and the only music had been the sound of bones breaking. Well, there had also been a Song. But she couldn't really remember that very well because she was dancing too loudly. Lenci had enjoyed dancing throughout her childhood, and it was simply wonderful to do it again. Karthik danced alongside her somewhat awkwardly, but at least he was sharing in the moment.

Twenty minutes later, they stumbled off of the dance floor, breathless with laughter. They made their way to a cocktail table and leaned on it to catch their breath.

"Oh *gosh*! You're worse than you were in high school!" Lenci gasped between breaths.

"Thanks," Karthik said. "You weren't t—too bad either."

He made no comment about the fact that she remembered him being a poor dancer in high school, and she let that moment pass.

Suddenly, an olive-skinned fellow with luscious, brown hair and the smile of a winner who never loses sloppily threw his forearms onto their table.

He leaned toward Lenci and said, "E-thik, man, who's your *friend*?"

Karthik rolled his eyes. "Lenci, this is my cousin Arjun. Arjun, Lenci."

A cousin, the Agent noted, who had not been among the relatives she'd met earlier in the whirlwind meet-and-greet.

"Thomas," she added. "Lenci Thomas."

"Karthik's mother's maiden name," Arjun smirked. "You related? E-thik, you didn't bring a cousin as your date? *Lame*, man!"

"No relation," Karthik replied. "She's my—"

"Lenci," Lenci smiled.

Thomas was Monica Chang's maiden name. She didn't know why she had said that.

"Mm. Lenci." Arjun studied her with what she considered to be excessive interest.

As he leaned closer, his perfectly pressed blazer sleeve rode up slightly to reveal a tattoo of a bullfrog on his right wrist. The tattoo seemed out of place on a guy whose day job could easily have been high fashion modeling. It must have been the result of some wild college escapade, she imagined.

Just to break the awkward silence, she said, "Nice to meet you."

"Pleasure is *all* mine." His gaze remained below her collarbones.

She felt like using her fist to turn his head away but resisted the urge out of politeness. After all, she felt the pressure to represent the Wilson family well.

"That *saree*," Arjun said, at last. "Where did you get it?"

"It's from Kerala," she replied, skipping the portion about how Karthik had picked it up for her while he was visiting his family.

Perhaps she would be able to skate by without pretending to be from India by allowing all of the facts of the situation to remain vague. Out of the corner of her eye, she saw Karthik breathe a sigh of relief.

"Really? Which city? The border design is incredible."

The man was undressing her with his eyes, but he couldn't stop talking about her clothes.

"You into fashion?" Lenci asked in an attempt to maneuver the conversation away from questions to which she did not know the answer.

"Well, I like a silken cravat as much as the next guy."

"Balaramapuram," Karthik interjected, "where Lenci's *family* is from."

Even after seeing the fierce look she gave him, he insisted, "She showed it t—to me when she came back from her trip last year."

Arjun's cocky grin widened. "No way! That's where *our* family is from. No doubt, E-thik told you that. A dance?"

Dance hopefully meant less talk. Lenci took his hand, and her heart skipped a beat. Arjun's grip was familiar in the way that his fingers hooked around hers, calm, practiced, and attentive but not necessarily caring. His hands were smooth yet full of strength—hands that she was sure she had held before.

Arjun laughed heartily and addressed her in Malayalam as they walked away, "Now you'll get to dance how *we're* used to. E-thik's watered down blood makes him a travesty on the dance floor."

She shot a dagger glare at Karthik over her shoulder. He looked down at the table to avoid her gaze but could not seem to look away for long.

"So, what are you *really* doing with my cousin?" asked Arjun.

"Hard to imagine anyone related to innocent old Karthik having a bullfrog tattoo." She mirrored his scrutinizing expression. "Are you *really* his cousin?"

"In the way that cousins can sometimes be." He smiled cryptically.

She had heard that phrase before, but plenty of folks probably used it.

"I find him useful," she said.

"Mm." He drew her closer, his smile widening. "I hope he hasn't been tutoring you. You speak Malayalam with a stutter."

"I tutor him, in fact," she found herself saying. It was a lie, though. Lenci had actually learned from hearing Karthik speak to his relatives on the phone. "You know how terribly afraid he is of our culture; he told me he didn't start speaking the language until he was thirteen, even though he could understand it all along."

"*Our* culture," Arjun echoed, adjusting his grip on her back.

Then, looking at her pointedly, he asked, "Are you *really* from India?"

"In the way that we can sometimes be," she replied.

He grinned, clearly delighted by the intrigue of his cousin's date.

Relishing her name in his mouth, he whispered, "Lenci."

It was not Arjun's overly familiar manner that unsettled the Agent but the fact that, as they danced, she had the increasing impression that she had danced with him before. His face was jovial and handsome, the type that any woman would like to think she might have seen before. That was of no consequence on its own. But his movements were strong, fluid, and unmistakably direct, too direct for a wedding dance floor. These were the movements of a person who meant business. And what business could Arjun have with Lenci Chang—or, more likely, with Agent Thomas?

She had to remain calm. For all she knew, this man was like her, trained to perceive an increase in rate of breathing, pupil dilation, and the slightest tension in the tiniest muscle or tendon. It was possible that he could read her as well as she could read him. And it was highly probable that he had tracked her down on someone else's behalf. But whose?

Her pupils were undoubtedly dilated by now. So, she smiled and gave him classic elevator eyes. After all, between fear and attraction the Agent knew there to be little difference. And where survival was concerned, there was no difference at all. There was only the drive.

Arjun smiled at her as if they had reached an unspoken under-standing, and she refused to break eye contact. Behind her smoldering gaze, he would never see the frantic search through her memory for their true connection.

When the song ended, Arjun put his lips to her ear and whispered, "At long last, sister."

The Agent bowed her head coyly and removed his hand from her waist. "Yes, it really has been too long. Your poor cousin will feel we've left him out of all the fun."

"My cousin," Arjun repeated amusedly, allowing her to drag him off of the dance floor. "Look at him trying to make eye contact with you to see whether his little white lie about the *saree* is still in tact."

"What lie?" she asked impishly.

She glanced at Karthik, who indeed had not taken his eyes off of them that entire time. Still put off that he had lied about the very thing that he had said he wouldn't, Lenci gave him no indication of whether she had exposed his secret.

Suddenly, Arjun spun her back into a dip and kissed her. She broke from his hold and slapped him across the face, which seemed to only moderately surprise him. She wiped her lips, perturbed by the feeling that she had indeed kissed that man before, and continued on her way to where Karthik was waiting. Arjun followed more slowly and pensively.

At the table, Karthik was shaking in speechless horror. Lenci feared that his stutter had taken him over completely. Now, poor, poor Karthik was just going to be one huge, walking stutter for the rest of his life.

"Well, Arjun, you *are* a character," she said. "I had a wonderful time, except for the kiss."

Karthik's quaking intensified at the very mention of the word.

"It's okay, Karthik," Lenci said, staring at Arjun coldly. "I *know* his type. A kiss means nothing."

"That is true for our type," Karthik's cousin agreed.

"*I* am not like *you*," Lenci responded.

"Aren't you, though?"

Her smile, though forced, appeared relaxed as she said, "Thank you again for the dance, Arjun."

Lenci could tell that Karthik was pleased with the fact that his womanizer cousin was about to be dismissed. His shaking lessened considerably.

Arjun, also sensing that he was about to get the boot, grabbed three glasses of champagne from the tray of a passing server. He offered Lenci one, but she held up a hand to decline his offer.

"Oh, come," he coaxed. "You don't seem like the type to pass up a cool flute of bubbly. And here, I've even gotten a glass for the subber."

"*What* did you call him?" Lenci's eyes flashed lightning with thunder shortly to follow.

Arjun jiggled the champagne flute in her face, and she seized his wrist.

But before she could throw him down and stomp him into the floor, Karthik blurted out, "She's pregnant, so you can put her glass aside."

"Karthik!" Lenci exclaimed.

Snapping out of his jealous protectiveness, Karthik looked away, saying, "I was just trying to help."

"I don't *need* your help," she sighed, releasing his cousin.

Arjun gave Lenci a stiff smile and looked between her and Karthik almost disgustedly.

After wrapping Karthik's hand around a glass, he raised his own and said, "To Lenci's beauty. And to her finding a *pureblood* to fulfill her dreams instead of this Naga subber whose mom is a half-breed and whose daddy is blacker than——"

Without thinking, Lenci smacked Arjun's hand. For such a small gesture, the spoilage was great. Champagne dripped down his face and ears and hair and even down his silken cravat onto his expensive shoes. She wanted to break the champagne flute over his head as well, but she refrained. Watching Arjun wipe the champagne from his face and swab his ears with the tablecloth would have to be reward enough.

He leaned toward Karthik menacingly. "The family will hear about this."

"It's not even *his!*" Lenci protested.

Without looking at her, he continued, "Enjoy the time you have with her, E-thik. She may just slip out of your reach one of these days."

His cocky grin returned before he smoothed his dripping hair and disappeared into the crowd of relatives.

"I need to eat something," Karthik grumbled.

Lenci followed him to the buffet table, saying, "I should have punched him in his pretty face."

After getting no response, she added, "If I weren't at your family's party I *would have* punched him in his pretty face."

"He's going to tell my aunt, and she'll tell my uncle," Karthik moaned. "It'll t–take years t—to repair."

"People were always talking about your family anyways," Lenci said, resisting the urge to apologize, even though she knew she should. "Don't you ever get sick of walking on eggshells?"

All of a sudden, the room seemed like it was spinning. Lenci looked around to see if anyone else appeared to be disturbed by it. Everyone continued to mill around her unperturbed. Taking a couple of deep breaths, Lenci found that the air felt thick and that it was rather revolting to think of drawing it into her lungs. Her stomach gurgled and not in a good way. Dr. Williams had warned her of this, although she had mentioned it under what was proving, that evening, to be a misnomer.

"Morning sickness," she gulped.

Without another word, she began weaving through the sea of people to get to the restroom. Karthik abandoned his plate of food and trailed her closely. After seeing the line snaking from the women's room, he steered his friend to the one-stalled family bathroom around the corner. They squeezed through the doorway together. He locked the door while Lenci rushed to the commode.

Having the tail of her *saree* pinned to the shoulder of the *saree* blouse was revealed to be a supreme advantage as she emptied the contents of her stomach. That *saree* was too nice to take a dip in the toilet bowl.

Behind her, Karthik was cradling his head with one hand and holding her thick, curly mane in the other. She had not noticed him smoothing her hair back from her face as she was retching, but she afterward mumbled her thanks.

"There are plenty of perfectly levelheaded families that came over from India, but my uncle's family is one of the unfortunate ones that's been tied up with the WCE," he said, half to her and half to himself. "It's not ideal, but it is what it is. And Arjun was just joking, in any case."

"No one should make jokes like that—*ever*." Lenci wiped her mouth on a piece of toilet paper and stood up, smoothing her hair.

"He's done it since we were kids. And everyone knows his parentage is dubious, anyway. Even though he's registered as a 3, he's probably subclass, too."

"Which is no excuse!" Lenci retorted. "And we're not subclass."

"It *is* the official term for our unregistered status."

She continued without acknowledging his comment, "And your mother is *not* half of anything. So, if that Arjun thinks he can just swagger around with his stupid eugenist slurs and his stupid champagne and his stupid smirk—"

Arjun must have known how Lenci would react to his eugenist comments. The image of his pained, champagne-dripping face replayed in the Agent's mind over and over. He had stuck the tablecloth in his ear when he thought no one was looking. But she had noticed. Of course, he hadn't expected it to be revealed that she was pregnant while he had the earpiece in. Perhaps he'd been looking for some other information. Whatever the case, the champagne was a clever way to fry an earpiece, however painful the feedback must have been.

So, someone had heard everything before that. They had heard her introduced as Lenci Thomas, an Indian American whose family was from Kerala. They had heard that she was pregnant. And they would undoubtedly have to report back to their agency what they'd heard. But which agency?

There was no good answer to that. Instead of having attempted to figure out why Arjun seemed so familiar, the Agent should have seen the signs that she was walking into a trap.

"He said that 'the family' would hear about this," she said. "His smirk, the champagne, the flirting, all of them were signs!"

Karthik was staring at her exasperatedly. In his mind, they were probably still in the middle of their discussion about eugenist terminology.

"Did you drink any of the champagne?" Her voice had lost its argumentative tone.

"Are you kidding? I wasn't going to drink to *that* toast."

"Good, because I think your glass had something in it," the Agent said.

Arjun had wanted a private moment with her. She had cut the dance short, and dismissed him before he could propose a time and place. If he had anything truly important to say, he would make a way for them to have their private moment. And the Agent did not like to think about how he might do that.

"Something like what?" Karthik followed her to the door.

She leaned out cautiously, looking in both directions before stepping into the hall.

Chapter 13

"COULDN'T WE AT L–LEAST T—TAKE fifteen minutes t–to say goodbye?" Karthik asked, his voice crawling with alarm.

She kept up her brisk pace. "Look, if you want to still be breathing in fifteen minutes, we need to get out of here *now*."

"I'd l—like to be breathing for the n–next half a century, if possible," Karthik muttered, rushing to keep up. "Why are you being so paranoid?"

The laughter and music from the reception hall faded behind them. They moved as quickly and inconspicuously as they could to the valet desk.

"Can you please give us the keys to our car?" the Agent asked with a smile.

"Oh, we'll get it for you." The attendant returned her smile. "Which number is it?"

"412."

Once the attendant had retrieved the key, the Agent snatched it, slammed a twenty on the counter, and ran. Karthik quickly followed.

"So, n–now we're st–tealing?" he whispered.

"You can't steal what already belongs to you," she replied. "Stay away from the edges!"

They darted through the shadowy garage in search of Karthik's jeep. When they found it, Lenci dropped onto all fours and crawled along the length of the car to get a look at its underside.

"What are you d—doing?" Karthik asked.

She jumped to her feet. "No bomb. Let's go."

"If you think we're in danger, maybe we should, you know, call the police?"

Calling the police was the last thing they should do. Arjun was likely an operative of some covert agency, the kind that the government contracted to have no accountability whatsoever. A police presence would do nothing for her and Karthik.

"Aren't we in Borschath Police Department's territory?" she asked in an empty voice. "They'd probably deport me, you know. Let's get in the car."

Karthik rolled his eyes as he unlocked the door. "What did you get us into this time?"

She ignored his dramatic sighing, went around to the passenger's side, and hopped in. Upon hearing a sharp breath behind her, she threw her arms up to shield her neck—and not a moment too soon. A thick cord caught her around the forearms.

Someone was in the back seat. Actually, two someones.

"Get out! Get out of the car!" she yelled as her assailant yanked the cord tight.

Her warning came too late. Karthik was already fully engaged with his assailant. The Agent slid her seat back and managed to trap her attacker between it and the back seat. As she climbed over to engage the other guy, he swung at her, and she fell backward into the space between the front seats. She kicked his head into the ceiling of the car. With him out cold, she rolled backward out of the passenger's side door.

The car lurched back and forth as the Agent's first attacker attempt-ed to follow her out of the car. He was a big guy in a tiny space, and he was wedged in there pretty tight. She smiled at him, closed her door, and waved at him through the window.

When she came around to the driver's side, Karthik was slumped over the steering wheel, looking a little woozy.

"What's going on?" he asked.

"We need to get a move on."

"But my car—"

"We don't have time for this." She took his arm and pulled him along.

Their attackers would be expecting them to go down to the street. So, she led the way upward. She had no plan for when they got to the

103

top, though. Luckily, their plan-less flight did not last long—or unluckily, depending on one's perspective.

Five men came walking down the ramp toward them. Arjun strutted at the front of the group.

"Get her," he ordered his roaches.

The four other men advanced on the Agent.

"I want her alive, though," Arjun said, "for questioning."

Karthik rushed forward to help her, but his cousin shoved him back. Reacting with a surge of puerile rage in lieu of protective instincts, Karthik flew at him. Arjun seemed to have anticipated this response and easily defended himself. Despite Karthik's flawless use of the training he had received at Canon, Arjun displayed a mastery of hand-to-hand combat that exceeded the offerings of any law enforcement academy.

"You're slow, cousin, for a policeman," Arjun jeered. "Did you have too many donuts, or is this pitiful display the pinnacle of your physical *prime?*"

He accepted a few blows with an amused look on his face, as if he thought Karthik's attempts to pummel him were cute.

The Agent rolled her eyes. She turned her attention to Arjun's four roaches who were putting a lot of energy into circling her menacingly. She decided they would be named Blitzen, Donner, Cupid, and Comet.

"But I'm no Vixen," she said aloud.

They didn't get it, obviously.

So, she continued, "This is an adorable little setup: multiple assailants and a dramatic cousin showdown, all in a public space. I'm assuming you looped the security cameras on a blank feed?"

The roaches did not answer her.

"Good," she said, twisting her hair into a low bun. "Let's do this."

Blitzen and Donner were behind her, and Cupid and Comet were in front of her. The sound of wind, traffic, and far away sirens faded, and the shaky breathing of her opponents became the only sound she could hear—that and the dragging of their feet on the cement floor of the garage. They were nervous.

At last, Blitzen and Donner grabbed for her. She allowed them to take her arms. Leaning on them for support, she kicked Comet in the face. And Cupid as well. She elbowed Blitzen's solar plexus while simultaneously stomping Donner's foot. Grabbing their collars, she slammed their heads together and recentered her weight to prepare for the oncoming attack from Cupid and Comet.

Meanwhile, Arjun had allowed Karthik to knock him to the floor, but he easily swiped his cousin's feet out from under him and dealt him a heavy blow to the gut.

"How much does she remember?" he demanded.

With the wind knocked out of him, Karthik was slow to respond. Arjun grabbed his face and turned it toward his own.

"I need to know, E-thik. Your life depends on it." Then, perhaps perceiving a softer entry point, he said, "*Her* life depends on it."

"She remembers *nothing*," Karthik recited, glad that those words could be used to spite someone other than himself.

"Look at her," Arjun said. He pointed at Lenci squeezing the air out of her last conscious assailant. "Does she look like she's forgotten anything from her dark time?"

"She's *told* me nothing, then," sighed Karthik. His breath was rattling and throaty. "Seems like a lot of people have been holding out on me."

"For your own good, cuz," Arjun said.

He drew his gun from its holster at his waist.

"Gun!" Karthik yelled. "He's got a g——"

Arjun hit him with the gun handle and knocked him out.

The Agent gathered her unconscious assailants into a neat pile in a nearby parking stall. She had not killed them because she could recognize an invitation to a conversation when it was extended to her.

So, she tied the roaches together by the neck first and then linked their arms with the length of her beautiful *saree*. She straightened the crooked elastics of the stockings and shorts that she had worn underneath it and regathered the curls that had escaped her bun. She never felt more herself than when she was thrashing a group of roaches. The heels of her stilettos clacked cheerily on the concrete floor as she approached Arjun.

"Stockings!" he exclaimed. "I'll be damned, Bathsheba. Modesty never really became a female like you."

"Woman," the Agent corrected.

"Enough for me," he replied with a sly smile.

He leaned in to kiss her, but she turned so that he kissed her cheek instead of her mouth.

"I assume you've come for a *purpose* or I'd be dead already," she said.

Obviously taken aback, he fumbled for words, saying, "To discuss— er, propose, well, I mean—of course, a conversation with you is always my pleasure."

Conversations with her generally included blood or screaming or some mix of the two. She did not entertain his banter.

"Tell me what you meant by 'the family.'"

"We *are* children of the same parents, are we not?" Arjun said, spinning his gun around his index finger. "The family's in a Vice—or, the other way around. Anyway, some of the kids are spoiled."

"I don't want riddles; I want answers." She knocked the gun out of his hands. The safety was still on, so the weapon didn't discharge when it hit the ground. "*Why* are you here? Who sent you?"

He shrugged. "Well, I'd be lying if I said someone didn't send me, but I've come with my own reasons."

She studied him suspiciously. "Where do you know me from? Before tonight, I mean."

"Interesting." His eyes glimmered. "You really don't remember anything, do you?"

There were only a few people who knew about her memory fade.

"So, SSI sent you."

"Your words, not mine," he said, "but to answer your question in a word: Warbuck."

Arjun Thomas from Warbuck's Warrior section, the partner Agent Thomas was assigned on her first and last mission with SSI. Yes, she remembered now.

"Of course!" Lenci exclaimed. "We went on a mission three years ago when I was seconded to Warbuck!"

He shushed her and looked around at the empty, shadowy garage. "Do you always talk about classified info like you're making a wedding speech?"

"I'm sorry!" she said, excitedly. "I just—after we got separated, I never thought I'd see you again. I thought you were, well—"

"Dead?" He laughed as he bent to retrieve his weapon. "I thought the same of you, yet here we both are. Funny how life works out."

She gazed at him, filled with the relief and joy of being reunited with a friend whom she had believed to be dead.

"Yes," she replied, watching him fumble with his gun. He seemed to be unable to fit his finger on the trigger. "Life can be so strange, really."

"Would you like to do the honors?" he asked, at last, holding out the gun to her.

She shook her head. "Can't compromise my mission with a murder trial."

"I would do the clean up," he said. "You won't get an offer like *that* very many times in your life."

"No, thanks."

As Arjun took a couple steps toward her, an uneasiness crept into the Agent's bones. She observed the subtle cross sway of his pelvis and shoulders as he shifted weight from one foot to another, and the deep, measured breaths he took through his mouth. It began to dawn on her that while this man's face belonged to Arjun, the rest of his body seemed not to be Arjun's at all.

It was a silly thought, but the Agent knew all too well that, in the world of the WCE, many nightmare-worthy scenarios were possible. Most importantly, Arjun Thomas was not a mouth-breather—well, he wasn't back when Lenci had known him, anyway.

"You're really Arjun?" she asked.

Behind his grin, she could see him straining to get a read on whether she was serious.

"You're registered as Class 3.5. Surely you wouldn't know any other Arjuns," he responded.

She demonstrated moderate amusement at his joke. He would have to be Arjun to her until she figured out who he *really* was.

She shrugged. "I'm just wondering because, well, Warbuck would be anxious to know the whereabouts of their missing agent."

"Didn't you hear?" Arjun asked with a smirk. "Warbuck was dismantled this very day."

"Don't kid me," Lenci said. "Warbuck's been in business for over fifty years. How could it be dismantled in a day?"

"Inside job," he said in mock sorrow. "Too bad, too. The whole agency imploded just on the day when their missing agent resurfaced."

His face was smug. *He* had taken down Warbuck from the inside.

She stared at him incredulously. "You—you're a double agent. How *could* you?"

"*Double* agent? You underestimate me." He clicked his tongue. "Besides, the pot and kettle are the same color, are they not? Given the fact that the memory drive you planted on me at that party was *empty*, I'm guessing you've got a scheme up your sleeve as well."

Lenci remembered nothing of a memory drive and certainly not of planting one on this traitorous man at a party coatcheck—if that was where it had happened.

She said nothing.

"And couldn't you have chosen something a little more modern than a flash drive?" Arjun asked.

Then, after noticing the hint of sadness in her otherwise blank face, he said softly, "You still haven't overcome the conditioning against new tech, have you? It's possible, you know."

Not quite understanding what he meant, she turned the conversation toward answering the question that gnawed at her.

"Where'd you get that bullfrog tattoo?" She motioned to his wrist.

He chuckled, shaking his head. "Look, I consider you a friend, especially given our past. Maybe we can help each other."

"I don't need your help."

"Don't you, Agent Thomas?" His eyes gleamed condescendingly. "Who do you think fried the drives to cover your tracks after you took the Songs?"

Her mind raced furiously to catch up, but to no avail. The only thought in her mind was that she resented that bullfrog.

"Whose side are you on, anyway?" she asked.

Arjun tossed his luscious hair. "Oh, keep up, will you? I'm on no one's side, really—except, well, *ours*. As subbers, there's really no one else we can trust, hm?"

How he knew that Lenci was subclass—and not Class 3, as Agent Thomas had claimed to be—was beyond her. She didn't bother denying it.

"I don't work with double agents," she declared, "and if you ever refer to an unclassified person as a 'subber' in my presence again, I'll throttle you."

"I get all hot and bothered just thinking about it." He laughed. "Alright, *Valencia*. Maybe I can convince you with a conversation!"

A conversation was what he wanted, and it would be a conversation that he got.

"Fine," she said, moving toward him. "Just, don't touch my face. I need it for work."

He swung at her so quickly that she barely had time to dodge before he'd swung again. Lenci remembered Arjun, but she did not remember him like this. His body was more agile and less broad, changes that caused her to find herself playing catch-up.

This man was a brawler, she observed. A smooth brawler but a brawler nonetheless. She evaded his wild outside swings effectively, taking note of his habit of winding his entire body nearly ninety degrees before striking. His strikes tended toward a pattern of *right, right, left, right, right, left*. Embarrassingly repetitive, she thought.

She blocked his left, raising her other arm in anticipation of a strike from his right only to double over in pain when he side-kicked her square in the midsection. He had been stringing her along with the shrugging strikes and the easy pattern. That hurt her pride a bit.

Deciding not to give any thought to evasive tactics, even for the sake of the cargo, Lenci recommitted herself to the fight. She grabbed Arjun's leg and flipped him onto the ground, but he was on his feet again in a split second. He faked with his left fist and jabbed with his right. She moved back but still absorbed some of the impact from the strike. Bringing a hand to her face, she realized that her lip was bleeding.

"Oh, ho! Ladies and gents," Arjun narrated in a sports announcer voice, "he's drawn blood! And from the *moneymaker*, no less! What are you going to do, Agentess? You want to hurt me because I marred your gorgeous face?"

The metallic taste of the blood in her mouth was familiar, comforting, even. She began to hum under her breath a tune that probably sounded to her opponent like the distorted melody of a popular lullaby sung underwater or through a fan.

"I've heard rumors," Arjun said tauntingly. "Rumors of a large-legged *female* with fishnet scars who rose to greatness from the bed of David Miller the Killer, rumors of a soulless weapon who leaves broken bodies in her wake. I am having trouble believing, Agentess, that those rumors have any substance to them at all!"

She spat her blood in his face and crouched down into a fight stance with her arms raised. Her pose oozed of David Miller's flamboyant fight style, which brought a devilish glint into Arjun's eyes.

"There she is!" He grinned. "Now, let's talk about joining forces."

The Agent sighed, lowering her arms. "I have no idea what you're talking about."

"Then, as you wish, I will say it directly," he said, taking a deep, sucking breath. He wasn't fatigued. That was just how he breathed, and it irritated the Agent. "I heard the WCE are in an uproar because all of the master copies of the Songs have gone missing, most likely stolen by an Amphibian."

"And you think I've got a backup?"

His eyes gleamed. "I think your cute little noggin *is* the backup. And, whatever your reasons for taking the Songs, it's ingenious to have that kind of leverage."

"Perks of having a new life," she said. "I don't remember a thing about your precious Songs."

He pulled her in by the waist. "Oh, come! I'll let you in on my plan if you let me in on yours."

The man certainly had a penchant for making anything and everything sound suggestive.

"Not interested," she replied.

"When did you become such a prude?" he asked, playfully snapping the elastic of her stockings. "If you need a little loosening up—"

She drove her palm into his nose. "Shut up and fight, Mouthbreather!"

This Arjun was too strong and too skilled to succumb to her in regular combat, but thanks to his jibber-jabbering, she had learned him—or relearned him, seeing as how they had known each other in some capacity before. It seemed that he could not, for all the goodness in the world, stop breathing through his mouth. So, she breathed his mouth-breaths with him, anticipating his every move and striking before he was ready.

At one point, she swept his legs, and he hit the floor with a *THUD*. She scuttled backward a couple of feet and squatted down, waiting. Once he was on his feet again, she nodded her chin at him as if to invite him to strike first.

Clearly frustrated, he tackled her and attempted to overpower her with sheer force. He stooped over her, low and crouched, trying to collect her unruly limbs, but she trapped him in an x-guard and took him down. Gaining the advantageous position, she gave him the good old ground and pound.

His right eye was bleeding and promising to swell when he finally flipped them, but she hooked her leg around his neck and took him to the floor once more. Then, she pinned his head to the ground by pressing her knee into the side of his face. Considering some of the spars she had had in the past, this was a relatively smooth ending, especially since there was no glass in this arena.

"For the last time, *why* are you here?" she demanded.

"I told you: I came because I wanted to. I'm a free agent now. No strings, unattached—free."

"No one is free," she retorted.

"You're so sexy when you're mad."

She pushed her knee harder into his cheek and searched through his nearest pocket for a zip tie. He always carried them, just in case.

Usually, though, the zip ties were for people other than himself. How she knew this was irrelevant.

"Old habits die hard, hm?" He groaned as she fastened the zip tie around his wrists.

"We can only be what we are made to be," she said gruffly.

"Whores?"

She pulled him into a sitting position and replied, "I survived, didn't I?"

"Didn't we all?" He sniffed. "You've got to start remembering, Agentess. Remember *everything*. There are more dangerous people out here than me, especially the ones expecting you to be the Relief."

Relief. The thought made her mind blank. So, she avoided it.

"What'll you do if I *don't* remember?"

"I'll find my way forward." He shrugged painfully. "But I'd rather have you along with me."

"Honestly," she said, "I don't even remember who you *really* are."

"I don't buy it."

Indistinct mumbling and grunting alerted them to the fact that Arjun's roaches were stirring. The time of free talk was coming to a close.

"How many more are there?" she asked, grabbing his collar.

"Of *us*?" He laughed wryly. "Precisely none—but according to rumor, more than the director knows."

The Agent had been asking about the number of roaches Arjun had brought with him, reason being: she had to prevent her secret from reaching the wrong ears.

"You know what I'm asking," she said.

Even though he didn't respond, she knew that she would probably find out by the end of the night just how many more men Arjun had recruited for this little fun fest.

She released his collar. "I want your word that you won't tell *him*."

"*The Killer doesn't know about—*"

"No one knows," she hissed. "And don't think I won't kill you if you tell the director or the Vice or whoever. Wherever you think you can hide, I will track you down, and you'll wish you'd never been born."

"Miss Bathsheba, always so gracious and gentle." He chuckled. "Sure, you have my word. I won't tell the 'director or the Vice or whoever' or *Father* about your little secret."

The Agent inwardly sighed with relief. "The men on the motorcycles were your techs, so they were the only ones on your team with an open channel to your earpiece, correct?"

He didn't answer her question, most likely because he already knew what she had in mind to keep her secret safe. It was nothing personal, just the way things had to be done.

"You'll want to search the compartments of the motorcycles when you're done with them," he said. "I brought you something."

"Gifts?" she said sardonically. "Sir, I barely know you."

"And yet, I know you well, sister. As long as you're playing this little memory game, you won't be able to get off anyone's radar. Just make sure you search the motorcycles."

She retrieved Arjun's gun and leaned down to whisper in his ear.

"You should have used this when you had the chance," she said.

"He conditioned me against guns, too," he replied, turning his face toward the floor. "Still working on breaking free of that. In any case, I've done what I came to do."

She whacked him on the back of his head with the handle of the gun, and his body went limp.

"Lenci?" Karthik croaked. "What happened?"

Lenci didn't know what to think or what to feel, and she certainly didn't know what had happened. Everything had happened so quickly, and the blank slate name had already wiped most of it away. But there were tied up men, only half-conscious, piled in a parking stall not too far away. They were tied up in her *saree*.

"I don't know," she answered. "I remember nothing."

She helped her friend to his feet.

"What are you doing with that *gun*?" he asked.

Oh, yes. The gun. The cool metal was soothing in her hot, sweaty palms. Lenci knew how to shoot. Bourghin had taught her. She'd take the gun and use it.

"It's your cousin's, remember?"

She slid it out of safety mode, then aimed and shot, casually obliterating Arjun's left kneecap as he slumbered.

"Whoa!" Karthik's hands flew to his mouth.

She shushed him as she piled Arjun on top of his associates. He was still out like a light. The pain had not awakened him, which was a curious thing.

Karthik watched with a sullen face as she drew a phone out of his cousin's pocket and dialed three numbers.

"Hello?" she said when the Borschath Police picked up. "There's a man in the valet parking structure of the Palm Tree Veranda in Niebla Beach. I think he's been shot. It looks pretty bad."

She slipped the phone back into Arjun's pocket and patted it with a tad more tenderness than Karthik seemed to appreciate. He didn't say anything, though.

"We should get out of here before they come," she said, stuffing Arjun's gun into the waist of her stockings.

"What about the *saree*?"

"He can deliver it when he's had it dry-cleaned. Let's go."

Karthik followed her mutely to the car. She dropped to the ground again to check the vehicle's underbelly.

No bomb. The back seat was empty. Their ambushers had left the doors open and the key in the ignition.

"Whew!" Karthik breathed, gripping the wheel. "Let's get out of here. I don't care where we go."

"Well, that's good because we may be going down some unexpected roads."

Lenci's gaze was fixed on the rearview mirror. There was nothing there. But from above them, she heard the faintest buzzing, humming, and sputtering of a pair of motorcycles coming down the ramp. She felt herself sinking, sinking through the seat of the car and into the depths. In the near future, some very hard decisions would need to be made.

"Start the car," the Agent said. "*Hurry!*"

Chapter 14

THE JEEP SCREECHED OUT OF THE PARKING STALL and swung right down the ramp that led from the seventh to the sixth level. From the sound of it, the motorcycles were about one hundred meters behind. Right again, onto the ramp that led to the fifth level. The motorcycles were gaining.

Karthik took the turn onto the fourth level a little wider than he meant to and narrowly escaped scraping the wall of the garage.

"We don't even know what they want!" he burst out, looking nervously at the pair of what resembled glowing eyes in the rearview mirror. "We don't know who sent them or if they're trying to chase us into a trap!"

"Just keep going *right,*" the Agent said, clenching her stomach.

She rolled down the window for some fresh air.

At the speed Karthik was taking the curves, their trajectory felt like a downward spiral. Just when the Agent was sure that her stomach was going to jump out of her throat, the jeep lurched out of the structure and onto the city streets.

"We need to get to a back road," she said, "somewhere without too many people."

"Are you kid–dding me?" Karthik protested. "This is a st–tandard evasive exercise. We *have* to st—tay on the main streets, l–lose them in the crowd!"

She did not have the heart to tell him that this most certainly was not a standard evasive exercise.

She insisted, "We *need* to get to a back road."

"I d——don't k—now an—ny back roads in this borough!"

"Good grief!" She looked at him with a face full of concern. "Is this what you were like when you were on patrol?"

His fingers were tapping the steering wheel furiously. Pinky, ring, middle, pointer, thumb, thumb, pointer, middle, ring, pinky. "N—never patrolled with my pregn—nant friend in the car."

Sentimentality—superfluous and highly counterproductive, but sweet nonetheless.

The Agent sighed. "Okay, they're not snipers, so they won't risk shooting at us on the street with all these people. Get us to the frontage road off the 507. By the time we get out there, it'll be empty enough."

"Empty en—nough for what?" His voice was girded with suspicion.

After glancing in the rearview mirror, she pounded his seat. "They're gaining, Karthik! You have to turn here!"

"It's not safe! I can't!"

"You can! Drive on the sidewalk!"

"No!"

"*Yes!*"

He turned the wheel just in time. The jeep bumped over the curb, narrowly missing a couple of pedestrians, and screeched onto the cross street. The motorcycles continued onward, probably planning to cut through one of the alleys to double back and head them off at the next road over. Karthik drove down the street until it dead-ended into an industrial plaza.

"Dead-end. Of course," he said, steering the jeep at just the right angle to hop the curb and enter the plaza. "Well, we might be able to hide here until they give up searching for us."

Lenci put her arm around her friend's headrest. "Ethan, how do you deal with a bee problem?"

"Stay inside," he said decidedly.

She crossed her arms. "No house."

Answering from the wealth of childhood experience they'd had with bees at Eucalyptus State Park, he replied, "Run, then, or jump into a body of water."

"Or get rid of the hive."

Silence and more tapping from Karthik.

At last, he asked, "Lenci, who are these people?"

"I don't know."

"Well, you've got t—to kn—now something," he said indignantly.

"Because I saw you cl–lobber four men without even breaking a sweat, and when I woke up, Arjun was out too."

"Yes, Arjun." The man who was Arjun but most likely not. She had been able to relearn him despite his outward appearance, but she could not—for the life of her—remember where they had first met. And now his roaches were after her.

She could hear motorcycles approaching. She looked out the window, but she couldn't see them yet.

"We should go out the other side," she said.

Ready to go with her hunch, Karthik drove to the far side of the plaza and made a right onto the empty street that bordered it. He anxiously gripped the steering wheel, looking ahead for a possible ambush.

"There's a l–lot you aren't t——telling me," he said.

They both started at the sound of glass shattering. The right side-mirror was hanging off of the car.

"They're behind us!" Karthik exclaimed, looking in the rearview mirror. "It's only two kilometers to the highway onramp, but unless we think of something, they'll likely catch up with us before we get there."

Lenci pulled the gun out of her stockings. "Keep your head down, and turn left here. Drive us toward the canal."

The canal was a cement conduit, which had once been used to transport water to Diablo from neighboring districts, but ever since Diablo became exempt, the canal had been dry and empty. It was, however, the perfect type of deserted place where one could do all that needed to be done.

"So, now you're an expert in cat and mouse chases?" Karthik asked.

"Not that I remember." Her eyes were glued to the rearview mirror.

"Auntie Monica's going to kill me."

"Not if Dasher and Prancer do it first."

"Who?"

She motioned silently back at the cyclists. Karthik cast her a frustrated glance, then turned onto the pothole-covered frontage road that ran parallel to the canal.

Another shot completely took off the jeep's left side-mirror. Lenci leaned out of her window, using the body of the car for cover, and returned fire. She got one shot off, but Karthik's creative maneuvering of the raggedy road caused her to miss her mark.

"Speed up!" she yelled.

The two motorcycles were gaining on them and moving further

116

apart. This was no time to worry about speed limits. To avoid being sandwiched, Karthik threw the car into fifth gear and punched the gas pedal.

"No! What are you doing?" Lenci cried. "The gun's no good at this distance!"

"We should have switched seats at the plaza," Karthik grumbled.

"And then, our moms would have finished the job for sure," Lenci chuckled. "I'll try to rein in the side-seat driving. Just try not to drive us to our untimely end, Lieutenant Wilson."

He cast her an annoyed glance, but there was a hint of amusement in it.

Behind them, the motorcycles had dropped into line, one behind the other, and they were now approaching on the driver's side of the jeep. This was not a particularly advantageous formation, but they were forced into it by the thinness of their cycle tires, which were too thin to maneuver the potholes very well. There was a narrow strip of smooth asphalt on the left side of the road on which they rode single-file.

Prancer was in front, and if he got taken out, Dasher would wipe out.

"I'm going to get in the seat behind you," Lenci said. "I'll have the best shot from there."

"There's not enough cover—"

Before he could finish, she squeezed through the space between the seats and into the back seat. She remained standing back there, slightly hunched with the back of her head pressed against the roof.

Karthik groaned. "Nice going, Big Butt! I can't see in the rearview mirror!"

"Well, you are getting a rear view." Lenci tossed her head as if to look over her shoulder. "Keep going straight."

Her backside pressed up against Karthik's headrest as she leaned out of the window. She fired three shots in close succession.

"Ha!" she said, pulling her head in. "Got one! And the other one, sort of."

Karthik's voice trembled. "You didn't kill them, did you?"

"Should have," she replied, leaning over the back seat to get a better look. "But no. I tagged Prancer twice in the vest. At least, it looks like he's wearing one just from the shape of his torso. He's off his bike. Dasher managed to avoid a wipeout, but I took out his gun arm. My guess is that he'll need to try at a closer range, if he wants to try with the other."

Karthik breathed more easily since the danger seemed to have subsided for the moment. Lenci continued to peer over the back seat with her rear end pointed toward the front of the car.

"Hey, Big Butt," Karthik said, looking in the rearview mirror. "You want to sit down or something? Your butt's in my face."

"Kind of like that one time when we were kids, hm, Buttface?" Lenci wiggled her rear end playfully.

Karthik's voice was suddenly serious. "You remember that, Lenci?"

"I remember nothing," she said, still staring out the back window. "Here he comes! Turn us, Karthik! Turn us!"

She was ending the chase, but she was risking a lot to do so. He cast her one last apprehensive glance, then floored the clutch, cranked the wheel hard, and pulled up the parking brake to execute a perfect boot-legger's hairpin turn. The car swung around and skidded to a stop as Lenci leaned out the window one last time.

Two shots were fired, but one was not from her gun. When she pulled her wind-blown head back into the car, she leaned heavily on her left arm to hoist herself into the passenger's seat.

"Got him," she half-smiled. "Just under the helmet. Sorry to disappoint you."

Karthik looked sick, almost as if he had killed Dasher himself. He was spending precious emotional energy on lamenting what had been necessary, but Lenci could sense that this was not the time to lecture her friend on the merits of compartmentalization. Silence enveloped them.

Then the Agent said, more to herself than to Karthik, "Their men will clean up. Leaving the body there would be worse for them than for us."

"Who's them?"

She followed his gaze to the blood dripping down her arm.

"It's a shallow wound." She shrugged her wounded shoulder. "A graze, really."

He looked unconvinced and sicker.

"Don't tell my mother," she said. Then, grinning, she continued, "Nice move with that bootlegger. They did teach you something at the police academy, after all."

Karthik smiled weakly. The Agent had an idea of what he was feeling, how confused he must be. In some sense, she felt that same confusion—or maybe it was a connection. She always had a hard time telling the difference.

"I hate to break it to you," she said, "but I actually need to get back to Prancer."

"What?"

"He's incapacitated now." She said that truly believing it should make him feel better. "Look in the rearview mirror. He collapsed after he fell off his bike and hasn't moved since."

The look Karthik gave her indicated that he did *not* feel better.

"I'll go back and talk to him, and you can stay here," she said. "Just lock the door, okay?"

He groaned. "I can't let you go alone."

"Well, hm." She thought for a moment. "I won't tell if you don't."

"I'm coming."

Afraid that the incapacitated roach might disclose information that could be dangerous for Karthik to know, she said, "Just, maybe drive the car back within twenty meters of him and then I'll get out. You can watch from there, and if anything seems off, you can run him over. Deal?"

"The reliability of this plan seems *very* low to me."

He would do what she wanted. She could tell by the look in his eyes.

"I'm a pushover," he sighed, starting the engine.

When they were within twenty meters of Prancer, the Agent hopped out of the car and approached him cautiously.

She could hear the downed roach's laborious, gurgling breaths. As she stood over him, she realized that she had missed his vest and instead hit an artery. He was bleeding heavily.

"Was this a loyalty test?" she asked grimly.

"C—c—class violation!" the roach choked. "Y—you traitor! Miscegenist!"

"Who sent you?" she demanded. "Who dares condemn me?"

"Y—you're two classes below the K—killer. Y—your own actions condemn you!" He slid the cap off of one of his molars and swallowed the cyanide pill stored inside. "Death to the subber!"

The Agent watched numbly as the roach foamed at the mouth and then became still. She knew that he had been referring to the cargo as the "subber." But what she had done to survive was not the cargo's fault.

Shoving away the feelings of offense, the Agent searched through the roach's clothing and found his phone. It was a standard SSI satellite phone. This roach was apparently a double agent who reported to the director of SSI but was loyal to the WCE. More than likely, Director

Gomez had commissioned this team to see how much Lenci remembered. However, she had failed to take into consideration that her agency had been infiltrated at this level.

So, this had started as a SSI surveillance mission, but when Prancer heard that the Agent was pregnant—with a WCE connection, it would not be difficult to deduce by whom—the surveillance mission became an execution under the WCE's interpretation of Neo-Eugenic law.

The Agent looked through the call log and messages in Prancer's phone and was relieved to find that the dead roach had not attempted any contact since that afternoon. This chase, then, was a result of his passion for Neo-Eugenic law. He had not been under orders to put her down. That was a relief.

She dialed the last number in the call log.

When the connection was initiated, the person on the other end did not speak. After listening to the shallow, expectant breathing for a couple of seconds, the Agent decided that the middle-aged woman who had answered must be Director Gomez.

So, she said, "At the end of a very poorly planned surveillance job gone wrong, I'm calling to warn you that you've got traitors in your midst. Now, if you have any further questions, let's do this the civilized way. Send me Bourghin."

And with that, she hurled the phone to the ground and stomped on it.

She went to the roach's bike and rummaged through the cargo compartment. There was a shoebox in it. The box was taped shut, and it thumped and rattled when she shook it. Before she could peel back the tape from the lid, she heard footsteps behind her.

When she turned around, Lenci found Karthik nervously shifting from foot to foot.

"What's that?" he asked.

"I don't know," Lenci said, tucking the box under her arm. "Let's go back to the apartments."

"The apartments? Are you sure it's safe?"

She hadn't gotten a chance to search Dasher's bike, but when she looked at where he had fallen, his body and his bike were gone. Someone had already started cleaning up.

After looking around the empty street one more time, she responded, "You know SSI is involved here, right?"

Her question was met with silence, but she could read in Karthik's face that he did know that. And she was fairly sure she would know just what his connection was to SSI within the next twenty-four hours.

She continued. "Then, you know that SSI believes it is in their best interest to keep me safe—for now. After this debacle, they will undoubtedly redouble their efforts."

Karthik looked apprehensive, but he probably couldn't protest without giving away exactly how much he was tied up with SSI. They walked back to the jeep and got in.

"That guy's name wasn't really Prancer, was it?" Karthik huffed indignantly. "Dumb code name. Sounds like one of Santa's reindeer."

He was unwittingly making fun of Lenci's marking strategy. Rather than explaining how it helped her to keep track of her opponents and their unique characteristics, she simply shook her head and smiled.

They rode the rest of the way to Central Diablo in silence. It was a tense, brooding silence in which—the Agent knew—Karthik was coming down from his adrenaline spike and reconnecting with the many emotions that he had had to ignore during the chase. She didn't pry. He would soon let his thoughts be known.

When they arrived at the apartment complex, he parked on the street instead of returning to his reserved parking stall in the garage. Lenci didn't blame him for preferring to stay out of echoey, shadowy places. His busted side-mirrors were a stark reminder of what could have happened to them.

With the engine off and the parking brake on, he finally erupted. "What the *hell* is going on here, Lenci? You disappear for five years, and when you come back, you can take down guys twice your size and shoot them to d—death like you're blinking or taking a breath."

"I don't know, Karthik!" she said. "I don't *know* what's going on."

That was apparently not the answer he wanted. His fingers were tapping on the steering wheel, tapping, tapping, pinky to thumb and thumb to pinky.

"In situations like tonight, it doesn't matter what's going on, not really." She rubbed her forehead. "I just do what has to be done. Survival is the name of the game, right? What is necessary must never be lamented."

Karthik cast her an exasperated glance.

After a brief silence, she asked, "Do you remember what happened the day I decided to sign on with SSI?"

"I'll never forget it," he replied.

"Hm."

Chapter 15

IN THE HALLWAY OUTSIDE their doors, Lenci and Karthik discussed their plan of action.

"Here, take my arm," Lenci said, linking elbows with Karthik.

Wiggling her wounded shoulder, she added, "Maybe she'll be less likely to notice when yours is blocking mine."

"This is a bad idea," he sighed.

Her shoulder began to throb when she took his arm, but she pushed away the pain, turned the key in the lock, and cautiously opened the door. Lorenzo was nowhere to be seen, and from the sound of it, their mother was washing dishes in the kitchen.

She motioned to Karthik that it was safe to move forward. They traversed the living room on tiptoe to the door to the inner hallway. Behind that door lay safety, namely in the form of a fuzzy, long-sleeved bathrobe.

The water in the kitchen stopped running. They had been detected.

"Hi, mama," Lenci said, turning slowly so that Karthik's shoulder could remain glued to her own.

"Hey, baby. Karthik." Monica nodded. "How was the reception?"

"Oh, the usual," Lenci replied, avoiding her mother's gaze. "Beautiful decorations, nice relatives, fun dancing—"

"You had fun?"

"Yes."

"Both of you?"

"Yes."

"I'm asking Karthik, too."

Lenci refused to look at him. She knew that his face had already betrayed the fact that he had *not* had a good time that evening. He had never been a great secret-keeper.

"Yeah." She could tell he was looking at the ground by the way his voice drooped. "Lots of fun."

"I see."

With a more than slightly amused tone, Mrs. Chang continued, "And did this 'fun' involve taking off large portions of your clothing?"

Lenci looked down at her awkward ensemble. Wiggling her stockinged toes, she smiled. The only run in the stockings revealed a patch of normal brown skin underneath. Her scars were safe.

Karthik—perhaps anxious not to look too much like he enjoyed the thought of any activity that involved taking off large portions of clothing—took a tiny step away from her.

Mrs. Chang gasped at the sight of the bloody, jagged slit in the sleeve of her daughter's new *saree* blouse. The wound had mostly stopped bleeding by that time, but Lenci had not had the time to clean it up.

"It looks worse than it is, Mama. *Mama!*"

Lenci's mother had always been lightning-fast in this type of situation. It seemed like she kept a bottle of isopropyl alcohol and cotton balls stuffed in her back pocket. As Lenci hissed and fidgeted, Karthik crept around behind them.

He had almost reached the front door when Mrs. Chang called out without so much as a glance backwards, "I'm not done with you either, Karthik Ethan-James Wilson! Sit down on the couch until I'm ready to speak with you."

Lenci smiled at her friend's glum expression. Her evening with him had been one large déjà vu on many levels.

"You're done," her mother said after cleaning the wound. "Go rest up. I got a call from the gym at the Resplendent Oaks Mall today. They confirmed your Monday start date and asked you to wear 'real gym clothes?'"

"Free gym memberships for all family members!" Karthik sang from the couch.

"And friends," he added quickly.

Lenci smiled and dropped her gaze.

"Did you say '*gym memberships*?'" Lorenzo barreled through the hallway door. "Hey, what's up with the bloody-shouldered freak show?"

Ignoring his insult, Lenci said, "I guess I can ask the manager about guest passes for you guys. Wouldn't get my hopes up, though. He's not very agreeable."

"Sweet!" Lorenzo pumped his fist. "This'll be *awesome*! Karthik and I can lift together *every* weekend and get ripped!"

"And *there's* incentive to get your homework done," Karthik said, high-fiving him.

Turning to her mother, Lenci whispered, "I know it's not the most impressive job. But it's just—"

"I know," Monica said, "until you can get back on your feet. Just take a breather and birth your baby. That's what this time is for."

Then, seeing Lenci's raised eyebrows, she continued, "I'm just saying that you're not a failure, even if you feel like one, sweetie. You're still so young, and you have plenty of time to figure out what you want to do with the rest of your life. Go rest now."

Lenci gave a sympathetic nod to Karthik.

"Thank you for a good time," she said.

He nodded back at her, undoubtedly wondering what on earth kind of crazy woman thinks a good time is getting beat up and shot at. Then again, she hadn't been the one getting beaten up.

Tucking her shoebox under her arm, she headed to her room. She peeled off her stockings and placed the shoebox inside of the box marked "Specials." When she slammed the closet door, she caught sight of herself in the full-length mirror. Those scars reminded her of music that she didn't like.

No, no, no, no. She was sinking to her knees.

Bow!

The next thing the Agent knew, she was washing her face in the bathroom.

"You've got to keep it together," she was saying. "If you get too involved, you won't do anyone any good."

She rubbed her face roughly with the towel.

KNOCK *KNOCK* "Lenci?"

The mother was calling her. She was using the blank slate name.

"Yes?"

Bewildered, Lenci looked around the empty bathroom. She had the feeling that she had just been talking to someone, but she couldn't quite remember the details of the conversation.

The mother was still on the other side of the door. "Are you okay?"

"Yes, just finishing up."

"Okay, baby, just checking." Monica's footsteps thumped softly toward the living room.

Lenci stood for a long time, staring into the mirror as if to search for something she had lost. Not finding it there, she wandered back to the room that had been provided for her. As she passed the door to the living room, she heard her hostess talking with the guy from across the hall.

"Tell me what's worrying you, Ethan."

"It's hard to explain," he replied.

"Boy, you better spill it before I spill you! And after I do, you know you're not too big for your mama to tan your hide either!"

Lenci grinned from ear to ear. She had heard that tone before, and it maybe even struck a little fear into her heart to hear it now.

She returned to her room, turned out the light, and jumped into bed. Eugenia the Ewe was still on the desk, probably smiling at her through the darkness. Lenci rolled onto her unwounded shoulder, hugged her pillow, and promptly fell asleep.

***

In the middle of the night, the Agent rolled over and grasped her pillow more tightly. As she did so, she found that the pillowcase was entirely soaked. In fact, the whole bed was drenched. Her face and arms were covered in a goopy residue and something slimy was wedged between her thighs. It was the rubbery, finger-like roots of a holdfast.

"Oh, no," she whispered.

As she pulled on the holdfast, it stretched and grew until she found that she was entangled in an entire bushy, slippery frond of giant kelp. The smell of saltwater mingled with stale sweat filled her airways until they began to constrict.

Come on, Bathsheba!
Come on, come on and
Give a little something too

All she wanted was to stop the music. But the kelp held her back and grabbed at her, taunting her and molesting her.

I know where Poison Arrow landed

"That's the wrong Song!" she cried.

In the act of writhing and struggling to free her limbs from the kelp, she jolted awake. The silvery beams of the moon shone softly through the window onto an unfamiliar bedspread that reminded her of something about a fake apartment and a fake family. Exhaling deeply, she brought her hands to her head. Her face was covered with sweat and slobber all the way up to her hairline. She must have been sleeping with her mouth open again.

Gross. She wiped her face on the comforter, threw the blanket back, and got out of the bed to turn on the light. With the darkness gone, she confirmed that she was not in the house in Chile.

After lifting her shirt and examining her torso, the Agent let out another deep breath. Just faint scratches and fading rope burns. No bite marks, though. If there was anything that could convince her beyond the shadow of a doubt that she was no longer in David's vicinity, a torso with no teeth marks on it was the winner.

She made a move to return to the bed but suddenly noticed that her pajama pants were sticking to her legs. They weren't just stuck to her because they were too small; the fabric was sopping wet.

She slid her hands over the bedspread. A patch in the lower half of the bedclothes was soaked. She had wet the bed.

Sighing, the Agent folded up all the bedclothes and put them in a laundry basket. She had seen a laundry room at the end of the hall near the elevator. If this building had been updated any time recently, the laundry room would take swipe cards for payment. Perhaps the mother kept the laundry card in a drawer in the kitchen.

As the Agent crept quietly through the darkness of the living room, the area was abruptly flooded with light.

"Lenci?"

"Mother!" She nearly dropped the basket. "Oh, you scared me! What are you doing up?"

"What are *you* doing up?"

Lenci gripped her basket a little more tightly. "Asked you first?"

Her mother sighed. "I never sleep well with you kids in the house."

"Thanks."

"I just mean that I worry about you. Why are you awake?"

Lenci dropped her head. "Laundry. I, uh, had an accident."

"Oh, sweetie!"

"No, I'm okay!" She drew back as her mother approached. "I just need to get to the laundry room. Do you have a swipe card or something?"

"I'll get it. Why don't you start loading up the machine, and I'll be there in a minute?"

"Okay."

Lenci turned toward the door, but she stopped in her tracks when her mother gasped aloud.

"What's wrong?" she asked.

"Lenci, you're bleeding."

At first, Lenci thought that her mother was referring to the ugly wound on her shoulder. But that shoulder was facing the opposite wall, and her mother was staring at her rear end.

Twisting around to see what all of the fuss was about, Lenci saw that on the seat of her pants, there was a growing red stain.

"Forget about the laundry. I'll get you a change of clothes," her mother said. "And when you've changed, I want you to lie down on this couch and *don't* move. I'm calling Dr. Williams."

Monica brought her daughter a flannel nightgown and a fresh pair of cotton underwear, then rushed back to her bedroom to make the call.

When the mother was gone, the Agent kicked the laundry basket of urine-drenched bedclothes and curled into a ball on the couch. If she had simply taken evasive action instead of engaging Arjun in that conversation, she wouldn't have sustained this injury at all.

One of the main purposes of lying low was to prevent any damage to the cargo. David had always trained her to cause the least amount of collateral damage possible during any mission. He called it "efficiency." However, he had also taught her—both intentionally and unintentionally—all that she knew about survival. And many recent events, including the conversation with Arjun, had in some sense been about survival. The complication in this whole situation, then, was that the cargo's survival hinged on the Agent's altruism. She was possibly sacrificing her own survival for someone she had never even met.

Someone, she dared to think. She had known enough of death to be able to sense life when it was present. Over the course of her short career, the Agent had ended many lives without regret, and yet she was reluctant to cause the end of a life that had never once had the chance to act with honor or dishonor, or even to defend itself.

From that moment in the Chilean clinic when she had learned that she was likely entrusted with the cargo, most of her decisions had considered the little one under her protection—save for the occasional flare-up of her pride. And it was that same pride, the insatiable desire to prove herself—even more than her drive to survive—that had prevented her from walking away from Arjun's invitation.

What more did she have to prove in this lifetime? And at what cost? She brought a hand to her abdomen.

"Hey, in there," she whispered. "I guess maybe you're leaving because you think our missions are incongruous. With my recent actions, I can see why you'd feel that way, but I'll make it up to you, Kiddo. Just, please, stick with me for a bit, and I'll keep you safe. I promise."

She lay back and smiled.

Kiddo. It was a nice nickname.

Chapter 16

DR. WILLIAMS' ORDER WAS STRICT bed rest for three weeks. The Agent named Lenci did not want anyone outside of her family to know about her condition, so she told Bread that she had an ankle injury. However, even though she had come up with a satisfactory excuse for her absence from work, she hated being confined to the living room couch where there was nothing to do but eat and feel useless.

One morning, three days into the couch sentence, Lenci's mother brought the clunky, cordless home phone to the living room. Without explanation, she put the phone on speaker and went into the kitchen to prepare a snack.

"Ey, Circus!" the phone squawked. "It's Racky and Theresa! Say hi, Theresa."

The silence on the other end was cut short by a *WHUMP* and a grunt of a hello that led the Agent to believe that Theresa's ribcage had been the recipient of an extra bony elbow.

"Anyway, we're hitting you up because *Bread* told us you were injured. We were looking forward to having you around to put him in his place. The fans are all bummed out, too. Get off your backside soon, so we can go to Chubba's Chicken to celebrate. Bye!"

There was some rustling, and the Agent was fairly sure she heard Theresa's voice calling Racky dumb, then the recording ended.

She smiled. Although it was imprudent to entrust herself to anyone, the Agent liked the thought of joining Racky for a meal at Chubba's Chicken. It gave her something to look forward to in this uncomfortable time. She was in a strange house in a strange place and didn't know if she could trust anyone. Everything that was familiar to her was far away. And then, there was the issue of Kiddo.

"I actually did tell him no, mother," she said aloud as Monica placed a turkey avocado sandwich on the nearby coffee table.

"What was that?" Monica sat down beside her on the couch.

"I took the beatings the first five times, if you include what was supposed to have been the initiation," the Agent said, staring over her mother's shoulder at the door. "And then there was the stone. Still have nightmares about that every night."

"Lenci, what are you talking about?"

The Agent named Lenci looked at her briefly. "I don't know. I'm sorry. Was I rambling?"

After Monica didn't answer, the Agent turned her attention back to the door. "There's someone out there. I could feel his footsteps thumping before, but now he's just standing there—breathing."

A knock followed shortly thereafter and Monica, astonished by this sequence of events, hurried to open it. Chandler Bourghin stepped into the apartment. He wore jet-black slacks, a belt with a silver buckle, and a crisp, white dress shirt.

"Chandler!" Monica said delightedly. "What a wonderful surprise!"

The Agent's focus snapped back to the mother. "You know him?"

"Of course she does, Lenci," Chandler said. "Your mom is the main reason Director Gomez added the Minority Familial Inclusion clause to SSI's confidentiality agreement. While we were recruiting you, Monica brought it to our attention that the agency might exclude a large portion of our country's young, gifted population if we mandated a complete cessation of familial contact—simply because there are many cultures in the States where family is a huge priority."

She glanced at her mother whose face showed no sign of deception or distress. What she knew of Monica Chang seemed to line up with Bourghin's claims. Lenci's mother was a woman of conviction and could be quite outspoken when she wanted to be. It was not inconceivable that Mrs. Chang had managed to convince the director of a covert organization to allow her to be involved in the affairs of her secret agent daughter.

"Well played, *mother*," she said as she turned her chilly gaze upon her.

"Hey, fix your face!" Monica snapped her fingers in Lenci's direction, causing her daughter's gaze to drop.

Then, smiling at Chandler, she said, "Girl lives outside the home for five years and comes back thinking she's big and bad."

Chandler returned her smile and said, "I'm wondering if I might have a few minutes with Lenci."

"Of course, Chandler," Monica replied. "I'll just step out for a moment, but please stay as long as you'd like. Our neighbor from across the hall asked me to help him get something out of the basement."

He nodded to her, and she excused herself.

"So, Brad told me you'll be off work with an ankle injury, hey?" He sat down in a chair across from the sofa.

"Yeah," Lenci replied. "My butt's glued to the couch for the next two and a half weeks."

"I see." His gaze was probing.

In the awkward silence, the Agent hummed a couple of warbling notes through her nose. At last, she straightened up in her seat and met his gaze.

"Why are you here?" she asked.

She saw the thought pass over his face. He was searching for something to say other than that she had asked for him through the phone of an agent that his director had sent to surveil her.

He sighed. "I don't intend to keep anything from you, Lenci."

The Agent's heart skipped a beat at such a tender use of the blank-slate name, but she held onto the mental image of Prancer's foaming mouth to keep her memory intact. She still had questions.

"You can start with telling me why we're in a fake apartment."

Chandler shifted uncomfortably. "Your request to come to Diablo caught us off guard since your entire family and the Wilsons moved to Windsailing a few years before you joined SSI. But I recognized that there must be some reason Windsailing was not an option—perhaps that Miller knew that we had recruited you from Windsailng. In addition, with your memory lapse, I thought maybe a familiar setting with familiar people would be helpful for your recovery."

His concern was precious, though rather naïve. The Agent smiled at the idea of a handler that thought something might be helpful for her recovery.

"Why was SSI surveilling me three nights ago?" she asked.

"Director Gomez has concerns about your loyalty, as you seem to have gathered," Chandler replied.

He paused to examine her expressionless face, then continued.

"Her anxiety is not about your character so much as Miller's methods of manipulation."

He paused again, then said, "You're aware that she, too, spent some time with him in her younger days?"

The Agent's eyebrows shrugged ever so slightly, but she did not show any other signs of surprise at this tidbit.

"It's true," he said. "But as divine plans would have it, she was recovered after six months. With the proper help, she was rehabilitated and is now the director of the largest and most successful covert agency ever to have a contract with the Western Government."

"Ah, it all makes sense now." She gave him a patronizing smirk. "You came here to convince me to let you rehabilitate me. Well, let me tell you: you taught me everything I needed to know to protect myself. And now I'm back and I feel fine, Chandler."

"Feelings aren't everything," he said, stiffening. "Chandler, still?"

His face was grim, and his eyes were sad. The Agent had not meant to upset him. He had only been kind to her since the day he had found her.

"So, what'll you do with me?" she asked. "You know, to get me field-ready again?"

"Well, what *can* I do?" He shrugged, trying to appear unperturbed. "If you're feeling fine, maybe we should just continue with business as usual. Can I count on you to stick around for a while?"

She shrugged as well. "I have to for the next few weeks, for my ankle. Few months would be ideal, though, if the family's up for it."

"You'd stay in this apartment after what you know?"

"Here's as good a place as any," Lenci said. "My family's here, and the food is really good."

"That is an *understatement*," Chandler smiled. "I once had Thanksgiving dinner here. Monica Chang is one of the best cooks I know. Her macaroni and cheese is to die for!"

"Yeah." She mirrored his smile.

Then, searching for something to contribute to this more light-hearted discussion, she summoned up the little bit that she knew from experience. "And the desserts are pretty great, too."

"Ah, yes, the desserts." Her handler's voice was cheerful, but his gaze was still probing.

The faint *DING* of the elevator was muffled in the tense air of the Changs' living room. The uneven footsteps of two people carrying something together thumped laboriously down the hall.

132

"Before your mother returns," Chandler began slowly, "I wanted to let you know—I don't know if this is the time. Well, I guess there's no time that would be good—"

"Somebody died," she finished with a wry smile.

People could often be uncomfortable with the idea of death, but the Agent had generally transcended that discomfort.

"Yeah," her handler said. "Do you remember Reece Ma who graduated ahead of you at the Academy?"

He pulled out a small, black contraption and squeezed it between his forefinger and his thumb. It projected a 3D image of a man who looked to be in his mid-twenties, with chestnut brown hair and olive-colored skin. He had a thin but angular jaw, a long, slightly rounded nose, and eyes the shape of perfect limes. His smile was cocky, like he'd never experienced a loss in all his life.

Lenci's heart sank. Reece Ma was a sopient from the SSI Academy. He had graduated at the top of his subdivision. While his official specialty was technology, he had also been a formidable opponent on the sparring mat. Well, before she had been trained by the Killer, anyway. She had grown fond of that cocky smile, a smile that she had recently seen on the face of someone else.

"Yes," she replied. "How did it happen?"

There was a soft thud in the hallway. Lenci's mother and Karthik had set down whatever they were carrying a few meters away from the door. They were resting.

"I was hoping you could tell me," Chandler said. "Gomez assigned Reece as head of the surveillance team three days ago. Now, the director understands why you terminated the operatives that were found to be members of the WCE, but it did raise some concern for us when we found Reece's body floating in the bay. His face was smashed in something terrible."

"Had he been around before all this?" Lenci asked, trying to remember why it was important that he most likely had not.

"Now that you mention it, no," Chandler said. "A couple years ago, during an operation in Siberia, he sent a 'strained but contained' signal, warning us that he had to go dark for a while. It was only last month that he sent us encrypted correspondence from Moscow to notify us that his mission had been a success. The director pinged him when you first arrived and asked him to return to check you out. He arranged to meet his team directly at the site and made plans to debrief Siberia after the surveillance assignment."

So, Reece Ma had gone missing. Then, he came back, but he didn't show his face. The face on the man who led the surveillance team was not Reece's face. And now, Reece's body had been fished out of the bay with a bashed in face. Chandler was studying her as she sorted through these thoughts. Perhaps he was baiting her.

"How do you know it was Reece's body?" she asked.

"DNA test."

"Hm."

The Agent wondered if Director Gomez was big and bad enough to bash a man's face in, but she did not dare verbalize that thought. Chandler was looking at her with those sad, honest eyes again.

"We found this in his hands," he said.

He pulled a water-stained scrap of cloth out of his pocket and unfolded it to reveal an intricate gold design. Lenci, bombarded with emotion, took the cloth. Before the tears could well up in her eyes, she pushed all the feelings down and began humming under her breath.

"Is it yours?" Bourghin asked.

"Of course it is," the Agent said. "I can't escape the feeling that there's a question you truly mean to ask me, Chandler."

He looked pained in asking, "Lenci, did you kill him?"

Sparks ignited in her eyes, and her voice shook violently as she replied, articulating each syllable clearly and emphatically. "I would *never*."

She didn't add that she had only knocked out the men in the garage. They didn't matter to her, anyway.

"Well, I didn't think so, Kiddo," Chandler smiled kindly. "But some questions are simply a matter of formality, especially where the director's peace of mind is concerned."

As she thought about it, the full length of the *saree* had been wrapped around the roaches. The leader of the surveillance team had never gotten his hands on it. The Agent wondered if the director was big and bad enough to frame her for murder.

The front door opened, and Karthik and Monica came in carrying a portable piano that was already set up on its stand.

"Look what we found in storage!" Karthik said. "It's just what we'll need for your couch potato month."

The Agent was perplexed by Karthik's assumption that she would want his company during her bed rest sentence.

"To be continued." Bourghin stood up.

After introducing himself to Karthik as "Chandler," he announced his intention to depart.

"I'll see you out," Mrs. Chang said.

Chandler gave the Agent his card and told her to call him if she ever wanted to talk. She doubted that she would, but she smiled and nodded politely, all the same.

When the door was closed, she looked solemnly at Karthik who was now sitting in the chair across from her. He had already plugged in the keyboard and was fiddling with the volume and bass dials.

"Pianist," the Agent said. "Makes sense—such delicate phalanges."

He gave her an odd glance.

"This old thing has seen better days," he said, plucking a couple of keys to test the volume. "I bought a real piano while you were gone, but I put it in storage when—"

He didn't complete that statement—the Agent presumed—because she wasn't supposed to know that he and his mother had moved into the apartment across the hall only a few days before. He was lucky that the Agent was not in the mood to interrogate him about his part in that.

She had weightier matters on her mind than trigger prompts and children's tricks. The news of her colleague's death was troubling enough, but even more troubling was what truly linked them—a forgotten secret that was in danger of being revealed before its time. Suddenly accosted by feelings she did not desire to feel, the Agent began to hum.

"Lenci," Karthik said softly.

The past melted away as she turned her gaze upon him.

"Are you feeling okay?" he asked.

She slung her arm over the armrest and smiled coyly. "Guess I don't quite feel myself right now."

"Well, then, you're in luck because I've got a song that cures all identity crises." He gave her a playful grin and dramatically plunked out the first few measures of Tchaikovsky's "Swan's Theme" on the keyboard.

"For real?" Lenci laughed. "Have you ever *watched* that ballet?"

"Only every time you performed it at school," he said. "But if the joke is going to detract from your enjoyment of my musical prowess, I'll play something else."

"Moonlight Sonata," she suggested.

"Excellent choice." His grin broadened as he effortlessly changed keys. "I haven't played that since you left."

As she listened, Lenci pointed her toes and stretched her legs. A dull pain had strangely settled on her limbs, or maybe she was only just now allowing herself to feel it. She lay back on the couch and closed her eyes. Karthik's touch was gentle—very light, in fact—for such a weighty song. Each phrase pulsed like a heartbeat, starting firmly but releasing softly, drawing her deeper and deeper into a familiar calm.

But, still, Poison Arrow waits for her relief!

She gasped and sat up. Karthik stopped playing.

"I'm okay," she reassured him. "I just—I almost fell asleep."

He eyed her apprehensively but resumed his playing.

She returned his gaze with some amusement.

Smiling impishly, she said, "I wish I could get up and dance to this. It'd make a great *developée* exercise."

He seemed to relax when she mentioned dance. Lenci had always loved to dance.

"I'll just do some *port-de-bras*," she announced, raising her arms with a flourish into a crisp fifth position.

Then, she flexed her hands to mimic the sad swan that Karthik had conjured with his hat tip to Tchaikovsky.

***

Monica walked Agent Bourghin to his car, but she continued to stand anxiously at the curb after he closed the door.

He rolled down the window. "Everything okay, Monica?"

"May I—May I—"

"Please, come in."

He unlocked the door and watched her calmly as she lowered herself into the passenger's seat. After pulling the door closed, she took a deep breath and smoothed some stray hairs away from her face.

"That isn't my daughter, Chandler," she said. "She looks like her; she talks like her sometimes; even her style of joking is the same, but she's different. Besides the fact that she has been quite forgetful, she walks differently and she—"

She thought for a moment. "Well, she was such a sweet, darling girl before she left. But now, she has these terrible mood swings and this heartless stare—"

"Trauma changes people," Agent Bourghin sighed. "Please try to be patient with her. When we discovered that she'd had the memory lapse, we knew that her road to recovery was not going to be an easy one."

"But she isn't—"

"Please, Monica," he said. "You have to understand that what your daughter saw—what her abductor put her through—it could have caused a psychological disruption unlike anything you or I can imagine. My assessment is that he attempted to use hypnosis to control her."

"Hypnosis?" Monica's tone turned up sharply in alarm.

"Well, it *is* what she was trained for at the Academy, but she was trained only to respond to me."

She crossed her arms. "*Only* to respond to you? Chandler, I did not see anywhere in our agreement that my teenage daughter was going to be subjected to psychological manipulation, by you or anyone else!"

"The director had Lenci tested for suggestibility after finding that her aptitude test results were off the charts."

"You changed our agreement without telling me?"

"I can understand why you would be upset," Agent Bourghin said patiently, "but we are a *covert* agency. We agreed to allow you to know the basic idea of what your daughter's duties would be. But you do understand why some things would remain classified, don't you? At the time we signed your daughter, our hypnotics program was barely off the ground. The methods we were using were cutting edge—"

Mrs. Chang took her head in her hands. "So, you're telling me that my daughter is just a lab rat to you? You want her back so that you can write down the results of an experiment?"

"Far from it," he responded. "I care for your daughter a great deal, which is why I am convinced that we have to *actively* help her to recover. The best way to do that is to reaffirm the identity she was primed to believe she lost."

"But how?"

He smiled. "Well, she may have helped us out with that already. I think she tethered herself. Basically, she held onto some element of her old life, one thing to remain real to her and to remind her of who she really is. That way—even if she's mainly living out of the hypnotized compartment—her old self, Valencia Chang, is still preserved."

Monica sighed and folded her hands in her lap. "I trusted you, Chandler, and you betrayed my trust. Now, I need you to be completely forthright with me."

He nodded in acquiescence.

"When did this happen? Her abduction, I mean. You broke the news about a year ago, but your progress reports were suspiciously vague for at least a year before that—more, though, I think."

"You're an unusually observant woman, Monica Chang."

"Like daughter, like mother. It's what you appreciate most about us."

Chandler sighed and glanced in the rearview mirror.

"About three years ago," he said. "We were trying to celebrate Lenci's seventeenth birthday, just to call her since she was training out of district. The director at the other site was bewildered because, supposedly at SSI's request, he had released Lenci to go on a mission with one of his own agents and David Miller. Of course, Miller had engineered the whole thing. We never would have allowed that."

"And this David Miller," Monica said grimly. "What kind of man takes a seventeen-year-old girl?"

"He was her combat trainer at SSI," Bourghin replied. "Of course, now, it's obvious that he must have been targeting her nearly from the beginning. But as we supervised them during that time, we never thought—I guess we only saw what we wanted to see."

Monica took a deep breath. "Yes. Well, to that effect, I appreciate all that you've done to get Valencia back to our family. But please do her a favor and stay away."

Before he could protest, she held up her hand and continued, "She's with her family now. That is what she needs most."

"I haven't given up on her," he said.

"I'm happy for you to do whatever research you need to do behind the scenes, but I implore you not to confuse her with your presence."

He nodded grimly. "We're on the same side, Monica. I'll keep my distance."

"Thank you for understanding, Chandler."

After she had walked back into the building, he saw on his car phone that he had a voicemail from Blair Lee-Smith. Rather than listen to her voice before having to call her again anyway, he punched in her number and pulled away from the curb.

"Lee-Smith."

"What gives?" Bourghin asked. "You called during my house visit."

"You should have stayed," she replied. "I would have loved to hear Agent Thomas' reaction to this news."

"What news?"

Her voice was shaking with excitement. "It's about the body from the bay."

"Yes, Agent Ma's body. Go on." Bourghin shifted into second gear irritably.

"It might not be Reece Ma's body," Blair said.

Bourghin released the clutch too quickly and killed the engine.

"Come again?" Cars were honking behind him.

"Theresa noticed an odd texture to the skin. So, we conducted a second test using a tissue sample from beneath the epidermis, and Agent Ma's record disappeared from our system!"

Bourghin scratched his scruffy chin. "Maybe we can contact his family to ask for a sample off of one of his belongings and then compare the two?"

"Theresa figured out a way. She's conducting a manual test now."

"Great."

"That's not all," Blair said, "but she said you'll want to come in."

***

Bourghin trudged into the conference room at HQ to find Ms. Lee-Smith, Theresa, and Director Gomez waiting for him.

"Oh, good, we can start," Blair said.

"Where's Racky?" Bourghin asked.

Theresa rolled her eyes. "Probably with Lenci's family or getting gifts for them or something. You should talk to her about getting too attached. In any case," she flipped some papers onto the table, "look what I found in the blood sample!"

Everyone leaned in to look at the dark blotches on the paper.

"What are we looking at?" Gomez asked.

Before Theresa could respond, Blair exclaimed, "They're nanobots!"

"Well, thanks for stealing my thunder," Theresa said sullenly. "Yes, they're nanobots. The body we recovered in the bay was chock full of them."

"But what does it mean?" Bourghin asked.

Theresa shrugged.

Blair picked up the papers. "When I was working at the FBI, these were just becoming popular."

"Popular for what?" Theresa asked.

"First nanosurgery, then, later, assassination," the director said. "That was before people realized how easily machines could be hacked."

In answer to Theresa's inquisitive look, she said, "It's marginally more difficult to program people, but it's *much* harder to hack them."

"These little guys certainly did their job, then," Theresa said, collecting her papers once again. "Given that there was no sign of trauma from a needle, the nanobots probably entered in the form of an

139

inhalant or something. They attacked the heart and ripped it to shreds inside of the chest cavity."

The director cringed. "But if Reece was already dead from nanobots, why bother smashing his face?"

"Oh, that's the other thing." Theresa handed over the lab results from her manual blood test. "Reece was a huge blood donor while at the Academy. So, we have existing records from his donations. Type AB-. Our body from the bay is O+."

Blair's eyebrows raised. "You're saying the epidermis really was a DNA mask?"

Theresa nodded. "I'm just surprised the mask lasted that long underwater. After twenty-four hours submerged good quality masks usually come undone."

"Superior design," Blair said. "That's tech this area won't see for another twenty years, at least. We're way out of our league here."

Director Gomez fiddled with her collar for a moment, then said, "Get me a sample of Agent Thomas' blood."

"But director," Theresa began.

"Just get it!"

Theresa nodded and left the room.

Bourghin cleared his throat. "I don't like the direction this is going. But if it'll clear all suspicion, I'll call and ask Monica to convince Lenci to give a sample."

"Thank you, Bourghin." Gomez nodded at him as he departed.

When they were alone, Blair turned to the director. "Someone could have put the mask on a cadaver to make us think Reece died. That's strange enough on its own, but what's it got to do with Agent Thomas' blood?"

"A handful of the agents that went missing in the same window as Lenci ended up resurfacing within one month of the downfall of their home agencies," the director said. "But what if they weren't actually the agents that had gone missing?"

"That's a stretch." Blair's jaw tightened. "But it's possible, I guess, with a good DNA mask and lots of personality study. So, we're getting the blood just to make sure?"

"Replacing the weak things," the director whispered, staring out the window at the cluttered street.

"What?"

"Nothing."

Chapter 17

THE BLEEDING STOPPED AFTER the first week of bed rest. Despite receiving Dr. Williams' permission to return to life as normal, the Agent insisted upon completing the remainder of her couch sentence—just in case— and she spoke to the affectionately named Kiddo every day for the duration.

Karthik played the keyboard for her every evening he wasn't working, and on the weekends she enjoyed watching him and Lorenzo play *Zombies With Protruding Umbrellas*. They begged her to join them, but she declined. She was content to watch them struggle, celebrating quietly from behind a fashion magazine every time they beat a level. The two worked hard at it, stopping mainly for bathroom breaks. They often ate pizza or cereal with their eyes glued to the screen and one hand still on the controller. They occasionally took lengthier breaks to grapple on the floor in front of the TV after completing a level as some sort of reward. The Agent found the whole thing amusing, at the very least, and rather heart-warming, if she allowed herself to consider it as such.

She decided during her couch sentence that she liked being Lenci. She liked having a mother and a brother and neighbors across the hall. She liked having festive meals and small talk and nights of listening to Moonlight Sonata. She liked that she could open up to her family about the mundane aspects of the odd jobs she'd taken in various countries without disclosing the darker details of her past. She liked sitting wedged between Karthik and Lolo to heckle horror movies on Fridays and eating noodle soup late on Monday nights. She liked the low hum of voices behind the hallway door after everyone else had retired for the evening. She liked the absence of bones breaking, millstones, and night training.

In fact, she couldn't really remember what the big deal had been about the night training. She remembered getting punished for her refusal, but the details of her life as Bathsheba seemed like immaterial dream-stuffs compared to the crisp, radiant tranquility of her new life as Lenci. There were days when the Agent became convinced that her time in WCE territory had indeed been one long nightmare. The only evidence to the contrary was Kiddo.

On the day that Lenci was to return to work, she heard a strange bumping and scratching at the front door.

Figuring that Karthik had forgotten his key at work again, she threw open the door and said, "I keep telling you to check your pockets before you leave—oh."

"Hey, Circus!" Racky squawked, shoving her locksmithing tools into the duffel bag slung over her shoulder.

Lenci motioned her in. "Were you just trying to break into my apartment?"

"Yeah, but it's not breaking in if you are coming to see the person who's already inside. Nice place!" Racky spun around in the living room to give it a decent once-over.

Lenci suspected that her coworker had just cased her family's apartment, appraising every loose object in it.

"How did you know where I live? And what are you doing here?" she asked.

"Interrogations are for killjoys," Racky replied, setting her bag down and unzipping it. "Besides, I brought lunch."

After looking in the paper bag that she handed her, Lenci set it on the table and grinned. "Chubba's! I thought you said we'd go out there together. You know, make an event of it?"

"Well, we could have done that," Racky said. "But we can't have you overexerting yourself. Besides, I wanted a private space to give you *this*."

She pulled a bundle of clothing out of her duffel bag and handed it to Lenci. Upon a quick examination of the clothing, all of the blood drained from the Agent's face. They were maternity clothes! She lunged for Racky and, closing one hand around her neck, took her to the floor.

"*How* did you find out?" she growled, holding a blue, frilly blouse with a pink floral pattern in her face.

Racky coughed, her arms and legs wriggling helplessly at her sides.

"I—I hacked your—medical records," she said.

The Agent tightened her grip. "Why?"

"Your—face!" Racky managed to eke out.

This woman who was being strangled had the nerve to get sassy with her. The Agent suppressed a laugh and released her coworker.

"What does that mean?"

"Your face," Racky repeated, rubbing her neck gingerly. "It was fuller than I remembered, but the rest of your body wasn't any different—just more muscular. So, I hacked Dr. Williams' records and confirmed my suspicions."

The Agent drew Racky to her feet, pulled out a chair for her, and sat down across from her. Her face was still expectant.

Racky continued, "I wasn't about to divulge your secret, girl. I'm not about that. It's just—I know what it's like to have that kind of secret, and I wanted to let you know you don't have to go it alone."

This aerobics teacher showed more interest in her than a random coworker would. The Agent knew she wasn't *that* charming. And how on earth would Racky have known what doctor's office to hack?

"We were teammates." The Agent meant her statement more as a question.

Racky nodded.

"At SSI?"

Another nod.

"Or, almost, I guess," Racky said. "More like pre-teammates. Theresa and I were assigned to you, specialized to you, but we were never commissioned because you didn't come back from Warbuck—until now."

"Does Theresa know about my secret?"

"Of course not! What kind of evil riffraff do you think I am?"

"So, you don't trust her either?"

Racky shrugged. "You can expect this will stay between you and me."

The Agent saw no signs of deception in Racky's face. A class violation, by Western Federal decree, disrupted all confidentiality laws, even in Diablo. So, if this hacker really was an SSI agent, she had broken protocol by failing to report the information she had discovered in favor of Lenci's privacy. It had been quite a while since she had encountered that kind of decency.

Lenci turned her attention to the clothing. "You bought these?"

"Favorites from long time ago," Racky chuckled.

She held out a pair of sweatpants. "These puppies will buy you some time even after the belly bump appears. They are real comfy, too."

After examining her for a moment, Lenci remarked, "You don't look old enough to have have been pregnant a 'long time ago.'"

"My Class 1 stepdad," Racky said. "Now you know why it was a secret."

Lenci frowned. "I'm sorry."

"My baby girl came out just fine. I even held her once before the district took her away from me."

"You don't ever get to see her?"

"She stayed with my grandmama while I was in and out of juvenile detention." Racky shrugged. "I haven't seen her since the day I signed on with SSI, though. I dropped in to let Grandmama know that I had a real and true job with the DoD minor recruitment program. Saw my baby, two years old, sleeping in a big girl bed. Damned if she didn't look just like I did at that age!"

Tears welled up in her eyes as she whispered, "Subclass 4.14s the pair of us, like step-twins in some twisted way. You know, when the dad is Class 1, they *divide* by one to get the subclass designation—like what he did was of no consequence. She's Subclass 4.14 just like me and my mother before me. It's backwards, I tell you—so backwards and wrong!"

Lenci, uncomfortable with this sudden burst of emotion, put her hand on top of her pre-teammate's in an attempt to console her.

"I want to punch that guy in the face for what he did to you," she said.

Racky wiped her eyes. "Girl, he is not even worth the knuckle ache. He was a low-down creep going nowhere fast, just looking for someone to dominate so he could feel like more of a man. I don't waste my time with people like that, and neither should you."

"Hm." That struck a chord in the Agent for some reason.

"Why did you stay with Miller so long when you knew Bourghin was out there looking for you?" Racky asked, cocking her head at Lenci. "You could have picked up some pretty bad habits, as suggestive as your silly head is."

Feeling self-conscious, the Agent blurted out the first excuse that came to mind, "You can only be what you're made to be."

"Mm." Racky's face scrunched up. "I guess that works if you are man-made—which you are not."

She was laughing her drunk llama helium laugh again.

Lenci smiled at her. Now she was sure that this peculiar woman could be her friend. She liked Racky's down-to-earth way of thinking about things. And that insane laugh was growing on her.

"We did train together a couple of times, didn't we?" she asked.

"At one of the bootcamps," Racky said, stretching casually toward the middle of the table. Her hand passed over a stack of ceramic coasters. "I wasn't sure you would remember me."

"That time *is* a little fuzzy for me." Lenci strained to get the right details. "Didn't we fight a locker room full of eugenists?"

"Yeah, a bunch of Class 1s and 4.14s dug up my file. They tried to jump me after finding out I was subclass."

Lenci shook her head. "Nothing brings the classes together like hatred for the Subclass."

"I guess," Racky said. "But I hadn't been trying to pass, for real! It's just I'm not always thinking about it, and no one ever asked."

"And people see what they want to see," Lenci added.

"And they get mad like you've been lying to them when it's really their ignorant selves that were assuming things," Racky huffed. "Anyway, that day you were on your way to some kind of conditioning, but you jumped into the mix because they called me a subber."

"Ugh," Lenci winced. "'Subber' is just such an ugly word. I prefer the term 'naturally unclassified.'"

"That's what you told those eugenists, too!" Racky laughed. "Didn't really do much to change their minds, though."

Lenci smiled as the facts came back to her. "Good thing you thought up the electroshock thing."

"Well, I couldn't have done it without your electro-resistant behind."

"We have the Killer to thank for that bit of training."

"I will thank that lecherous numb-nut for nothing," Racky said. "He's only ever been trouble to anyone in his path."

To keep from dwelling on such things, Lenci said with a grin, "I got written up big time for that fight *and* two days in solitary."

"Me too, but I enjoy my own company."

"Me too."

The two women laughed heartily.

Suddenly having a spark of memory, whether from the report or from actual events, Lenci asked, "Hey, didn't I call you 'Commando' or something?"

"A couple of times, now that I think about it," Racky replied. "But I never could comprehend why."

Lenci shrugged. "Locker room profiling, I guess. Probably for the same reason I called Theresa 'Satin.'"

"Oh! I thought you meant 'Satan.'"

They laughed again.

"Anyways," Racky said, "plenty has happened since that time, so you can do away with the underwear nicknames, if you want."

She reached into the bag of Chubba's goodies. She handed Lenci a chicken thigh and pulled out another one for herself.

"To new beginnings," she said, extending her chicken thigh towards Lenci.

Lenci extended hers as well, and the pieces of chicken met with an awkward squish.

"I kind of like 'Circus' as my nickname, though," Lenci said.

"Maybe I will keep calling you that, then," Racky said, biting into her chicken thigh.

"Also, you can put it back anytime, Racky."

"Put what back?"

"The coaster you took off the table. I saw you swipe it when you were stretching."

"Can't get anything past you, Circus," Racky said, pulling the coaster out of her pocket and placing it back in the middle of the table along with a small blue box. "Except for these *lovely* two-carat, SI2 diamond earrings of your mom's."

"How did you get those?" Lenci snatched the box.

"I came in through one of the bedroom windows first," Racky said nonchalantly.

"And then you climbed down the side of the building and took the elevator up so I could catch you pretending to break into my apartment from the front door?"

"What can I say?" Racky took another bite of chicken. "I mainly do it for the challenge. And the thrill. And the equilibrium, in a minor way."

***

K. Ethan Wilson was sitting in the reception area when Director Gomez leaned out of the conference room.

"Mr. Wilson!" She beckoned to him.

He rose and followed her into the room where Agent Bourghin was waiting. "Chandl–ler said you wanted t—to see me? I'm hoping you can make this quick because I t—took emergency l–leave to come d—down here."

They sat around the end of a long table in the center of the room.

"Thank you for taking the time, Mr. Wilson, K. Ethan," Gomez said, smiling winsomely. "May I call you Ethan?"

He gave her a scrutinizing glance and then looked at Bourghin.

"L—lieut–tenant Wilson is fine."

Gomez's expression sweetened. "Lieutenant Wilson, then. How is Lenci?"

"As well as she can be, und–der the circumstances. Auntie Monica says th—that Lenci still sleeps with the l—light on, so she's probably still having n—nightmares. But she seems t–to have adjusted well enough to civilian l—life."

"Have you noticed anything unusual about her behavior?"

Lieutenant Wilson's forehead wrinkled. "Unusual? Well, everything has been about as unusual as it can be. But I guess you'd expect th—that since we haven't been together in five years. N—none of us are the people we were back before she l—left."

He was good. His manner was professional and pleasant enough, but he certainly didn't seem to want to volunteer any more information than was required of him. Bourghin gave her a look that said, *We're wasting our time here.*

She changed her tactic.

Folding her hands on the table in front of her, she said, "Lieutenant Wilson, allow me to be frank with you. We are coming to you because we are desperate. Now, I don't normally do things like this, but desperate times call for desperate measures. What I am about to tell you *must not* be repeated outside of this room, least of all to Lenci herself."

Bourghin's gaze flicked up at her. She pressed forward.

"There are agencies out there less scrupulous than SSI, who are experimenting with a new kind of weapon. Have you heard of DNA masks?"

Lieutenant Wilson nodded.

"Well, their existence has made DNA-testing fairly unreliable these days, and these other agencies are taking advantage of that. In fact, I

147

suppose you could say that they are *people-masking*. We've already got one unidentifiable body that was masked as one of our own agents."

Shifting in his seat, he asked. "What's your point?"

"My point," Gomez said, "is that we have reason to believe that the woman we brought back from Chile is not our agent, *your* Lenci, but a specially trained and *deadly* substitute. We need you to get a current blood sample and another DNA sample off any of her belongings—pre-disappearance, of course."

Lieutenant Wilson laughed out loud. He laughed so hard that he shook, but Gomez took note that his eyes were still very grave.

He cleared his throat. "You d——don't really believe that, d–do you? Even if they could come up with a d—DNA masker that l—lasted l—longer than a few weeks without renewal, a substitute couldn't possibly fool Lenci's closest friends and family."

"Love is blind, Lieutenant," Gomez retorted. "Family and friends are the prime example of this."

"What she means," Bourghin cut in, "is that it is possible to study about someone and to become a lot like them, especially with cosmetic procedures and intense psychiatric training. We're wondering if there are any memories that only Lenci would have known or remembered, anything of great emotional value, or routines that she seems to have forgotten since her return?"

A shadow crossed Lieutenant Wilson's face.

"N—nothing I wouldn't give an arm and a l—leg to forget, myself," he replied. "N–now, I really should—"

Gomez interrupted. "Recently, we took a sample of Valencia's hair and tested it against the DNA sample we had on file."

Lieutenant Wilson stood up and made for the door. "I d–don't have t–to l–listen to this."

"Don't you at least want to know what we found?" she asked.

"I d—don't care what you found," Lieutenant Wilson said over his shoulder.

"We didn't find anything," Gomez said. "We ran the test, but as soon as we did, her existing record was deleted from our system. It was irrecoverable, even by our best tech staff. Do you know what that means?"

Lieutenant Wilson did not respond. He stood with his hand still on the doorknob. His back was to them, but it was clear that he was listening.

"It means that *someone* doesn't want us to know her identity," she continued. "And wouldn't it be strange to delete someone's record if they were indeed who they said they were?"

"With all d—due respect," Lieutenant Wilson said, turning around. "Here in the Western States, n—nothing is as it should be. I d—don't know why your records were d—deleted, but I d—don't see what that has to d—do with me."

"Well, wouldn't you want to know that the woman who has wormed her way into your life is not your long-lost childhood friend?"

"She *is* my friend!" Lieutenant Wilson snapped. "N—now it's my turn to be frank with you. I d—don't l—like being surveilled or ch—chased by strange men on motorcycles. And d—don't try t—to t—tell me that they weren't from your agency. I saw the initials that are on this building on the phone of one of the cyclists."

Gomez remained silent.

"So, I don't know what kind of game you're playing here, but d—don't expect me to play along. Lenci's recovery has been rough, and it's only just now beginning to smooth out. The l—last thing we need is for you all to confuse her with this n—nonsense."

"If you ever change your mind," she replied calmly, "you know where to find us."

"When you approached me about being a part of Lenci's recovery process, I signed on for Lenci, n—not for you. Stay out of our lives."

He nodded brusquely to both her and Agent Bourghin, then took his leave.

"He's rattled," Bourghin said.

"Indeed," Gomez replied. "But that's the same reason he's going to test her current DNA against her public record. When he does, her record will likely be erased from all available records, which means he will need the test done manually. He'll produce a sample of DNA from before she was abducted, just to make sure. Since he knows now that we have the means to do it, he'll hopefully come to us. Then, we'll have our answer."

"How do you know?"

The director smiled. "I know young love when I see it. It believes the best until there's no other option. That is when love turns to desperation. And that is when it's most easily exploited."

"That's a gamble," Bourghin said.

"My life has been one huge gamble after another, Samir. I don't intend to stop now."

Chapter 18

LENCI'S FIRST DAY AT WORK WAS A BLAST. She took on four new trainees whom she learned quickly from observing their warm-ups. From there, she was able to create a routine that was tailored to the particular needs of each one. Her trainees enjoyed their workouts so much that they were singing her praises in the locker room. Ten more people requested training with her for various days of the week, much to Bread's chagrin.

At the end of the day, Lenci walked into the women's locker room to check for anyone who may not have heard the final closing announcement. The room was lined with lockers, and the showers were in an alcove on the far end. Lenci wandered through the locker room and made sure each shower stall was empty. Then, she headed back the way she had come.

Suddenly, she was encompassed in darkness. The Agent had begun many ambushes with the surprise of total darkness in order to instill fear in her target. She used to let them marinate in that fear as they intuited her presence and the fact dawned on them that they had become prey. Rejecting fear for the moment, she crouched behind the lockers nearest to the entrance and waited.

I know where Poison Arrow landed
In a desert near the sea
She dreams beyond a life of swimming
But her legs lack strength
She fails

The Agent did not like the darkness that surrounded her. It was an unfriendly darkness, a darkness in which unfamiliar songs bombarded her. She heard footsteps. Someone was coming down the hall toward the locker room, three someones from the syncopated rhythm of the footsteps. She hummed under her breath.

Come, Bathsheba. She could take three assailants and still shield Kiddo, if she prioritized her core correctly.

But I know where Poison Arrow landed
Despite the power of her venom
Her will grows weak
I know where Poison Arrow landed
And, still, Poison Arrow waits for her relief!
Sweet relief

"You go in, and I'll get the lights," a male voice said.

Two people approached, but one was much closer than the other. With a fierce yell, the Agent flew from behind the lockers and pinned the person who had just entered the locker room to the wall. An amused and contemptuous breath puffed in her face.

"*Now, Bread!*" a familiar voice squawked. "Turn on the lights, you cretin!"

The Agent heard the generator thump and whirr, then the locker room became light again. The person she had pinned to the wall was none other than Theresa. Racky stood a couple of meters away, her face full of concern.

"Did we spook you, Lenci?" Theresa smirked. "Guess they didn't have rolling blackouts in Chile, did they?"

Lenci released her roughly, trying to remember what she had been so riled up about. She wasn't actually scared of the dark.

"Leave her be, Theresa," Racky said.

"Hey, she attacked me, remember?" Theresa rubbed her neck where the Agent had dug in with her forearm.

She looked happier than Lenci thought she should for someone who had almost died.

"Only because you didn't announce yourself," Racky retorted. "You okay, Circus?"

"I'm alright," Lenci said hurriedly, brushing past her pre-teammates into the hallway.

She found herself face-to-face with Bread.

"I knew you would be trouble," he grumbled. He wasn't talking about her reaction to the dark. He was talking about her aptitude as a trainer. "Now none of my guys are going to be able to train anyone."

"Well, if you want, I can train your 'guys' to get them *up to par*." She smiled mischievously.

"Get out of my sight!"

Lenci chuckled as she walked away. She wondered what Bourghin could possibly have on that guy that made him so committed to employing her when he so obviously hated her.

Good old Bourghin.

"Ey, wait a minute, Circus!" Racky called, jogging to catch up. "I can give you a ride. Catch you later, Theresa!"

"Oh, it's okay," Lenci said. "It's late-night noodle night. My brother and my—Karthik, and I, we're going to get noodles at this place we like. It's a tradition. You know, bring a little cheer to the start of the week? And tonight is special because it's the first time that we don't have to eat it from takeout containers in our living room."

Racky's eyes lit up. "I *love* noodles! Like those ones with the flavored powder? *Damn* good! Just message your brother and let him know that we're swinging by for them."

"It's not really like instant ramen," Lenci said hesitantly.

"Oh, so it's that fancy stuff with the oil packets and all that?"

"Kind of," Lenci replied. "You'll see. Can I borrow your phone? I lost mine."

***

"Well," Blair said. "You called it! Lieutenant Wilson sent in a sample to be tested at the district lab this afternoon."

"The predictability of young love," the director smiled.

"Is Lenci's record still in the district database after the test?" Bourghin asked.

Blair shook her head. "And I asked Racky to replace it, but the replacement wouldn't stick. The system is rejecting any record linked to Lenci's picture, name, or DNA. Racky is arranging Lenci's papers and driver's license, so she'll have those, at least. But it looks a lot like someone is trying to make her into a ghost."

"That's doesn't look good," Bourghin said glumly.

"No," the director said. "It doesn't."

"You really think Wilson will bring us samples for a manual test?" Blair asked.

"Time will tell," the director responded. "But remember, I was right about him once already."

Chapter 19

IN THE DARK OF THE PARKING GARAGE, Racky and Lenci watched as two figures approached from the elevators. They were two guys, both roughly the same height, although one was skinny as a string bean and the other more filled out.

When they reached the car, Racky pressed the button to unlock the back doors.

"Hi guys!" Lenci called backward over the passenger's seat. "Racky, this is my brother Lorenzo, and this is Karthik, our across-the-hall neighbor."

"It is very nice to meet you," Racky said in her most professional tone.

She gave Lenci a thumbs-up as the guys slid into the back seat of her small, champagne-colored sedan.

"What's up?" Lorenzo said.

Even though he was trying his best to sound bored and uninterested, his voice cracked slightly when he addressed Lenci's coworker. Apparently, he found her attractive.

"Aw," Racky said, responding to what he hadn't said.

She grinned sheepishly at Lenci who rolled her eyes.

"N—nice t—to meet you, t—too." Karthik shook the hand Racky extended over her shoulder. "'Racky,' d–did you say?"

"Yeah, like the boxer, except bony."

Much to Lenci's relief, Racky did not mention her breasts.

"Racky's my friend," Lenci said. "We work together."

"Your friend?" Karthik echoed.

Like she couldn't make a friend if she wanted to.

"Well, in the way that friends can sometimes be," Racky said, stifling a giggle. "So, what's this place we are going, Circus? And *where* is it?"

"It's this great Chinese place that serves people of every class, lawfully but dangerously including members of the Subclass." Lenci looked out the window coolly before continuing, "It's about ten minutes away, off a tricky intersection in some sketchy alleyway. I don't remember the name of it."

"I d–do!" Karthik piped up, seeing where this conversation was going.

But it was too late.

"Better let me drive," Lenci said, "if you don't mind."

"Okay." Racky unbuckled her seat belt.

"Wow, didn't see that coming," Lorenzo said sarcastically.

"This is a bad idea," Karthik whispered as the women switched seats.

"It's a fine idea," Lenci said. "I don't get motion sick when I'm driving. Besides, I know how to get to the restaurant."

"So d–do I," he replied, not commenting on the fact that the last time Lenci had been to that restaurant was before they moved away to Windsailing.

"*And* I'll do it in record timing."

Karthik and Lorenzo groaned.

"Now, let's see if I can get this contraption to work," Lenci said, fiddling with the buttons on the radio.

There was something about that odd, old technology that reminded her that she might have driven a car once before. Music blared from the speakers, shooting electrifying beats through the car and its passengers. Soulful voices, rich as butter and clear as bells, hauntingly wove in and out of the energetic baseline.

"Do we *have* to listen to this?" Lorenzo complained.

"Ey!" Racky said, recognizing the voices of her favorite Korean choir-band in their new hit song. "I didn't know this album was out in the States yet!"

Suddenly, Lorenzo seemed much more appreciative of the music. Karthik did not.

"Can you turn it d—down just a l—little?" He took off his seat belt and moved forward to turn the dial.

Lenci shifted the car into reverse, pressed the accelerator and then slammed on the brakes, sending him whipping forward and then back into his seat.

"Buckle up, Karthik," she said, looking past him through the back windshield as she backed up more slowly. "We can listen to your favorite music on the way home."

"Great," he mumbled, putting on his seat belt again. "Just drive carefully, so we d—don't d—die before we get there."

"I didn't tell *you* how to drive during the car chase."

"Actually, you d–did. As I recall, one of your specific requests was that I not 'drive us to our untimely end.' I held up my end of that deal, so maybe you can d—do us all a favor and do the same tonight."

She winked at him before facing forward.

"I'll do my best." She punched the accelerator, extracting screams of terror from her passengers—and, in Racky's case, possibly screams of delight—as the car screeched out of the parking garage and shot onto the street.

***

They parked in an alleyway across the street from the Chinese restaurant that was their destination. The restaurant had no name, or at least no name that was posted. In the dirt-streaked windows hung roasted ducks and parts of pigs. There was a pawnshop next door on one side and a hybrid pet shop and animal euthanasia center on the other, both with "no questions, no refunds" signs posted.

"Classy," Racky commented, stepping over a puddle of something that looked like it had once been in someone's stomach.

"The food is really good," Lenci reassured her.

"Better be, Circus," her coworker replied. "This looks like the place I got my very first job as a gunk runner."

Lenci gave her the kill sign and looked anxiously at Lorenzo. Thankfully, it seemed that he hadn't heard or understood what Racky said.

"You ever had real wonton soup, Racky?" Lorenzo asked, holding the door open for her. He was trying to deepen his voice.

"That's the one with the lard base, right?" She winked at Lenci. "Soup that makes you weigh one ton?"

"Wow, you don't know anything about Chinese food," he said, taking her arm and dragging her up to the counter to look at the menu. "Don't worry; I'll help you."

"How thoughtful," Lenci said, sharing an amused glance with Karthik.

His eyes were smiling again. She was glad to see him happy. And

155

gladder still that Racky was so good-humored about Lolo's peacock-like preening.

"Maybe we should sit," Karthik suggested. "No telling how long those two are going to be."

They sat across from each other at a table for four. Lenci piled up the menus because they already knew what they wanted. Karthik was tapping his fingers again, but Lenci noticed something was different about the pattern.

"Your tapping's not like normal," she said, aware of how abrupt that sounded only after it came out of her mouth.

"Nothing ever is with you around," he grinned.

She watched his slender fingers for a minute.

Then, she declared, "It's Moonlight Sonata!"

"So it is," he said. "D—do you remember telling me that I should put my t—tapping tic to good use by l—learning to play the piano?"

The corners of her mouth twitched upward. "You mean, the tapping caused the piano-playing and not the other way around?"

"*You* caused the piano-playing!" Karthik laughed. "You're the best problem-solver I know. Bossy as hell, but a good problem solver."

"Hm."

She looked down at her place setting. Her brother and Racky were still at the counter, admiring the pastries through the glass. She could hear Lorenzo's boastful teenage "man" voice and Racky's friendly "isn't he cute" voice weaving in and out of the sounds of the dishwashers and the cooks conversing over their duties.

"I d—didn't want you to go," Karthik said.

She met his gaze. "I can't imagine why I would have wanted to. Why *did* I leave?"

He was quiet for a while. The Agent had expected to see thousands of thoughts whirl across his face in that moment. Instead, it seemed that there was only one, and Karthik was just deciding whether or not to out with it.

At last, he said, "I was afraid."

"Hm."

The Agent took a sip of ice water and set the cup back in the middle of its ring of condensation.

"I was a flake, and I'm sorry," Karthik said, trying to make eye contact with her again. "If I had it to d—do over again—"

"Don't be sorry," she replied, still looking at the water cup. "We were just kids, anyway. What did we know about—well, anything, really?"

156

Something was off about his story. It didn't make any sense that Lenci would run away just because Karthik had been flaky about some random plan they'd had. Surely they had been through worse in all the years that they had known each other.

"Lenci," he began with a wavering voice, "what happened t–to you while you were gone? What were you d—doing?"

"I don't know," she said truthfully, relieved for once that the blank-slate name hindered her retrieval of information that would probably scar Karthik for life.

Just then, Racky and Lorenzo came to the table and took their seats across from each other.

"So, now I know what a *char siu bao* is," Racky said proudly, "and *har gow*, which sounds *delectable*."

"Did you order for us, Lolo?" Lenci asked.

"Renzo," he corrected stiffly.

While he put up with her calling him by the childish nickname at home, it seemed that it was simply unacceptable to call him that in front of a woman whom he was trying to impress.

"And yes, I did. Wonton noodle soups all around, except yours without the wonton, which makes no sense at all."

"Okay." She smiled but cringed inwardly as she wondered if his rejection of her nickname for him had to do with the fact that he wanted no part of her at all.

That was probably jumping to an unfair conclusion, but she couldn't help wondering.

"Racky'd never had a *don tot* before," Lorenzo said cockily. "So, I got the guy at the counter to give her a sample. I mean, because we're good customers, right? Come here regularly and stuff. It's just good business."

"How was it for you, Racky?" Karthik asked, just to be polite.

"I'm not too big on custard," Racky admitted. "But it was really nice of you to get the sample, Renzo."

Lorenzo beamed proudly. "Have you ever been to *dim sum*?"

She scratched her head delicately with one finger and then resorted to patting the itchy spot. "Is that like sushi?"

"Not really."

As Lorenzo embarked on a long exposition about *dim sum*, Lenci quietly slid her hand across the table and linked Karthik's little finger with her own. Then, they simply enjoyed Lorenzo and Racky carrying the conversation for them.

When the food came, everyone was excited to dig in. Racky had never used chopsticks, and while Lorenzo was keen to instruct her, she ended up asking for a fork. To smooth over his feelings of rejection, Racky diverted the conversation to the fact that Lenci had two bowls in front of her.

"Are you really going to eat all that, Circus?" she laughed. "We had Chubba's this afternoon and now you are going to eat two bowls of extra high carb water?"

"I could help!" Lorenzo piped up.

"No one comes between me and my noodle soup," Lenci said. "Besides, my job is to exercise hard all day every day, so I think I deserve a carb binge every once in a while."

Karthik smacked his chopsticks on the brim of his bowl for emphasis, saying, "Don't underestimate her, Racky. This woman can seriously throw down."

"Okay, Ms. Personal Trainer." Racky twirled another bunch of noodles around her fork.

"You mean 'Ms. Greedy Gut,'" Lorenzo said, getting up to go to the bathroom. "I'll be right back."

Lenci burped curtly in his direction before picking up one bowl to drain the ginger-infused, garlicky broth. As she started on the second bowl, a group of men barreled through the door. There were five of them, and they were all large, muscled, and menacing.

The men wandered around the dining area ridiculing the decorations and making rude comments about the aromas coming from the kitchen.

When the guy behind the counter asked how he could help them, one of the rude men, a fellow with a pink bandana tied around his head, responded, "What'd you say, yellow skin? I don't speak that ching chong talk. Don't you speak Engarish?"

Pink Bandana Man's friends laughed.

"Hey!" Lenci said. "Don't bring that mess in here. Have some respect!"

"You got something to say to me?" Pink Bandana Man stalked over to her table.

Karthik was already giving her the "please don't make any trouble" look. His hand over hers was an attempt to get her to think before challenging this guy and his gang to a duel. It worked. The truth was that she didn't *really* want to start a fight in the restaurant, especially with her little brother due to return from the restroom any second.

Swallowing the insults that were bubbling up in her throat, she finally said, "These guys work really hard all day in here. I'm just saying that you could treat them with more respect."

"Well, no one was asking you, Hula Brownie," Pink Bandana Man told her. "But I might let you off easy tonight. I've got a taste for exotic females."

A wave of tittering spread through his small entourage.

He motioned to Lenci's noodle soup and said, "And my, what *exotic* food you're eating! What's this?"

To her horror, he stuck his hand into her bowl and pulled out a handful of noodles. There was a green onion on the tip of his index finger, which he extended toward her.

"Oo," Racky said under her breath, "he done did it now."

Lenci brushed Karthik's hand from her own and stood up. She glowered at Pink Bandana Man. His companions were snickering and whispering to each other behind him. She knew that she could make quick work of them. But not in the restaurant. There wasn't enough space in there to entertain a fight that would allow her to protect her midsection *and* beat these guys into the ground.

"What is *that?*" she asked, sticking her finger into Pink Bandana Man's sternum.

"What's *what?*" He looked down to see what she was pointing at.

"This!" She threw the remainder of her hand-soiled noodle soup onto his chest and clapped the bowl over his head.

Spouting many uncharitable words, Pink Bandana Man threw the bowl on the floor, and shaking his finger in her face, he said, "You got more beauty than brains, Hula Brownie. You don't know who you're messing with. Better pack a gun in your coconut bra from now on."

She said nothing in response to his inaccurate hate spew but took her seat again and stared her ice-cold stare up at him. He was too flustered to stare back, so he stormed out with his posse in tow.

Racky and Karthik exhaled deeply. That had been a close call.

"Subclass, all of them," Lenci said, shaking her head. "Some pure-bloods might not know any better yet, but subclass people should never stoop so low!"

"None of them looked mixed with Class 2, though," Karthik replied.

"Being the product of multiple classes, *any* classes, should make it easier for people to engage in cross-class relations," she said. "Knowing that the love of two people of different groups brought us into the world should empower us to know that class designation never has to be a cause to hate or mistreat anyone."

"Not all subclass people are brought into this world by love," Racky said with a far away look in her eyes.

Her comment was born of personal experience, which Lenci ought to have considered given their earlier conversation about Racky's secret pregnancy. Furthermore, the three of them at that table knew from the treatment of their slave ancestors that it had been so, even from before the Subclass was officially labeled as such. It was an indelible and ugly truth that the history of Class 4.14s as a group included sexual relations between slave masters and slaves, relations which clearly never could have been consensual from the slaves' side. Most, if not all, Class 4.14 people had some Class 1 ancestry due to this kind of abuse. It was a tragic fact, one that many people overlooked in everyday life because of the pain it brought up.

Lenci bowed her head silently to acknowledge that she had spoken far too broadly.

Then, seeming to return to the present, Racky added, "And, in any case, people looking to hate will always find a way."

When Lorenzo returned from the bathroom, he did not seem to notice the mess on the floor by the table.

"Ready to go?" he asked.

"I'll get the check," Lenci said, standing up.

Karthik stood up as well. "No, I'll do it."

"Absolutely not," Lenci replied. "You've been paying for the past three weeks!"

"Yeah, but it was my idea to make it a tradition. So, I'm paying."

"No way!"

"Look," Racky butted in, "*I* will pay just so you two will stop arguing and let us go home."

"No!" They said in unison.

"It's a cultural thing," Lenci explained in a hushed tone. "We're almost done, aren't we?"

"Only if you let me pay," Karthik said stubbornly.

"Not happening, Buttface."

"Argh!" Racky brought her hands to her head.

After five more minutes of that, Lenci and Karthik split the cost of the meal halfway. The owner of the restaurant, grateful for Lenci's defense of the staff, comped the soup that Lenci didn't actually end up eating and gave them a free box of leftover baked goods.

Lorenzo and Racky went to the car ahead of the other two because Lenci insisted on staying back to apologize for the mess. She had actually offered to mop the floor herself, but she settled for keeping the busser company as he mopped up the noodle soup and porcelain smithereens. Karthik, of course, stayed with her.

Chapter 20

WHEN KARTHIK AND LENCI EXITED the restaurant, they found themselves surrounded by a triangle of men. Pink Bandana Man was with them in the middle of the triangle, wearing a new shirt that was presumably borrowed from the now shirtless fellow behind him.

"Nice change," the Agent said.

"I owe the new shirt to your superior soup-sloshing skills," Pink Bandana Man replied.

"I was talking to the guy with the emperor's new shirt over there." She nodded to the guy behind Pink Bandana Man. "Nice pecs."

He grinned goofily.

Pink Bandana Man scowled.

"Might be better n—not to infuriate the really big guy who's with a bunch of other really big guys," Karthik whispered.

Then, he addressed Pink Bandana Man, "Look, I think we can still work this out respectfully and nonviolently."

Pink Bandana Man and his crew laughed.

"Too late, Lieutenant Wilson," the Agent told him. "We're going to have to scrap our way out of this one."

At least her brother and Racky were secure in the car across the street. If things really went poorly, Racky would know what to do.

"No way," Karthik said, pulling out his phone and dialing. "I'm calling the police."

"This is Pyrite Valley Police Department's side of the district," she reminded him. "*If* they show up, they'll probably join the beat down."

This elicited a couple of snickers from Pink Bandana Man and his gang as they slowly converged on the two friends.

"Well," Pink Bandana Man said, "let's see if Pyrite picks up. I'm feeling a game of police roulette tonight."

The phone rang and rang.

"Fifty-fifty chance they'll join our side, if they come," Karthik said, backing up.

The Agent stepped back with him, keeping an eye on the advancing thugs.

"I don't like those odds," she replied.

They'd retreated as far as they could while maintaining some room to maneuver. Their backs were to the storefront, which was completely dark. The workers had either gone home or found a place to hide and wait out the impending violence.

Pink Bandana Man and his friends were getting antsy. They were starting to make intimidating and lewd gestures at the Agent—behavior that could only be overcompensation for inadequate fight skills. If this scuffle would ever get started, she would lay them out.

The phone rang a couple more times, then the call dropped. Karthik dialed again, but they all knew where this situation was heading.

"Good old Pyrite," the Agent said, sounding more cheerful than she should have. "Guess we'll have to do it the down-home Diablo way."

"Pin her down while I take care of this wimp," Pink Bandana Man ordered his roaches. "Then, she's *mine*."

The Agent named the three roaches Banana One, Banana Two, and Pecs Guy. They were all ogling her and jeering at her to make the first move.

"First things first, Karthik," she said. "You hold your own for a little second while I deal with these gunkheads. Then, I'll come help."

"Be careful," he told her as Pink Bandana Man approached him.

As soon as he was within reach, Karthik landed a hard right hook to Pink Bandana Man's jaw. Not bad—the Agent thought—for someone whose only training had been the rough streets of Diablo and the Canon Police Academy.

Pink Bandana Man recovered quickly, but Karthik was light on his feet and well able to predict that the thug's next strike would mirror his own for pride's sake. He dodged and struck again while Pink Bandana Man was off-balance, sending him hurtling onto his rear end.

Lenci smiled. Her friend had come a long way since their days of flight rather than fight. They both had, she supposed. The three roaches assigned to her were also watching Karthik and Pink Bandana Man. She swung at Pecs Guy, then at the Bananas. They dodged disinterestedly, like she was obstructing their view. This was to her advantage, however, because while they were gawking, she was studying their breathing patterns.

As Pink Bandana Man struggled to get up, Karthik offered him his hand and asked, "Had enough?"

Pink Bandana Man slapped his hand away.

"Guess that was a 'no,'" the Agent said. "Beat his behind, Karthik."

"So much for trying to d——deescalate," he said, casting her an annoyed glance as Pink Bandana Man jumped to his feet.

"Get that big-mouthed witch!" Pink Bandana Man snarled, prompting Pecs Guy and the Bananas to leap into motion.

The fight between him and Karthik was on again, more intensely than before, but the Agent didn't have time to watch because she was now engaging three assailants of her own.

Pecs Guy took the first swing, which she dodged easily. His beautiful pecs were slightly distracting, which is why she miscalculated the angle of his next strike and walked right into it. She stumbled backwards and scrambled to collect the hair that had been knocked from her ponytail.

"Always with the hair!" David exclaimed. "Focus, Sheebs! You look beautiful as always. No need to fix your 'do during a fight."

As always, his advance was aggressive. As always, she started the session in defensive mode. He pushed and punched and kicked at her all around the borders of the lawn. It took both of her arms to block one punch, but her flexibility and strong legs made up for her lack of upper body strength. She frequently blocked with her legs. One minute was her adaptation time with strangers. Once she had successfully defended for a whole minute in this drill, she would be allowed to attack.

When David threw his next punch, she knocked his arm away over her shoulder and jammed his nose playfully. He attempted a side-kick, which she easily kicked back. She hooked his supporting knee, drew his leg out from under him, and twisted his dominant arm behind his back. Before she could pressure him into submission, she was interrupted by the beeping of his watch. The drill was over.

"That's nearly the right spot," he said. "Just put pressure on the hand here, then twist—Ah!" He tapped her shoulder lightly, the sign that he had allowed himself to reach his pain threshold. "Good. Let's go for it again."

The Agent did not intend to return to bed rest. So, she took special care to shield her core when the Bananas came at her from both sides. As Banana One kicked at her, she yanked him off-balance and swung him around into Banana Two. She could hear Pecs Guy preparing to grab her from behind.

He set his timer again, and they were back at it. She never looked at him when they sparred. She didn't need to see his face or even his body to predict what his next move would be.

He would draw a sharp breath before he attempted a strike. That breath would be shallow when he was about to use his dominant arm, but slightly deeper with the other. She could hear him shifting when he was about to execute a roundhouse kick. When their bodies were close, she could feel his ligaments and tendons creaking as they stretched and released. They spoke to her, telling her how to respond.

She had known these things from the very first time they sparred. Her adaptability was the main reason he had chosen her as his protégé, but under his tutelage, her lethal capability had increased dramatically. She no longer hid in the shadows of defensive fighting. He had taught her to attack, and she had absorbed it all. He had made something of her. And for that, she was eternally grateful.

She cried out in surprise as he took her down.

"You good?" he asked.

She smiled up at him without a hint of fear.

"There's my girl," he said.

She cuffed him in the eye, and as he recoiled, she grabbed his head with her knees. Twisting him downward, she pinned his shoulders.

"I've got your neck," she laughed. "Had enough?"

His voice, dripping with sarcasm, came muffled and strained from between her thighs. "You don't think I can be dangerous with my head between your legs?"

He tapped her thigh to indicate that he no longer wished to be choked, and she slid off of him. Hopping to avoid his playful grab at her ankle, Bathsheba giggled and twirled out of his reach. David was slower to get to his feet.

"Night is coming," he said. "Let's get your physical therapy done."

A faint, earthy aroma filled her nostrils.

She could not bear to dwell on such things. For what had been forced upon her, she had taken to extremes. And while it was Bathsheba who had done what was necessary, that bitter, bitter smell reminded her that there had been someone before her. She did not want to be reminded.

Someone grabbed a handful of her hair. She smashed his hand to her scalp and threw him over her shoulders onto the ground. It was Pecs Guy again. As he lay winded, she untangled his hand from her hair and looked around for Karthik.

He had held his own pretty well with Pink Bandana Man—as in, Pink Bandana Man was kneeling on the ground, holding his midsection.

That was a good sign. And yet, the Agent saw that, while she had been mindlessly rampaging, Banana Two had abandoned his companions to their fate at her hands. He was currently approaching Karthik from behind.

"Behind you!" the Agent shouted, only a little too late.

She tried to move toward him, but Pecs Guy and Banana One drew her back into a fight that they were taking much more seriously than they had at the beginning.

Karthik had been able to dodge the powerful part of Banana Two's strike, but he still caught the followthrough on the back of his head. He pitched forward into a head-butt from Pink Bandana Man. Grabbing Pink Bandana Man's shoulders, he fell sideways and brought him to the ground. Banana Two tried to kick him while he was down, but Karthik swung around and swept his legs.

The Agent struck Banana One in the throat, causing his hyaline cartilage to break and pierce his trachea. He folded to the ground and gasped for breath like a fish. Pecs Guy continued to be a nuisance, but the Agent finally wrestled him down and began to fold him into submission.

Banana Two was now lying on the ground behind Karthik, but Karthik appeared to suffer from the blows to his head. He managed to get up, but from the way he was staggering, the Agent figured he must be trying to decide which Pink Bandana Man to swing at. Finally, he began to back away from his opponent, which was the smart thing to do since he wasn't in any shape to take another blow.

Banana Two grabbed his ankle, sending him reeling backward onto the ground. In a sloppy but effective motion, the roach enveloped Karthik into a spinal lock.

"Good grief." The Agent banged Pecs Guy's head on the sidewalk and knocked him out.

"Now, stay down," she told him before running to help Karthik.

Pink Bandana Man had taken to kicking wildly at Karthik who was still woozy and wrapped in Banana Two. Sometimes Pink Bandana Man hit his intended target, but it seemed from the other voice that sometimes yelped upon contact that he was also striking his own roach.

"Hey, Pinky," the Agent said, patting the top of his head. "I think it's time for me to be 'yours.'"

He grabbed at her. She seized his outstretched arm and twisted him onto his stomach.

"Now, I don't know what kind of madhouse you were raised in, but

166

let's get one thing straight," she said, digging her knee into his back. "Sticking your hands in people's food is in poor taste, as is making disparaging comments about people's language and culture. Are we clear?"

He grunted in response.

"Was that a 'yes?'"

"Yes. Now, let me up."

The Agent released him roughly and went over to detangle the woozy Karthik from the more-than-intermediate grappler who held him captive. As she pried them apart, she could hear someone helping Pink Bandana Man up. The Agent kicked Banana Two in the side to make him release her friend. She pulled Karthik to his feet.

They turned around to find themselves staring into a sleek, old-style revolver. So, that was why there were only four guys in the fight when there had been five in the restaurant. The bearer of the gun must have been instructed to stay out of the fight unless something went wrong. Something like the Agent and Karthik beating all the other rude guys into the ground, for instance.

Karthik, who was already beyond lightheaded, began to buckle at the knees. The Agent clutched his arm to steady him.

"Not so tough now, are you, Hula Brownie?" Pink Bandana Man snarled.

The gunman snickered and added, "Yeah, Island-Style! Want a face full of bullets?"

She sighed. "I was willing to let you off with a mild butt-kicking, but now I'm going to have to beat both of your faces in. *And* I'll have an excuse because this is definitely in self-defense."

She was already calculating how she would disarm and incapacitate the extra man, but the sound of a car trunk popping open startled them all. They looked toward the champagne sedan across the street from the restaurant.

In front of the car stood Racky with her wild, honey-colored hair glowing in the streetlights like a glorious golden nimbus. She had a large shotgun pointed in the direction of Pink Bandana Man and his extra man. The shift in attention afforded Lenci the split second she needed to snatch the extra man's gun and disassemble it.

"Say aloha to Bambina Extraordinaire, you ill-behaved ignoramuses!" Racky called as both men put their hands up. "Ey, Circus, didn't anyone ever teach you to look out for the extra guy in a fight?"

"Once upon a time, I think," the Agent laughed.

167

She added, "Woman, that's got to be the biggest shotgun known to all of humanity. Does it also shoot grenades?"

"Could probably t—take out a whole city block," Karthik murmured in agreement.

"Without even aiming," Racky said, sucking her teeth. She hadn't taken her eyes off of Pink Bandana Man.

He and his extra man backed away down the street. The Agent would have liked to follow those guys and finish the fight in a way that would teach them a lesson, but she figured that perhaps there had been enough excitement for one evening—especially for Karthik and Lorenzo. In Diablo, it was common knowledge that surviving to see another day was often more rewarding than the pursuit of retribution or justice.

She watched until the thugs rounded the corner. Then, she gently guided Karthik toward the car. They went slowly but with purpose. His movements were choppy, and his eyes were still a little unfocused.

"You n—need to check your ego," he said, his speech slurring slightly as he hobbled along. "J—just can't keep your mouth shut and walk away."

"I'm sorry," Lenci whispered to him. "I should have sent you to wait in the car. You shouldn't have to be in a fight every few weeks on account of me."

"*You* shouldn't be in a fight every few weeks," he grunted. "Anyways, n—no way I would have l—let you fight those guys on your own."

"I could have handled it by myself."

"But you shouldn't have had to," he said. "Are we in this together or are we n—not?"

Lenci smiled, but deep down she felt a pang of regret. Karthik's clothes were torn, and his jaw was swollen. Little pieces of skin dangled from his knuckles. The blood was sure to follow shortly. This poor man was constantly in harm's way because of her. And although she didn't like to be criticized for her arrogance and temerity, she began to wonder if a different response from her in that situation could have spared her friend some physical agony.

After her prolonged silence, Karthik said, "Well, *I'm* in it with you."

"We are all in it together, lovelies," Racky said, hopping into the driver's seat. "Now, let's get out of here before something else happens."

Lenci opened the door of the car and helped Karthik into the back seat next to Lorenzo.

"Dang, man!" Lorenzo exclaimed. "You look awful."

Karthik shifted painfully to put on his seat belt. "T——tends to be a trend when I'm hanging around your sister."

Groaning, he added, "I'm a pushover *and* an en–nabler."

"You're not a pushover," Lenci said, climbing into the passenger's seat. "Except for when you were *pushing over* those bad guys!"

He didn't laugh at her bad pun. Apparently, getting a bit roughed up made him humorless.

Lorenzo, who had been quite stiff around his sister since her return, surprised everyone by bursting into laughter. He hadn't so much as cracked a smile at any of her jokes, but here he was uncontrollably chortling his little heart out. It crossed the Agent's mind that this could be Lorenzo's way of dealing with the stress of the situation. After all, he had spent most of his life in Windsailing and didn't have the same exposure to street violence as she and Karthik had had at his age. Still, humor was humor, and Lenci had made her little brother laugh. She smiled.

She had been wondering if Lorenzo would ever warm up to her. And all it took to win his heart was her pummeling a bunch of insignificant roaches. Small price to pay—for her anyway.

"My sister is a bionic superwoman!" he guffawed. "Sure am glad I'm on *your* side."

On my side. How about that, Kiddo? Lenci's smile broadened.

"Best choice in any fight," Karthik admitted.

"Well, you didn't do too bad yourself," Lenci told him. "You can really handle yourself in a fight."

He chuckled wryly. "Yeah, but not enough to handle being double-teamed by dirty fighters."

"That's why it's a good thing you had me there to watch your back," she replied.

Karthik grinned at her. "If you hadn't been there, I wouldn't have been in the fight."

When Racky pulled onto the main road, she was happy to tune the radio to the classical music station to honor the promise Lenci had made to Karthik on their way to the restaurant.

"This isn't really my type of sound," she said, moving her head to the tempo of the music. "But it's got a kind of fun beat to it."

"It's Rachmaninoff," Karthik said indignantly.

"If that means 'catchy,' I concur," Racky replied.

"Hey, hey, hey, Lenci, can you teach me your *awesome* fight skills?" Lorenzo begged, tapping the passenger's seat like a crazed woodpecker.

"Nothing offensive," Lenci said. "But here's my favorite defensive move. Saved my life many times, you know."

She reached over the seat to show him how to layer his hands in front of his throat to block a chokehold or a surprise throat strike. It wouldn't do much against a full-grown opponent, but it could helpful if he was as prone to fights as she had been in school.

"Girl, that's nothing!" Racky said. "You ought to show him how to get out of a guillotine choke! That would be useful."

Lorenzo's eyes began to shine. "You grapple, Racky?"

She amusedly looked out her window into the side-mirror and did not answer.

He didn't seem to notice but continued to practice the defensive posture that his sister had taught him, occasionally adding a loud exclamation of some kind to make it seem tougher.

They rode the rest of the way in silence, apart from Racky's beat-boxing accompaniment of Rachmaninoff's Piano Concerto Number 3. She even threw in a few "eys" on the offbeat just to spice it up.

During the ride, the Agent's mind wandered back through the memory of sparring with David. Most importantly, she remembered that that particular evening with him had marked the beginning of the night training.

It was a bitter, bitter thing to remember. She remembered the darkness and the bed and some sheets. And between the sheets was the darkness. And in the darkness was the night training.

*****

Racky said goodnight at the curb, and all the way up the elevator, Lorenzo was still going on about his favorite moments of the fight. The other two were content to pretend they were listening. When they reached their apartment doors, Lenci unwove her arm from Karthik's, and they stood in silence without breaking eye contact. They shared a not-so-secret smile.

"Argh! Blegh!" Lorenzo burst out, pounding dramatically on the Changs' door. "Mom, let me in! Karthik and Lenci are being *weird*!"

"Put a muzzle on it, Lolo," Lenci said, handing her keys to him. "You'll wake up the neighbors."

Lorenzo turned the key in the lock and threw open the door.

"Bye, Karthik!" he yelled without looking back.

He crossed the common area quickly, stopping every few steps to practice his new defensive posture and exclaim loudly like he was in a comic book. Soon, he disappeared behind the hall door.

Lenci smiled at Karthik.

"I'm sorry, again," she said. "Don't forget to put some ice on your jaw."

"I've t–taken a beating before," he replied. "Remember how we used to wrap our heads in toilet paper l–like old-fashioned bandages after the Rump Bumpers beat the snot out of us?"

She gave no indication that she did or didn't.

He continued, "Well, from growing up in Diablo, I kn–now how to ice a jaw. And I'll just t—tell mom that I broke up a fight between a couple of folks we took in for processing."

"But—"

"Don't worry." He waved his hand dismissively. "Just, *please*, try n— not to escalate a situation when we're outnumbered. I don't know how many more beatings I can take."

She laughed. They wished each other a good night, but neither of them turned away.

After another moment or five, Lenci tucked her hair behind her ear and said, "I should go."

"Me too."

"Good night," she said again, this time willing her legs to move.

"Good night," she heard Karthik say as she closed the door.

Shortly afterward, the door to his apartment also opened and closed.

Lenci let out a deep breath and looked around the empty living room. Her mother had left the kitchen light on. She must have gone to bed already. Lenci's keys were splayed out on the dining table where Lorenzo had tossed them on the way to his room.

Glad that her mother wasn't there to extract the details of that evening's tussle from her loose-lipped little brother, Lenci rolled her tense shoulders and stretched her aching arms. It was time for a shower! She went to her bedroom and stripped off her baggy clothes. Her abdomen had not yet become round, but it did protrude a little more than it had before. And it wasn't the noodle soup that was doing it.

Her gaze wandered to the jagged scars on her legs. She touched the cream-colored skin, wondering what could have caused such grotesque tearing.

In front of the bathroom mirror, the Agent became bothered by the enormous smile that plastered her face. She enjoyed a lovely night out as much as the next woman, but the feelings that were coursing through her were inefficient and possibly counterproductive. Regardless, the face in the mirror continued to beam.

"Down girl," she said, turning around to pull back the shower curtain.

The water needed to run for a while so that it could heat up.

She patted her abdomen and said, "How do you like it, Kiddo? Uncle Karthik got his butt whupped tonight, didn't he? We'll have to take better care of him next time."

The sound of the refrigerator door opening alerted the Agent to the fact that someone was in the kitchen—probably Lorenzo, rummaging for a late night snack to take back to his room. Monica Chang had superhuman hearing when it came to household misdemeanors such as this. She hated it when he ate in his room because the inevitable piles of crumbs attracted ants. The Agent expected to hear Monica's bedroom door fly open at any second. But the apartment remained quiet.

As the Agent thought about it, the mother probably would have heard them come in, even if she *had* already gone to bed, and she would have wanted to ask them about their evening. A wave of panic pulsed through the Agent. If someone was in the house, if someone had gotten the mother—she stuffed the fear down and rummaged through the bathroom drawers in search of a weapon only to find a small, pink razor. She could do more damage with her bare hands.

As the Agent put her ear to the bathroom door, the lights suddenly went out. She listened for a moment, but she heard only the water running in the shower. Someone had planned an ambush, only they had found the mother first. They were still in the apartment, waiting for the Agent. She stood up slowly, her heart racing.

Then, sensing movement beside her, she whirled around to strike her opponent first. The sound of glass breaking only registered in her mind after the strange pressure in her right fist.

Bringing her left hand to her right, she confirmed by touch that there were indeed small chunks of glass embedded in her fist. She had broken the mirror.

"Lenci?" Her mother was calling her. Yellow light crept in beneath the bathroom door. "You alright, baby?"

"Mother!" She threw open the door. "You're okay!"

"Of course, sweetie," Monica said. She was holding a camping lantern. "I fell asleep with my audiobook playing. Strangely, I didn't hear you two come in, but the blackout knocked out my stereo and *that* woke me up."

"Rolling blackouts," the Agent breathed. She had learned about them at work earlier that day.

"Yes," her mother said. "They've been more common of late. Our building doesn't have a generator, so we're just going to have to wait this one out."

"Good luck with that," the Agent said, folding a towel over her right hand. "Lorenzo just opened the fridge."

"Did *not!*" he yelled from his room. "Besides, Lenci broke the bathroom mirror. I heard her do it!"

"Did *not!*" the Agent yelled back, slipping into her room while the mother stepped into the bathroom to investigate.

Once the bedroom door was closed and locked, the Agent pulled back the curtains to let the moonlight in. She searched through Lenci's desk and found a pair of tweezers. Then, sitting on the edge of the bed, as close to the window as she could get, she leaned on the windowsill and used the light from the moon to examine the cuts on her hand. After wiping the blood away, she sighed with relief. She had seen worse.

She used the tweezers to grasp the first shard of glass.

"See?" she muttered. "This is why you don't get attached to them, whore."

"Lenci!" It was the mother again, but her voice was muffled on the other side of the door.

The doorknob jiggled.

The Agent made every effort to sound patient. "Yes?"

"Open the door. I want to talk about the mirror."

"Couldn't we talk tomorrow, mother? I'm really tired."

"Saying it in Spanish won't deter me, young lady." Had she been speaking Spanish? "Your father and I know Spanish better than you do! Now, open this door!"

The word 'father' inspired fear in the Agent because it was one of the names she had called the man who was now hunting her. But she knew that Monica was not talking about the husband of Bathsheba. She was talking about Kingston Chang, Lenci's dad.

In English, "Mother—"

"If you don't stop calling me that, you ratty little fake…" The mother's voice reduced to a mumble as she walked away.

The Agent turned her attention back to her fist. The light from the moon was bright enough that she could see the glass shards jutting out of the torn skin. Thankfully, she did not feel any pain, just pressure.

Suddenly, the door behind her flew open. It appeared that the mother had a spare key.

"Mama," Lenci said, shuffling across the bed on her knees. "I'm sorry about the mirror. But I just need to—"

"I'll do it," her mother replied gruffly, snatching the tweezers.

The light from the lantern enveloped them with soft, golden light. It reminded Lenci of when her mom used to stay up late with her to remove splinters. It wasn't the removal process that took so long, just the soaking beforehand. And she used to yowl like a mortally wounded cat if she happened to look while her mother used a pin or needle to fish the softened wood out of her flesh.

This extraction was eerily silent in comparison.

"How did it happen, baby? How did it happen?" Monica whispered.

She sat with her daughter's hand in her lap and tugged gently but firmly on each and every shard, one after another, until they were all sitting in a pile on the bedside table.

Lenci hissed quietly as her mother dabbed at the cuts with an alcohol-soaked cotton ball.

After her hand had been bandaged and her mother was standing up to leave, she blurted out, "He loved me, Mama."

Her mother stared at her pointedly. "He *what?*"

"Because I'm gifted," Lenci said, cradling her bandaged hand. "That's why I stood out to him at the Academy, more than the others."

"You think *that's* why he took you?"

Lenci chose not to think about the Killer's obsession with her appearance. She defended her position with no small amount of pride, "I was at the top of my subdivision. When it came to aptitude results and field tests, I had no equal!"

Her mother sat down on the bed beside her. "And what kind of work did he have you doing that built you up? Did he teach you anything life-giving, or did he just use you? What did he give you that you didn't naturally have?"

"He taught me everything I know!" the Agent snapped.

"No, he did *not!*" Monica retorted. "He abducted you and abused you. He took you away from everyone who knew you and loved you."

"Well, yes," she mumbled, "we had to train far away, because if his wife found out about the class violation—"

"His *wife?*"

174

The mother was unhappy. Her tone suggested what the Agent herself had fought not to believe throughout her time with David: she had been nothing but a pet animal, a thing, and an easy target given that she was beholden to him for having taken her on as his protégé.

Lenci waited for the reprimand she knew was coming. Her mother had raised her better than to be with another woman's husband. She had raised her to stand up for what was right and not to bow to the fear of abuse. She should have resisted. She should have fought back. Why hadn't she? Maybe she had. She couldn't remember. Her fist hurt. And there was something welling up inside of her that the Agent could not hold back any longer.

The mother was not reprimanding her. She did not even say one word. She simply held her daughter and let her cry. She sat with her until her breathing normalized. Then, she collected all of the bloody shards into a towel and left the room. When her mother was gone, Lenci dropped off into a deep and peaceful sleep.

Chapter 21

THE NEXT FEW MONTHS WERE quiet for Lenci. The nightmares and flash-backs had dissipated, for the most part. Since the day she had learned of Reece Ma's death, she only saw Chandler in passing at the gym. He greeted her with a firm nod and always walked away with a hint of melancholy.

Home life was comfortable and stable. Lorenzo continued to be a smart-mouthed jokester that brightened Lenci's days. And Karthik, in particular, was a steadfast and unobtrusive presence. Lenci did not speak about the Killer, and Karthik never pried. He seemed content to let bygones remain as such and did not condemn her for any foul play he could very well have suspected. Thus, he became a safe and trust-worthy companion.

Likewise, Racky also had proven to be a loyal friend. She was always hanging around with the family, bringing her fresh perspective and soul-raising laughter. And since no one else from SSI or the WCE came knocking on the Changs' door, it seemed to Lenci that her secret was safe after all.

Perhaps, though, the most curious characteristic of her new life was the lack of intrusions of any type of Song. There were many new rhythms that brought joy to Lenci's life. Aside from going to work, she also looked forward to going to Dr. Williams' office every four weeks for Kiddo's checkups. After Racky showed her how to remove the GPS locator on a mobile phone, she finally agreed to carry one in order to stay in touch with her family. She hardly ever got into fights, which made Karthik happy. Overall, Lenci welcomed these new rhythms because they instilled in her a rather pleasant sense of humanness that grounded her and gave her peace.

Despite having adjusted so well to living with her family, she still felt apprehensive about returning to Windsailing as the holidays approached. While David Miller's current significance to her was more akin to that of a closet monster, she could not shake the feeling that her abductor had posted surveillance teams at the Windsailing airport, waiting to alert him of her presence in the district. They might not know her under the name that currently protected her, but they would recognize her on sight.

Lenci feared to think what would happen to her family if David Miller encountered them all together. While her memories of him were vague, she did remember this: he was a harsh man who could be quite cruel when he was angry. Seeing as how he had been searching for his runaway protégé for months, he would undoubtedly be angry—angry enough to cause unspeakable harm, she imagined. To give Lenci some peace of mind, her family arranged to celebrate the holidays in Diablo.

Kingston Chang and James Wilson rode in from the Forsythe airport late in the evening on December 24th. They couldn't stay long because they needed to be in Windsailing to present their big project on the 27th. In preparation for their arrival, Lenci had taken the day off from work to help with the baking of desserts.

Her body had undergone a few changes due to the pregnancy, the most exciting of which was the appearance of a small, melon-like belly bump, which she carried fairly low. It had been present for a while, but it had grown to the point that even Racky's magic maternity clothes only partially concealed it. This would not matter for the duration of their short family holiday. Lenci decided she would not keep Kiddo under wraps during that time. After all, with her family, she had no reason to hide. So, for the special debut, she wore a tight tank top under which Kiddo could properly be showcased.

When her dad and Uncle James finally arrived, their reunion was joyous. Lenci threw herself into her dad's arms and squeezed him tightly. She had been looking forward to meeting Uncle James and told him so, though with an awkward blush since she knew that this was not their first encounter. It was simply the only one she could remember. Uncle James took everything in stride. He was a tall man of closely shaved hair and blue-black skin. His face was like the midnight sky, featuring a couple of sparkly stars and a very friendly crescent moon.

After all of the formalities, Uncle James kept shaking his head saying, "Our little Lenci's all grown up. How about that?"

She didn't remember a time when she had been called "little Lenci," but she liked his deep, resonant voice and figured that he could keep calling her that as long as he said it in that same voice.

By that time, Racky was basically considered a part of the family. So, on the 25th, the Changs and the Wilsons had her along for their celebratory day out at Fairwaves Beach. Everyone knew the water would be too cold for a swim at that time of year, but the sun would still be worth enjoying. So, Lenci, Racky, Karthik, and Lorenzo all piled into Karthik's jeep while Mr. and Mrs. Wilson and Mr. and Mrs. Chang rode in the Changs' car.

When they arrived, Lenci hopped out to help Karthik unload the towels and beach chairs. She came around the back of the jeep and found him in a dreamy haze with the chairs hanging loosely over his arm. She pinched his face playfully, and his eyes focused on her.

"Penny for your thoughts?" she smiled.

"I was just thinking about all our memories here as kids."

He didn't ask her if she, too, remembered.

Turning to admire the golden-brown incline and the dark green expanse beyond it, she remarked, "You live so much in the past, Karthik."

"It's sometimes happier there," he said, gazing at her wistfully, "and more predictable than the present."

He added, "Still find myself popping back and forth between the two, though."

"Understandably," she said. "But I guess the present's got some things worth staying for."

He grinned. "Like what?"

"Well," she said, leaning toward him until he became stock-still and wide-eyed, "I can think of at least one."

After lingering for a delicious moment, she snatched the chairs from him and took off running.

"Races where losers get tossed in freezing cold water!" she shouted over her shoulder.

Lenci had never been fast, even before she got her melon bump. She had to dump the chairs at the halfway mark and dedicate all of her energy to turning on the speed. The warm, crumbly sand became progressively cooler and firmer as she grew closer to the finish line. Behind her, she could hear measured, amused breathing approaching.

Karthik caught up with her at the water's edge where they simultaneously screeched to a halt.

"Tie means I win!" she said, lunging for him. "Prepare to get tossed, Lieutenant Wilson!"

"Tie means anything goes!" he replied, evading her easily. He scooped her up, and dangled her over the water. "And the only way you'll ever toss me is in your dreams."

"Oh, my friend," she said, watching as a blue-green wave curled up before them. "Get ready for dreams to become reality!"

When the wave crashed into a freezing sheet of water that probably made Karthik cramp up from the waist down, Lenci flipped backwards. She gently grabbed his head with her knees and forced him to the ground. Another wave overtook them in a whirl of bubbles and kelp.

The chill of the saltwater and the slimy sensation of kelp wrapping around her arms drew her briefly into a shadow. In this shadow, the cold of the water penetrated to her bones. A deep desperation and paralyzing fear rose within her. The fear confused her because she had just been having so much fun. What could she have to fear in this moment?

The wave drew back, and Lenci found herself planted on her hands and knees in the coarse, wet sand. She shivered violently because of the breeze, but she remained alert and tethered in the present moment. Here, at Fairwaves Beach—where she had spent many holidays as a child—there were no shadows. Here, she was only given to enjoying time with her family.

"Come on, Lenci!" Karthik was calling.

He sounded happy but out of breath, like he had been laughing and accidentally inhaled some seawater.

She squinted in the glare of the sunlight coming off the water and saw him kneeling a few meters from her. When their eyes met, they both began to laugh. He held a hand out to her, and she began to crawl toward him. They were too slow to reunite, and the next wave bowled them over. When they regained their footing, however, they scrambled out of the water as fast as they could.

By that time, their parents, Lorenzo, and Racky were sitting in beach chairs just out of reach of the water. Karthik and Lenci ran up to them, laughing between teeth-chattering breaths.

"Oh, Lenci," Monica said, staring exasperatedly at her daughter. "Why don't you take off your stockings? You've gotten them all sandy!"

Lenci had kept the scars a secret successfully all this time, although she could not even remember why she had to do so. At some point in her life, she had been an avid rock climber, and rock climbers sometimes have accidents. Accidents cause scars. There's nothing shameful about that. Nevertheless, she tied a frilly, teal sarong over her stockings, the waist of which sat comfortably nestled beneath her belly bump.

"Don't worry, Mama," she said. "I'll rinse them out before I put them in the washer."

No one else did any more than dip their toes into the water, just to say that they had. The parents bundled up and huddled together to talk about the maintenance of the Windsailing properties and the probability that both James and Kingston were in line for a promotion by the end of the year as long as everything went well with this next project.

While the parents talked, Lenci, Lorenzo, Racky, and Karthik drew a line in the sand and began to play volleyball. At first, Lenci and Racky played against the guys, but Lorenzo began to complain.

"Too much girl power," he said.

"Fine, Big Baby," Lenci replied. "Come be my partner, and you can be on the winning team."

He sat on the ball. "I don't *want* to be on your team. I want to beat you."

Would you look at that, Kiddo? Lenci laughed. *Uncle Lolo is blowing us off, so he can be on a team with Racky.*

"I see how it is," she said aloud. "Alright, Karthik, come be on my side. It'll be just us rejects against the chosen ones."

Cracking her knuckles, she added, "And we will *crush* them."

Karthik high-fived her. "In it to win it, partner! L—let's kick their butts."

"Hey, hey, hey!" Racky protested. "I am an innocent bystander over here!"

Motioning for her brother to serve the ball, Lenci responded, "My apologies in advance. Sometimes collateral damage is unavoidable."

That sentence felt strange in her mouth, and she wished she hadn't said it, even as a joke. Nevertheless, when Lorenzo served the ball, she switched into kill mode. It was a specialized kill mode, which resulted not in broken bodies but a rather effective synergy with Karthik and a score well above that of Lorenzo and Racky.

When Karthik scored the final point, he and Lenci shared a congratulatory hug. Caught up in the excitement of the moment, she kissed his cheek. It had seemed like the natural thing to do at the time, but upon realizing what she had done, she quickly slipped out of the hug.

She looked away, her lips still burning. Karthik stood frozen on the spot where she had kissed him, but everything else in the world was in motion around them. Lorenzo picked up the ball just to throw it into the sand again. Racky had dropped to the ground and was melodramatically rolling back and forth, laughing and moaning that her life was over.

"Aw, man!" Lorenzo exclaimed. "The only reason you won again is because I'm hungry."

"Oh, no," Lenci grinned. "We can't have you so *weakened by hunger* that you can't play a decent game of volleyball. Maybe Racky and I will have to go and get you a snack before our rematch."

"Yes, food!" Racky bounced up. "Let's go, Circus! I think I saw a burger place somewhere near the parking lot."

Karthik was still standing in shock with his hand on his cheek when the two women left in search of burgers.

Once they were out of earshot, Racky nudged Lenci and said, "I saw you slip that kiss in there. You go, girl!"

Lenci turned slightly pink. "It's dangerous to get involved with assets. I know better than that."

"That boy is not anybody's asset," Racky said. "But his are nice and tight, though, hey?"

Lenci smiled sheepishly. "He's a nice guy, too, Racky."

"What's the problem, then?"

Before Lenci could answer, two women in crisp pantsuits stepped into their path. If she had not been so engrossed in egging her brother on, she would have seen them, sitting in the silver car that had been facing their volleyball game. But then again, if she had noticed them there, she would most likely have noticed that same silver car following them all the way up the Coastal Highway to Fairwaves.

Maybe she had noticed them, but she just hadn't wanted to believe that they were a threat. She now knew that her hope for a drama-free holiday had been a vain one.

"Nice day to be out at the beach, isn't it?" Blair Lee-Smith took off her sunglasses.

Her gaze wandered to Lenci's abdomen, and her face became ashen. She was accompanied by Theresa. Theresa kept her shades on, probably believing that they gave her a menacing presence.

"It was," the Agent responded icily. "Is there something I can do for you ladies?"

"I think Blair and I have seen all we came to see," Theresa said.

Motioning to the belly bump protruding over the top of the Agent's sarong, she asked, "Where'd you get that?"

"Swallowed one too many watermelon seeds," the Agent replied.

"I know where she got it," Blair said numbly.

Theresa shrugged. "I knew, too. I was just—"

"We know what you were doing," Racky said. "Just stop."

It was obvious to the Agent that the assistant director had not been expecting to find her in this condition. Perhaps Ms. Lee-Smith had had a hunch that she was hiding something, but she had been unsure of what it was. Well, now she knew.

"What are you going to do?" the Agent asked.

Blair had not taken her eyes off of the belly bump. "I don't know."

Racky and Theresa stared at her in disbelief. From the constipated look on the assistant director's face, it was obvious that she had a personal connection to the issue at hand. The drooping of her shoulders suggested a lack of confidence and possibly a fear of exposure.

"Look," the Agent said, "I don't want any trouble. I'm just trying to carry Kiddo to term, and then I'll be out of your hair."

Theresa snorted disgustedly. "How precious! She's even got a pet name for the love-fetus she's incubating for the one-eyed assassin."

The Agent lurched forward, but Racky stepped between them.

"Enough, Theresa," Blair said. "Let's go. We've wasted enough time here."

"Later, premie-teammies," Theresa said, smirking at the Agent.

As they got into their little silver car and drove away, the Agent turned to Racky.

"You know, suddenly, I don't feel so much like burgers."

"Don't get all bent out of shape," Racky said. "I lifted Blair's phone while she was acting like a zombie on account of your kiddo. If she calls anyone, we will know right away."

"She's not the one who'll make the call," the Agent said. "Theresa was chomping at the bit to pass along that information."

Racky grinned. "Oh, well, that's even better. Well, I mean, it's not good, but it's fortunate because I cloned her phone *ages* ago. We will know the instant she makes a call."

"And it won't be until she's away from Blair, so we have a little time," the Agent said. "I need to get home, though."

"On it, girl. I'm messaging Karthik now. The families should be packed up and ready to go by the time we get back to them." Racky smiled sympathetically. "If you are afraid Blair and Theresa will harass you, you can crash at my place."

"I'm not afraid of them," she said, more to herself than to her friend. "I'm not afraid of anyone."

Well, there was one exception to that, but he was probably halfway around the world searching for her.

"That's good," Racky said. "But just know that if you ever need a place to crash, you can always crash with me."

"Noted. Thank you."

The families were packed and ready to leave when they got back, although everyone was slightly put off by Lenci's urgency to return home. However, remembering that pregnancy was often accompanied by certain hormonal spikes, they didn't ask too many questions.

Karthik drove the 'kids' car home. After Lorenzo and Racky had fallen asleep in the back seat, Lenci stared out the window at the ocean beyond the highway railing. Her heart calmed as she watched the waves dance up and down, spraying white foam against the rocks. Yes, even the ocean had a dance to perform. It was a comforting thought.

"I'm glad you're here," Karthik said, breaking the silence. "I missed you when you were gone all that time."

Lenci smiled at him in an attempt to mask her sadness. "Me too."

"Everything okay?"

Of course, he could see through her mask.

Evading the question, she straightened up and broadened her smile. "I'm just really glad to have you as a friend. You're like a brother to me, and I don't ever want that to change."

"It won't," he replied, trying not to look injured.

His heart was sinking; she could tell. But she was not sorry that she had said that. Situational tides were changing once again, and she wanted to be sure that, when the waters got rough, all that she held most dear would be preserved.

***

When they got back to the Changs' apartment, Lenci rushed to her room. Her family remained in the living and dining area and attempted to salvage their holiday cheer. Karthik and Lorenzo turned on the game console and showed their dads the skills they'd unlocked on the newest level of *Zombies With Protruding Umbrellas*.

After putting some *tamales* on the stove to steam, Monica set out cookies and a custard pie for snacking. Racky had brought her own pumpkin spice rooibos tea to share, which both Monica and Preeti found to be delightful when mixed with milk and a dash of nutmeg, at her suggestion. She also brought pork rinds.

"You are a surprising young woman of eclectic taste," Monica remarked.

"I will take that as a compliment," Racky said, smiling broadly.

"It was meant to be one," Monica replied. "Now, you can put back those teaspoons you swiped while I was at the cabinet."

Pulses of laughter shook Preeti's frail body as she rocked back and forth in her chair. "Oh, Monica, the girl is a supreme cat burglar, isn't she?"

"Only the best of the best," Racky said proudly, taking the teaspoons out of her pocket and placing them on the table. "I'm just no match for the Chang women and their powers of observation."

This had become a sort of game for them. Racky often took random objects from their apartment just to see if they would notice. If she ever made it out the door with anything, she always brought it back the next time she visited. In this respect, taking things from the Changs was understood to be more for the fun of it than for the equilibrium of the universe, which was good because Mrs. Chang would not have been too pleased if any of her possessions were replaced with an item of comparable market price but of lower sentimental value.

The three women had a good laugh over the spoons and sipped on their tea in order to ignore the elephant in the room that was Lenci's absence. When they had run out of things to talk about, they watched the game of *Zombies With Protruding Umbrellas*. Karthik had set up another screen so that they could have four players instead of just two. The teamwork between the fathers and sons was effective, and they were beginning to advance through the levels much more quickly than before.

"Karthik really is like a big brother to Renzo, isn't he?" Racky said after watching them for a while.

"Yes," Monica responded. "I think he makes his best effort to be a role model. And he's had an amazing influence on Lorenzo. Karthik moved away from Windsailing to come out here a couple of years ago, but he still kept in contact with him."

Preeti nodded. "Every couple of days, they talked. And it did warm my Karthik's heart so. I think, in a small way, he thought of taking care of Lorenzo as a way to redeem his friendship with Lenci."

"Which we all know he didn't *need* to do," Monica added. "But I know that Lorenzo has appreciated his friendship and advice over the years."

Seeing that the two older women were touching on a topic that she had long wondered about, Racky cleared her throat. "If you don't mind my asking, what exactly happened between Karthik and Lenci?"

Monica and Preeti exchanged a sorrowful glance.

"We don't know," Monica said. "They came to our house after school one day, and she wouldn't let him in. They argued at the door for a while and then he left. Neither of them would explain what happened, and that same day Lenci asked me to sign the form for her enrollment at the SSI Academy."

"It's so sad," Preeti said, tearing up. "They were quite close."

Embarrassed at having brought up such a painful memory, Racky attempted to switch the topic.

"Tell me about them," she said. "What was it like when they were little?"

Immediately, both of the older women smiled nostalgically.

"It was wonderful," Preeti said.

"They were the sweetest." Monica put an arm around Preeti's chair. "You know, Racky, Preeti and I met in the maternal care unit at the hospital in Central Diablo."

Preeti began to laugh. "The nurses mixed up our babies! You see, that was before Western law forced miscegenists to join the Subclass. So, I was still Class 3.51 and Monica was still Class 4.14. I guess Lenci looked like she belonged with a Class 3 woman, and Karthik looked like he belonged with a Class 4.14 woman."

"Our husbands were traveling at the time, so that was where some of the confusion came from," Monica explained. "Back then, just like now, interclass couples were not well understood or in the forefront of anyone's mind."

"I like it that you call non-Class-1 women 'women' rather than 'females,' Mrs. Wilson," Racky chimed in. "And Mrs. Chang, I don't think I ever heard the term 'interclass' before?"

"In this family, we do not acknowledge class hierarchy." Monica smiled kindly.

"It's nice," Racky nodded, eager to get back to the story. "So, Lenci and Karthik were switched at the hospital?"

"Yes," Monica said, "but I told the nurses that I distinctly remembered holding my baby *girl* in the delivery room. And, after the woman in the room next door to me also seemed to believe that her child had been switched for one of the other sex, the hospital staff finally believed us."

"It helped that we had already named them, though," Preeti added good-naturedly.

Monica chuckled. "Yes, that helped. And after the whole ordeal, we each were curious to meet the would-have-been adoptive mother of our child. Preeti and I hit it off, and in our first conversation, we found out that our husbands actually worked for the same company. And, well, we've been together ever since."

"You mean you've been living together all this time?" Racky asked incredulously.

"Near each other, at least," Monica said. "Even when we moved to Windsailing for James and Kingston's job, we lived five minutes' walking distance from each other. Karthik and Lenci transferred from Forsythe's School for the Gifted to Windsailing's Gifted together."

"That sounds like a decent switch," Racky said.

Monica nodded. "Things were better in the Eastern states, but even Windsailing's Gifted forced them to wear a distinct uniform and eat lunch in a separate room from the pureblood students. Karthik and Lenci had lunch together every day, though, even after Lenci started skipping grades. They always found time for each other. I think it was their way of coping."

"Maybe, but it was just their way of being, too," Preeti said. "At a younger age, sometimes they wouldn't even play or talk; they'd just sit quietly. They just *were* together—very strange for such young children."

"Whoa," Racky breathed. "No wonder they are so comfortable together."

"I suppose," Monica smiled. "They laughed together, cried together, and argued with each other. It did breed a certain intimacy."

"Yes, yes, it's true. I tell you, girl"—Preeti patted Racky on the shoulder—"at school, outside of school, at any activities they did, they simply could not be parted. When they were young, they had sleepovers multiple times a week. That is why it was very difficult when they turned eleven."

Racky's eyebrows raised.

"We had to tell them they couldn't sleep in the same bed anymore." Monica said, smiling a little. "You know, they were just kids; they didn't think anything of it. But it wasn't appropriate anymore."

Preeti shrugged. "Their little hearts were broken for a while, but they survived."

"So," Racky said pensively, "Lenci and Karthik grew up sort of like siblings?"

"I guess you could say that," Monica said.

"We've always shared them," Preeti agreed. "It takes a village, you know, to raise children."

Chapter 22

In Lenci's room, the Agent pulled the "Specials" box down from the shelf in the closet and emptied it onto the bed. She knelt and began to sort through the pile in a mix of reverence and frustration. These mementos were pieces of Lenci's life—a dried rose from her very first performance of Swan Lake, a rock from the bottom of Lake Intención where she'd once vacationed with the Wilsons, and a lock of Karthik's hair from the Non-Violence Pact they'd made at age seven, among other things.

It was precious junk, and yet, upon seeing it and experiencing it, she was not overcome with the emotions she had expected to feel. In fact, she felt very little, other than the pressing need to find the item that she'd stashed there.

At last, she came to the shoebox that the man with the bullfrog tattoo had given her on the night of Karthik's cousin's wedding reception. With brutal impatience, she bypassed the time-consuming tape that sealed the package and instead ripped open the box at its seams. Out popped a purple, cloth pouch. It landed on the bed with a *PLUNK*. With shaking hands, she poured out its contents: a handheld tape recorder, a bunch of dried kelp, and a journal.

"You dear, strange bullfrog man," she breathed. "How did you get these?"

When she pressed the play button on the tape recorder, there was only a low hum. Disappointed, she ejected the tape and picked up the journal. Its peach-colored cover was made of a thick, pulpy paper, probably handcrafted. A handprint of rusty, flaking residue folded around the spine as if someone had grabbed the journal after dipping their hand in rust-colored paint—or blood.

The Agent closed her hand over the spine of the journal and confirmed that the handprint was the same size as her own. A startling image of bloody palms, hers, flashed before her eyes. She shook the image from her head and opened the journal.

There, below I see her
So lonely in her pool

Upon a quick flip-through, the Agent determined that the lyrics of her Song were scrawled sloppily on every single page of the journal—repeating over and over—even onto the inside of the back cover.

She put her head down on the open journal and sighed. Then, upon drawing a deep breath, she was overwhelmed with the fragrance of myrrh. As it mingled with the scent of the dried kelp, the Agent was suddenly bombarded with a series of iconic memory spurts—memories of being trained for a specific purpose, memories of being kissed and beaten until she no longer knew her name from her alias, memories of the millstone and night training, and memories of frantically writing the Song lyrics over and over to counteract the intrusions of the information that she had been studying. These intrusions were unruly images from recordings of a trainer who had cared for Lenci before her abduction and images of her training with him at the SSI Academy where she had called him by his true name.

Samir.

By rote the Agent had learned to trust a handler who did not know her and, in the past few months, by necessity she had learned fondness of a family who had not raised her. And that made her terribly sad. Because now, she could not remember if it had been pain or pleasure, fear or love which compelled her to forget or to retain. She was unsure of all that she had learned and gained as well as of the hearts that she had won so effortlessly.

And what if she had done it purposely, however unintentionally? What if she had used them as tools in her mission, the one that had been forced upon her? It was a terrible thought.

No tears. The Agent would not allow it.

In her avoidance of the impending sorrow, she had a wonderful idea about the tape recorder. It was a trick she had learned during her antique tech training. The azimuth angle of the tape head had been tampered with during the recording of a secret message, but someone had straightened it again afterward so that the tape appeared to be blank. When she knew to listen for it, the Agent could actually hear the faint, garbled echoes of music. She hurried to Lenci's desk and rifled through it in search of a screwdriver.

Once she had adjusted the azimuth angle of the tape head to a position that would have made any other tape recording unrecognizable, she inserted the tape and pressed play. Upon hearing the music from the Song, the Agent was seized with anxiety, but that was to be only the first concern of many.

In a voice that sounded like her own, the recording relayed a message that had probably been made toward the beginning of her memory intensives and long before she had discovered the need to escape.

Hey, whore. She cringed at *that* word. *Have you bedded the stuttering hunk yet?*

She turned pink at that description of Karthik and shook her head as if her interlocutor were right there in the room with her.

Good grief! You sure are slow when you think you're better than what you are made to be. The Cull must begin, and Poison Arrow won't relieve herself. Not ringing a bell? Of course, it isn't, 'blank-slate Lenci.' But you remember me, don't you? You'd better. This is the part where you remember that you are just a pawn in someone else's plan. Now get a move on!

The recording ended with a *CLICK* that made the Agent jump. She was bristling in reaction to the way the voice on the recording had spoken to her. David had spoken to her that way, and the use of the Song was his method, but the recorder of the message had apparently adopted his style and was attempting to manipulate her with the same tools. Maybe that would have worked before the Agent had realized that she could not trust anyone—least of all herself.

A million thoughts and questions ran through her mind, the most prominent of them regarding how many of her recent actions had been of her own volition. There was only one way to find out. She wondered if she could deviate from a mission once it had already been drilled into her. The Agent knew what was expected of her, but after spending all this time as a person rather than an animal-slave-weapon-thing, she just wasn't sure if she was *willing* to do it. Even so, she would have to confront Poison Arrow, if she didn't want the WCE actively hunting her.

As fate—or plans—would have it, she had recently met someone who had been in the Killer's grasp before, someone who sought safety under an abnormally high collar. Lenci was positioned fairly well, having won the trust of all those around her, and now she had a clear path to Poison Arrow herself.

She collected the rest of the irrelevant trinkets and stuffed them back into the "Specials" box. Standing up, the Agent glanced at Eugenia the Ewe. The stitched-on smile was so inviting that she couldn't help hugging the stuffed animal. Suddenly, she felt a strange sensation in her midsection, like a tiny jab from the inside.

A couple months before, Dr. Williams had told her that the weird flicking feelings she had been experiencing were a sign that Kiddo was practicing some kicks. Now, though, Kiddo's kicks had grown to feel more like real kicks, even if with such a tiny foot. There was some real strength to the movements.

"That's right, Kiddo," the Agent whispered. "We are fighters, aren't we?"

There were many things that needed to fall into place before the mission could be completed. And at the moment, the Agent very much enjoyed being Lenci. In fact, she thought perhaps that Lenci was the only person she knew how to be at this point. So, Lenci put on her biggest smile and went out into the common area to spend the rest of the holiday with her family.

To her surprise, with the help of their dads, Karthik and Lorenzo had made it to the final level of *Zombies With Protruding Umbrellas*. Lenci fetched a bowl of spicy chips from the kitchen, wedged herself between Karthik and Lorenzo, and cheered them on to the victory of survival and safe passage to a protected colony of uninfected survivors.

If only life were that easy.

Later, Lenci's mom brought out Mexican hot chocolate, and Karthik set up his keyboard. The evening flowed by peacefully with the medley of hymns and carols that Karthik had arranged himself. Lorenzo fell asleep on the floor beside the game console, but everyone else sat around the room soaking in the music and the contentedness of a holiday spent together.

Racky, who had never before had Mexican hot chocolate, hacked and wheezed her way through a cup of it before helping herself to a cup of black tea. She had just poured a spot of milk into it when her phone began to vibrate. Theresa was making a call!

Without a word, Racky tapped Lenci on the shoulder. She showed her the number on the screen. It was a number that neither of them recognized, but when Racky looked it up later, it was just a pizza joint.

***

Later that night, Beatriz Gomez was preparing to leave HQ and head home. Her briefcase was on her desk, and her files were strewn about the room. These were the files of the missing agents from all around the country. Half of the files were for agents from her own agency. Although she had looked over them time and again, she could not escape the feeling that something had been taken out of them.

There had to be a common link among these agents that made them prime targets for the WCE. All of the ones from SSI, except for Agent Thomas, were subclass. But that was no pattern at all. One outlier brought her all the way back to square one.

What would the WCE want with subclass agents, anyway? They preferred elite agents who were well born or pureblood, at least, like the other twenty from around the country. They were purebloods of different classes, all top-of-the-line agents, well respected at their home agencies.

Since the resurfacing of Bourghin's hypnotic, the director had spent more time in her office than she could remember having done in the past. She couldn't explain why Agent Thomas' case seemed more urgent than any of the others. Maybe it was just that Valencia was the only lead she had right now, her only hope of finding out what the WCE had planned for the others—or maybe she was a threat.

Lieutenant Wilson had not yet tired of protecting her. So, for the time being, Director Gomez knew she had to continue researching the other lost agents, using any and all clues from their files.

Still, she had to sleep sometime. She unbuttoned her high-collared blazer, laid it over the back of her chair, and gathered the files into her briefcase. Just as she was about to lock up, though, the landline rang. It was her direct line, so there were only a few people that could be on the other end.

She picked it up and waited for the caller to speak.

"Poison Arrow," a male voice whispered. Though low in volume, it sounded like a command.

She stiffened and said, "Wrong number." But her ear was glued to the receiver.

The voice on the other end remained quiet, but it was somehow still menacing. "Timetable for the Cull has been moved up. You have seventy-two hours to comply."

"How did you get this number?" she demanded.

192

"You think just because you've gone off and made your own agency that you're strong enough to break away?" He chuckled. "It's been twenty years, but you're still marching to the beat of *my* drum, Poison Arrow."

"I never marched to your drum," Director Gomez said defiantly. "Just like Agent Thomas has allowed *your* seed to grow in her womb—yes, the Assistant Vice herself told me about that—no one's *marching*, Killer. So, you can take your drum elsewhere."

"Brave words," he replied, "but ultimately ineffective, as you will see, because—"

I know where Poison Arrow landed
In a desert near the sea
She dreams beyond a life of swimming...

Everything inside of her urged her to hang up the phone, but she could not. He recited the words in rhythmic waves that coursed through her veins so naturally that she wondered how she had gotten along all these years without him, without the sound of his voice or the ferocity of his caress. Overcome with the intoxication that comes with being strangled for pleasure, she went weak at the knees and knelt by her desk.

"Sweet relief," he repeated at the end. "You understand, you useless hag? Now, tell me where she is. If you're reliving some fantasy born of the regret of your youth, snap out of it. You can't save Bathsheba's offspring any more than you were able to prevent the medical miscarriage I ordered for you."

After a moment's silence, he said, "You let her slip through your fingers, didn't you? You're not even worth the six months I spent training you. Never mind, then. I'll *make* her come to me."

Breaking from her ecstatic haze, Poison Arrow responded indignantly, "I can't believe you *had* her beyond initiation. She is, at least, one and a half classes beneath you!"

He laughed condescendingly. "Are you jealous, Poison Arrow?"

When she didn't answer, he continued, "You should be. She's twice as gifted as you ever were."

"But it's a class violation!" Poison Arrow protested. "You both should be—well, I'll kill her myself!"

"Sure, give her a reason to snap your neck!" He was smirking. She could tell. "You wouldn't last ten seconds one-on-one with her."

"I would if I had a gun," she said. "And you know that my aim is sure. According to the agency tenets and in adherence to true Neo-Eugenic law, I will punish her for having seduced you into this class violation."

"No." His word was always final. "For her disobedience and her pregnancy, she deserves worse than the gun. I created her, so I will crush the life out of her myself. It is the only way."

"Killer, let me redeem myself in the agency's eyes," Poison Arrow pleaded. "I'll kill the whore!"

"She's mine, Poison Arrow," he said. "So, after she kills you, I will kill her. And the world will be spared the subber progeny."

"But—"

He gave a sinister chuckle. "Do yourself a favor and forget this whole conversation. I don't need you in hysterics right now. Just remember to stay out of my way when it comes to the female. She's mine."

The line went dead, and Beatriz found herself alone, kneeling on the floor of her office. Perhaps she had dropped something under the desk. But why was she holding the phone? She couldn't remember.

So, replacing the receiver on the hook, she collected her belongings and left for home, mumbling, "Stay out of my way when it comes to the female. She's mine."

Chapter 23

A COUPLE OF DAYS LATER, AFTER THE LAST APPOINTMENT of her workday, the Agent was starting her own personal workout at the free-motion calf machine. Her training sessions always left her in a reflective mood because of how earnest her trainees were. They worked doggedly, returning time after time, triumphing over each exercise little by little, and when they had mastered one, they begged her to teach them another. For many reasons, the Agent wished that she had been taught to approach learning with that humility. At the Academy, the Killer had only taught her to be proud and to use the pride of others to bring about their demise.

"Chang, you need to cover Theresa's aerobics class at 1900," Bread said, leaning into her line of vision.

She didn't look at him but continued to breathe deeply and focus on her form. Somewhere to her right, a couple of women were discussing the midseason statistics of the best team in the International Ballet League. The Agent had not been able to keep up with the League since she left Spain for Chile. From the sound of it, the principal dancer was so much of a diva that the coaches of last year's champions were considering trading her for three younger, harder working dancers.

"Are you listening, Chang?"

For a while, the team would suffer as fans stopped attending the matches, but the Agent assumed that true fans would regain enthusiasm when their team actually began to win matches with good technique and less drama.

"*Chang!*"

Bread's face, red and shaking, was only centimeters from her own. A vein was popping out on his forehead. She grabbed his nose and held on to it.

"*What, Bread?*" she asked irritably.

Bread's arms flailed helplessly as he leaned into her grip to keep her from doing something crazy like ripping his nose from his face, which at this point, he believed she was fully capable of doing.

"Ub, ub, cad you—"

"No," she said, still pinching his nose as she continued her weights routine. "I know this must be hard for you to get through your butter-brain, but just because Theresa and I are both brown and beautiful does not mean that we are interchangeable. Besides, she really ought to cancel her classes if she's not going to come in."

"But—"

"Sh!" The Agent twisted his nose slightly to silence him.

The two women who had been discussing the ballet league were now talking about the news.

"Did you hear about that double murder suicide that took place on Philemon Avenue early this morning?" one asked.

The voice of the other drooped as she replied, "Yeah, and what about that house right next door? Burned straight to the ground, I heard. Kind of makes you wish you had the means to move to the Free-East, hey?"

The Agent released Bread and patted him roughly on the cheek as she stood up. He sniffed contritely, and although he really looked like he would rather be anywhere else, he didn't move away from her.

"I've got to go," she said. "Ask Racky if she can fill in for Theresa."

"Ask me what now?" Racky squawked from the lat pull where she had been watching Lenci and Bread's interaction with some amusement.

"If you would fill in for—"

"I know, Bread," Racky said, walking over.

She pulled Lenci away and whispered, "But you know I can't take over the class if you need to go home. I'm your ride."

Bread skittered away, probably ready just to cancel the class. He had finally been trained.

"I'll take the bus," the Agent said, avoiding eye contact.

Racky put her hands on her hips. "Girl, I may not be the brightest bulb on the block, but I do have eyes. I saw your face when those ladies were talking about what happened on Philemon Avenue. What does it mean to you?"

"You are one of the brightest bulbs I know, Racky," the Agent smiled. "No one else could have hacked my medical records and then encrypted them to the moon and back."

Well, maybe Reece Ma could have, but he was dead.

"It's nothing, really," she said in response to Racky's question. "The Killer's call sign is double murder suicide with arson next door."

"His *who* now?"

The Agent sighed. "If we were ever separated and he got a tip that I was in a certain area, he would kill three people and make it look like a double murder suicide. Then, he'd burn the property next door to the ground. That's a pretty unique combination to have on the same night, so if I was in the area, I knew to meet him at the burnt out property within twelve hours."

"So, it's like an email except with killing people and arson?" Racky's face scrunched up. "That's downright nasty!"

"He doesn't think of life in quite the same way as we do," the Agent gulped, feeling embarrassed at the lame excuse. She stroked her belly bump soothingly as Kiddo seemed to be doing a wiggle-dance in there.

"Well, you're not going to *meet him*, are you?"

Lenci smiled. "I'm just tired. The news shook me up a little, so I'm going home to rest for a while. Some time with my brother will do me good."

"Okay, Circus," Racky said, studying her intently. "Well, get some rest. I will call you later."

"Sounds good," Lenci replied, giving her a hug. "See you."

"Bye."

Since Kiddo was gyrating on top of her bladder, the Agent had to stop at the restroom before heading out. When she finally got to the bus stop, she was horrified to see Karthik's jeep pulling up to the curb. He put on his hazards and got out of the car.

"Well, well, well," he grinned. "What's a girl l—like you d—doing at a bus stop like this?"

She stared at him wordlessly.

He cleared his throat. "Racky said you weren't feeling well and that you'd decided to go home early. I wasn't feeling too good myself, so I thought I'd take the rest of the day off. I'd much rather have a headache with you than with the slobs at my office."

Lenci both loved and hated the sight of her friend leaning against the jeep, his eyes begging her to choose life, life with him, life with their family, life that gave to her more than it took.

"I'm sorry that you're not feeling well," she said sweetly. "I can't say I'm sad that you came, though."

She squeezed his hand but quickly released it and folded her arms. He opened the door for her, and she avoided eye contact with him as she got into the car.

The Agent knew that she couldn't run from the Killer forever. He was calling her, and sooner or later, if she did not go to him, he would come to her. But how could Lenci explain that to Karthik? How could she break his heart by telling him that she had to leave him, their entire family, again, to be—what was it?

An animal, a slave, a weapon—what she was made to be.

On the way home, Karthik talked to her about the interesting people that he had processed at the corrections facility that day. A man with a fork tongue, a woman with a blue mustache, and more. He talked about his police buddies, guys that had gone through training with him, a couple of whom had been his and Lenci's schoolmates before they left for Windsailing.

The Agent let his chatter dull her anxiety. The sun was going down. In a few hours, the twelve hours since the double murder suicide and arson call would be complete. After that, the Killer's patience being what it was, he would find a new way to get in touch with her. She wished that he would take another couple of months to try to find her, just for the sake of Kiddo. But she knew that, while the Killer did not have the highest level of technological savvy, he was a supreme tracker. He would find her—soon.

When they got home, they found that Monica had taken Preeti down to Sandland on a day trip. With their husbands back in Windsailing, the two women went about their normal business as if the holiday season were already over. Preeti loved to sit in the bookstore of the air-conditioned mall while Monica did check-ups on the baby camels at the Sandland Zoo.

Lorenzo was home, though. He and Karthik had their customary grappling session. After allowing himself to be pinned twice, Karthik struggled to his feet and pulled Lorenzo up after him.

"Okay, champ, I'm too old to continue these battles without some nourishment!" He laughed.

"Right," Lorenzo agreed. "Woman of the house, make us sandwiches!"

"Make them yourselves, you slobs," Lenci replied without looking up from the fashion magazine she was reading.

She was sitting at the dining room table, enjoying a plate of leftover *tamal* and black beans. Having grown up so close to the southern border, Lenci considered *tamales* to be right up there with noodle soup and fried chicken on the list of her top comfort foods. And at that time of year, there were plenty of *tamales* in the house.

"Touchy," her brother said. "I mean, what does a guy have to do around here to get some food?"

Karthik chuckled. "Well, my friend, I'm happy to inform you of a secret life-saver for any bachelor in the Western States: the microwave!"

Lenci snorted disgustedly at the implication that the microwave was to be used as a last resort when there was no woman to prepare fresh food for helpless men.

"Just joking," Karthik sang in an apologetic tone.

"Mostly," Lorenzo added, pouring himself a bowl of cereal.

"Not helping, Renzo," Karthik said.

"Fine, Lenci," Lorenzo said. "If you're not going make us food, you can at least share some wisdom or stories from your *mysterious* travels with us."

"Well, when I did a brief tour in the Sovereign Nation of Hawai'i, I learned not to solicit information I couldn't handle."

Seeing the disappointment in his face, the Agent sighed and put down her magazine. The Killer was coming for her. Goodness only knew how long she had left on the earth. If there was a way to satiate her brother's curiosity without endangering him, she was more than willing to oblige.

"What do you want to know?"

Lorenzo pulled up a chair across from her. "What did you do? I mean, I know that you had a bunch of odd jobs, but what was your *actual* job?"

Karthik's mouth dropped open, but he dared not pull up a chair— the Agent presumed— because he didn't want her to change her mind about revealing the information that everyone, including SSI, had been seeking since her resurfacing.

"I was a relief worker," she said, thinking herself clever for having found a way to describe her life's work without tainting Lorenzo's innocence.

"A relief worker, hey?" Her brother munched thoughtfully on his cereal. "But you also learned to beat people up."

"Yes," she said, "only when they really deserved it, though."

That was probably mostly true.

"And the relief you brought was, like, food and stuff?"

"Not exactly." She spoke slowly, searching for the right words. "I brought people relief from suffering, or fear, trouble that they were in. I brought an end to their pain."

"Like euthanasia? Isn't that illegal?"

"Um, no. I mean, yes, but—well, it depends on where you are," she stammered. "WCE-sponsored districts are friendlier to it. That's not what I was doing, though."

"Oh," Lorenzo nodded knowingly. "So, basically, you were popping people off and stuff, right?"

"Whoa, bud!" Karthik interjected. "Where'd you get an idea like that?"

The Agent shook her head to keep him from trying to defend her.

"It's just, you know, Lolo, there are bad people in this world, and they hurt innocent people," she said quietly. "And sometimes, for whatever reason, the authorities that were put in place to protect the innocent people aren't able to. When that happens, someone's got to stop the bad people from hurting innocent lives."

"And you're one of those someones," Lorenzo said, more to himself than to her.

He said it as if the logic made sense in his mind, which confused the Agent greatly. She supposed, though, that his definitions of "bad" and "innocent" probably differed from what hers had been back when she had trained with the Killer. Now, though, maybe their definitions didn't differ so much, after all. And that, for better and for worse, was sure to change the course of the Agent's life. In fact, that change had already begun.

As if sensing that his sister was a rapidly fading apparition, Lorenzo threw his arms around her. Forcing back tears, Lenci held him tightly and wished that she never had to let go. She wished she wouldn't have to break his heart. Over his shoulder, she made eye contact with Karthik who looked as if he were heartbroken already.

The moment passed and, all too soon, Lorenzo was back to his normal wisecracking self. Lenci and Karthik humored him by trying out the new game he had brought home: *Aliens From Outer Space Who Love Pizza.*

It was late when Karthik announced that he should head back across the hall. He had to work the next day, and Lorenzo, despite being on holiday break, had band practice early the next morning. Their mothers were due back at any moment, but they had stayed up as late as they could waiting for them.

As Lenci locked up behind Karthik, Lorenzo bounded off to beat her to the bathroom. The Agent found herself alone in the living room with the reality that she would eventually have to face the Killer if she ever wanted a chance to live her life.

Kiddo moved inside of her, bringing a smile to her face.

"Now, don't you worry, Kiddo," she said quietly. "I told you I would protect you if you stuck with me, and well, you held up your end of the deal. I'm going to make sure we're safe. I promise."

***

In a dark arena, the Agent struggled forward, pulling the weight of her opponent's limp body. The long, curly mane that entangled her fingers was matted with sweat, dirt, and blood. When she reached the doorway, she laid the body down against the door. The head, adorned with a face very much like her own, was twisted at an unnatural angle, but the Agent felt for a pulse on the jelly-like neck nonetheless. Feeling nothing, she arched her back and let out a guttural yell, a message for the spectators that had arranged this event.

After a couple of moments, the door opened a crack and a peach-colored journal protruded through the space. With a bloody hand, she took the journal, accepting the mission that had been assigned to her. It was only then that the door opened fully, but there was only darkness on the other side.

It was around 0400 when the Agent's eyes popped open. The darkness in the room was stifling. With her heartbeat thumping in her ears, she sat up, breathing shallowly. The child within her was motionless, perhaps still asleep, unaware that something was clearly amiss.

The Agent silently crawled out of the bed and put an ear to the door. Not a single noise came from the other side. She turned the knob as quietly as she could and stood aside to let the door swing inward. When no menacing form filled the doorway, she peeked out into the hall and looked both ways.

The moon shone softly through the open window at the far end of the hallway. A chilly breeze was causing the sheer curtains to billow. They were like tangible rays of moonlight, ghastly white and wavering fearfully.

It was the wind, she decided. The wind's blowing through the hall had caused her to believe that there was someone pacing around out there. She marched over to the window, shut it, and latched it with a firm *THACK*. But when she was reentering her room, she could hear breathing nearby, possibly in the bathroom. He had finally come for her.

Come, Bathsheba!

Rather than confront the Killer in the hallway, the Agent ran for the door to the common room in an attempt to lead him away from her family. His steps were close behind her as she burst through the door. She willed herself to move more quickly, but her legs were becoming lead-like.

Someone had left one of the lights on in the living room. The Agent scrambled to the light switch to turn it off. The switch was already down, even though the room was bright with light. So, she flipped the switch upward and the light went out.

But that wasn't right. She flipped the switch down again and the light came on, so she quickly flipped it back up. It made no sense! *Down, up, down, up, down, up.* David was most likely coming to strangle her any second now, and she couldn't make the damn light go out! *Down, up, down, up, down, up.*

"Lenci?"

She shrieked and, falling against the wall, slid to the floor. There, she curled up with her arms and legs folded to protect her head and her belly bump.

Her brother, who had come into the kitchen to grab a late night snack, ran to get their mom. Together, they helped Lenci to her feet and led her back to her room. She was trembling from head to foot and muttering about Poison Arrow and the Cull. Monica stayed with her for a while to examine her head and body, which had not sustained any injuries. When her daughter's quaking had stopped, Monica wished her a good night, turned out the light, and went back to bed.

Alone once again, the Agent was bombarded by lyrics from the Song interwoven with whispers about Poison Arrow. The darkness was loud and unbearable until, at last, the Agent jumped out of bed and turned on the light. Immediately, there was silence. Fetching a piece of paper, she scribbled a note with shaking hands. She then collapsed onto the bed and fell asleep.

The next morning, Lenci awoke peacefully in her room. She stretched and glanced over at her bedside table. All of the blood drained from her face. In her own handwriting, the words "Sweet Relief" were scrawled on a piece of paper. She grabbed her phone from her desk and stroked her belly bump as she dialed a number

"I need to see you," she said when the call connected. "Fairwaves Beach. 1400 today, please."

Chapter 24

THAT AFTERNOON, THE AGENT TOOK the purple cloth pouch from the box inside the closet and stuffed it into her windbreaker. She called a taxi, which took her straight to the parking lot of Fairwaves Beach.

Scanning the beach from the top of the sandy incline, the Agent finally caught sight of the man who had pulled her out of the water a few months before. That was how she felt she knew him, although she understood that their history was much richer than that.

He was standing with his back to her, staring out at the green-blue waves. His shoulders were slightly hunched, as they had been in recent times, but the Agent thought that she might remember a time when he had stood taller and straighter.

As if sensing her presence, he turned and rested his sad, honest gaze upon her. She slipped out of her shoes and jogged down to meet him. When she arrived, she stood before him with the glow of recent revelation on her countenance.

"Samir," she said, touching his face softly. "Your name is Samir."

She had no memory of him under that name, but Lenci had trusted him once upon a time. He had done his best to prepare her for life as an agent, and she was grateful. Besides, after all of the compassion and honor that he had shown her since her resurfacing, gratitude was the very least she owed him.

He took her hand from his face and squeezed it fondly. "I knew you'd get it eventually. You have something to tell me, Lenci?"

"I have something to show you," she said. "A few things, actually. First of all—"

She unzipped her windbreaker and took it off. The curvature of her abdomen was quite pronounced under her skintight tank top. Samir brought a hand to his gaping mouth.

"Meet Uncle Samir, Kiddo," Lenci chuckled. "Samir, meet the only mistake ever to save my life."

Samir shook his head in astonishment. He ran his hands through his hair and turned away from his agent, then back toward her. For a moment, Lenci was unsure whether he was going to cry, laugh, or reprimand her.

"Divine intervention," he whispered.

Then, grinning broadly, he declared, "Kiddo, you are one rambunctious young lady! You mean to tell me that you gave David Miller the slip because—"

"Yes."

"And you've been hiding all this time because—"

"Yes, Samir," she smiled. "Turns out the World Council of Eugenics doesn't take too kindly to naturally unclassified offspring, especially that of their operatives."

"*Their* operatives?"

She pretended not to hear his indignant exclamation.

"It was a miracle enough they didn't know my true heritage while I trained with him." She swallowed uneasily, then resumed her smile. "I guess I have you to thank for that since you registered me as Class 3.5. The Killer never had a clue."

Bourghin recoiled when she mentioned the Killer. Maybe it was because she had said it with a tad more reverence than he wished she would. Maybe he had noticed someone else doing that recently as well.

"I want to know why you registered me with a false class designation and why I played along," she said, looking at him intently.

Bourghin's response was empty. "Why else? You know that survival is the name of the game. The less people know about you, the better. They see what they want to see. And you were in a unique position to use that to your advantage."

"But it was more than that, wasn't it?" Lenci insisted. "You suspected that SSI had already been infiltrated by the WCE at a higher level than any of us had previously thought."

He looked out toward the ocean. "I don't know what you mean."

Samir had always been forthright with her about everything, but he was suddenly very uncharacteristically evasive. The Agent was fairly sure that he was protecting someone, probably that same person who spoke with forced reverence when she said the Killer's name, the person whom Samir probably considered to be more like Lenci than either of them would have liked.

"We are not the same, she and I," she said.

"Who?"

The Agent took the purple pouch from her pocket, saying, "There's no use in trying to protect her. The Killer is in Diablo. He called for me, and since I didn't answer, it's only a matter of time before——"

"David Miller is *here*?" Bourghin looked panicked. "What if he's been watching me? I could have led him right to you!"

She stroked her belly and said, "If he wanted me dead, I'd already be dead. But I have a feeling that he's not going to try to put me down until after I've done his dirty work *and* cleaned up after his mess. That's where the director comes in."

Bourghin crossed his arms. "What are you trying to say?"

"Ever heard the name 'Poison Arrow?'"

He didn't respond, and his kindly face became the kindliest version of stony that the Agent had ever seen.

She continued, "You should look in the files from her resurfacing, if you can access them. I'd bet my life that the director has an incriminating tattoo somewhere on her body."

Samir's face softened. It seemed that he already knew about Director Gomez's tattoo.

"She did call herself 'Poison Arrow' when she resurfaced," he said. "Reports say she had the hardest time learning to answer to her legal name again."

The Agent nodded grimly. "Everyone thinks that her condition was reversible because she only spent six months with the Killer. But what I'm trying to *say* is that her rehabilitation was not successful and now a whole lot of people are in danger."

"But how could she still, over twenty years later——"

"Hold that thought." She opened the purple pouch and handed the journal to him.

His eyebrows raised at the sight of the bloody handprint along the spine, but he opened the book nonetheless.

Sniffing, he asked, "Is that myrrh I smell?"

"I made an oopsie with the myrrh oil during physical therapy," she lied. "Please pay attention. It's the writing on the pages that's important here."

He flipped through the entire book. Then, puzzled, he turned back to the first page and began to read aloud.

There, below I see her
So lonely in her pool

"Stop! *Stop!*"

The Agent knocked the book out of his hands. It landed in the sand with a muted *THUMP*.

Bourghin regarded her in bewilderment. "What?"

Sighing, she retrieved the journal and dusted the sand from its cover. "Remember how you trained me to respond to certain rhythms and patterns of intonation?"

He nodded.

"The Killer used music and poetry instead, and this book contains my Song. It helps me to be a good soldier."

Her handler frowned. "But you were trained only to respond to me, to *my* voice."

"Well, when it comes to my Song, I'm trained to respond to the Killer's voice."

"But, I'm not him!" Bourghin sputtered. "So, what does it matter if you hear the lyrics of your 'Song' in my voice or anyone else's other than his?"

"*Every* voice is his," the Agent said darkly.

Perhaps this was a mistake. If Bourghin decided to take the journal and managed to read enough of the Song aloud, he could prevent her from finishing her mission.

But Samir made no move to take the journal.

Instead, he said, "So, Miller took you because he knew that you were gifted and had tested high for suggestibility. And then, he proceeded to groom you with music—"

"The WCE trained a whole group of agents to respond to specialized Songs," she interrupted. "There were some from other agencies."

Bourghin's face flooded with relief at the mention of the other missing agents. "If we can get copies of those Songs, we might be able to develop a plan for rehabilitation for our own missing agents."

She looked down at the ground, wondering how she could tell him that such a plan would not be necessary.

"Do you know where we might obtain copies?" he asked.

"All official copies of the Songs have been destroyed," she replied.

She left out the part about how the agent with Arjun's face had suggested that *she* had locked them all away in the depths of her patchy memory.

Disappointed but not ready to give up just yet, Bourghin asked, "How many were there?"

"Enough chitchat. I asked you here because the Killer primed me to take down one of those agents."

He stared at her incredulously. "From SSI? Which one?"

She responded by handing him the tape recorder.

He pressed the play button immediately. She couldn't look at him as the recording played. In fact, she turned her back to him as if she were refusing to receive the message that had been left for her. But when she heard the *CLICK*, she turned to face him once again and saw in his face that he had put together most of the important bits of the story.

"So, that Mirra really knows how to press your buttons, hey, Lenci?" he grinned wryly.

"Who?"

Lenci had been under the impression that Operation Mirra must have been the plan to douse the peach journal in myrrh for memory's sake. After all, wasn't *mirra* Spanish for 'myrrh?'

"Mirra," Bourghin repeated. "Or, you know, the one that disrupted our trust bond with this garbage?"

"Oh," she looked down. "We don't talk about her."

"We who?"

"No one. Just forget it," the Agent said quickly.

Samir, ever tactful, changed the subject.

"What's the Cull?"

"Not completely sure," the Agent said, sifting through her memory as fast as she could. "But whatever it is, the first phase is a test of some kind of antipersonnel weapon. Biotoxin would be my guess, given the direction of WCE research in recent years."

His brow furrowed. "When?"

"If I have anything to do with it, never," she replied. "Also, you can do us both a favor by staying home tonight. I need to have a conversation with Director Gomez."

"Can't I come along to facilitate the dialogue?" Bourghin asked.

As she turned toward the parking lot, her facial expression told him that she greatly appreciated the thought but that the dialogue she'd be having with the director was not the type where he could join in with an objective viewpoint.

She started up the sandy hill without even saying goodbye.

"What are you going to do, Lenci?" he called after her.

She responded without looking back, "I'm going to stop her."

Chapter 25

AFTER A BRIEF SHOPPING SPREE, during which she had picked up a green backpack and a few gadgets for that evening's entertainment, Lenci stopped by her favorite Chinese restaurant to enjoy a bowl of noodle soup. Just one bowl because that evening's activities would best be completed in the absence of a soup-sloshy stomach. She looked longingly at the beverage menu but patted Kiddo affectionately and stuck with the tinny-tasting ice water.

As she ate, she messaged Racky to ask for assistance in fortifying the security protocols for accessing missile launch codes at the SSI headquarters. The next thing she knew, her phone was ringing. It was Racky.

"Hello?" Lenci slurped a couple of noodles into her mouth before devoting her attention to the conversation.

Racky also sounded like she was eating, possibly a candy bar or something else chewy and crunchy at the same time. "What's all this about 'missile launch codes at the SSI headquarters?' HQ only has two wings: admin and the gym, and not one of them is weaponized."

"I'll bet you a bag of Chubba's chicken thighs," Lenci said.

Racky huffed, but she didn't say anything.

So, Lenci continued, "It shouldn't be too hard to get in the network or whatever and find the building's blueprints, right?"

"'Get in the network or whatever?' Girl, this is not some kind of magic trick where I just say 'abracadabra' and we're in. Do you know what kind of virus I would need to get through the failsafes, booby-traps, and firewalls?"

"No, but you do. I've never been good with tech stuff, but that's why I'm asking the best of the best to help me out."

"Can I ask why—"

"No," she answered abruptly. "This has to be done on trust, at least right now."

"You know I got your back, Circus," her pre-teammate said.

Lenci sighed with relief. "Thank you, Racky. I don't care how you get it done, but just make those launch codes inaccessible, please."

Racky sighed a different kind of sigh. "I will message you."

After hanging up, Lenci resumed her enjoyment of her noodle soup. It was a fairly safe bet that the biotoxin would be diffused via some kind of projectile. And a projectile would need to be launched. So, the best possible turnout would be if the launch codes were simply inaccessible.

She had nearly polished off her soup by the time she got Racky's message.

It consisted of a single word: **Done**.

Lenci wondered what her pre-teammate had found that had caused her to be at such a loss for words, but she pushed away that distracting thought. On a basic level, she knew what she was walking into, and she needed to get her head in the game. She put her phone into her backpack and looked out the window.

Darkness had fallen, and the streetlights in front of the restaurant, whose bulbs had been shot out long ago, were just shadows of what they had been. Their only function, now, was to serve as a reminder of the absence of light. In some strange sense, Lenci felt that she had been robbed.

"You never know, Kiddo," she said stroking her belly. "Who's to say a person can't change?"

Suddenly, the air around the Agent began to smell like myrrh. She knew it was just a phantom sensation, but it filled her with a strength that she did not understand.

Despite the task at hand, she couldn't help wondering what Lorenzo and Karthik were doing, what Racky had been eating on the other end of the phone, and what on earth kind of virus could infiltrate SSI's security. Whatever Racky had done, it was sure to be a riot.

***

At precisely 0045, the Agent showed up at the Sopient Solutions, Incorporated headquarters. She went around back and hid in the bushes beside the maintenance entrance. The night air was chilly, and she

211

shivered in her light clothing. She was beginning to regret only wearing a windbreaker over her gym clothes and stockings. The ensemble was supposed to be unrestrictive, but she felt more restricted by the cold than anything else. She adjusted the shoulder straps of her backpack. If only she had thought to pack a heavier jacket along with her climbing gadgets.

Her shivering stopped when the door opened.

Showtime. The night cleaning crew shuffled out the door and down the stairs, talking and laughing as they went. As the door was swinging shut, the Agent threw her left hand out to stop it. The door closed on her palm, so it didn't latch. Although she couldn't feel anything but the pressure, she knew that she'd have a sizable bruise in a few hours.

She didn't mean to, but she swore aloud. The word soured on her tongue and stung like a slap in the face. She turned her attention toward the cleaners to see if there was to be any confrontation. They continued on their way, chatting as they went, unaware that the door had not shut behind them and that someone who had been in the bushes was now in the building.

As the darkness in the entryway engulfed her, the Agent breathed a sigh of relief. She hadn't expected it to be that easy to break into the headquarters of a covert organization. As she was congratulating herself on a sneak-in well done, a red light shot out of a contraption in the ceiling and spread over her face. She tried to duck out of its reach, but she wasn't fast enough.

"Scanned," a synthetic voice said. "No facial recognition match available. Please provide voiceprint verification."

Apparently, SSI had invested in better technology than most of Diablo could afford. The Agent knew better than to speak and risk identifying herself, especially as it seemed that the scanner hadn't recognized her face. She looked around to see if there were any weapons protruding from the wall or ceiling. Not finding any, she concluded that this part of the security system must be all bark and no bite—or someone was helping her.

A few heart-pounding seconds later, there were a couple of high-pitched chirps, then the same voice said, "Package has been delivered. Say, 'yes' to add tip now."

The security system had been tricked into believing that the Agent was a package that had been delivered. Someone was definitely helping her. It wasn't beyond Racky's ability to pull something like that. The Agent made a mental note to later ask her friend how she'd done it.

For now, she had a mission to complete. If there were any weapon-ized projectiles to be sent off from this building, they'd have to be stored somewhere cool and where no one would think to look. She elected to take the staircase down to the basement.

Behind her, the synthetic voice said, "Okay, add tip later. Goodbye!"

The basement was a dark, cement-walled, underground room filled with mops, brooms, and other cleaning supplies. It did not look like the type of place one might keep a missile. After a few moments of creeping around in the cobweb-filled shadows, the Agent nearly gave up hope. That was when she saw the emergency exit sign over an old, rusty, metal door. The sign wasn't illuminated.

She tested the door and found it unlocked. Someone must have been in recently and forgotten to lock it. The Agent dropped to her knees and pushed the door open a half a meter. It opened upon what had probably used to be an old panic room. The cement walls, metal door, and shelves stocked with canned food suggested that that was indeed what it had been once upon a time.

So, emergency, yes. Exit, no. In the center of the room, there stood three massive glass cylinders, and in each cylinder stood a canister. All of them were lined up on a shared console.

"Oh, my, my, Director," the Agent breathed. "You *have* been busy."

Forgetting the need for stealth, she stood up and walked straight across the room to the canisters, which were connected to some kind of long-range diffuser. Hundreds of tubes and tubules branched off from the cylinders into the walls. While it looked like the director had rigged an old missile launch system for her purposes that evening, the Agent had been wrong about projectiles being the director's instrument of choice. Gomez was going to release the biotoxin into something under-ground, probably the sewer or a water source. Coming from below would draw less attention, until it was too late.

As the Agent examined the console, her heart sank. Lights were blinking everywhere and the tangle of wires and circuitry made the whole getup very impressive.

"Let's see what this does," she whispered, taking a running start and hurling all of her weight into the middle cylinder.

It made a great crash, and the glass went everywhere, but the canister didn't burst. That was a good sign. It must not have been armed yet.

There came a loud humming, and she turned to find that a protec-tive shell had descended around each of the remaining cylinders.

213

Inside, a loud hissing indicated that the canisters were depressurizing and preparing to release their contents into the diffuser.

"Oh, Racky, I hope you really were able to disable those launch codes."

The Agent stuffed the one canister she had into her backpack and looked for a quick, undetectable way to the top floor. The elevator would eliminate the element of surprise, and there were thumbprint scanners on the entrances to the stairwells.

Outside the door to the panic room, she found the solution, which quite literally stank. It was the trash chute.

Chapter 26

AROUND 0110, SAMIR BOURGHIN poked his head out of his office to see if anyone was around. He had spent his evening pretending not to be there. In fact, he had even gone so far as to make a big deal of leaving the office at 1700 sharp, per usual, secretly parking his car a kilometer away, and jogging back to "retrieve his phone."

"Got all the way to the highway this time," he had told the director as he passed her in the hall. "I'll just grab my phone and run down the stairs. I could use the exercise."

He went into his office until she had gone back to her own. Then, he scanned his thumbprint at the stairwell to sign out—only he didn't leave. Gomez had no reason to suspect that Bourghin was still in his office when she looked down the hallway to make sure all the lights were off before going home. According to all official records, he was not in the building, and that was the way he wanted it.

If there was any truth to Lenci's story, he would discover evidence of it in the director's office. Although Gomez had had twenty years to find ways to cope with her condition and to conceal it, Bourghin was sure that he would find something.

He'd actually been wondering for some time if the director was acting under her own power or if she was just like the sopients they were training, a time-release capsule that would eventually wreak havoc in whatever capacity her commissioners wished. Her lack of memory regarding the commissioning of the twenty missing agents as well as her recent obsessive behavior with respect to Lenci had been points of concern for Agent Bourghin. Lenci's report had confirmed his fears and driven him to take action.

After establishing that there was no one else on the floor, he moved quickly and quietly down the hall to the director's office. To his surprise, the door, though locked, was slightly ajar. He entered and headed straight for the filing cabinet behind the desk. When he found it locked, he turned to the desk to look for the key. He froze, however, upon the sensation of cold metal pressed against his kneecap.

"Who's there?" a female voice asked from beneath the desk.

"I could ask the same thing," he replied.

"Bourghin?"

The woman with the gun emerged and stood up. Their bodies were uncomfortably close in that dark space between the desk and the filing cabinet, but she was not bothered by their proximity in the least. In fact, she might have been enjoying it.

In the dim light that squeezed through the slats of the blinds, Bourghin could just barely make out the features of a familiar face, a face he did not want to see at that moment.

"Ms. Lee-Smith!"

"How many times do I have to tell you to call me Blair?" she said coyly. "Now that you've stormed into a dark room to be alone with me, there's no need to be shy."

He ignored her banter. "What are you doing here?"

"That's classified and out of your jurisdiction," Blair responded, pulling back the edge of her blazer so that he could glimpse the faint gleam of a golden badge attached to her belt. "Now, I'll have to ask you to head home, Agent Bourghin. The Cooperative FBI will be contacting you within a couple of days, so don't leave town or anything."

Just as he opened his mouth to defend or accuse or interrogate, the bell on the elevator rang. Someone was coming! From the sound of the confident, high-heeled footsteps, it was not an unreasonable conclusion that Director Gomez had returned to the office.

Blair switched her gun out of safety mode and pointed it at Bourghin, motioning for him to get under the desk. He momentarily considered resisting, but he thought better of that as he imagined cooperation might lead him to more information.

Blair squeezed under the desk after him, placing an authoritative finger over his horrified mouth. The director's footsteps stopped at the door of her office. In the silence that ensued, both of the intruders concluded that she was reasoning with herself over the already open but locked door.

After a few seconds that seemed like an eternity, she grabbed her brief case off of the desk and clip-clopped to the conference room.

The air under the desk had grown hot and stuffy. Bourghin let out a deep breath and brushed some of Blair's hair out of his mouth.

"Well, I can't leave *now*," he whispered.

"That's true," Blair replied, equally quietly, as she crawled out from under the desk. "Lucky you."

"I just want to know what's going on."

He used the desk for support as he got to his feet.

"You and me both," she said, moving to the door to get a look down the hall.

There was something draped over the back of the director's chair. Upon closer examination, Bourghin discovered that it was the director's high-collared blazer. He slowly folded the blazer, lamenting how the director had used it to keep her alternate identity out of sight and out of mind.

"Poison Arrow," he whispered aloud. "Like a frog. Amphibious."

Blair whipped around to face him. "What'd you say?"

"Poison Arrow," he repeated. "Lenci implied that Poison Arrow is going to attempt to initiate the Cull."

He dropped the terms 'Poison Arrow' and 'Cull' nonchalantly, hoping that his confidence would put the federal double agent at ease.

"The Cull, hey?" Blair smirked. "Well, Bourghin, you *are* in the know."

"I'm not trying to step on anyone's jurisdictional toes," he said dejectedly. "But I have a responsibility to my agent as her psychiatric trainer. I took an oath, you see."

The oath to guide and to teach, to fortify and to help. For this particular situation, saying he was acting strictly in honor of the oath may have been a stretch, but he felt that he was within the spirit of it.

Blair sighed. "Okay, just stay out of sight and out of my way. I have spent my whole life training for this, and I can't have you messing it up."

It was then that Bourghin noticed a familiarity about the shape of Blair's face, namely her high cheekbones and pointed chin. These were features that graced the face of the director. And it was only in recognizing this resemblance that he began to understand that the roots of Ms. Lee-Smith's dedication to her job at SSI—and apparently, her investigation of the agency—were more personal than they were professional. He wondered how long it must have taken her to track down her birthmother whose whole life had been dedicated to covert activities.

When Blair ventured out into the hallway, Bourghin waited five seconds, then followed after her to listen outside of the conference room door.

***

The Agent watched from the shadows as Gomez entered the conference room. The director paced back and forth, mumbling to herself a list of things to do and things she had already done.

"I put it in the canisters in the basement," she said, glancing up at the ceiling with shining eyes. "Hooked them up. Still need to activate the codes. But where did I get them all in the first place? Oh, never mind. Never mind."

She moved to the computer at the far side of the room and turned it on.

"Oh, try it with the projector," she whispered. "It'll look great wall-sized."

As the light from the projector flickered on, she double-clicked and, much to Lenci's dismay, the launch codes began to load, plotting a route from the tubules in the building to the underground water pipes of a certain borough. The director turned to admire her work as it was projected on the big screen behind her.

The Agent moved to the center of the room and sat cross-legged on the table behind the director. She cleared her throat. Gomez whipped around, but she had only begun to reach for her concealed pocket pistol when the Agent pounced on her and trapped her in a one-armed headlock.

"Greetings, Director," the Agent said, forcing her to her knees. "What are you up to this lovely dead of night?"

"What are you doing here?" Gomez's tone was indignant despite her undignified position.

"Couldn't sleep."

The Agent smoothed the director's hair out of the way, and there, at the base of her neck, was a small, full-color tattoo of a golden frog.

She continued, "So, I thought I would come and see what you were working on."

She plucked the pistol from the director's pocket and placed it on the desk next to the computer.

"I have no patience for your audacity tonight, girl," Gomez said irritably as she grasped at the Agent's arm. "Go home, and I'll forget you were ever here."

The Agent released her. The director would not engage in hand-to-hand combat, even when provoked. It seemed that, without a gun anyway, she was just a limp noodle. The big screen showed that the launch codes were almost completely loaded.

So much for Racky's safeguarding. Friendship could only be counted on so far and no further. And perhaps their friendship had been engineered from the beginning. That was a terrible thought.

Since programming was not the Agent's strong suit, all she could do to prevent the contents of those last two canisters from being diffused was to convince the director that she was still under the Killer's influence and persuade her to pursue a different path.

Gomez approached the computer once more, eyeing the Agent to see if she would make another move. The gun was on the desk in front of the director, but the Agent was unworried.

She took her seat on the table once more, and said, "I'm disappointed to see that you're actually initiating the Cull."

Gomez froze.

"The Cull," the Agent repeated. "Twenty years ago, you were the first of the Amphibians commissioned by the World Council of Eugenics, so it's your job to initiate the Cull. I *had* hoped you were past all that by now, though."

Silence from the director.

"Yes, yes, I know who you are," the Agent said. "The golden frog on the back of your neck kind of gives it away. I thought your high-collared suits were a little conspicuous, Poison Arrow."

The normal pallor of the director's face gave way to a fierce, red glow.

"I never intended to accomplish that heinous mission, and I am *not* Poison Arrow, Agent Thomas." Her top lip curled back slightly upon pronouncing the name of her competition. "You have no idea the strength it has taken to get this far!"

"Maybe I don't," the Agent conceded, "but a bunch of people are going to die tonight if I don't stop you."

"So, you came to kill me?" the director asked haughtily

"Not if I don't have to," the Agent replied.

"I'm not affected." Gomez was beginning to shake. "I can handle myself. I mean, look at you! You spent *years* on tour with the Killer. And now, you're pregnant, which is against Neo-Eugenic law *and* the WCE tenets."

The launch codes were now completely loaded. The network was initializing a permissions box for the launch itself. Time was running out, and yet, the Agent sensed that she might be close to a breakthrough.

"But you spent long enough with him. Long enough to break the same rules I did, am I right?" she asked.

"I don't know what you're talking about."

"I'm *talking* about your long-lost daughter!"

Just then, Samir and Blair tumbled into the room. They were wrestling over a firearm, which Samir snatched and tossed. Blair dove after it, grabbed it, and sprang to her feet, trying to look as professional as possible.

"Bourghin, I am warning you to stand down! You are skating *this* close to obstruction of justice. I said, 'stand *down*,' and I mean it!"

She smoothed her hair back nervously as she looked between Director Gomez and the Agent.

"There's that unforgettable face!" the Agent said. "The cheekbones and chin of a Director and the brow of a Killer, all framed with chemically lightened hair. As for you, Agent Bourghin, I thought I advised you to stay home?"

"Agent Thomas," he replied, staring at the large screen behind the director. "I didn't see you come in."

She grinned, motioning toward the hall. "Wiggled up from the basement, twenty-one floors through the trash chute—using suction cups, of course."

"You rambunctious young lady!" he exclaimed.

The director glared at him, and he looked at the floor.

The Agent chuckled. "It was the funniest thing: I was wandering through the basement when I found *this.*"

She pulled the canister from her backpack.

"Looks like a big, bad carrier of an experimental biotoxin that could be diffused into a neighborhood, probably targeting some group of people that the WCE thought no one would ask questions about. That's just to my untrained eye, though."

Turning to look at the screen behind her, the director's eyes grew wide. A dialogue box had popped up over the fully loaded launch codes.

Instead of launch permissions, it read: **Self-destruct HQ: yes or no?**

That was most certainly Racky's doing! The director selected 'no,' but when she tried to click the launch button, the dialogue box appeared again. She did this over and over until, at last, she turned her gaze upon the Agent with a scathing malice.

"You just want me to fail," Gomez declared. "You want me to fail, so you can replace me!"

"Mm, yes and no," the Agent replied. "I do want you to fail as in I want you *not* to cause the deaths of millions of people. But I don't want to replace you."

"Millions of people?" Bourghin echoed.

"I'm afraid so," the Agent said. "The World Council of Eugenics has selected Princess Pollywog here to demonstrate their power to enforce Neo-Eugenic law on the rest of the unaffiliated and exempt world. They were intending to start small with Diablo tonight, but the plan is definitely to go larger-scale. In Darwinian terms: a chance to prove that an entire class is unfit. Sound about right, Director?"

The director did not answer.

Glancing at Blair, the Agent said, "Memorize the coordinates on the screen and look them up later. You'll see that the WCE was targeting the public housing developments in the Philemon borough, which has a predominantly 4.14 population. Ms. Lee-Smith, your mommy has been a bad, bad girl."

"Beatriz Gomez," Blair said a very professional tone, "I am a federal agent and, through the Cooperative FBI, I have a warrant for your arrest for treason, collaboration in war crimes connected to the World Council of Eugenics, involvement in international terrorism and smuggling, and at least three counts of murder."

"I *knew* there was something off about your story about transferring out of the FBI!" the Agent interjected. "So, you're Cooperative, though, not Eastern. How diplomatic!"

Blair ignored her once again, addressing her birthmother instead. "Ms. Gomez, you're undoubtedly facing life in prison. However, if you will come with me and cooperate, I might be able to get you a deal regarding your choice of prisons as well as long-term rehabilitation options."

But Director Gomez was not looking at Blair. She was looking at the Agent, the reason her organization was unraveling, the Relief she had dreaded.

"I've been on my own for over twenty years, for goodness' sake!" she cried. "I ran this agency *against* the WCE. We've consistently served our country by uncovering terrorist plots and taking down major crime syndicates."

"You're under his thumb, and you know it," the Agent challenged.

She did not need to say whose thumb she was under. There was only one *him*.

"I am only what I have been made to be," the director growled. "Just like you: a whore made by whores *for* whores!"

There was a smell, something bitter, an aroma—the Agent could not think about that at the moment.

She said, "Alright, I see how it is. You think you've got everything under control, but—"

I know where Poison Arrow landed
In a desert near the sea

"No! *No!*" Gomez grabbed her gun from the desk and waved it in the Agent's direction. "No one is supposed to know my Song!"

Blair cocked her weapon in response. "Drop it, Ms. Gomez. I'm no fan of Agent Thomas, but I can't have you gunning down an unarmed pregnant woman on my watch."

"Thanks," the Agent grumbled.

"Director, with all due respect—" Samir started.

"Oh, shut up, Bourghin!" the director snarled. "Blair, you're not going to shoot your own mother."

"You're not even surprised," Blair said, her gun wavering. "You've known who I was since I showed up here. Haven't you?"

The director's face was hard, calloused, and angry. She did not respond.

Her daughter's voice faltered. "You never said anything, but you knew the whole time."

"Well, the federal agent bit was a surprise." Gomez shrugged as she aimed at Blair and pulled the trigger.

Although she was only hit in the shoulder, Blair was unconscious before she hit the floor, likely overwhelmed by the shock of the whole situation. Bourghin knelt to examine the wound.

The director turned toward the Agent. "Agent Thomas, do you know how poison arrows are made?"

The Agent said nothing. She motioned for her handler to take Blair and exit the room. He didn't move.

Gomez continued with pride, "Left alone, a poison arrow frog wouldn't do much harm, only to predators maybe. But Man, with his insatiable need for war, knows every way to maximize on a natural defense mechanism. Torture the frog to the point of extreme distress, and she excretes copious amounts of her potent neurotoxin for his arrows. You see, being only what she is—yet in the hands of Man—she can cause whole systems to shut down."

The Agent sighed. "Look, I get it. It wasn't your fault that you became Poison Arrow. The Killer has a way about him. I guess I thought by reciting your Song, I could help you understand how far his influence—"

"Oh, you have made your intentions perfectly clear," the director said, turning her gun back toward the Agent.

"And now that my Song has been compromised, I have no choice but to eliminate the threat. Pity." She smiled condescendingly. "We have so much in common, you and I."

The Agent leapt toward the director the instant she saw her trigger finger twitch, a risk she had calculated and was willing to take, but she suddenly found herself shoved to the ground at an angle at which she had not intended to fall. The ensuing *BANG* was accompanied by a man's voice crying out and the sound of glass shattering.

The floor-to-ceiling window nearest Gomez was now in pieces on the floor, and the director herself was sprawled out among the shards. Heart pounding, the Agent rolled over and glanced at the spot where she had been standing, the spot where Agent Bourghin's body now lay. A thin trail of blood was already crawling away from him.

Chapter 27

RESISTING THE URGE TO HURRY to Bourghin's side, the Agent crawled first to the director who lay motionless amid the glass by the window. It did not take a long examination to determine that the cause of Beatriz Gomez's death was a single shot to the head. And it did not take much imagination to conjure a guess at who had killed her. The Killer had made the shot from the eastern tip of the building across the street. He had been watching the whole time.

Suddenly feeling exposed, the Agent scrambled away from the window and back to Bourghin, who lay prone in his blood. She felt for a pulse and was relieved to find it, although it was quite faint. Her windbreaker would not be absorbent enough. She had to use her stockings to wrap his wound as tightly as she could to stop the bleeding. Her scars were the least of her troubles at this point.

She marched to the computer and clicked 'yes' to start the self-destruct sequence. Racky's plan was indeed a riot. Disabling the launch codes and replacing them with a self-destruct sequence was ingenious! A whole pile of rubble on top of the disease-filled basement would keep people safe for a while longer. And the heat from the explosions might just destroy the biotoxin altogether. She guessed there might be such thing as true friendship after all.

The self-destruct counter on the screen indicated that she had ten minutes before the building would be destroyed. That was more than enough time.

Humming to keep focused, the Agent retrieved a large coil of rope from the backpack that she had brought with her. She sat down between Samir and Blair and attached the rope to her own ankles, leaving two leg-lengths between the knots. After testing the strength of the knots, she measured out a few arm-lengths and then looped the rope around the assistant director's waist. To make everything neat and tidy, she stuffed the canister she had stolen into her green backpack, she situated it on Blair.

"I'm no fan of yours either, Assistant Director," the Agent said, "but I cannot allow you to be destroyed by the mistakes your mother and I have made."

Then, she gently wedged herself between her handler's body and the floor, and once she bore the majority of his weight, she pushed up onto her hands and feet. Samir groaned quietly and extended his right arm. The Agent balanced on three limbs in order to grasp his hand and bring it to her lips.

"Hold on, Samir," she whispered. "I'm going to get you out of here."

He murmured something incomprehensible before his body went limp. The Agent ignored the feeling of his blood seeping through the back of her shirt and pressed forward, her massive legs straining to adjust to the weight of the two bodies attached to her. Arm after arm, leg after leg, she crawled out of the conference room and down the hall, pausing only to recenter Samir's body on her back and to make sure that she didn't bump Blair's head too many times as she towed her along. A wavy trail of blood followed in their wake.

"I'm sorry," she muttered over and over. "I'm so sorry."

If only she had remembered sooner, if only she had considered more fully the consequences of provoking the director with the use of her Song, if only she had thought to push Bourghin away and take the bullet herself... But she had not. This man had honored her, believed in her, and had compassion on her for as long as she could remember, and she had rewarded his kindness with reckless endangerment.

She scanned Samir's thumbprint at the doorway to the stairwell and crawled onto the top landing. When she had pulled Blair's body over the threshold, she took one of her special climbing gadgets from her backpack. It was a small, black device with a large button in the center and a wound-up cord attached to a hook.

The Agent peered over the railing at the spiraling staircase, all twenty stories down to the ground floor. Sighing, she pressed the button on the compact device, and it unfolded into a harness. She attached the hook to the railing of the stairwell and then pulled Blair to her feet. Blair's body was still limp, dead weight, but the Agent managed to secure her to the front of her body with the ropes. Then, with Samir on her back and Blair on her front, in an animal-slave-weapon-thing sandwich that resembled a ball more than anything else, she threw herself over the railing and plunged downward at a dizzying rate.

As the zipping sound of the cord filled her ears, the Agent screwed her eyes shut and hoped that the advertisement on the gadget's packaging was right about the fifteen thousand kilo weight limit. She knew nothing of physics, only that their combined weight amounted to much more at such a rapid speed. The air whooshed up through her hair, but it was mostly obstructed by the bodies tied to either side of her. She clung to them tightly because she did not trust the harness that held them. She should have bought three harnesses that afternoon.

She was jolted from her thoughts as the cord seemed to have run out. The cord was slightly stretchy, but it was not like a bungee cord. It stretched and bounced a couple of times, then began to sway calmly. She, and her associated ball of persons, hung suspended from the stairway railing about two meters above the ground floor. Looking up, she decided to be grateful that she only had that far to fall.

After taking a deep breath, she unhooked the harness and dropped to the hard, cement floor. She checked her unconscious passengers briefly, then continued onward in her bear walk with Samir on her back and Blair dragging along behind her.

It was seven minutes from her start time when the Agent crawled out of the maintenance door. She heaved the two bodies down the steps of the back porch and continued down the block. Just when she reached the far corner, the basement exploded, and the building began to crumble. A cloud of ash rose up and lingered in the air.

The Agent untied the knots around her ankles and laid Blair, still unconscious, across the sidewalk. A lone car pulled up to the curb.

The driver rolled down the window and squawked, "Ey! That weaponization program I uncovered in the system really was legit. Serves the whole backwards agency right!"

"Remind me never to get on your bad side." The Agent grinned in spite of the situation. "Thanks for all the help, including at the maintenance entrance. I wouldn't have gotten past that, if it weren't for you."

The blank look on Racky's face told the Agent that her pre-teammate was not the one who had been helping her. She'd have to look into that later. There were more pressing matters at hand.

"I need you to take the assistant director to the emergency room," she said.

"What happened?"

"You owe me chicken thighs," the Agent grunted, stuffing Blair with the backpack into Racky's passenger's seat.

She took her phone out of the backpack and put it into the pocket of her shorts.

"Take Blair across the district to Resplendent Oaks or something. I have to take Samir to the hospital on this block and, well, you know protocol. Can't have people knowing their injuries occurred at the same place."

Responding to Racky's confused expression, she added, "She's got a slug in her shoulder, but she'll be fine. I have to go."

She hoisted Samir's body further up on her back and gripped his arms more tightly.

"You got it, Circus," Racky said. "Ey, listen."

The Agent glanced back at her.

"I know you must be shook up, but promise me you will not do anything stupid."

"Can't make promises I don't intend to keep," the Agent said, moving toward the hospital. "Hide the backpack somewhere safe!"

The low beams of Racky's car slanted, then disappeared altogether as she did a three-point turn and began to drive to the other side of the district.

Not too long afterward, the Agent arrived at the emergency room of Diablo Memorial Hospital and began her role as the scared bystander.

"What happened, ma'am?" one of the nurses asked as a gurney was wheeled out for Bourghin.

"I—I—I—" The Agent began to shake and then burst into tears.

As they positioned him on the gurney, his lips were moving, but no sound came out.

After lifting up Samir's shirt, another nurse announced, "I have a gunshot wound here!"

Another nurse was tapping the Agent's shoulder. "Ma'am, are you family?"

"F—f—friend! M—my—Samir Bourghin!" She threw in a couple of extra theatrical sobs, hoping that people would stop interrogating her.

Samir's lips were still moving as they rolled him away. He was saying the same thing over and over again.

As the Agent mimicked the movements of his mouth, she added the voicing and told the nurse, "Mirra."

"Excuse me, ma'am?"

"Mirra," she repeated to herself.

Then, getting one last glimpse of her handler as they wheeled him through the doors of the operating room, she read his lips and said, "Rambunctious young lady."

The nurses left her alone to wait. An hour later, a short woman with caramel-colored skin, black and gray hair, and a rather severe regard came into the waiting room and sat down across from the Agent. Her eyes widened at the Agent's disorderly appearance, but she did not address her.

Twenty minutes later, the surgeon came out of the operating room. He removed his gloves and mask. He looked exhausted.

"Dr. Bourghin?" He extended his hand toward the woman who had been waiting across from the Agent.

"Yes." The woman stood grimly.

"I'm so sorry. We did our best, but he was nearly gone when we got him on the table. He flatlined, and we weren't able to get him back."

"You tried, and I am grateful," she said in a sensible tone. "I would like to see my husband now."

The two exited the waiting room together, leaving the Agent alone with the unbearable truth that she had not gotten her handler help soon enough. She had let him down—again. And this time, there was no making up for it.

"I'm sorry," she whispered.

She felt the strange and wonderful sensation of Kiddo moving in her womb, but it did little to comfort her.

"I let him down, Kiddo," she said, rubbing her belly as she jogged for the door. "I'm so, so sorry."

Maybe there had been no reception in the waiting room, or maybe she had been too worried to check her messages during the surgery. Whatever the case, as she exited the hospital, all of the messages seemed to arrive at once.

Karthik had messaged multiple times to ask where she was and what she was doing. Her mother had asked her the same questions. Auntie Preeti had left a voicemail, and so had Karthik, and so had her mother. They all were worried about her, but there was something else, too. She could not quite understand between the bad reception and the background noise in the recordings, but the little bit that she understood caused her heart to sink.

Lorenzo had been admitted to Diablo's Central Hospital, had undergone surgery, and was being held in the intensive care unit. This—the Agent knew—was the beginning of the end of her happy life as Valencia Chang.

***

She found Karthik waiting for her lobby. His eyes widened upon seeing her bloody, bare-legged, and disheveled.

"Blood's not mine," she said gruffly. "Where's Lorenzo?"

"Room 3968," he replied. "This way."

He grabbed her hand, but she quickly wrenched it back.

"It'll be better if we don't touch," she said, quickening her pace.

She arrived at Room 3968 ahead of him, but she could only bring herself to peek through the doorway. Her little brother was lying in the hospital bed, bruised and unconscious, with a halo crown fixed to his head and tubes everywhere. Their mother and Auntie Preeti were sitting silently at the bedside.

Lenci drew back from the doorway and gasped upon finding herself face-to-face with Karthik, who had just arrived behind her.

"I can't go in," she whispered. "I don't know what to say to them."

"They just need you to be with them," he said. "The family can't face this alone."

He was close to her, but he respected her wishes and did not touch her.

She crossed her arms, unable to look him in the face. "What happened?"

"We d—don't know," Karthik replied. "Auntie Monica said she was listening to an audiobook in her room when she heard a th—thump."

He swallowed hard. "She just thought it was Renzo playing with the football in the house again, but when she went t–to check on him, he was on th—the kitchen fl—loor."

A difficult silence wavered between them as he fought back tears.

"He was just getting a sn—nack," he choked.

"What injuries did he sustain?" Lenci asked, trying to focus on anything that might get her more information faster.

"Injuries sustained?" Karthik parroted. He sighed. "Broken n–neck and hands."

"Which vertebrae?"

229

He looked at her fiercely. "C4–5. D—does it matter?"

"Yes," she responded, "because now I know for certain who did this."

Targeting C4-5, one strike to the back and one to the front—the Killer's typical, arrogant, two-step kill. He enjoyed killing and did it every so often to remain sharp. A kill like this, if he weren't to be paid for it, would be as casual as scratching an itch. Most importantly, however, a kill like this would be easy for the Agent to trace back to him. The Killer wanted her to know that this was his work.

Smoothing her hair, Lenci straightened up and entered the hospital room.

"Hello, mother. Auntie Preeti." Then, not knowing what else to say, she announced, "I'm here."

The two women rose and enveloped her with love. She unfeelingly brought her arms to hang loosely around their shoulders. It was only when the mothers drew back with blood on their hands that the panic began.

"What happened to you?"

"Where have you been?"

"What were you doing?"

"Why didn't you answer our calls?"

"We were so worried!"

"And what happened to your *legs*?"

She looked at the two older women wearily. "Agent Bourghin is dead. The director is dead. And the agency is dead."

Monica and Preeti fell silent. Karthik, who had been watching from outside the room, entered and took a seat near the door.

After a moment of silence, Monica burst out, "Baby, just us tell what happened!"

How can I tell you that I'm not your daughter, that I've endangered this whole family for my own selfish gain?

"I can't," Lenci said, moving toward the bed. "I've caused enough destruction already."

"Don't say that," Auntie Preeti said. "This was a senseless, random act of violence. It had nothing to do with you."

Little did she know, it had been very intentional and it was anything but random.

Lorenzo looked so small in the vastness of the hospital bed. His lanky frame, which had never truly been still in all his life, lay motionless like a pile of skin and bones. The hint of breath that remained in him was barely noticeable underneath all of the equipment and tubing.

"He's such a smart boy, you know," Monica said, coming to stand by Lenci. "Doctor said if he hadn't had his hands in front of his throat, his spinal cord would have been completely severed. Really quick thinking on my baby's part. There's no damage to the cord at all—so no paralysis—and his hands will heal right up in no time. "

Lenci avoided looking at Karthik, even though she knew he was looking at her. He wanted to share a hopeful glance over the fact that the one defensive move she had taught Lorenzo had saved his life. But she did not feel hopeful.

"Did you see him, mother?" she whispered.

"Who?"

The him. "The one who did this. Did you see him?"

Monica closed her eyes momentarily, then opened them wide as if that could erase the horrific scene from her memory.

"He climbed out the kitchen window before I could see his face," she said. "I think he heard me coming. But he was Class 1, very tall, wiry, and had long hair for a man. I can't imagine how he got down the side of the building without a rope or anything, but he was nowhere on the property by the time first responders showed up."

Lenci didn't take her eyes off of Lorenzo. "Did he say anything?"

Monica stammered, "Well, he—he said something about a brother. Maybe 'brother won't love you' or something? I don't know. He was probably high. You know, gunkheads have the highest number of convictions for eugenist hate crimes."

The mother thought a eugenist, gunk-crazed, Class 1 man had crawled up the side of the building just to murder Lenci's brother. Well, she had most of it right, anyway. The Killer did not approve of gunk-use, though.

Covering her dread with a chuckle, Lenci said, "Congratulations, mother. You are most likely the only civilian ever to witness David Miller the Killer at work and live to tell the tale."

"I'm not feeling very festive right now," her mom responded.

"Look," Lenci said. "I can't explain everything, but I think it would be best if you left. I don't care where you go, back to Windsailing or to Sandland or wherever, but please don't stay here."

"We're not going anywhere," Monica said resolutely. "We're family. And if there's anything you're facing, we'll face it with you."

Lenci looked back at the figure in the bed. "The Killer thinks that Lolo's the one I'm tethered to. So if we separate, he'll think he succeeded in cutting me loose."

"But if Lorenzo is the tether—"

"He's not!" she snapped.

Then, regretting having spoken so harshly, she lowered her voice and continued, "I never should have stayed with you all. But now we've been given a second chance to do this right. Please, take him away."

Monica sighed. "We'll talk about it tomorrow. Why don't you get some rest? Preeti and I have already checked into the hotel just across the street. Take the key and go."

"I'm going back to the apartment," Lenci said, rubbing her eyes with her bloody hands. "That's where I need to be."

"You're not thinking clearly, girl," Auntie Preeti said. "It might be better for you to be outside of the apartment—just to not be in a place that reminds you of your brother."

Little did she know, to be reminded of her brother was exactly what Lenci needed.

"Besides, if this Killer knows where we live now, what's to say he won't come back for you?" her mom chimed in. "We just want you to be safe."

"He won't be coming. In any other situation, I would be in the wind by now. He'll be leaving the city in search of me. Won't return unless he has reason to believe I'm here, like if you're here."

"Lenci, please, just calm down and think about this, now."

"I don't want to stay in the hotel! I want to go *back to the apartment*."

Mrs. Chang was unfazed. "I had the locks changed while Lorenzo was in surgery. I've got the only key, and I'm staying at the hotel. You can deal with it."

"You think I can't break into my own house?"

Lenci shuddered at her mother's glare, then turned her attention to Lorenzo. She could not hold his broken hands or kiss his cheek because of the braces and tubes. So, she gently placed her hand over his heart.

Karthik drew Mrs. Chang aside.

"Auntie Mon—nica—"

"Don't you gang up on me, boy," she said. "I lost my baby once already, and I'm not about to lose her again. You choose her side this time and you will lose."

He sighed and took her hand. "L—let me t—take her home. If she n—needs anything, I'll be right across the hall. Maybe I can even pull a few strings d——down at the police station and get us an armed guard."

Mrs. Chang looked doubtful.

"Please, Auntie Monica. We only just got her back. *Our* Lenci, n—not that emptied out shell that dropped back into our l—lives earlier this year. Maybe staying at home will give her the stability she needs to d——deal with everything."

Monica briefly pondered the possibility.

"Don't pull any strings at the police station," she said, at length. "It's probably better if you lie low. Police presence would draw attention."

That was all the permission Karthik needed. He gave Mrs. Chang a squeeze as a silent thank you.

"Bring her by the hotel tomorrow morning for breakfast," she said.

"Okay," he grinned. "Ready to go home, Lenci?"

Lenci lingered for a moment, her hand still over her little brother's heart.

Then, as if coming out of a trance, she turned calmly and replied, "Yes, let's go."

After embracing their mothers, the two friends trudged down the hall to the parking elevators. Karthik's jeep was not far from the exit. They both looked in through the windows before getting in, but Lenci did not bother checking the underside of the car.

"He did this to break me," she said as Karthik backed the jeep out of the parking stall. "And he might have. He just might have."

Karthik glanced down at her scarred legs, then turned his eyes back to the road without saying anything. He wanted to ask her about the scars, but he wouldn't—not now. And for that, she was very grateful.

The rest of their ride was silent. For the Agent, the past day or two had been a blur—the reminder of a mission that she had well forgotten, the news that the Killer had come for her, the fall of her sponsor organization, the death of her dear handler, and the news about Lorenzo, all bringing into focus one horrid realization that happened over and over and would not stop. If she wanted her loved ones to be safe, she had to stay away from them. She could not have the life that had made her come alive.

A void that had once been filled with the details of survival plans—and which had, of late, been filled with the mundane joys of civilian life—finally presented itself for what it was. This emptiness was an invasive macrophage of nothing. It ate into every part of the Agent's self, every thought, every emotion, and it would not stop until she was completely hollowed out.

When she and Karthik arrived at the apartments, they paused in the space between their entryways, enveloped by a familiar and comforting feeling. This was the feeling they felt after every adventure they ever came back from, the feeling of reluctantly parting ways so that they could dream up their next adventure. The corners of Lenci's mouth turned upward slightly. She noticed a small echo of her smile resounding in Karthik's eyes.

"I—" Karthik was startled by the sound of his own voice. He began again in a lower volume, "Would you l–like to come in? Just for a while?"

Lenci let her hand fall away from the handle of her front door. The apartment would be eerily empty. And although she had been hoping to spend the evening scrubbing every area of the apartment, fresh paint on the walls and mopping the kitchen floor could not clean up the blood that was on her hands.

She sighed. "Okay. Yeah."

Her friend nodded, turned the key in the lock, and pushed open the door. The Wilsons' apartment was quiet. Without asking, the Agent went straight to the shower where she washed off all of the ash, sweat, and blood of her failed mission. Then, she went to Karthik's spotless, well-organized room and found some sweatpants and a T-shirt to wear. Lenci paused briefly to admire a photo at his bedside, a photo of their families at Fairwaves Beach some years ago. She could not recall the details of that trip, but she deduced from her and Karthik's snaggle-toothed smiles that they must have been about seven years old. That was the year of the Non-Violence Pact.

Dear, dear, mature Ethan. The pact had to have been his idea, given the way she tended to resolve conflicts. He had always been at work, helping Lenci to be a better version of herself. The Agent touched the face of the boy in the photograph before placing it back on the bedside table.

She returned to the living room. Karthik was sitting on the couch and, when he saw her, motioned for her to take a seat anywhere. She chose the loveseat next to the couch.

One thing Lenci had always appreciated about her friendship with Karthik was that they could just be. They never had to make up awkward conversations for politeness' sake. If neither of them had anything to say, they would say nothing. And so, that night, they said nothing because there was nothing to say.

She breathed deeply. There was something about the musky fragrance of those raggedy couches that soothed her. This apartment had become like a second home to her, but she could not escape the feeling that, very soon, she'd have to become someone else again. Someone who had no home, someone who was no one at all.

A sob broke her reflection. It appeared that Karthik could no longer contain his emotion over the evening's events. He brought a hand to his mouth to try not to disturb her, but she had already noticed.

She felt so empty, but of what she was missing, he was so full. Crawling over the arm of the loveseat, she slid onto the sofa next to him and stared at his tears as they flowed down his face unhindered, free. Then, against what the Agent would have deemed good judgment, she pressed her lips to his cheek. As she did so, one small tear ran down her face, and she did not attempt to hide it.

Karthik was no longer the spindly teen that Lenci had left behind to join Sopient Solutions, Incorporated. This proved something of an obstacle as she realized she could not stretch her arm around his shoulders in the way she had been able before he had joined the police force. She settled for wrapping her arms around his waist and resting her head on his shoulder.

She could feel his every shuddering breath and hiccup thronging through her. Perhaps comforted by his willingness to feel what she could not allow herself to feel, she drifted into the most peaceful rest she had had in a long while.

**

The next morning, Karthik awoke to find that he and Lenci had indeed spent the entire night on the couch. They seemed to have slid sideways during the night. Though slightly astonished, he was comforted by the warmth of their closeness, a closeness which they had shared throughout their childhood.

Lenci's head still lay on his shoulder and her right arm was somewhere under his back. Her belly bump pushed softly against his abdomen as she breathed, and her left hand rested on his chest. The dark purple bruise that ran around the middle of her hand and the phantom mark of a wedding band on her ring finger caused a pang of sadness in his heart. These tempted him to believe that there was no escaping the past. There were so very many factors he could not control—try as he might—for his best friend's good.

After a while, Lenci stirred and opened her eyes. Her satisfied expression from having gotten a decent night's sleep was quickly replaced with a look of horror.

She bolted upright. "Oh, no! Oh, no, no, no."

"What?" Karthik sat up, too.

"What did we *do*?" She catapulted off of him, feeling her borrowed sweatpants as she went.

She seemed to calm down when she realized that the twisted waist was still tied tightly. He instinctively felt for his belt buckle but shook his head to clear his thoughts.

"Nothing," he replied with certainty. "Pretty sure I would have remembered if—"

"I have to go!"

"Lenci—"

She was out the door before he could stop her. Sighing, he ran his hands through his hair, grabbed a couple of fistfuls of curls, and lay back to stare at the ceiling.

He was unable to reach her by phone for the rest of the morning, so he ended up going alone to meet their mothers at the hotel.

"Lenci wasn't feeling well this morning," he told them. "So, she's resting, but she sends her love."

"She ran out on you, didn't she?" Monica smiled wryly. "I was afraid of that."

"Oh, Monica," Preeti said. "Don't be upset."

"I drove around to all of her regular spots, even to the gym," Karthik said. "I don't think she wants to be found right now."

He avoided bringing up the possibility that she had left for good.

"I knew I shouldn't have let her out of my sight!" Monica brought a hand to her head. "What will I tell Kingston?"

"A lot has happened," Preeti said, taking her hand gently. "No one blames you, and Kingston certainly will not. Lenci is an adult woman now. She makes decisions for herself. These kids, they are intelligent and good-hearted. We must hold them with open hands."

Having waited for a safe space to bring up an idea, Karthik took his chance, "Please hear me out on this, Auntie Mon—nica. I have a police buddy who owes me a favor. He has a friend who can arrange for a medical transport t–to get you and Renzo and my mom down to your place in Sandland—just while Renzo recovers. Then, you can all return to Windsailing t–together."

"I guess there's no point in staying here if the trigger-prompt therapy is no longer needed," Monica said slowly.

"But what about you, Karthik?" Preeti asked. "You broke your lease so that you could move into that old apartment with me. Will you be able to find something before the end of the month?"

"I can check and see if my old place is still available," he replied. "Anyway, my priority is getting you to a safe place. If Lenci comes back, I'll let you know. But will you please go?"

"Okay," Monica said. "I'll take them down to Sandland. And you take this, Karthik."

She handed him a balled up towel. When he opened it, he saw it contained shards of glass covered in what appeared to be dried blood. He looked at her inquisitively.

"At one point, Chandler told me that they needed recent blood samples from Lenci. I couldn't bring myself to turn these in at the time, but now—"

He didn't need her to finish the thought that she was heartbroken and did not know any longer if the young woman who had been with them was indeed her daughter; that she couldn't bear not to know; that she still hoped against hope that that young woman was her Lenci.

So, the two mothers each embraced Karthik and said goodbye. The next day, Preeti, Monica, and Lorenzo traveled to Monica's property in Sandland. Karthik resumed his role as a patrolling officer at Canon Police Department. The world was returning to the empty normal to which they had become accustomed in recent years. Just like that, their precious Lenci had dropped into their lives and out again—not seamlessly but effortlessly. And that, perhaps, was what hurt above all.

Chapter 28

A FEW DAYS LATER, Lenci and Racky were sitting across from each other in the living room of Theresa's two-bedroom rambler. The room was fairly dark, save for a patch of afternoon sun that shone in through the screen at the front entrance. Every window that had a curtain was covered.

"Isn't it strange that Theresa left her door unlocked?" Lenci asked, slurping a spoonful of soggy cereal from a bowl that sat in her lap.

"She's probably not coming back," Racky replied. "SSI is a pile of rocks. It would make sense to be in the wind by now, Circus."

"I know," Lenci sighed. "But I couldn't leave without paying my respects."

"You're not really going to Agent Bourghin's grave in broad daylight, are you?"

"I saw the obit in yesterday's paper. The service finished at 1300 today. If I can get a cab to wait for me, I can be back here by 1700 for a short dinner and 'in the wind' by 1730. Will you be here?"

"I'll have to be, but—"

Lenci shushed her and motioned toward the front door. A car was pulling up in front of the house. It was Karthik's jeep. And it was too late to close the door. So, the women dropped to the floor and crawled into the hall to get out of sight.

"Hell–lo?" Karthik called from the porch. "T–Theresa Cravenly? Hello?"

Cravenly? Lenci looked at Racky. Racky shrugged.

Karthik cleared his throat. "My n—name is Lieutenant Wilson. I'm a friend of your coworker Rackelle? She's gone missing, see. Your gym manager didn't seem to know much, but when he heard I worked for the Canon Police D——Department, he gave me your address t—to see if you might be able to help."

Racky motioned toward the door. He was trying the handle on the screen.

"D—do you mind if I step in for a moment?" he was saying.

"Go talk to him," Lenci mouthed.

Racky shook her head emphatically.

Lenci nodded equally emphatically and began to push her toward the entryway. Racky wriggled back, and the two had a frantic, wordless exchange after which Lenci fluffed Racky's hair and pulled her camisole straps off of her shoulders.

"Element of surprise," she whispered. "Get him out of here."

Racky glared at her, then shouted, "Wait a minute! I'm coming!"

She bounded around the corner just in time to intercept Karthik in the small entryway. She pulled up her camisole straps with the kind of agitation that couldn't be faked.

Lenci stifled a laugh.

"Oh!" Karthik said, sounding terribly embarrassed. "Racky! What are you d—doing here?"

"Uh, well," Racky stammered, "I was actually searching out Theresa, too. I hadn't seen her in a while. So, I came here to see what was going on."

There was an awkward pause.

"And I have been staying here—to wait for her."

"Oh."

The Agent's heart leapt into her throat because the emptiness in Karthik's voice sounded too much like the emptiness inside of herself, an emptiness that she had never intended for him to experience.

"Sorry I disappeared," Racky said abruptly. "I saw on the news about Lorenzo."

"He'll be okay. My mom and his are staying in Sandl—land until he's stable enough t—to go back to Windsailing, so—" He dropped off.

"So," Racky said slowly, "Why are you here, again?"

"Oh, uh, I came here t—to ask Th—theresa if she'd seen you. The manager, uh, Bread? Said you two were pretty close."

"Bread!" Racky laughed. "Lenci calls him that, too."

His voice brightened immediately. "You've seen Lenci?"

239

"Not of late. I meant she *used* to call him that," Racky said. "Let's talk on the porch where there's more light and air. It's kind of stuffy in here."

The hinges on the screen creaked as she shoved him through the doorway.

"N—no, I d——didn't think you would have," he said glumly. "Seen Lenci, I mean. Well, since I ended up finding you after all, I guess I should give you this. Auntie Monica was th—thinking about giving it to you before, but she couldn't bring herself t—to, you know——"

Lenci heard something that sounded like glass wrapped in fabric drop onto the porch.

"Oh, my," Racky said, her voice rising to a near squeak. "For my glass garden? That's right decent and genuinely thoughtful of her!"

"Glass garden?" Karthik repeated.

After a moment, he said hurriedly, "Oh, right. The junkyard d—— decorations you t—told us about. Yes, Auntie Monica saw them and thought of you. Um, anyways——"

It was fortunate that Karthik could be rather emotionally obtuse at times—the Agent thought—because any other investigator might have noticed that Racky was hiding something. But anyway, the conversation had turned away from Lenci, so what did she care if Karthik wanted to chat about glass gardens?

"Karthik," Racky was saying, "I can't accept this. See, SSI assigned me to spend time with your family so Lenci would have a connection to the agency, but these kinds of gifts are really not what it's about."

"But I——let me explain——"

"I got a new number," Racky interrupted. "How about we exchange info, so I can message you if I happen to see Lenci?"

The Agent smiled. She took her chance to sneak out of one of the bedroom windows. It seemed that Racky had everything under control. But she had some explaining to do about that glass garden. The Agent wondered what on earth kind of benefit could come from having a glass garden and why Racky hadn't ever shown it to her during her many visits.

***

It was 1600 when Lenci's taxi pulled into the cemetery. After studying a map of the place, she asked the driver to take her to the hill directly across from the one where Agent Bourghin was buried. The sun was still up, but it was beginning to move behind the row of eucalyptus trees that marked the far boundary of the grounds. The trees cast long shadows over the grassy hills.

"Hey, lady," the driver said, "you sure you want to be walking around here by yourself?"

"It's not the ones that are dead and buried that we have to worry about, friend," she replied. "Please stay here. I'll be about five minutes, and then I'll need a ride back."

"Just be careful, alright?"

He gave her an uneasy glance as she heaved herself up and out of the back seat. She smiled at him through the window, then turned and ambled down the grassy hill.

At the foot of Samir's hill, she stopped, suddenly filled with dread. She had come to pay her respects and say goodbye, but now she wasn't sure that she could. She convinced herself that she must be allowing the taxi driver's apprehension to get to her.

"We *will* be careful," she said, patting her belly bump through the blousy fabric of her maternity tank top. "Won't we, Kiddo?"

The baby responded to her touch by kicking back at her hand. Feeling reassured, Lenci fixed her eyes on the balloons affixed to the grave next to Samir's and marched up the hill.

Her heart and her feet turned to lead as she approached her handler's grave. Upon seeing his name carved on the headstone, she buckled at the knees and knelt in front of it on the dirt that would one day become grassy and uniform with the rest of the lawn.

"Here lies Lieutenant Colonel Samir Bourghin, faithful soldier, husband, uncle, friend—" Her voice faltered.

She needed to get a handle on her emotions. She attempted to steady her voice as she added to the list on the tombstone in a croak, "And—and handler."

When the word came out of her mouth, she knew that she would not be able to finish reading the rest of the epitaph. She grabbed both sides of the headstone and touched her forehead to the name it bore.

"I honor you!" she whispered. "I honor you because you saw me with compassion from the beginning to the very end. And I will honor you by being the agent you knew Lenci could be, that you strove to help me to become. If only you knew—"

She suddenly felt self-conscious about kneeling in the dirt and talking to a stone.

"I feel so lost!" she concluded forlornly.

Kiddo moved inside of her, and it was only then that the Agent became aware that they were not alone. She pushed down the oncoming rush of anxiety and addressed the newcomer.

"We can make this a four-way conversation, but as my center of gravity has recently shifted, I'll need a little help—if you wouldn't mind."

Using her left hand to maintain her balance, she lifted her right into the air as an invitation. A small, strong hand gripped the Agent's and pulled her to a standing position.

"Your Hindi is very good," the newcomer said.

Lenci did not realize until that point that she had not been speaking English. She turned around. The stranger was a short, caramel-colored woman in her fifties. Her black and gray hair was pulled back into a low bun, which added to the severity of her angular jaw and stern gaze. Despite only having seen her once before, Lenci knew who this stranger was, and she was no stranger at all.

"Dr. Bourghin!" she exclaimed, her voice cracking as she jolted back into English. "I didn't know you spoke Hindi?"

"Urdu, for my husband," Dr. Bourghin replied. "I speak Spanish with my family of origin, though. Samir's service was hours ago, and I did not see you here."

"I wanted to attend," Lenci said. "I was one of his students at the Air Force Academy, so I wouldn't have missed it for the world, really. It's just that I had a familial conflict that I needed to work out."

"I know who you are, Valencia Thomas," the older woman said. "And I know that you were with my husband the night he passed away."

"I keep going over every detail of that night," Lenci said, swallowing the lump in her throat. "I wanted to keep him from harm, but I let him down."

Dr. Bourghin grabbed her hand and squeezed it. "Don't you dare! Samir saw you as a daughter. And especially since we never had little ones of our own, you meant a great deal to him."

Lenci dropped her head.

"He was always raving about this girl," Dr. Bourghin continued, raising Lenci's face. "'She has such potential, honey! Honey, do you know she leg pressed three hundred and sixty-two kilos today? Honey, do you know she recited, from her brilliant memory, *all* of the postal codes of the Western States this afternoon? Honey, do you know my kiddo Lenci is a little knucklehead, always getting in fights with trainees much larger than herself? She's such a ram—'"

"Rambunctious young lady," Lenci finished with her, smiling a little.

The older woman smiled as well. "So, there. We'll have no more of this guilt business. You know why my Samir put himself in harm's way? He did it so that you could have a fighting chance. Now, you remember *that* before you do anything rash."

As Samir's wife turned to walk away, Lenci called after her, "Dr. Bourghin!"

"Esperanza."

"Esperanza." Lenci felt comforted just saying the name. "I *will* honor your husband's memory. I'll make sure that he didn't die in vain."

"Don't you understand?" the older woman replied. "You already have."

Dr. Bourghin left Lenci perplexed by the graveside and walked up over the side of the hill. Lenci remained, stroking her belly for a while, wondering what possible purpose there could be in Agent Bourghin's life having been traded for hers. At last, still not having come to any clear conclusion, she bent and kissed the headstone.

"I won't let you down; I promise you that."

Then, she went her way, down the hill and up the next, back to where the taxi was waiting.

After fighting through rush hour traffic, the taxi dropped Lenci off a couple of blocks away from Theresa's house. She enjoyed the short walk, making a game of tapping her belly and seeing how quickly Kiddo would react. When she reached the house, she found a silver sedan parked in front.

With a pounding heart and shallow breath, the Agent climbed the porch steps and knocked. Racky opened the door and welcomed her with a smile. Behind her, Theresa sat on the couch with her signature scowl.

"Look here, Lenci!" Racky said excitedly. "Theresa came back and she wants to join us for our last hurrah dinner!"

"Great." Lenci did not do a very good job of sounding excited.

"Well," Theresa said in her monotone, "at least I won't ever have to see you again. Let's get this party started."

"Aren't you guys heading out, too?" Lenci asked.

Theresa shrugged. "Racky said it'll take another few days to get us set up with new identities for international travel."

"I could change things in the system easy," Racky said. "But getting physical ID cards and passports has been difficult since SSI collapsed. All my regular contacts have gone underground."

"Besides," Theresa said, "I don't know about you, but as a free agent, I actually wouldn't mind looking into *why* our very healthy and successful agency suddenly collapsed. And sticking around here might lead me to some clues. You know what I mean, Lenci?"

"On second thought, no party necessary. We could just say goodbye right here," Lenci said, walking down the steps.

"And miss out on an evening of fun and excitement?" Theresa skipped after her. "Not for the world!"

"Don't let her bend you out of shape, Circus," Racky said.

Chapter 29

RACKY DROVE THEM TO A PLACE that Lenci had suggested in the Philemon borough. For the whole ride, Lenci sat in the passenger's seat, watching Theresa in the side-mirror. Theresa preened smugly for Lenci as though she enjoyed being watched.

"You sure this is the place, Circus?" Racky asked, gazing with some uncertainty at the time-eroded storefront with a crooked sign that read: **Indigo Jazze**.

"Being naturally unclassified like myself, you should know not to judge a book by its cover," Lenci responded. "And yes, I'm sure. Didn't you know that jazz spelled with an 'e' makes it classier? It might even be pronounced 'jazzay.'"

Theresa snorted. "Figures you'd bring us to a dump like this. Couldn't we have gone to Resplendent Oaks or somewhere trendy?"

Side-glancing her indignantly, Racky opened the door and motioned them in. "If it's a special place for you, Circus, then I'm glad we are coming here for your *last night with us.*"

Theresa shuffled in behind Lenci who was already asking the hostess for a booth in one of the quieter alcoves.

Racky shoved past them both and tapped the hostess' shoulder. "Actually, we already got a table. One of our party is already seated. We will find our way, but could you please get us some menus?"

Astonished by Racky's abruptness, the hostess wordlessly handed them each a menu and stood aside as they made their way into the restaurant. The jazz quartet that was to provide entertainment that evening began their act with an upbeat tune.

"One of our party?" Lenci whispered to Racky. "What are you not telling me?"

Before Racky could answer, they rounded a corner, and Lenci saw the additional invitee. She immediately drew back around the corner, dragging Racky with her.

"You *told* him I'm leaving?"

"Of course I didn't," Racky said. "I told him that I had seen you. You would have regretted it if I hadn't. And at least *you* know that this is goodbye. So, just—say goodbye."

Lenci opened her mouth to protest, but Racky stared her down.

"Okay," she said. "I'll do it. I'll say goodbye."

"Good," Racky said, patting Lenci's shoulder. "Because he already saw us, and it would have been in poor taste for you to turn and walk out. Plus, Theresa looks like she's moving on in."

And indeed she did. She had positioned herself next to Karthik in the booth. He was politely chatting with her, but he expectantly glanced toward the entrance every so often. When Lenci and Racky emerged from around the corner, his face lit up, and he waved energetically.

"Your friend Ethan is so pleasant," Theresa said as Lenci and Racky sat down across from them. "And his speech impediment is adorable."

"Ethan," Lenci repeated, piqued by the usage of his middle name.

"Yes, it's the n—name my mother gave me," he replied.

Her eyes narrowed. "Don't use that uppity tone with me, *Ethan*. Us common folks who doesn't have access to the same *choices* you do'll have a hard time understanding."

"You have some nerve. I was worried sick!"

"Sick is better than murdered on your kitchen floor."

"And you know what's better for me?"

Racky cleared her throat. "Maybe we will let you two work this out. Theresa, want to see what they have for drinks at the bar?"

"Oh, no," Theresa smirked. "I'm quite enjoying this."

"Theresa!"

"It's okay," Lenci said frostily. "We were just about done. Weren't we, *Ethan*?"

He sighed. "I have n—nothing more t—to say."

"Good," she said. "You were invited here because I'll be leaving soon. So, let's just have a good time."

"Hear, hear!" Theresa said, pounding the table a little too animatedly. "About having a good time, of course."

She smiled slyly at Karthik who turned his eyes toward Lenci pleadingly. He looked so helpless and sad, squished between Theresa and the wall. And the expression on his face, that annoyance with a hint of terror, was one that tugged on her heart. Though taller and more muscular, Karthik was in many ways the same boy with whom Lenci had grown up—from the fact that he was uncomfortable when someone flirted with him right down to the fact that he was insecure about his heritage.

Lenci grinned in spite of herself. Karthik smiled as well, seeming to relax a little, although he continued to lean as far away from Theresa as possible.

When the server came, Racky ordered a Tequila Sunrise. Theresa ordered a Bloody Mary. Karthik ordered a coffee, and Lenci ordered a lemon-lime soda with a cherry.

"She's pregnant," Racky apologized as the server gave Lenci a judgmental glance in response to her drink choice.

"And he's a police officer," Lenci explained, motioning to a bewildered Karthik.

The server shook her head mutely and trudged away to put in the drink order.

The next hour or so was actually fairly pleasant. Everyone got along well together. Theresa made an insensitive or crude comment here or there, but the other three settled into a decent pattern of letting those utterances pass without engagement. They shared a large platter of chili cheese fries with lots of jalapeños and onions. Kiddo liked the chili cheese fries—or, Lenci assumed that must be the case, considering the baby's prolonged happy dance after she'd finished her first plate.

Karthik looked happier and more at peace, and Racky was having a good time, too. This was how Lenci wanted to remember them. It was a beautiful way to say goodbye. But she knew that all things beautiful could not remain so forever, and this beautiful goodbye suddenly took an ugly turn.

"So, Lenci," Theresa said with a mischievous glint in her eye, "now that our gig with SSI is over, why don't you tell us about your role in its downfall? You left the Killer knowing that you were going to bring down your home agency, didn't you?"

"Theresa!" Racky hissed. "There is a *civilian* at the table."

"Well, that isn't ent–tirely true, but I get the point," Karthik said, attempting to stand. "Covert agencies are contracted by the government and accountable to no one, so my police officer ears don't need to hear this. I'll just go t—to the restroom while you finish up your d—discussion."

Theresa moved closer to him so that is was impossible for him to get past her.

"Um, excuse me," he said, struggling to remain polite.

"Excused." She didn't budge.

"Theresa, stop being rude. Let him pass," Racky implored.

Theresa chuckled. "I guess he's just going to have to force me. Isn't that how efficient women get it done, Agent Thomas?"

"Th—thomas?" Karthik echoed, still awkwardly half-standing.

Racky grabbed Lenci by the wrist before she could lunge across the table. Her grip was tight but more beseeching than prohibitive. The Agent tried not to look at the various utensils, glasses, and other objects that littered the table. Each represented a unique and interesting way to cause bodily harm. That was what she had been taught to see, what had become second nature for her to see, what she wished she could not see.

Fists balled and arms tense, she growled, "If you think I don't have ways to incapacitate you from my current position, you're wrong. Now, let him pass or you will spend the next six months learning to walk again."

Theresa seemed pleased to have gotten this reaction out of her. Without another word, she slid out of the booth and allowed Karthik to exit as well. She smiled coyly at him as he excused himself and hurried off toward the men's room.

Taking her seat once again, Theresa folded her hands on the table and said, "Okay, let's start with an easier question: What exactly *did* you do with the Killer? Did you have a role *besides* 'whore?'"

The Agent bristled at that word but remained silent.

"What is this?" Racky asked. "An interrogation?"

Theresa shrugged. "Months ago, Blair said that there were WCE operatives among us. Our subdivision was suspected to have been infiltrated. I can't imagine who else she could have been talking about."

The Agent's eyes were glued to her in a cold, analytical stare. In all honesty, she could not remember if she had left the Killer intending to bring down SSI. She liked to think not, especially since she had gone to the trouble of trying to help the director to know that she was compromised. Admittedly, though, she had seemed to have conflicting goals at some points along the way. Theresa's interest in the matter was not surprising. However, her boldness in this sudden interrogation was.

"I'm just saying," Racky said, "even though SSI no longer exists, it is not productive at this point—"

"Actually, Racky, it's okay," the Agent named Lenci said, still staring at their pre-teammate.

She saw an opportunity to bend this interrogation in her favor.

"Theresa thrives on drama," she explained to Racky, "because she craves excitement in her otherwise dull life. So, we can only expect her to pry for details of a life she hasn't known. You see, she hoped in vain—once upon a time—that the Killer might choose her to work one-on-one with him at the Academy. Isn't that right, Theresa?"

Oh, the things she could remember when the situation called for it! That was possibly a partial memory gleaned from Academy reports, but she gambled on it, and the risk was worth it.

A hint of pink appeared in Theresa's cheeks, but recognizing that she had hooked Lenci into her game, she masked her embarrassment with a saucy smile.

"Without you there to seduce him into choosing you, he *would* have chosen me."

"Counterfactual," Lenci said dismissively.

Theresa's eyes began to gleam. "So you admit that you seduced him?"

"He taught me to find people's weak points and exploit them," Lenci replied. "I just learned the tactics he taught me and used them against him."

"Yes, well, seems likes his tactics worked fairly well on you, too." Theresa nodded judgmentally downward in acknowledgement of Kiddo.

Lenci crossed her arms and said, "No one is immune."

"True among weak-minded fools," Theresa said scornfully.

"Is that so?" Lenci asked.

Theresa sniffed. "Well, if I were a guy, your parlor tricks wouldn't work on me."

Motivated partially by pride but mostly by a desire for information, Lenci took a moment to make a few mental calculations.

"I could break you in sixty seconds," she said.

"No way!" Racky burst out.

"Sure could," Lenci replied, staring coolly into her drink. "But that kind of stuff is dangerous. Shouldn't do it unless there's simply no other option."

"What a load of BS!" Theresa said. "Just like everything else about you. Bourghin might have sung your praises, but you're nothing but a fraud."

Lenci's eyes blazed. "You accept, then?"

Theresa's face dripped with contempt, but she said nothing.

"Good." Lenci put down her drink and stood up.

"Give us a some room, Racky," she said softly, not breaking eye contact with her target.

Her pre-teammate hurriedly popped out of the booth to let her pass. The sound of Racky's analog watch clacking onto the table for easier viewing soon followed. The jazz quartet was taking a break, and over the cocktail chatter around them, Lenci could hear the watch ticking.

TICK *TICK* Domination was Theresa's game, so the Agent had to stay above her. Leaning with one arm on the table and the other on the backrest of the booth, she erased all traces of a smile from her lips. Theresa was the type that criticized jokes and fun. A teasing enticement was not the way to get under her skin.

"Sixty seconds to prove you're not weak-minded," Lenci said. "Just, whatever you do, don't look down my shirt."

She broke their locked gaze to wink at Racky and pull up the slouching neckline of her maternity tank top. The fabric immediately began to recede to its original position, rippling in a way that accentuated the fullness of her breasts. *TICK* *TICK*

"This is so dumb," Theresa pouted.

Her eyes fluttered, though, indicating that she was uncomfortable. That was a good start.

"I'll tell you what's dumb," Lenci said. "I told you *not* to look down my shirt, and you can't seem *not* to do it!"

She lifted Theresa's chin to make her meet her gaze. *TICK* *TICK* Theresa scoffed and turned away.

"I haven't even asked any questions, yet," Lenci said. "Talk about weak! Is that what they taught you at the Academy? I guess, contrary to what *my* mentors taught me, cowardice is a great defense mechanism."

Theresa's head snapped back toward her interrogator. She said nothing, but her fierce glare and heavy breathing declared her full engagement of the interrogation. Still, though rattled, she had not rid her face of its resting contemptuous smirk. *TICK* *TICK*

Lenci knew that Theresa's world was one of comparison. Theresa felt confident as long as she believed herself to be better than those around her, but that confidence would wane if the right kind of pressure were applied. And in the space created by the shrinkage of confidence, there would be room to maneuver.

So, Lenci mirrored Theresa's contempt but replaced the dismissive aspect of it with intense focus. After all, between jealousy and attraction, she knew there to be a fine line. It was time to find that line.

She did not break eye contact and leaned in until she could feel the heat radiating from Theresa's body.

"You were the top trainee in the Academy, weren't you, Theresa?"

Theresa continued to glare into her eyes.

"Yes," she answered with a tight jaw.

"But it wasn't enough for you, was it? You wanted the Killer's attention."

Theresa did not say anything, but Lenci could see that her pupils were dilated. This was a touchy topic for her, so it would be a soft entry point from which to make room for the real question.

"You didn't know me, but you wanted what I had, didn't you?" she said, cocking her head to the side in mock-sympathy, a gesture she knew Theresa frequently put to use. "Is *that* why you hate me so much?"

Theresa did not answer the question. Most of her energy seemed to be spent on keeping eye contact with her. Noticing that Theresa's eyes had begun to wander to her shirt again, Lenci put her hand under Theresa's chin and raised her face, this time leaning in until their noses were on the verge of touching. Theresa's breathing had become quick and shallow, almost drowned out by the *TICK* *TICK* of Racky's watch.

Lenci's hair brushed lightly against Theresa's face as she hovered there, with her soft, full lips only a couple of centimeters away from her pre-teammate's open and quivering mouth.

"I get it," she whispered, letting her breath mingle with Theresa's short, hot puffs of air. She allowed a sensible smile to grace her lips and continued in a quiet, sympathetic tone, "It's *not* hate, is it?"

Sensing movement, Lenci pulled back but not quickly enough. Theresa's mouth latched onto hers instinctively yet passionately. The Agent, not wanting to appear flustered, pushed Theresa's lips off with her own. Brushing away the slimy feeling that plagued her whenever she used her body as a tool in such a way, she grinned with all of the disdain she could muster.

"As I said, 'no one is immune.'"

Racky's laughter rang out over the music, which had only recently restarted.

"Woo!" She gasped for breath. "Oo, Theresa, girl, I did *not* know you swang that way!"

Theresa's eyes widened in surprise and anger since she had just apparently 'swang' in a way that had been hitherto unprecedented in her experience. This was the Agent's chance.

"Are you working for the WCE?" she asked.

Racky's laughter halted at this turn in the discussion. The sudden force of the question caught Theresa off guard.

Her eyes fluttered as she stuttered, "W—what? I—um—no! Of course not? What are you talking about?"

Stuttering, questions, fake indignation, et cetera. So, Theresa was not currently a WCE agent, but she *was* in the process of becoming one or had been courted by the WCE at some point.

"I know you reported my pregnancy," the Agent accused. "The night you called a 'pizza joint,' who did you *really* call?"

Theresa had already mostly regained her composure. All emotion had drained from her face. She *was* good.

But the Agent, encouraged by her non-answer, threw out bait. "Was it the Vice?"

There was a tiny spark in Theresa's eyes. It was not much, possibly just recognition of a title she had heard before, but probably more.

"Vice?" Theresa's voice took on its typical scornful tone. "Like the Vice President? Agent Thomas, what delusions of grandeur you *must* have if you think you're important enough for the Vice President to send a sniper to punish you as a miscegenist."

Interestingly, she seemed to interpret Gomez's execution as a fate intended for Lenci, a mistake. But the Killer never made that kind of mistake.

"The Vice President d—did *what?*"

Karthik was standing awkwardly beside the table. He shifted uncomfortably.

"It was a joke." Lenci shrugged. "Theresa was making a funny."

"Yes, I'm so funny," Theresa said coyly.

"You don't fool me," Lenci told her.

"Just like you can't fool us," Theresa replied grandly. "At least, not after I do a manual test from *this*."

Lenci glanced at the bundle Theresa produced from her handbag.

252

She didn't need a reminder of where she had previously seen those shards of bloody glass and the towel that enshrouded them. Her hand still ached occasionally.

"Damn it, Karthik!" Racky exclaimed. "We are not SSI anymore, and we do *not* want that."

His brow wrinkled. "While we were waiting for you, Theresa t——told me she was Lenci's other pre-teammate. And she said you guys d—*did* want it."

"I did say that," Theresa agreed proudly. "We want it as proof."

"No, we do *not!*" Racky insisted.

"And that bundle proves what?" Lenci said, doing her best to ignore the feeling of a knife in her back. "That the people closest to me don't trust me?"

She looked at Karthik, who looked at the floor.

Theresa, delighted by the direction of this conversation, was eager for a chance to twist the knife.

"Well, it *would* prove nothing except when paired with this hair." She held up a long lock of black, curly hair. "Hair from your—what did you say it was, Ethan? Ah, yes, your Non-Violence Pact. We'll test these two things against each other, and *that* could prove plenty."

"Why would you give her that?" Lenci asked Karthik.

"Maybe t——to prove that you're not the fraud they think you are?" He met her gaze. "T—to get all of these people who are hunting you off your t—tail? You know, to *help* you?"

She looked at him imploringly. "You could *ask* me what would be helpful. You know, help me on *my* terms?"

"Generally speaking, your t—terms have included my getting beat up or my complete n—non-involvement."

Lenci sighed. "There is just so much going on here that you can't understand."

"Only because you won't l—let me in on it!"

No, you could never understand the world of sopients and hypnotics and Amphibians. You could never understand the power of deception or the true bliss of ignorance. You could never wrap your mind around the idea of a soldier made to replace the weak things of this world with strength, a manufactured substitute so real that the real thing is undone.

"Fine," she said. "If you want to know so bad, I'll tell you: I'm not Valencia Thomas, and I'm not Valencia Chang."

Karthik looked cut to the heart. "You *would* say that t—to get rid of me."

"You can apparently take a hint, so why aren't you gone?"

"You d—don't have to ask me that t——twice," he said, slapping a bill onto the table to cover his coffee. "Goodbye, whoever you are! I hope you have a n—nice l—life."

At least you'll have a life. The Agent stared after him as he marched out the door. When he was gone, she turned her gaze back to her pre-teammates.

"I bet you also killed Reece," Theresa said, ready to ramp up again. "And you disappeared him so that other fake agent could take his place, is that it? And then you killed him, too! And then, pretended he was Reece!"

The Agent, knowing that she was being baited and not having the energy to engage, just shook her head.

Theresa continued, "If *you* could best Reece, then I guess he got what was coming to him."

"That is just nasty, Theresa!" Racky exclaimed. "Can't you show some respect for a fellow classmate?"

"I have no respect for people who ranked below me on the aptitude tests," Theresa said haughtily.

Then, glancing at the Agent, she added, "Or people who weren't ranked at all."

"Classless," Racky said, shaking her head.

"I think Lenci prefers the term 'naturally subclass,'" Theresa smirked. "Excuse me. I'm going to see if there's a decent little girls' room in this hellhole."

"I like this place," Racky mumbled as she walked away. "It's better on the inside than it looked on the outside."

Lenci offered her a tiny smile of gratitude, but her mind was racing with the possibilities that their conversation had produced. Theresa definitely had ties to the WCE, and her gloating about Reece made the Agent wonder if perhaps she knew more about the suspicious circumstances of his death than she had originally let on. Even so, Theresa did not seem to know about the more significant connection that Lenci and Reece had once shared.

Racky's voice jolted Lenci from her thoughts. "You won't try that tomfoolery on me, right? If there is anything you want to know, all you have to do is ask!"

She was talking about the interrogation.

"Don't worry," Lenci said. "It only works on the weak-minded."

Then, a mischievous spark igniting in her eyes, she hooked Racky's neckline with her fingertip and snapped it playfully. "But I could give it a shot if you *really* want me to!"

Racky screeched incredulously, and both women began to laugh.

"Get the hell away from me with that!" Racky giggled. She put a protective hand over her sternum and declared, "These tidbits are off limits."

"Noted," Lenci nodded, throwing back her head to finish the rest of her drink. "Also, are you wearing *two* bras?"

"One is a bikini top," her friend replied. "It actually holds the girls. The bra is just for storage and for show. It's authentic faux chain mail."

Lenci wondered why on earth Racky would make a habit of showing her bra to anyone, even if it *was* authentic faux chain mail, but Theresa came back before she could ask.

"Well, this has been fun," Theresa said. "But I think I've had my fill of fun."

"Right," Lenci agreed. "Me too. Let's get you guys back to Theresa's place. Since you both had drinks, I'll drive."

"You'd do that for us?" Theresa asked.

"*Some* folks in this world have a sense of decency," Racky said.

Theresa put the bundle of glass shards back into her handbag. "Yeah, I just didn't expect *her* to be one of them."

Chapter 30

THERESA SCREAMED BLOODY MURDER and pounded the back of Racky's seat as the champagne-colored sedan tore down the highway.

"You *knew* she drove like this and you still let her drive?" she shrieked.

"Didn't have a choice," Lenci said, calmly swerving into the exit lane in order to pass a slower car. "I'm the designated driver—courtesy of Kiddo."

"She just passed on the *right*!" Theresa squeaked.

"This is actually an improvement," Racky told her. "You should have taken a ride with her back when she first resurfaced. That was downright kaleidoscopic!"

"No, no, no, no, no, *no*!" Theresa yelled as Lenci steered the car across six lanes to get to a lefthand exit.

"Next time, you can take a taxi," Lenci said. "Now, I'll thank you to shut your face. I need to concentrate."

"Oh, great," Theresa groaned. "She's finally going to concentrate on driving now that we're exiting the highway. Help me, please, somebody."

"There's no help for people like you," Racky guffawed.

Lenci slammed on the brakes just in time to skid to a stop at the red light at the end of the off-ramp. She and Racky turned on the radio and began to shoulder-dance to an old K-pop song. Theresa rolled her eyes, leaned against her window, and exhaled deeply.

Then, looking out of the window, she drew a sharp breath.

"Lenci," she said. "Whatever you do next, please try to pretend that you know how to drive."

"I do," Lenci said with an apathetic glance at the Borschath Department police car beside them.

"Just don't get us pulled over," Theresa grumbled. "We can't afford to get booked under our current identities. SSI residue could be searching us out for cleanup."

Lenci figured that could actually be true. When the light turned green, she accelerated smoothly.

"See?" Theresa said, thumping Racky's seat. "I knew she was just being difficult before."

"Don't make me swerve this car," Lenci said, jiggling the steering wheel playfully.

"No!" Theresa cried. "The cops are still next to us."

"That's weird," Racky commented.

Lenci had noticed that as well. The police car had not pulled ahead or fallen behind. It was still cruising at an even pace directly beside them. Lenci braked slowly to allow it to pass, but the police car also slowed, remaining even with her. So, she sped up to try to pull ahead, but the police car, too, accelerated.

"Oo, look!" Racky squawked. "The cop is waving at you, Lenci. And he's cute. Wave back!"

"No," said Lenci. "He's harassing me. I absolutely will not encourage that behavior."

Theresa snorted from the back seat. "Oh, but *seduction* is your game, isn't it? What happened to 'no one is immune?' You might as well use it for something good this time."

"I'm not going to flirt with him," Lenci responded, keeping her gaze forward.

She was searching for a natural place to turn. After all, as much as she hated to admit it, Theresa was right about her and Racky's identities most likely being flagged for cleanup.

Lenci still went by 'Chang' in these parts, which would make it more difficult for anyone searching for Agent Thomas. However, her skin color was not going to be helpful in a confrontation with the Borschath Police Department. Borschath was extremely hierarchical with respect to class and rather ignorant of the Subclass altogether.

The police car whooped, and its lights began to flash.

A cocky, male voice called over the speaker, "Ma'am, pull over right here."

Lenci seriously considered punching the gas and seeing how far she could get in a highway chase to the southern border. Out of respect for her pre-teammates, however, she grit her teeth and did as the officer had ordered.

He parked behind them, and as he got out of his car, Racky said, "Now, Lenci, play nice."

"Don't mess this up for us," Theresa added.

"I'll do my best," Lenci mumbled, fishing for her license in her purse. "Not to, I mean."

Borschath officers were known to be belligerent and eugenist. The fact was, even with the Value 4.14 Lives Act that had been passed the decade before, Lenci's chances of avoiding a conflict in which the officer used excessive force were slim. It didn't matter that her mother was 4.14. Under Neo-Eugenic law, she was subclass and not protected under the act.

In any case, the officer was unlikely to ask about her class designation. He would undoubtedly assign one to her—unofficially, of course—and probably a Class 3 one. The rest of their interaction would depend on which kind of Class 3 he perceived her to be and how much fear was attached to that perception.

She rolled down the window. "Good evening, officer."

"License and registration," he said roughly.

Lenci handed them over, saying, "May I ask why you stopped us?"

"You were speeding," he replied without looking up.

"Respectfully," she said, "it was only ten kilometers an hour over the limit, and I was trying to keep from driving side-by-side with you like two toddlers on tricycles."

"Ma'am, I don't need to hear your excuses. You can take this ticket and set up a court date when you get home."

"Just take the ticket," Theresa whispered. "You can deal with it later."

"No, I don't think this is fair," Lenci said. "If you hadn't been—"

"What she means to say, officer," Racky interjected, "is that there has been a misunderstanding, and we are hoping that you can let us off the hook for our honest mistake."

Lenci glared at her sideways but kept quiet.

"Well," the officer said, shining his light in Lenci's face. "Maybe I could look the other way tonight, if you make the time for a routine body search."

"So, this is all about a *grope* session?" Lenci exploded. "You harass

258

us into getting a speeding ticket, then you offer to *rescue* us by being a sleaze?"

The officer's attractive face turned ugly really quickly.

"Hey, *mamaseeda*, don't you know that I could get you sent back to where you came from? I'm giving you a chance to help yourself, brownie."

"Oh, good," Lenci said. "So, you're ignorant *and* a eugenist sleaze."

"That's it!" The officer threw the license and registration on the ground. "Step out of the car!"

She unbuckled her seat belt. "I thought you'd never ask."

"Play nice!" Racky called after her.

The car rocked as the officer thrust Lenci against it, but she threw out her arms to catch herself before her belly bump could make contact. When he came at her with the cuffs, she twirled to the side and did some fancy footwork after which the officer himself somehow ended up in the handcuffs.

She dragged him to his car, whispering in his ear as they went, "I can guarantee that my roots are in the States just as much as yours are and most likely *more*—not that that's ever a reason to mistreat anyone."

She opened the driver's side door and shoved him in. "Now, be a good boy and go back to where you came from."

It was only then that she noticed his partner sitting in the passenger's seat. He must have had the seat reclined before, which is why she hadn't seen him. But now, the seat was upright, and his partner looked very unhappy.

***

"Let us go, you hellions!" Racky said, stumbling into the large, crowded cell after her friends.

"We don't even know her!" Theresa cried.

"And you also probably don't know the people who cooked up a driver's license for her when she doesn't even have a district record."

The corrections officers slammed the door in their faces.

"I was born here in Diablo!" Lenci said indignantly. "Someone must have erased my record."

"That's what they all say. You'll stay here until we can confirm your citizenship."

As the officers turned away, Theresa reached through the bars, saying, "Please don't leave me with her."

"Last chance to put me in solitary!" Lenci called after them. "I reported Guantanamo Bay during booking!"

"There's no *record* of you being there, sweetheart!" one of the officers chuckled.

"Is there ever a record of anyone being at Gitmo anymore?" Lenci shot back. "It would be smarter to put me in another cell, just in case."

"In case some *extremely dangerous* person also escaped from there and is waiting in the cell to kill you?"

"It's for their safety, not mine," Lenci said. "Suit yourselves, though."

"You're just saying that because you want a space all to yourself," Theresa grumbled.

"Exactly."

Racky popped Lenci on the back of the head with her open palm.

The officers laughed and moved down the line to check on the inmates in other cells. The three women turned to face their cellmates. Most of them were unconcerned with their presence. However, one handsome fellow made his way through the crowd to get a better look at them.

"Well, well, well," he said. "How nice that our paths have crossed again!"

"Is he talking to you?" Theresa asked Lenci.

Lenci shrugged, then said to the guy, "I'm kind of bad with faces. Have we met?"

"Now, that hurts," another voice said. "I thought our last encounter was fairly memorable."

Another man emerged from the crowd. He did not have any color of bandana on his person, but Lenci recognized him as Pink Bandana Man.

"What's up, Hula Brownie?" He grinned.

She turned to his companion.

"I get it now." She patted her chest. "The pecs. Didn't recognize you with your shirt on. Nice to see you again, too."

Pecs Guy looked a little flushed.

Pink Bandana Man stared condescendingly down into Lenci's face. "I'm the alpha here. Even the guards steer clear of me."

"How nice for you," Lenci said, remembering how she'd neglected to teach this guy a lesson the last time they'd met. "Now get out my face before I have to——"

"Play *nice*, Lenci," Racky urged.

Their other cellmates were starting to get charged up, and the whole cell began to hum with nervous energy. If a fight broke out, the officers would come back, and that didn't seem like a bad deal to Lenci. Maybe they'd let her out.

"Listen to your friend. Be a good girl, now," Pink Bandana Man said, tucking Lenci's bra strap under the sleeve of her tank top.

Lenci grabbed his hand.

"And be *smart*," he continued. "In a place like this, you think anyone's going to rescue you with a bazooka-sized weapon?"

With an ice-cold stare, the Agent responded, "I *am* the weapon."

And with that, she shoved him hard against the wall. When he tried to lunge at her, she struck his shoulder and dislocated it. Pecs Guy, who was approaching her from behind, received a kick in the gut and crumbled to the floor.

The other cellmates were hooting and hollering, jostling about excitedly.

"Damn it, Lenci!" Theresa said, backing up against the door to stay out of the action. "You're going to start a free-for-all."

"No," the Agent said, stomping Pink Bandana Man into the floor, "I'm ending this now."

"Help! This brownie's trying to kill me!" he screamed.

She rolled her eyes. "Racky, I need your bikini top."

"You *what* now?" Racky crossed her arms.

"No one needs a bikini top under a bra. Just give it!"

Sighing, Racky undid her bikini top, pulled it out of her shirt sleeve, and handed it to her friend. The Agent tied Pink Bandana Man's hands with it and then looped it around his neck in such a way that he could not move without pulling his shoulder further out of joint.

"What did you do to me?" he cried as she propped him up with his back against the wall. "What the *hell* did you do to me?"

"There," she said, turning to the other cellmates. "Any remaining questions about who's the alpha here?"

"We're her friends," Theresa announced.

Racky nodded in agreement.

Everyone quieted down. Word about the fight had apparently gotten out beyond the cell walls. Murmurs confirmed that corrections officers were on their way from another wing. Everyone withdrew to the edges of the cell and talked quietly about what they had seen.

After helping Pecs Guy to his feet, ruffling his hair, and giving him a thump on the back, Lenci joined Theresa and Racky near the door.

"I feel naked," Racky said.

"No one needs two bras," Lenci replied.

"This one is for storage and show only."

Lenci sighed. "I'll replace the bikini top—promise."

"You'd better."

"Borschath Correctional Facility." Theresa covered her face with her hands. "This isn't happening."

"Oh, but it is," Lenci said, shivering mockingly. "We're *criminals* now."

"It's not funny," Theresa told her. "You know we can't go on record."

"Maybe we *can* go on record," Lenci replied pensively. "It's been a few days since SSI collapsed. Everyone's busy scrambling to get underground, right? They probably don't have time to keep an eye out for folks like us." She hoped.

"Well you're all fine and dandy because you don't have a record to be flagged."

"Like you had nothing to do with that."

"I *didn't*!" Theresa snapped. "When we tested your—"

"Sh!" Racky said, motioning with her head toward their other cellmates.

"I'm just saying," Theresa whispered, "we don't know who's out there or whether they're planning to do a cleanup or a startup or anything. But now that Racky and I have been flagged, anyone who's looking can know we're here. And if they have people inside here, *all of us* are sitting ducks because of you!"

Lenci frowned. "So, now it's my fault if we're disappeared because I don't like being harassed?"

Racky sighed. "Well, they would have allowed us to stay in the short-term holding block if you hadn't grabbed that one officer's butt during the strip search."

"He grabbed mine first," Lenci said.

"But breaking that desk with his head—"

"Accident."

Racky threw her a look.

"I *told* him beforehand to play nice," Lenci explained.

"Like I told you?"

Theresa groaned. "Why am I here? Why?"

"You invited yourself!" Her pre-teammates said in unison.

"That's when I thought this was going to be fun."

"Who's not having fun?" Lenci asked.

"Us," said Theresa.

Racky nodded in agreement.

Lenci smiled mischievously. "Well, I have the keys if you want to get out."

Her pre-teammates looked at her incredulously.

A broad grin spread across Racky's face. "During the strip search."

"He grabbed my butt first," Lenci said.

"You are a chip off the old block," Racky beamed. "I knew I would have a good influence on you."

"Are you crazy?" Theresa hissed. "An escape from here would be too high-profile. Even if we made it out, we'd have half of Diablo's police forces snapping at our heels!"

The whole block suddenly became quiet. From the sound of the approaching footsteps, Lenci knew that someone was coming to visit her. In fact, she had a fairly good idea of who it was. He appeared at last, still in uniform, having taken another couple of hours of emergency sick leave. The corrections officers that were with him looked into the cell, but they made no move for the door.

Lenci and her friends stood back as the officers confirmed that everyone in the cell was alive and in one piece. Having heard stories about the crazy, pregnant female and her two friends, none of them were terribly anxious to be near them. There were rumors circulating that electroshock weapons wouldn't work on her.

"'T–two gym employees and an und–documented booked this evening at Borschath Correctional,'" Karthik recited, crossing his arms.

Then, he said, "If this is your way of getting my att–ttention, you'd better have something pretty d–damn important t–to t——tell me."

"*Ethan*," Lenci said, leaning in close, "I didn't *ask* you to come here. So, d—don't treat me like some d–damn child."

He ignored her jab at his stutter.

"You kn–new that this n–news was going to get t–to me all the way at Canon, and n–now you think I'm going t–to get you out," he told her.

She said nothing. His presumption of her dependence upon him was infuriating.

"I t—told you that I'd always be there when you needed me!" he continued, his face twitching as he fought back angry tears. "But you've put our families through hell. I will *n—not* allow you to keep t—— torturing us l—like this! And I'm *n——not* going t–to rescue you."

She threw the keys she'd stolen through the bars at him.

"I don't need you to rescue me," she said. "I don't need you at all."

While his face was asking how on earth she'd gotten the keys, Karthik was unable to bring himself to say anything to her at all. He laughed humorlessly, turned on his heel, and walked away.

"Oo, Circus," Racky said. "I don't think I have ever seen him that mad."

Lenci didn't answer. She didn't care if Karthik was mad. Maybe she was glad that he was. Maybe now he'd stop running after her and showing up in places where he ought not to be.

Chapter 31

A COUPLE OF HOURS LATER, many of the Agent's cellmates, including her pre-teammates, had settled down to get some shut-eye. It was in the silence and the dimmed lights that she became more aware of the sounds in the cellblock. Somewhere above her, people were laughing, probably having found some way to gamble or otherwise amuse themselves. In other cells, people were snoring.

"Bathsheba?" a voice croaked. "Eh! Miss Bathsheba?"

The Agent, slightly taken aback at hearing that name in this setting, stood up and peered through the bars at the cell across from hers. There, a man was beckoning to her.

When she leaned against the door of her cell, the dim light illuminated her face, and the stranger laughed raspily.

"It *is* you!" he exclaimed. "I'll be damned. The Agentess herself! Bathsheba, my lady!"

Her stomach fluttered, though not in a bad way. This man was a friend. Yes, he had helped to trained her once upon a time.

"You remember me?" he asked. "From G—"

"Guantanamo Bay," she breathed. "LeFabre, how nice to see you again!"

"Miss Bathsheba," he laughed aloud. "What are you doing out here? My goodness. From Gitmo, Bathsheba the Agentess!"

"Quietly, please," she said, possibly in French or Spanish, although she could never quite tell what language she spoke until she had switched. "I am called by a different name in these parts."

He probably knew her as a Spanish-speaker since the field trip to Guantanamo Bay had taken place only the year before.

"Still as lovely as ever, though," he remarked.

"You're kind," she replied. "What are *you* doing out here?"

He shrugged. "There is a season for everything—a season for imprisonment and a season for freedom, a season for breaking in and a season for breaking out. Eh, my lady?"

She nodded and a peaceful contentment settled between them.

LeFabre broke their silence with an incredulous laugh. "I never thought I'd see you out and about without the Killer. Why, just a while ago, I told him you'd do him proud with the new operations up at his Forsythe site."

"His Forsythe site?" The Agent's ears pricked up. "LeFabre, do you know for certain that he is in Forsythe?"

"I—I assumed you knew, my lady," he stammered. "Since I saw him in Central Diablo and now you here, I thought you two must have been traveling together."

"But Forsythe?"

"Yes." LeFabre's voice wavered anxiously. "He wants me to join him on a project. Just consultation: bruising the pancreas and puncturing the bladder in hand-to-hand—the rudimentary stuff. But if you didn't know he was working on a project, you didn't hear that from me."

"Oh, I knew he would be starting the project soon," she lied.

It was a natural feeling to her, putting people at ease to get the information she wanted.

"I just didn't know he was in Forsythe *now*," she said. "We had been planning to meet here in Diablo, but there was a complication and we lost track of each other."

LeFabre accepted her excuse willingly. "My sympathies for when you finally catch up with him. With respect to, ahem, complications, he is a hard man."

"But he told you he was traveling to Forsythe?" the Agent asked pointedly. "Directly?"

"Yes, my lady," he responded. "I was on my way to seal a deal when I saw him casing out an apartment building in Central Diablo. A man of his stature is difficult to miss, so I pulled over and greeted him. That's when he gave me the invitation to go to Forsythe. He's preparing things now, but I am to meet him there in three days."

"Thank you, LeFabre," the Agent said, modulating her voice so as to sound friendly and benign. "I guess I'll have to work on my winsome smile before going up to meet him."

"Oh, do not worry yourself about *that*, Agentess," he said. "The Killer has always been quite taken with your beauty, as any man would be. You just be yourself. You just be lovely. Everything will be okay."

She smiled coyly.

"Between the two of us," LeFabre continued in a loud whisper, "a woman of your talent might find many wonderful opportunities as a solo act. What could keep you with a man like him?"

The Agent had often wondered the same thing, but recently, fear of ending up like Beatriz Gomez—or worse—had kept her from entertaining the thought further. In that moment, though, LeFabre's words touched something deep inside of the Agent. The truth of her capability, even against the Killer, had lain dormant for far too long. Now, it was awakening. Her chances of ending her connection to the WCE with liberty rather than with death were actually fairly good. All she had to do was find the strength to confront the master assassin who had trained her.

After all, the survival game consisted solely of agents and patients—no winners—and in it, achievement looked only like action. It was possible that Gomez had understood that on some level, and she had achieved much, despite her limitations. Being acted upon was what had held her back and led to her demise. So, rather than waiting to be acted upon, the Agent decided to act.

"Miss Bathsheba, I did not mean to offend you by asking."

"Love, I suppose," she answered vacantly. "That is probably what has kept me with him all this time."

Or fear, or pain, or pleasure. She didn't know whether there was any difference among those.

"Well, then, one cannot argue with that." LeFabre gave a raspy laugh.

The cellblock door opening caused them to fall silent once again. Someone important was approaching. The Agent could hear the clip-clopping of sensible dress shoes and a group of boots echoing through the block.

When the echoing came to a halt, she was surprised to find Blair Lee-Smith staring at her through the bars. Some corrections officers stood behind her and her roaches.

"I'd say that I'm surprised too, but I like to be honest whenever I can," Blair said in response to the Agent's gaping mouth.

"What can I say?" the Agent sighed. "I've always been a hot head. Maybe it's better that Theresa, Racky, and I were never officially a team."

"I don't buy that you feel bad," Blair said, "not for a moment."

The Agent dodged her smackdown, determined to get her to play. "How'd you find us?"

"I had the names of your pre-teammates flagged in the system, so they popped up when you all were booked. I also got Borschath's announcement, which included the info on an undocumented that claimed the name of Valencia Chang."

The Agent gasped. "So, it was *you* that erased my—"

"No," Blair's voice became authoritative, "but we won't talk about this in public, Ms. Chang. Now, wake up the other two. They are very valuable assets to the Cooperative FBI, and they're coming with me."

The Agent's heart nearly jumped out of her chest. David was in Forsythe, just one district over from Diablo, and she would not be denied this chance to meet him.

"But you have to take me too!" she said.

"I don't *have* to do anything," Blair replied. "My problems may well diminish if you get deported."

"Blair!" The Agent swallowed, trying desperately to think of something she could use to tantalize the Cooperative FBI agent. "Ms. Lee-Smith, I know where he is. I know where the Killer is!"

Blair motioned for the guards to have their weapons within reach as they unlocked the door. "Where?"

The Agent stood behind the door while the roaches pulled Theresa and Racky to their feet.

"Oh, thank goodness!" Theresa exclaimed sleepily. "Blair, you wouldn't believe the mess this idiot got us into!"

"Shut your mouth, Theresa," Racky mumbled, rubbing her eyes.

"Windsailing," the Agent said at last, clinging to the bars of the cell with wide, innocent eyes. "The Killer is looking for me in a borough in the northern tip of Windsailing. Get me out, and I'll take you to him. That arrest could catapult your career to the next level, you know."

Blair looked her up and down, then sighed. "Okay, boys, this one is mine too. I can have the paperwork cooked up within the hour. It's not safe for her in here."

"Guantanamo Bay," the Agent shrugged as she brushed past the bewildered guards.

"Hey!" Blair grabbed her arm.

As the Agent resisted the impulse to twist out of her hold and throw her to the ground, she sensed movement that she did not understand. Then, she felt a sharp pain in her hamstring. She gasped and seized the throat of the roach who had stabbed her with a sizable needle.

"Too late," Blair smirked. "The tracking device is already in. No point in killing the guy."

The Agent begrudgingly released the roach who quickly jumped behind his companions.

"Why?" she asked Blair. Despite her best efforts, she still sounded hurt.

Blair began to walk back the way she had come. "Because I don't believe that the Killer is in Windsailing, but I do believe that you will lead me to him."

"After this treatment?" The Agent followed her, huffing indignantly. "I saved your life, you ungrateful brat."

"I'm grateful," Blair said as they exited the cellblock. "That's why I'm not condemning you to life in a maximum security prison—yet."

The Agent frowned at her. "That, and you're hoping to exploit me."

"That, and well—you're kind of like a weird, same-aged stepmother to me."

"Great," the Agent muttered.

They fell silent as they passed through the well-populated staff lounge. Aside from a couple of fleeting glares from the officers that had booked the former SSI agents, no one really paid them any mind. The Agent found a lonely pair of handcuffs on the snack table by the door, so she adopted them when no one was looking and followed Blair out of the staff exit.

And just like that, she was outdoors in the chilly Diablan twilight. The sun would be up in a half an hour, at the most.

"Well, I've appreciated our candid discussion," Blair said, "but I guess this is goodbye for now. I need to take my assets to HQ for processing."

"Well, mine would be too big to fit in the back seat of your car, especially if I'd have to share it with those two." The Agent motioned toward her pre-teammates. "Mainly Theresa—no offense, of course."

Theresa rolled her eyes and slammed the door.

"Ey!" Racky squawked. "You calling my butt bony?"

"If the yoga pants fit," the Agent laughed.

Blair got in the driver's side and started the engine.

"Girl, you are a stanky mess!" Racky called out the window. "Don't forget: you owe me a bikini top!"

"And you owe me chicken thighs!"

The car pulled away, leaving the Agent alone in the dim, gray light of the parking lot. She shivered and folded her arms across her chest. The path ahead of her was sure to be difficult, and she would only succeed if she remained free of distraction. In that sense, she was glad to be alone. But solitude was something to which she was no longer accustomed. She dared not entertain the thought that she was afraid of it.

Kiddo shifted inside of her, and she patted her belly in response. She was not *completely* alone. She sniffled but smelled no hint of myrrh in the chilly air, just the fresh scent of eucalyptus leaves. She had told LeFabre that love had been the cause of all this.

"What *is* love?" she whispered.

Suddenly, a pair of headlights shone upon her.

Who now? She shielded her eyes and waited silently as the driver of the car opened the door and got out.

"You?" Lenci stared at Karthik incredulously.

His angular jaw was drawn tight, and his face looked smeared. He had been crying. She had hurt him. She had wanted to hurt him so that he would leave. But he hadn't left. He had waited there for her, probably expecting her to break out. If she had, he would have been there, but what would he have done?

Karthik drew a wavering breath and opened his mouth to speak. Nothing came out. So, he drew another breath and tried again.

"Your terms," he said gruffly.

She threw her arms around him. This surprised him, but he yielded to her embrace willingly. Kiddo kicked back at the meeting of their bodies, perhaps with a hint of indignation. At last, the Agent pulled back, kissed Karthik lightly on the lips, and ran around to the passenger's side of the car. After he stood frozen for a couple of seconds that seemed like three eternities, she tapped on his window and he hurried into the car.

"I d—didn't think you were going t—to get out l——legally," he said. "That was a welcome surprise. You have friends in high places."

"Or enemies," she replied, buckling her seat belt. "Sometimes, I can't tell the difference."

He side-glanced her. "So, where to?"

"Forsythe, please."

270

"What's in Forsythe?"

Pain? Death? Freedom? Some fateful mix of the three?

"Well, for one," she replied, "tacos."

"*Tacos?*" He chuckled. "I thought you were going to say something harrowing and probably illegal."

"Oh," Lenci said, "that'll come later. Let's get food. Is that place we went after our elementary school promotion still in business? The one that doesn't use Neo-Eugenic law to determine their seating charts, at least on a good day? Their tacos were amazing."

"Yeah, I know the way." Karthik started the car. "Tacos I can do. Just let me know when the plan changes, so I can prepare myself."

She looked out the window and did not respond.

She was planning to confront the Killer. Actually, she was planning to do more than that. She was planning to take back her life from the Killer, and to do that, she was prepared to end his.

Chapter 32

LENCI SLEPT WHILE KARTHIK DROVE. She even slept through the border crossing. Karthik hadn't had the heart to wake her, so he flashed his Canon badge at the border agent and lied that they were plainclothes cops on a cross-district sting operation. He felt truly terrible about the deception, but there was really no telling what Lenci would have done if she had been awake.

Anyway, the deception was harmless from a legal perspective since they were both subclass and could not affect the district class ratios. The border agent let them through without inquiring about Lenci's identity.

The sun was just coming up when Karthik pulled into the parking lot of a small taqueria on the outskirts of Forsythe. As soon as the car stopped, Lenci sat up and stretched. Her face was full of a fear that Karthik did not understand. Upon meeting his gaze, she quickly masked the fear with her brilliant smile.

"It's nice not to be alone," she said, "especially right now."

"We're in this together," he reassured her.

She held out her pinky, and Karthik linked it in his own for a precious half-moment. Then, Kiddo must have kicked her bladder or something because she went bursting from the vehicle and around the side of the restaurant where a restroom placard was posted.

Karthik entered the restaurant, took a number from the dispenser at the door, and seated himself. He summoned the menu by keying his number into the keypad in the middle of the table.

The holographic menu shot up out of the table and floated in front of his face. This was an older model of the tech he had often used in Windsailing, but it was more advanced than the dated tech to which he had grown accustomed in Diablo. Even so, he quickly figured out how to navigate the holographic menu and ordered an appetizer of black beans to eat with chips. He figured he'd wait to order a main course since Lenci would undoubtedly want to look at the menu for herself and not have him presuming to know what she wanted.

As he waited, he studied his surroundings in fascination. He had only moved back to Diablo a couple of years before, but in that time he had forgotten how technologically advanced the other Western districts were. Robotic servers rolled back and forth through the restaurant, bringing food to tables and bussing empty dishes. Holographic advertisements hovered just below the ceiling in green, red, and blue lights. Payments here would be purely electro-fund transfers—no cash accepted. Karthik checked to make sure his fund card contained all of his updated financial information.

More than half an hour later, Lenci appeared with a stony expression on her face and sat down gingerly across from him.

"I was beginning to think you'd fallen in," Karthik joked.

She rolled her eyes. "I couldn't even get into the restaurant toilets. The door had some kind of fancy lock on it that kept buzzing and locking me out, even though it was vacant. So, I ran across the street to the truck stop outhouse. I hate Forsythe and their illogical tech advancements."

"Heavens forbid anyone try to better the conditions of the Western States," he responded.

"I just mean we shouldn't have tech for tech's sake," she shrugged. "Why not use technology to better our healthcare or make auto-cars more compatible with the infrastructure of poorer districts?"

"Why not all of the above?" Karthik said, anxious not to offend any Forsythers who might have been listening. "You want to order something?"

Lenci looked sick as she examined the holographic menu, but she eventually shook off whatever was bothering her. She ordered *al pastor* tacos, and Karthik made that two orders. Afterward, the two friends fell silent. Karthik could tell Lenci had something on her mind, but he decided to wait for her to reveal what it was.

"I'm glad to know you, Karthik," she said, at length. "And I'm sorry for all of the grief I caused. I don't ever say it enough, but I really treasure you."

He laughed. "You dying or something?"

"No," she replied, looking exposed. "I need a spoon!"

She stood abruptly to track down a server. It was then that Karthik noticed the bloodstain on the back of her stockinged right leg. It looked like a puncture wound of some kind.

"The red button on the table is the hail button—your confounded technology at work," Karthik said. "What happened to your leg?"

"I got in a fight with one of the inmates at Borschath Correctional," she responded distractedly. "It's not as bad as it looks, and you should see him. Oh, excuse me, Toaster Man! Spoons, please!"

She hailed the robotic server by pressing the red button on the side of the table but still waved as if the server could see her. It rolled up to the table. Karthik wouldn't have said it before, but the machine did indeed look like an enormous toaster on wheels with bright lights of all primary colors flashing up and down its sides. Its front bore a screen that read: **How may I be of service?**

She sighed. "If you'd been listening at all, you would know I want some *spoons*?"

The server responded by spitting three spoons onto the table.

"Spot on, if you're counting heartbeats, Toaster Man," Lenci said, "but there are only two of us that can manipulate utensils at this time."

Karthik laughed as she searched for a hole in the large machine through which to return the extra utensil. There was none, so she rested the spoon on top of the machine and pressed the red button to dismiss it. When the server left, Lenci turned her attention back to the table.

"Mm, black beans," she said in a high-pitched, empty tone.

Karthik eyed her suspiciously, but he munched quietly in tentative agreement to the deliciousness of the black beans. They never used utensils when eating black beans and chips—not before she had disappeared, anyway.

Lenci tapped the spoon a couple of times on the edge of the bowl they were sharing, then said, "I'm going to have a conversation with an old friend tonight."

"A friend or an enemy?"

"Someone from my past—my old trainer."

She wouldn't maintain eye contact.

Filled with dread, Karthik asked, "He's the one that made you forget?"

"He's the one who made me *have* to forget," she replied.

"And he's the one who—who—"

"Threatened Lorenzo's life? Yes, the very same one."

"Are you afraid of him?"

"Shouldn't I be afraid of someone who can control me?"

Karthik considered this for a second before responding stoutly, "No one has that power. If you're going to be afraid of him, be afraid about something practical."

Lenci said nothing.

"You know, you could come to my place instead," Karthik offered. "Your teammates will think you've gone on the run, and you'll be safe. I could make sure you're safe."

"You?" He found her smile condescending.

She tossed her hair. "You can't protect me. *I* can't protect me."

They settled into a mixed silence—his confused and sorrowful, hers resolute.

"It's just a conversation," she said, probably more to herself than to him.

They both knew that her conversations tended to be more physically involved than most. After all, she had always been of the mind that actions speak louder than words.

"Please think of the baby," Karthik said, trying not to upset her by suggesting that she was unfit for a fight at this point. "Remember what happened when you had a 'conversation' with my cousin?"

"If I don't go, I'll be a sitting duck and the baby'll be done for, anyway," she replied. "I have to end this."

She was so stubborn. She always had been, and she always would be.

Karthik sighed. "You've pretty much done whatever you wanted for as long as I've known you, but just this once, would you please let me give you some input?"

"What kind of input?"

"SSI isn't around to help you anymore, if they ever actually did. Now, I know you don't like the idea of the police, but if we just—"

"No police!" she snapped.

"Why are you so afraid of the police?"

"I'm not afraid of them," she replied stiffly. "I'm not *afraid* of anyone. I just don't need government roaches overrunning my operation and messing up what they don't understand."

"Government *what?*" Karthik exclaimed incredulously.

"It's the reason Bourghin is dead," she sniffed.

They sat in silence for a moment, then Karthik whispered, "If I decided to call the police, would you kill me?"

She laughed and patted his hand, saying, "I wouldn't have to kill you to ensure that you were unable to dial 911."

He couldn't tell if she was joking and didn't want to find out. He drew his hand back.

"How do you even expect to find this guy?" he asked. "I mean, you said in the car that a mutual friend from Guantanamo Bay told you that he's in Forsythe, but this is a huge district and it's not like he gave you a house number or even a street name."

"I know that my old trainer only likes two-story houses," Lenci said, staring at the bowl of beans between them. "I know that he prefers moderate climates, if he has a choice about it, which means somewhere coastal or by a lake. I know that he prefers to be on higher ground to avoid flooding. He often has a cover as a teacher or professor because, well, word on the street is that is what he was before he started in our line of work."

"*Your* line of work?"

Lenci paid him no heed. "He's probably somewhere not too busy, small-townish in a way, but just lively enough that he can blend into the normal hustle and bustle of everyday life. He's been in and out of Forsythe since before I knew him. It's some kind of hub for him, which means that his residence must be fairly permanent, owned by him."

"Yeah, but—"

"He's in hills of the northwestern university borough within biking distance of the campus to keep in shape while he's not training vigorously," she said decidedly. "So, all I have to do is find a two-story house in that area, one that has a lot of windows and unprotected skylights, one practically *begging* to be broken into. It won't have the modern safeguards of most homes in the area."

"But wouldn't he have a lot of security?" Karthik asked. "I mean, a guy in his line of work would want to be careful, right?"

Lenci side-glanced him. "A person in *our* line of work wouldn't need to be careful. They could kill any intruder before he even knew what hit him and make it look like an accident. And they would enjoy it."

Karthik raised his eyebrows.

"Do your research." She gave a wry laugh. "Humans are one of a handful of species that kill for fun. And there's a reason why the Killer has made a whole life for himself under that name."

Staring off into space, she remarked, "Weird that he drilled into me the efficiency of only killing when necessary, even though *he* often goes out of his way for an entertaining kill. That's just one of many discrepancies in his teaching. He used those discrepancies to create an unequal flow of power, to control me. But I'm done being controlled."

Karthik didn't know what to say, so he said nothing. Their tacos came, and they were done talking about her old trainer.

***

Karthik paid for the meal, and the Agent did not protest because the only thing she had in her pocket was a pair of handcuffs—no wallet, no phone.

"I'll get you next time," she winked.

He laughed. "I'll hold you to that."

When they reached the parking lot, they stood smiling at each other but found themselves unable to say anything. There was so much to be said, and yet the Agent's time had run out. If there was love or truth or any kind of goodness between them, it soon would not matter. She had a mission to complete, and this time, nothing would stand in her way.

"Well, I should get going," she said, breaking the contented silence between them. "I appreciate all that you've done, Karthik. And I think it will be good for you to get on with your life without me introducing moment after moment of chaos."

She reached out for a hug, but to her surprise, he evaded her.

"Hold on," he said. "I have to pee."

She followed him and stood outside the door of the bathroom. He had had no trouble getting in there at all. The keypad stared smugly at her as if to say, *I only work for hunks, not whores.*

She scowled back at it.

"You know, Karthik, I'm really glad to have had you along up until now, but I don't think it's a good idea for you to come with," she told him through the closed door.

The tinkling sound inside stopped. "Well, you're still here, so you must actually want me to come with you. You're waiting."

The tinkling resumed. Why *was* she still there? If she cared about Karthik at all, she would leave him here while he was peeing and disappear forever. But here she was, waiting.

"I wouldn't want you to get hurt," she said. "I don't know what I would do if something happened to you."

The tinkling stopped. "Lenci, we've been through nearly everything together since the day we were born, excluding the past few years— which was mostly my fault, I'll admit. So, just let me make it up to you."

The tinkling resumed. She didn't feel that Karthik owed her in any way because she didn't remember what had happened all that time ago. But she liked his company. He made her feel more normal. The only problem was that her life was so abnormal, too abnormal for the likes of a well-meaning neighbor boy.

"I mean, we were born together, so we might as well die together, right?"

He chuckled, but she did not laugh with him.

"Lenci?"

That was precisely why she couldn't allow him to come with her. Once her abnormal life collided head-on with his normal life, if he didn't die, he might never recover. She slid her hand into her pocket and felt the comforting coolness of the metal handcuffs.

"I told you we'd do it on your terms," he was saying. "Gosh, what was I thinking when I said that?"

"On my terms, hm?" she said, pulling out the handcuffs and positioning herself behind the door.

The flush came, then the sound of running water. The doorknob jiggled, and just as the door began to swing open, the Agent threw herself into it with all her might. Her timing was just right. There was a thud on the other side of the door. Karthik was down. She entered to find him out cold with his face to the floor. She cuffed his hands behind his back.

"*My* terms are that I handle my own business, and no one else gets hurt," she said, propping him up against the wall. "I'm sorry, Ethan."

After fishing through his pockets for his car keys, she closed the restroom door and jammed the keys into the keypad. She didn't know much about high-tech restroom locks, but the fireworks display of sparks shooting from the keypad indicated that she had probably broken it. The screen displayed a flickering message of 'Occupied,' so Karthik was sure to be undisturbed for a while.

The Agent threw the car keys into a nearby trashcan and took a deep breath. She had almost succumbed to the inefficient desire for friendship and let a *civilian* walk with her into the most dangerous mission of her life.

Catastrophe avoided.

Chapter 33

WITH BARE LEGS UNDER her shorts, the Agent trudged slowly up the sloping street. She had dumped the stockings about a kilometer away from the restaurant, and she was glad that she had. Her scars reflected the pale blue light of the holographic advertisements that popped up and buzzed around her. She was no longer in hiding. It was a wonderful feeling to be unafraid, unrestricted, and less itchy.

It was less wonderful that she had to keep brushing the advertisements away from her face just to get a good visual on the sidewalk. She didn't know how anyone lived a focused life in Forsythe.

Night was falling, and although the Agent had not yet found the Killer's house, she was in good spirits. David was a predictable man with a routine that he followed religiously. If she could make it to his house by 1900, she could break in while he was showering.

She studied the rows of houses silhouetted against the blue-gray sky and smiled. In her time with the Chang family, she had forgotten how much she enjoyed this work, the challenge of the hunt and the promise of a gratifying kill. The Agent never thought in all of her life that she would turn on the very one who had brought her up, but why not? She had learned him like she had learned any other man—and he had hurt Lenci's brother.

None of the houses that she had seen so far matched her prediction of the Killer's Forsythe residence. All of them, every single one, had a sign for an alarm system. Some of them had tall electric gates with automatic weapons pointed down at the street. Their windows were made of plexiglass.

It seemed these hills were full of houses with valuable things inside them, a burglar's dream come true. The Agent smiled, thinking of her aerobics teacher friend who had made a hobby of bringing equilibrium to the universe, but she quickly brushed the thought away when she saw something move out of the corner of her eye.

She glanced to her side. No one was there, but there had been someone there before. Of that, she was fairly certain. The hairs on the back of her neck stood on end, filling her with that dread that comes between codes yellow and orange. It was delicious and terrible all at once.

Still, there was no sense in confronting the person. If it was just a random passerby, the Agent did not want to draw attention to herself as an out-of-place character on the night that a major crime was committed in the neighborhood. And if she was actually being followed, she would need some time to assess the situation.

So, she walked onward, pretending to move with purpose. The advertisements continued to accost her, but she swiped them away as nonchalantly as possible. *Cleaning products, online prep school, two-for-one hazelnut milkshakes.* She turned left at the next corner and walked down a block.

Buy life insurance and get it passed down in the will, three pairs of chain mail bikini cuts for the price of two, vacation in Forsythe's best resorts for the cheapest prices. She could hear the shuffling footsteps and the same hushed breathing about fifteen meters behind. She turned left at the next corner and at the next.

As she began the fourth left turn, her follower addressed her, "Okay, so I guess you know you're being followed. We can stop going in circles now and talk about this like adults."

"You again?" She turned around in disbelief. "How did you find me?"

"You're not the only one who can play this game," Karthik replied, stepping out of the shadows. "You'd already told me that you'd be in the northwestern university borough. After waking up with a mild concussion on th—that germ-ridden restroom floor, I followed the most likely route that you would go."

"I think I'm impressed," she said, raising an eyebrow, "and not just by your ability to play detective while mildly concussed. Tell me more."

She sat down and patted the curb beside her.

He accepted her invitation. "I know, for instance, that you know better than to walk around an area predominantly inhabited by Class 1 folks when it's n—near dark. So, I figured you'd try this hill first rather than the next one over where no one would question your presence after sundown."

"But why this particular section of the hill?" she asked, intrigued.

"Well, I also know that you prefer straight paths up the hills and not winding paths where you can't see the end. You always hated the switchbacks on the trails at Eucalyptus State Park. So, I figured you'd try a straight path first and then work your way over to the winding areas afterward."

"There are three straight paths up this hill," the Agent said.

Karthik grinned as he responded, "I have clear memories of the day delivery drones were reintroduced to the Western States. We were still at Forsythe's School for the Gifted."

The Agent smiled. This, she had learned about as well, although she had not managed to consciously recall it until this moment.

"I was afraid of them," she said, in awe of this recollection. "I didn't like the noise."

He nodded. "So, I watched the drone routes all afternoon. This particular street just happens to be in a small blank space outside of all of the routes. Listen."

Silence settled between them, silence in which—the Agent happened to notice—there was absolutely no background whirring or beeping from the drones.

Karthik's predictions of her behavior based on his childhood friend's preferences had been spot-on. At this, she felt neither a warming of the heart nor a gladness of any kind but a sturdy respect—and a sense of accomplishment, as it seemed that all of her hours of memorization and behavioral training had paid off.

"Just let me be here for you," Karthik said. "I might have an indispensable role to play, as long as you d—don't kn—knock me out again."

He swallowed hard before adding, "Or kill me."

The Agent opened her mouth to laugh at him or reassure him or threaten him, but the sight beyond her friend stole her breath away. Across the street from where they sat was a two-story house with no alarm warning sign. Karthik turned to see what she was gaping at.

"That's the one," she said.

"How do you know?" he asked, looking up at the charming wooden panels and the red and blue trim.

"It looks exactly like our house in Chile."

Karthik's forehead wrinkled. "You mean, he decorated his house here to look exactly like the one in Chile?"

"The one in Chile was a replica," the Agent replied. "It's what you do when you live a manufactured life, but you want to remember something important."

She'd once had some replicas of her own, but David discouraged her from using them. Maybe that's why she had forgotten so much.

"But, most often," she continued, staring stonily up at the second floor of the house where a light was on in what she knew to be the bathroom of the master suite, "the useful things tend to come back anyway, when you need them."

Karthik was watching her anxiously. However, this was not a time that she could comfort him. She had tried to protect him, but he was grown enough to make his own decisions. He had made his choice, and she could not be responsible for him any longer.

She marched across the street with Karthik in tow. They stopped by the gate at the side of the house and gazed up at the yellow light coming from the second floor. The bathroom window was open, and the sound of running water confirmed that the Killer was indeed in the shower. The Agent had arrived at the prime time for her break-in.

"Well, the deed isn't going to get any dirtier," she said in a voice that had only tiptoed around the edges of Lenci's for the past few months.

It was a husky, rich voice, resolute and dismissive of the very idea of fear. And it felt good. When she stepped toward the gate, Karthik grabbed her wrist. Months ago, before she had been drawn from the ocean, the Agent would have knocked him off-balance and snapped his neck. Or, if she had been in a bad mood, she would have broken all of his bones and left him as a pile of jelly in the middle of the street. At this point, however, she had enough experience to know that Karthik meant no harm. But he was distracting her from the road ahead, a road devoid of caring hearts and concern for anyone's wellbeing.

Her muscles tightened to counteract the reflex to damage him.

"Release me," she said frostily. "Right *now*."

He stiffened. Yes, yes, she knew: her voice seemed soulless and angry, and it scared him. Finally, it was getting through his thick skull that the woman before him was not the girl with whom he had been raised.

"Lenci," he whispered, releasing her arm.

The Agent looked at him, grateful that she would not have to physically harm him. Enough blood would be shed that night. None of it needed to be his.

"I didn't want you involved at all, but you're here now," she said. "And you said before that you were ready to do things on my terms. Now, you'll kindly step aside, so I can do what I came to do."

"But if you don't succeed—"

She chuckled wryly. "If I *do* succeed, we'll chat about it over a bowl of noodle soup. What do you say?"

He sighed. "If we were doing this my way, I would be calling for back up right now. When would it be *helpful* for me to call the police?"

"After I'm done, so maybe in a few minutes," the Agent shrugged. "I just came here to have a conversation, and if the police want to clean up afterward, they can be my guest."

Karthik looked sick and remained silent, rooted where he stood. She gently moved him aside so that she could unlatch the gate. It swung open quietly, and her heart sank. On the ground inside the gate was a chain—not a thick, iron chain but a slim, steel chain, long and winding. It snaked around the corner of the house, and she had a terrible feeling about what was attached to the other end of it.

Sure enough, plodding footsteps and the clinking of the chain against the ground filled the air. The Agent was glad that the water was running in the bathroom. She hoped it would be loud enough to drown out the noise of the upcoming confrontation.

A gigantic Rottweiler bounded around the corner and stood before them menacingly. It was a very muscular animal, so much so that the chain attached to it seemed quite insignificant. The dog barked mutely, probably due to a noise-reducing shock collar. But its inability to bark had no bearing on the sharpness of its teeth. A low, rumbling growl shook its entire body. Karthik turned to flee, but the Agent held him back.

"Don't run," she whispered. "It only makes things worse. Remember Professor Reymundo's Pomeranians?"

The fact that she had thrown that memory at him was totally lost in the terror of the moment. Besides, his mind seemed to be in a different space entirely. He was looking at the bedroom window that was open just above the garage roof.

"You're going in through that window, right?" he asked.

"If we don't get mauled to death first," she replied, not taking her eyes off of the dog.

Karthik removed her hand from his arm.

"You're not going to get mauled to death," he told her.

And with that, he dove onto the dog, knocking it onto its side. It snarled silently and struggled under him briefly, but it lay still after recognizing that it was pinned.

"I got him!" Karthik exclaimed.

His voice and muscles were strained, just like the tense muscles of the massive beast beneath him. His wrinkled brow and wide eyes told the Agent that he had acted impulsively and that he was not sure what to do next. She hated to leave him in such a position.

"*Go!*" he urged.

This was her chance, and she had to take it. Dodging the onslaught of concern over what would become of her friend, she leapt up onto the roof of the garage and climbed through the open window.

***

"The things you do for love," Karthik grunted as the giant animal wiggled underneath him.

The grip that he had learned in his canine safety course at the Canon Academy had proven useful, but he was unsure of how to proceed. No one had ever taught him how to get out of such a situation, and he had never thought he would need to know that since he was so good at avoiding confrontations with dogs—at least, when Lenci wasn't around.

He sighed.

The dog, sensing Karthik's momentary relaxation, bounced onto its feet. Karthik, too, jumped up. As he backed away, the dog advanced on him, growling silently. Karthik's eyes wandered to the dog's chain, which he hoped would eventually restrain it somewhere near the edge of the property. That was another thing he had learned at the Canon Academy: dogs are territorial. If you get off their property, they'll leave you alone.

They were now at the edge of the street. Much to Karthik's relief, the dog's chain was pulled taut. The dog strained against the chain, then braced its neck and lunged forward. At the sound of a snapping link somewhere along the chain, all thoughts of canine safety training flew from Karthik's mind, and his childhood street smarts took over. He ran, and the dog pursued him.

As the breathing behind Karthik grew louder and louder, the urgency to find a good hiding place became apparent. But there were only houses as far as the eye could see. He could not afford to be identified in conjunction with this whole messy situation because someone would surely bring him in for questioning, and he had never been a good liar.

So, he tore down the sidewalk, knocking over trashcans and hurdling parked cars. If Lenci's confrontation would really only be a matter of minutes, then he would run until either his heart gave out or the dog gave up.

"The things you do for love," he said, this time with a hint of despair.

Suddenly, two headlights lit up the intersection in front of him. The car stopped at the corner, and the passenger's side door swung open.

"Ey!" the driver squawked. "Need a ride?"

Karthik put on one last burst of speed and dove into the car, shutting the door just in time. A *CLUNK* ensued as the dog collided headfirst with the closed door. Then, there was silence.

"Where's Circus?" Racky asked.

"With—with—" Karthik wheezed, leaning his seat back.

"Now, don't move on in just yet," she said, putting the car in park. "Let's get that bear cub into my trunk."

He stared at her incredulously.

"It won't be too hard to tie him up when he's unconscious," she said. "Besides, I suspect he might be useful, in an indirect kind of way."

Karthik groaned but got out of the car with her nonetheless. Racky pulled a roll of twine out of her bra. The perplexed expression on his face changed very quickly when she flicked him in the temple.

"Extra storage," she explained. "Mind your manners."

They worked together to tie up the unconscious dog.

"Notice the manicured nails," Racky said, "and the expensive leather collar. This is one pampered pooch. We can use him as bait to buy us some time to get Lenci to a safe place."

"She said she needed a few minutes." Karthik grunted as they heaved the animal into the trunk. "She didn't even have a weapon. I tried to dissuade her, but—"

Racky shook her head, closing the lid. "When that woman gets an idea in her head, there is no stopping her."

"Exactly."

"Well," she said when they got back into the car, "I'm just glad you kept that tracking device. I knew she was fixing to dig it out, but Blair, our boss, wouldn't listen to me. She was real self-congratulatory when our monitor showed that the device was moving!"

Karthik side-glanced her. "And you persuaded her to let you come here alone?"

"Well, I may or may not have slipped her and Theresa a little something."

He laughed. "You gunked them?"

"It was all natural stuff!" Racky said. "We were about ready for breakfast, anyway. So, I served them poppyseed muffins, heavy on the butter, and chamomile tea with some whole milk while we were waiting around at my place. They were asleep in twenty minutes."

"So, you gunked them in a trendy, all-natural kind of way."

"I guess," she shrugged, "but you would have been puppy chow if I hadn't."

"Thanks, Racky. So, can we go back for Lenci now?"

"She needed a few minutes," Racky said. "So we will give her a few minutes. In the meantime, I have an idea about what we can do with the cub."

"Then, we'll go back for Lenci?"

"Boy, if you don't stop badgering me—it's like you think I've never done anything like this before. Shut your mouth!"

And he did.

Chapter 34

THE AGENT CLIMBED THROUGH the open window into a tastefully decorated master bedroom suite. There was a wood fire burning in the fireplace. Beyond the closed bathroom door, the muted sound of running water told her that she had some time to prepare.

She crept through the suite and opened the door that led to the hall. There was a hardwood stairwell no more than a couple of meters from the doorway. She took the lightbulb out of the lamp near the stairs, then tiptoed down to the ground floor.

She did not think the fight would make it to that stage, but she needed to plan for every possible scenario. Using a box-cutter from a drawer in the kitchen, she cut a piece of carpet from the shadowy part of the entryway and laid it across the last stair step. After making sure that the carpet's pattern followed a natural progression from the entry to the bottom stair, she went back up to the master bedroom. The water was still running in the bathroom.

It took twenty seconds for the Agent to mentally note each weaponizable object and identify all potential exits. Then, she sat on the bed. This was a familiar feeling to her, sitting on the bed, waiting for David to come out of the shower. Usually, though, she was waiting for night training or a beating. Those had been the only occurrences in her life as Bathsheba that happened reliably, though often not predictably.

As she thought about that, the fear came to the forefront of her consciousness. Yes, she was afraid. It was not every day that a person attempted to murder the master assassin who had controlled her for as long as she could remember—and in said assassin's own residence, no less. But the Agent's only hope of gaining freedom from the WCE depended first on her gaining freedom from the Killer. She thought that reminding herself of that would make her fear dissipate. But it didn't.

Suddenly, she noticed another complicating factor. The matching decor, red satin bedspread, neutral tones in the carpet, the accent wall painted a tasteful, warm color, and the ornate candle holders on the desk all informed the Agent that David did not live alone in this house. He had never had much of an eye for home decorating. And judging from the bucket of ice with the bottle sticking out of it, the pair of champagne flutes on the desk, and the fire in the fireplace, it seemed that the woman of the house was due to arrive quite soon.

The water in the shower had stopped running half a minute or so ago. That meant the Agent's target was probably half-dressed by now.

Never mind the woman of the house. She pulled her hair into a low ponytail. It was showtime.

A billow of steam swirled out of the bathroom, revealing the Killer. He wore only a pair of black slacks, as usual having left the choosing of his shirt for last. The Agent smiled knowingly as he ruffled the towel through his hair on the way to the closet.

"Hey," she said casually.

Admittedly, announcing her presence took away a huge advantage, but she knew that she could take the Killer, even in the fairest of fights. She reminded herself that he had chosen her as his protégé for a reason.

"Hey, Sheebs," he responded, leafing through his dress shirts.

Then, seeming to realize that she was the one thing out of place in the perfect evening he'd planned, he whirled around to face her. "You're here!"

He tried to look angry to scare her, but she knew that he was really very unsettled.

She slid off of the bed nonchalantly and approached him. "You called, didn't you?"

His gaze flickered to the poker on the hearth. He was calculating his distance to the weapon, her distance to him, and the time their ensuing scuffle might take. She had already made those calculations before he came out of the bathroom, and she had moved the poker away from the closet to ensure she'd have the advantage.

"Yeah, but you didn't come when I called," he said.

He grimaced, trying to get a better read on her face, to see if she was there with intentions to harm him or not.

In order to seem like he was in control of the situation, he could not back away from her. The Agent knew this, so she met him nose-to-nose. She could not be afraid of him. This time, it was her mission not to be.

"I had some family things to take care of," she said.

He seized her by the neck in his rough-but-tender way, and she let him, never breaking eye contact.

"I don't care what you're into with some fake family that Bourghin set up for you," he said. "I wouldn't care if it were your real family. When I call, you *come*."

She kissed the Killer because she could.

"This a bad time for you?" she asked.

"Still got fifteen minutes before she's here," he mumbled, sucking at her lips.

As the Agent felt the Killer's hands tightening around her neck, she noticed a familiar hardness in his face. This was the expression he wore before mercy killings. After all the time he had spent training her, he still thought she was just a clueless, trusting, little pet, ready to be slaughtered whenever he pleased. And she hated him for that.

Although she previously never would have dared to strike him outside of a spar, this evening the Agent found herself more than willing to dare. At this point, it was not logic that compelled her. It was something else—something that he had always trained her not to acknowledge, something that made her a whole lot more like him.

She dropped downward out of the Killer's grip, swept the his legs, and grabbed the poker from its stand on the hearth. While he was still getting up, she swung at his throat with all her might and ended up breaking all of the metacarpals in the hand he used as a shield.

"I've come here for a conversation, *Father*," she announced, brandishing the iron rod. "And I intend to have the last word."

To her surprise, the Killer dove away from her, toward the bed. She watched him perplexedly as he frantically searched for something underneath it. Whatever he was looking for under there was something powerful, maybe a gun, because he gave no reaction as she brought the broad side of the poker down on his ankle. His pain management would keep him from feeling the broken bones until a more convenient time. She raised the poker again, looking for a bunch of nerves to damage that might cause convulsions. That would get his attention.

Finally, with a flamboyant flourish, the Killer proudly presented his secret weapon. It was a tape player.

He pressed play, and said calmly and authoritatively, "Bow."

As the first few lines of the Song danced on the air, the Agent felt her knees going weak. She backed away, wondering if he could really reclaim her so easily.

"There's my girl," David said, watching her intently. "Don't fight it. Just take it like a good soldier."

Crumbling onto the hearth, the Agent threw the poker toward the wall opposite the door to get it out of the Killer's reach. This was not necessary, though, because David was an artist. He knew the most efficient ways to kill, but he was—when it came down to it—a slave to style and drama. He had created Bathsheba. So, in this execution, he could not simply stop her life; he had to unmake her. He had breathed life into her once upon a time, and now, he had to crush it out of her. The Agent decided she would use that against him.

As the Song drained her strength, David pinned her on her back by the fireplace. Still struggling feebly, she looked around for anything she could use as a weapon. The smell of burning hair filled her nostrils as the fire singed the tip of her ponytail. It was bitter—bitter like myrrh. And the bitterness gave her strength.

"I had higher hopes for you," the Killer whispered.

"Like I had for my brother," she grunted, grabbing a handful of live coals from the fireplace and shoving them into his face.

He recoiled, only lightening his grip for an instant, but it was enough. The Agent drew her legs up and kicked him in the abdomen, breaking a couple of ribs from the sound of it. He flew backward into the wall and collapsed onto the floor as the Agent put out the fire on her ponytail and retrieved the poker.

David rose to his feet, drawing hoarse, uneven breaths.

He turned up his recording of the Song, looked the Agent directly in the eyes, and commanded her, "*Bow!*"

"No, *you* bow!"

The Agent was angry—angry about her brother, angry about her mission, angry about the person she had become. And the anger felt good. A primal scream flew from her mouth as she swung the poker again. She broke one of the Killer's knees, and when he fell to the floor, she shattered his dominant wrist. The tape player flew from his grip, and she heard it clatter onto the tiled hearth.

After that, she saw nothing but her target, and she desired nothing but to shatter him in the way that she had been shattered. So, although David tossed makeshift weapons at her as he side-crawled toward the door, she did not stop swinging.

In the hallway, he reached under a piece of furniture and pulled a gun, which she immediately knocked out of his hands. The best chance the Killer had at winning this fight was in avoiding physical contact with the Agent, but now he had no more surprise weapons on this floor of the house and his back was to the stairs.

The next time she swung at him, he grabbed the poker and, in so doing, earned himself a kick in the face. He held on, though, and used the poker to pull the Agent off-balance. The weapon sailed from her grip, skipped down the stairs, and landed in the entryway. She fell into the Killer, and they plummeted downward together. During their tumble down the stairs, the Killer remained on the defensive because the Agent pursued him unrelentingly.

Kiddo moved inside of her, perhaps expressing discontent at being jostled around in such a manner.

"Sorry, Kiddo," she whispered, patting the belly bump. "Mama and Father are just having a little chat. I promise it'll be over soon."

The Killer pulled himself up using the banister and began hobbling down the last few steps in a frantic attempt to reach his next mid-range weapon. In the dark of the stairwell, his makeshift depth perception was useless, and even though he had managed to stay on his feet most of the way, he tripped off of the last step, having believed that it was the ground floor. The Agent's carpet trick had worked! She retrieved the poker.

The phantom aroma of myrrh hung in the air around her. Now, she finally understood.

She swung at the Killer again and again, and his blocks became slower and sloppier. One well-placed blow to the head would have ended it all. But he had made her to become her opponent, and how well she did it! How well she *liked* it! She did not want to stop.

The Killer, having realized that he was not going to reach the hiding places of any of his other emergency weapons, resorted to the next best thing.

He caught her in a double underhook and quoted the third verse of her Song in a wheezy, pained voice, "Wives secure my legacy—"

"But beauty will be my ruin," she quoted back at him, shoving her knee into his injured ribs and sending him crumbling to the floor. "She thinks she's so forbidden. Oh, honestly! She knows no power!"

Now, the Killer abandoned all attempts to control his protégé and began to crawl toward the front door. The Agent dove onto him and wrestled him onto his back.

As it had become second nature for her to do, she caught his neck between her thighs and began to squeeze. His sinewy shoulders were trapped beneath her shins, and she could feel the rest of his body vibrating with rage and panic. His shallow, uneven breaths were even shallower now, and rapider. His body—at least the Agent thought it was his body—squirmed under her, begging wordlessly for her to allow him to breathe. Still, she squeezed.

"Now you know how it feels," she growled.

"Lenci?"

Her heart skipped a beat. She looked up to see Karthik standing just inside of the open front door. She looked for a place to put the poker, as if that were the most incriminating weapon in the room. She had nowhere to put it.

"Lenci," he said again, his voice shaking. "D—don't d–do this."

"I tried to spare you the trouble," she told him, struggling to keep her grip on the Killer's sweat-slicked neck. "But you wanted to *help*."

Karthik was breathing incredibly fast. He was frightened because he had never imagined that his friend could be capable of something like this.

"I kn—now," he said, crossing his arms to hide his trembling hands. "But I know that you're better than this. I *know* that you are! You d–don't have to d—do it."

"Yes, I do," she grunted.

"N—no!" Karthik exclaimed, shaking even harder. "You have a *choice*!"

"Go home, Ethan."

He gulped, probably wondering how quickly the Agent could shift targets. "I d—don't believe that you're a killer."

"I am only what *he* made me to be."

Animal, slave, weapon. She had been made to destroy life, and if that was all she could do, she would do it for a good reason. She could no longer smell the phantom fragrance of the myrrh, but she knew it was there, intoxicatingly thick in her lungs. It caused her throat to tighten, even as her thigh muscles continued to constrict.

Karthik could not stop her, and yet he could not turn away.

"Lenci? Lenci!"

What is necessary must never be lamented. The squirming beneath the

Agent increased in intensity and speed, and Karthik continued to protest.

She had feared for so long, not understanding that she had had the power to tear through the Killer like he was tissue paper. Now, though, she was beginning to realize that perhaps the Killer had not been her true opponent all that time. She had been her only opponent, preventing herself from reaching her true potential because of a misplaced desire for affirmation and a fear that she had blown out of proportion.

David had been still for nearly thirty seconds and counting, but the squirming beneath her continued. Horror and shame flooded the Agent as she realized that it was *Kiddo*, then, who joined in Karthik's plea for her to choose a different way—a way that led to life. The Agent stopped squeezing immediately.

"I will not *be* you," she whispered to the Killer.

He was unconscious and so did not respond. She gave his face one last smack for good measure and set about getting to her feet. With a sigh of relief, Karthik moved forward to offer her a hand, but she declined. As she jerked upright, there came a *SNAP*, and she sank back to her knees over the Killer's body.

All was still.

In the stillness, previously compartmentalized sensations trickled into the Agent's awareness. The poker was cool and soothing in her left hand. But her right hand, the hand that she had used to grab the live coals, was blistering. She could not see it, but she could feel the bubbly skin on her palms screaming at the floor about personal space. The insides of her thighs were wet, probably from the Killer's sweat and saliva.

"What happened?" Karthik asked in a voice barely above a whisper.

She groaned in response. Something was wrong. She hadn't twisted the Killer's neck, so she shouldn't have heard a snap. Beneath her, she could feel his chest moving up and down shakily. Leaning forward onto her good hand, she looked down to discover that a black fluid had pooled around the Killer's neck and head.

"Oh, no," she said, feeling the insides of her thighs.

That fluid had come from her womb. Something was very, very wrong.

"Come on," Karthik said, moving forward. "Let's get out of here."

To the Agent's trained ear, a sound very much like that of a muffled gunshot pierced the silence. Instinctively, she thrust the poker backward into the thigh of the Killer. He didn't move or cry out, but his face twitched into a pained expression. He was still unconscious, much like poor Karthik, who was now balled up on the floor with a hand over his bleeding abdomen.

"What is going on here?"

An older woman with a gun stepped out of the shadows on their right. She must have entered the house through the back door.

The Agent examined the dull-skinned woman with the tight, silvery bun and pointed nose. This was not Mrs. Miller. No, she recognized the prim, tight lips and disdainful gaze, although she had least expected to see them outside of Chile.

"Hello, Faye," she said.

"You may call me 'Assistant Vice,'" Faye the Eugenist Witch responded curtly.

"Figures," the Agent said. "But only the assistant because the WCE tenets state that the Vice can't be female. You actually run the show. Am I right?"

The Assistant Vice wrinkled her nose, which the Agent figured was her version of a smile or nod. Faye the Eugenist Witch was apparently above answering questions with words.

"So, you are an Amphibian, I'm guessing," the Assistant Vice said, "judging by your demonstrated lethal capability. What is your symbol?"

"He called me Bathsheba."

"The name of a *woman!*" The Assistant Vice scoffed. "But what happened to the animal you were assigned by the WCE? Don't you have a tattoo under those ragged clothes?"

The Agent grinned impishly. "If you wanted to get me undressed, all you had to do was ask."

"With a body like yours," the Assistant Vice replied with a lascivious stare, "I would not stop to ask permission—tenets aside, of course, and carnal pleasures a-center."

The Agent's cheeky joke had backfired on her. She had known too many of that kind: powerful, eugenist, and of experimental taste.

The Assistant Vice pursed her thin lips. "Now, explain what you are doing to my lover."

"I guess Errol doesn't know you're here," the Agent said.

"Errol and I married for political power, but David gives me what Errol can't." The Assistant Vice chuckled. "In any case, Errol seems fine entertaining Mrs. Miller on our yacht while I am on business here."

The Agent could not comprehend the complicated lives of people with too much power. She rubbed her belly painstakingly, finding herself surprisingly short of breath.

The Assistant Vice examined her for a moment, then said, "You are the one I have been told about."

"Not from *him*, I'm imagining."

The Assistant Vice's nose wrinkled again. "David would be the last to tell me of *another* of his indiscretions, especially with a Class 4 or whatever you are. Last thing this world needs is another subber."

The Agent bristled at that ugly word but remained silent.

The Assistant Vice continued, "In any case, I wouldn't need him to confess. I have ears pretty much everywhere nowadays."

"I figured as much. Own a pizza joint?"

"I own a lot of places—and people."

"Not me."

The Agent said it before she'd had time to think about the consequences. But after the words were out, the truth of her statement really began to sink in.

"No?" The Assistant Vice's mouth turned up on one side.

"You think the Killer didn't try to use my Song to defend himself?" the Agent asked. "My Song is no longer of any effect."

"You're cheeky for a lower-class female perched atop the body of a Class 1 woman's lover, especially when said woman is holding a gun."

The Agent gave a wry chuckle, looking her interlocutor up and down to see just how serious she was about using the gun. The safety was off, and her finger was firmly on the trigger.

"Listen," the Agent said, "I'd love to stay and chat, but David's barely got a rat's breath left in him, and my asset's bleeding out all over the floor. What do you say we table this discussion for a more advantageous time?"

"You're not going anywhere until you answer for this class violation." The Assistant Vice readjusted her grip on her weapon. "You seduced a Class 1 man!"

The Agent sighed and patted her belly to see if Kiddo would respond.

"Maybe he seduced *me*," she said absently.

"I'll speak for Mrs. Miller in reminding you that a man is never at fault for a woman's wiles, Agentess, much less a female of a lower class. As the Assistant Vice—"

Before Faye could lecture the Agent on the WCE tenets, she was interrupted by the cocking of a very large shotgun from somewhere in the shadows behind her.

"Enough with the eugenist, misogynistic pontificating, already!" Racky said, flourishing Bambina Extraordinaire. "I'm taking my Circus and her asset out the front door. And when we are gone, you can deal with your cheater-pig lover and spring his fur baby from the pound across the way."

"Young lady, how dare you—"

A swift, hard swat across the face with the butt of Bambina Extraordinaire was enough to render the Assistant Vice unconscious.

"I hate sassy, evil broads," Racky said, bending over the Assistant Vice's body disgustedly.

"This one had a mouth on her, too," Lenci muttered, struggling to her feet. "Just yammered away like she didn't even *want* to kill me."

"Or, she wanted to talk you to death."

"Damn near succeeded, too. I can't stand that Neo-Eugenic crap."

"Me neither." Then, motioning to her pre-teammate's ripped clothing, ratty, wild hair, and the black streaks running down her legs, Racky asked, "You okay, Circus?"

"Been better," she said. "We need to get Karthik to the hospital."

"Holy damnation!" Racky exclaimed, stepping over the pool of blood by his body. "I was just parking around the corner. I told him to wait *outside* in case you came running out of the house and needed him to lead you to the car."

"Yeah, well, he kept me from doing something I probably would've regretted."

The two women pulled Karthik to his feet and shared his weight. Lenci's knees nearly buckled on the way down the porch steps, but she clenched her thighs and sturdied them for his sake.

"'Probably would have?' You mean, you didn't even kill the Killer's nasty behind?"

"Where's your car, Racky?"

"Out this way, on the left."

Racky and Lenci got Karthik to the car and laid him in the back seat. Lenci sat in front but twisted around to keep an eye on him.

"Better not bleed all over the seats, Buttface," she told him. "Someone has to clean them, and it's *not* going to be me."

"Or me," Racky tossed in as she buckled her seat belt.

"Who you calling Buttface, Big Butt?" he replied weakly.

"Don't die on me and I'll consider sticking around. You know, to hang out. Deal?"

"Deal," he wheezed.

Lenci cradled her crispy hand, palm up, close to her chest. It hurt enough, but even worse: a throbbing had begun in her lower regions.

"Hold on, you two," Racky said, punching the gas pedal. "There's a hospital a kilometer away from here. And a good thing, too. You don't look so hot."

Lenci gripped her abdomen. "I don't feel so hot. I think—I think Kiddo is trying to make an early debut. Doesn't he or she know we're never early for anything? Subclass timing, right?"

Her laugh was gravelly and pained.

"It's Kiddo's Class 1 genes coming into play," Racky responded, accelerating through a yellow light. "He or she has a whole life to get it right, though."

Lenci's next laugh was more like a gasp. "Last time I saw Karthik, he was spooning a grizzly bear next to the Killer's garage. How'd he find *you*?"

"I happened to be driving by, and he jumped into the car."

"Happened to be driving by?"

Racky kept her eyes on the road and answered the real question Lenci was asking.

"Your 'asset' picked the tracking device that used to be in your leg out of the trash of the outhouse across the street from the restaurant you ate at. I drove up here to meet him, which was lucky for *both* of your behinds, if you ask me."

"I didn't."

"He's a good one, girl," Racky said. "His first thought was of you, even after waking up with a headache on the restroom floor. When he messaged me, his only priority was to make sure *you* would be safe tonight."

Lenci glanced back at Karthik lying across the back seat. His breathing had grown shallow, and his face was drenched with sweat. She closed her eyes and cradled her burnt hand against her chest once again.

Racky rounded the last corner far too quickly and drove over the tip of a traffic island to get to the emergency room drop-off area. Lenci jumped out of the car before it had come to a complete stop.

"Come on, Karthik," she said, pulling him out of the car. "Every adventurous path runs through the hospital at some point, so don't make a stink about it. And don't you go back on our deal now."

He was murmuring indistinctly, whether to himself or to her she was not sure. She slung his right arm around her shoulders and half-dragged him toward the doors of the emergency room. Racky leaned on the car horn until a group of ER nurses came to the door to see what all the racket was about.

Racky the Racket. Lenci chuckled, patting Karthik's shoulder with her non-crispy hand. Suddenly, she became aware of the warmth between their bodies—the remnant of a closeness that she could only remember having experienced once, recently. It was the warmth of an authentic intimacy, the replica of which she had known only as a longing during her time with the Killer.

A wave of dizziness came over her, and the intense pressure in her abdomen became pain.

"Too early," Lenci breathed, grasping her belly bump. "Stay inside for Mama, Kiddo. Just stay inside."

One nurse grabbed Lenci's blood-covered shoulder. "Ma'am, can you tell me where you've been injured?"

Lenci swatted her hand off.

"Take him, *first!*" she ordered, pushing Karthik into the arms of the nurse. "He's got a gunshot wound to the left lower quadrant of his abdomen. And he's been bleeding for about ten minutes. Damn it, woman, don't you have a stretcher or something?"

The nurse immediately barked out orders to her team. A gurney appeared, and Karthik was lifted onto it. As the nurses rolled him away, Lenci pushed down the sense of déjà vu and the fear of abandonment that rose within her.

"Kiddo's too early," she told the nurse who had greeted her, the First Nurse.

She patted her belly bump and doubled over. Karthik was gone, but for some reason, that pesky pain would not go away. The pain was not a continuous pain but one that came in terrible, overwhelmingly strong waves.

"I told him or her to stay, but—well, I never listened to anybody either. Rambunctious Kiddo," she gasped.

A wheelchair appeared out of nowhere. The Agent sat in it calmly. As soon as she was rolling into the hospital, Racky's car zoomed off into the parking structure. The wheelchair went *BUMP* *THUMP*. Then white light and white coats and white ceilings and white floors and white sheets and white walls bombarded Lenci and thrust her into an uncomfortable place between past and future that wasn't quite present.

The night she had lost her handler was the second worst night of her life. She could not bear the thought of losing Karthik, too.

"I told him not to come," Lenci murmured.

"You need to focus, now," came the voice of the First Nurse. "'Kiddo' won't have a chance if you don't pull yourself together and get into the right frame of mind."

At the mention of a mission for which she needed to be strong, the Agent felt a new resolve.

Come, Bathsheba

The nurse smiled as her patient took a deep breath and seemed to engage the task at hand. A group of strong hands lifted the Agent onto the table and began to undress her. The nurses wanted to give her an epidural, but they'd have to get her out of the gym shorts first. She doubted that she would see them again. It was unfortunate to lose perfectly good shorts, but she still had a strong conviction that it would have been harder to strangle David while wearing a skirt.

"Look at the black streaks on her legs."

"The baby's in distress. We need to work fast."

"Make sure there's an incubator ready to go in the premie unit."

"Prep the epidural!"

"The contractions are pretty close together. I don't know if we've got time for that."

Where was Bathsheba, anyway? The Agent did not generally feel pain, but the pain in her pelvic region was stubborn and escalating. And it was a pain unlike any she had ever felt before, intensified by the fact that poor, lovely, sincere Karthik was in some other room on a surgeon's table because she had failed to protect him.

Lenci never should have gone to Diablo and endangered her whole family. Because of her return, her brother would never talk to her again. And now her mother was going to miss the birth of her first grandchild, a birth that Kiddo might not even survive.

Come, Bathsheba

"Doctor, it's too late for the epidural," another nurse gasped. "The baby's crowning!"

299

The doctor, a tired-looking blond woman who had just entered the room, cried out, "Ma'am, you need to push now!"

The Agent had been alone in practically every endeavor she had truly cared about, but this would, by far, prove to be the most difficult. And Bathsheba was nowhere to be found.

"Push, now," the First Nurse encouraged her. "Push for Kiddo."

"Poor, poor Karthik," the Agent murmured.

Then, succumbing to the pain, she gripped the sides of the hospital bed and wailed, "Bathsheba, you *coward*!"

The world rushed and whirled around her. She felt and heard so many things that she experienced none of them. She knew only the emptiness of the growing loss that consumed her life. She was soon to be completely alone.

"I got it!" the First Nurse said in triumph. "It's a—it's a—"

The Agent had saved the revelation of Kiddo's sex for the day of his or her birth. She craned her neck to hear the nurse's next words over the noise of the crowded delivery room. But the nurse stopped short and looked up at the doctor, who was standing at the Agent's side.

"What are you doing?" the nurse asked.

Everything had already been blurry before, but the Agent noticed that her eyelids were becoming quite heavy. She opened her eyes wide and looked first at the IV that was in her arm, then up at the doctor who had just turned up her meds.

"It's just a little pain-killer," the doctor said. "Mind your business, nurse."

The nurse stood up straight, clinging tightly to the little, red body that had just entered the world. "At that dosage, you'll kill her. That's too high!"

"Kind of the point," the doctor said dryly, pulling out a gun and firing two silenced shots into the nurse's heart.

She then finished off the rest of the staff in the room, one shot each.

The Agent attempted to remove the IV from her arm, but the room was wiped away from her eyes like a mess of tears into a tissue. Darkness met her as an old friend with open arms. She beat it back with sloppy hands, knowing that this was a fight she would ultimately lose.

Through the darkness, she heard the sound of shuffling feet and the voices of men.

"Hinny, it's still alive!" one of them exclaimed.

"Not surprising, considering what the mother was rumored to

be," the doctor's voice replied. "We may yet be able to use that to our advantage. Now, clean up this mess."

***

Racky pulled into the first parking spot she'd found, which was actually two spots that she parked across diagonally. She had always hated those spots with the lines. And she hated whoever had come up with the idea for them, too.

Circling around to the trunk to get her extra cash, she began brainstorming about where she could buy get-well presents for Karthik and a gold chain for the baby. She figured Lenci probably wouldn't like it if she bought a chain from a pawnshop. The hospital gift shop would have to do. She hoped they'd have eighteen-karat gold.

She froze upon hearing the safety being switched off of a gun. She gripped the door of the trunk with both hands to keep them in plain sight.

"Okay, take it easy, Theresa," she grumbled. "But please try to remember that it was for a good cause. Theresa?"

"Guess again," a gruff, male voice said.

Strong hands shoved her into the trunk and slammed it shut.

"Ey!" Racky pounded on the side of the trunk that was closest to the cabin of the car.

The vehicle started up.

"Ey!" she shouted again. "Let me out of here, you degenerate!"

A hole appeared in the wall of the trunk beside her head, then another appeared out the back of the trunk. Apparently, her abductor was in the type of mood one had to be in to use a gunshot to tell her to be quiet. So, she was quiet. But as the car started to move, she wriggled toward the far side of the trunk where she kept Bambina Extraordinaire. When that guy opened the trunk, he would be in for the surprise of his life—the last surprise of his life.

Chapter 35

WHEN THE AGENT OPENED her eyes, she was accosted by the morning light coming in through the window.

"The shades!" she cried to anyone who might be around. "Please, pull the shades—my eyes."

The light dimmed, and she sensed someone sitting down in a chair next to the bed. She took a deep breath, which was tinged faintly with the aroma of familiar spices. After listening to the breathing of the older woman for a couple of seconds, Lenci knew who this visitor was.

"Auntie Preeti," she whispered. "When did you arrive?"

"Two days ago," came the voice of her dear family friend. "James got a call about Karthik, so I came as soon as I could. It wasn't until I got here and he was out of surgery, that I found out about you. They messed up your last name, though."

"Hm." Lenci squinted, trying to look around the room. "Is my mom here?"

"She wanted to be," Auntie Preeti said. "But your brother could not be left alone in his condition, you understand."

"I understand," she replied.

It was better that they stayed away from her. She did not want any more harm to come to them.

Auntie Preeti's cold, frail hand slipped into hers and squeezed. "I'm ready to report the incompetent hospital staff for overdosing you. Karthik told me how the nurses found you hooked up at such a high dosage. It's a miracle you survived!"

At the mention of the near-overdose, the Agent's eyes popped open. She gasped in pain and shut them immediately, but her mind was racing, trying to put all of the pieces together.

Auntie Preeti smoothed Lenci's bedclothes and continued, "I'm sorry to hear about the false pregnancy, dear. One might have liked to have a new life to brighten this tragic time. And you are so young to have trouble with fibroids."

"Pregnancy was real," Lenci murmured. "Birth was premature, but I heard them say it: my baby is alive."

She felt Auntie Preeti's hand on her forehead. "You've had a stressful past few days, girl. Don't upset yourself now."

"No!" Lenci said, weakly banging her fist on the side of the bed. "They took my Kiddo, but he or she is still alive! I heard them."

"Who, dear?" Auntie Preeti sounded accommodating but tired.

"There was this blond lady doctor with a haggard face, about one point seven meters tall, and maybe sixty kilos, and—and—some other people."

The Agent knew she couldn't disclose these things to a civilian. Not if she cared at all about Auntie Preeti's wellbeing. In any case, it was probably for the best that her family would be shielded from the severity of this loss. She would have liked to shield herself from it.

"You have always been very strong, Lenci," Auntie Preeti whispered. "This will not best you."

Those words struck a part of the Agent that could not be shielded, and she began to weep.

"I thought I'd changed," she sobbed. "But I couldn't—not even for my Kiddo! I could not stop being what I am."

Animal, slave, weapon—what she had been made to be. *Why couldn't there have been another way?*

"There, there, girl," Auntie Preeti said, caressing her face and wiping the tears from her cheeks. "Our Lenci. Our precious Lenci."

Another hand fell on her shoulder. She did not need to open her eyes to know whose hand it was. Even if she hadn't heard him breathing beside her, she would have known that it was Preeti's son.

"Don't look at me," she said, turning her face away from him.

She had heard him walk into the room, shuffling with the aid of a walker. This was the result of her being what she had been made to be—and Karthik was lucky. Others ended up like Lorenzo or, worse, like Samir Bourghin. It was foolish to have believed that she could lead a normal life with friends and family. It was selfish to have believed that.

And now her Kiddo, the child with whom she had been entrusted, was in the hands of her enemies.

"We're here for you," Karthik said.

He was still looking at her. She was sure of that. The scraping of a chair ensued and a soft thump.

After a moment of silence, he tried to ease the tension in the room with a little humor. "They let my mom see you because you were checked in as 'Valencia Thomas.' I guess that's the privileged life of the naturally unclassified yet class-ambiguous individual. Haha?"

"I told them I was your mother," Auntie Preeti said, relishing the craftiness of the scheme. "They didn't even check my ID."

The Agent smiled wryly. "Did you slip in behind her, Karthik? Or did you tell them you were a Thomas, too?"

"Life partner," he said very seriously. "And then, yes, I slipped in behind my mom."

A small chuckle escaped from the Agent. She squinted to get a glimpse of her friend. He was propped up in his chair with a pillow. His shoulders were slightly hunched to protect the stitches in his abdomen. He was clearly in pain, but when he saw her looking at him, he smiled. She closed her eyes again.

Their conversation for the rest of the day was full of jokes and laughter. Karthik and his mother limped around the subject of the birth to avoid upsetting Lenci. She knew that they did this out of love for her, hoping that they could help her to have some constancy in relationship, even when her entire world was in smithereens once again.

She appreciated their efforts, but her focus was divided. On the one hand, they were her family, the only good and beautiful thing left in Lenci's world. On the other hand, she had made Kiddo a promise that she would make sure he or she was safe. And now Kiddo was in the custody of WCE agents. The Agent could not abide the thought.

At last, visiting hours were over. Karthik, preparing to head back to his own room in Wound Care, hugged his mom and then turned to his friend. Since the sun had set and the only light in the room came from the hallway, she was able to meet his gaze.

"About what happened," he said, careful not to say too much with his mother there, "I still believe that you can be more than what circumstances and bad people try to force you to be."

"You can say that, even after seeing me in action?" she asked.

"Well, yeah." He shifted uneasily. "I mean, I *saw* you make a choice that night. It seemed hard for you to make that choice, but you did it."

Yes, she supposed that was true. She had made a choice against the purpose for which she had been primed, a choice *not* to become her opponent or to operate as he would, even when it would have been most advantageous for her to do so. But had she made the *right* choice? The Killer was still at large, and he would most likely be hunting for her as soon as he recovered. Her family was heartbroken and divided. And her Kiddo was in danger. If she had won any victory at all for herself, she had lost everything else.

Karthik's hand slipping into hers summoned the Agent back from the depths. "Plus, I know at least one thing that you are that the Killer d—didn't make you become."

She regarded him amusedly. "What's that?"

"You're l–loved. That guy n—never l—loved you. But I—mean, our *family* loves you. And that's got to be worth something."

"You're right. It is," Lenci said, holding out her pinky for him to link. "You all are so precious to me."

"Wow." He laughed, linking her pinky. "Mom, did you see that? She just told me I'm right. Got something to record with? I want this moment documented, so I can remember it forever."

Auntie Preeti smiled silently and did not take her eyes off of Lenci.

"Good night, Lenci," Karthik said. "I stuck to the deal and survived. What do you say we have breakfast tomorrow? You know, hang out?"

"Sounds like a plan," she grinned. "Goodbye, Karthik."

He shyly kissed her on the cheek and gave her one last giddy glance before wheeling his walker out the door. A tiny pang shook the Agent's heart, but she reminded herself that she had been trained to identify and exploit the weaknesses of others. Karthik could be no exception in that respect, especially when she would always know what his greatest weakness was.

"I should go as well before these nurses kick me out," Auntie Preeti said.

"Are you staying near here?" the Agent asked.

Auntie Preeti grunted as she rose to her feet. "The hotel across the street. Let me hug you, Valencia."

They embraced, and the young woman inhaled deeply. She did not know when she would have another opportunity to take in that love.

"Promise me that you will come back for him," Auntie Preeti whispered. "He has always been there for you, when you allowed it."

"What?" The Agent tried to empty her voice to sound innocent and sincere, but she knew that her friend's mother was not fooled.

Auntie Preeti pulled back and looked her in the face. "My son is blinded by what he wants to see, by love. I love you, too, but a child cannot fool a woman who raised her. Now, if you need to go, take care of all that you need to. But then you come back for him, girl. You know that you need each other."

The Agent had thoroughly enjoyed her stay with the Wilsons and the Changs. Karthik's friendship had majorly contributed to her enjoyment. So, she figured that—if she survived long enough—it would not be too much of a burden to look in on him the next time she was in Diablo.

"Okay," Lenci said. "I promise."

Auntie Preeti smiled. "Goodbye, our Lenci."

"Goodbye, Auntie Preeti," she replied, trying to ignore the tugging inside of her chest.

Their parting was slow and tender. Auntie Preeti walked to the door and looked back just once. Then, she went out and was gone.

As soon as the door clicked shut, Lenci burst into tears. She had not meant for the mission to end this way. She had not meant for anyone to get hurt, least of all her family and Kiddo.

A tightness settled in her chest, and a wave overtook her. Her breath was crushed to nothing, and a cold terror penetrated to her bones. However, as she slowly sank into the depths, her sobbing tapered off. The scent of myrrh settled around her, filling her lungs with its bitter, spicy aroma.

"Poor, poor Lenci," the Agent said consolingly. "You bind yourself with promises faster than you can begin to make good on them."

She slung her feet over the side of the bed. "But your Karthik was right about one thing: you made a *choice*."

That would be useful later—she was quite certain—since she was not what she had been made to be, nor was she what others perceived her to be. In fact, she was not even the person she had once been but someone else entirely.

Epilogue

THREE WEEKS LATER, IN THE midwestern district of Corpus, Racky sat across from Blair in the conference room at the Cooperative FBI headquarters. While Blair worked off of a holographic screen, Racky was still using the laptop SSI had given her for the Diablo mission. New equipment was on the way, but HR was slow about assigning new equipment, especially given that Racky's background check had raised a few red flags.

"And you were just waiting in there with your shotgun when the WCE agent opened the trunk?" Blair asked incredulously.

"Gunned him down like he was a rabid dog," Racky said without looking up from her screen, "and took his cyanide tooth, so I could study the spring-loaded ejectors."

"Any idea why he wanted you?"

"Nope. And the only reason I knew he was WCE was because of the cyanide tooth."

Blair side-glanced her. "Well, I'm glad you're okay."

Turning on the holodevice that was built into the table, she said, "I think I might know at least one reason why the WCE was after you. Take a look at this."

A large 3D image of a collapsed building popped up out of the table. The building, which must have been at least three stories high at one point, was completely leveled.

Racky's eyes flickered briefly to the image, then back to her laptop. "Is that Dr. Williams' office?"

"Yeah, good eye," Blair said. "Did you ever successfully encrypt Lenci's medical records?"

"Yes, but I didn't see much."

Blair continued, "We searched the ruins. All of the computers were missing."

"They wanted me to decrypt her files," Racky said quietly.

"Because you're the only one in the world that can do it."

"Damn straight." She double-clicked emphatically. "And, they can kiss my subclass buns of steel if they think that I would—"

She froze, her eyes locked on the screen of her laptop. "I knew it!"

Blair crossed her arms and waited for the big reveal.

"Remember how I hacked into the Forsythe Memorial Hospital cloud to take a look at the security recordings and see if I could get an ID on the people who took Lenci's baby?"

"You're still going on about that?" Blair asked. "You know that the hospital records say that she had a melon-sized fibroid removed that night, right?"

"That's the WCE's eugenist humor coming through," Racky replied. "They tampered with the records. I had a baby once. I know pregnancy cravings and labor when I see them. Plus, her face was fat."

Blair looked at her skeptically.

"Look here!" Racky turned the computer screen toward her. "Right here!"

Blair leaned over the table to get a better look. In the recording, there was a group of people lifting an incubator into the back of a truck. Inside it was a small lump.

"Can you make it bigger?" she said, squinting.

"It will take some time to clean it up," Racky replied. "They corrupted some of the data by imposing footage of a garbage run over it. For now, it will just have to be grainy. Now, see that blond lady at the front? She matches Karthik's report of Lenci's description of the doctor who was in the delivery room!"

"The doctor that the hospital said never existed?"

"That same one," Racky said, sucking her teeth.

Blair's eyes grew mournful, and her thin lips pressed into a grim line.

"Okay, so, Lenci had a baby," she sighed, at last. "The WCE was not transporting a fibroid in an incubator. But what would the WCE want with Lenci's baby?"

"I can't think of anything good," Racky said, "You would think they just would have left him or her for dead, but they used an incubator. It's like they *wanted* to keep the kid alive."

"I guess I should be glad since that's my half-sibling," Blair said, "or worried."

After a respectful pause, Racky clicked her mouse a couple of times. "Let's see if I can get this picture of the license plate cleaned up. Maybe we will get a lead."

Blair straightened up.

"I can't believe Theresa isn't here busting her butt alongside you," she said. "I thought she'd take my threat about sending her to prison more seriously."

"We know that you need us too much for that," Racky said. "But don't get bent out of shape. She's hard at work. Karthik gave her a sample of Lenci's blood, and she's testing it."

"Oh." Blair sat on the table beside her. "He finally decided to turn her in, hey?"

Racky kept her gaze on the screen. "He was fuzzy in the brain and vexed because she disappeared when SSI collapsed."

"I pretty much never find her absence terribly upsetting," Theresa said, trudging into the room. "But I guess you already knew that."

"Find anything?" Racky asked hopefully.

Theresa nodded. "The blood test is intriguing."

"Did you find an untainted record to compare the DNA?" Blair asked.

"No, but Lenci's friend Ethan gave us a lock of her hair from when they made some kind of dumb kid pact." Theresa yawned, then looked at her nails. "In any case, the DNA matches, but the weird thing is that her blood is chock full of those weapon-grade nanobots—kind of like the not-Reece body."

"So, it *is* our Lenci!" Racky beamed.

Blair snatched the report from Theresa and stared at it incredulously. "But those nanobots are designed to kill. How is she still alive?"

"Maybe they got turned off," Racky suggested.

"Not likely," Theresa said, "but I would need a live blood sample to confirm exactly what's going on."

Racky shook her head. "Someone tried to kill her."

"Understandable." Theresa shrugged.

"But she survived," Racky continued, "and now she's pretending that she's not herself?"

"Or she doesn't know she's herself," Theresa said matter-of-factly. "She's kind of an idiot."

Blair pensively leafed through the pages of Theresa's report. "The fact that she survived a nanobot assassination attempt *is* pretty impressive. I can also see how the WCE would want to investigate whether the nanobots in Lenci's bloodstream were passed to the baby. The implications of an event like that could be huge!"

"Wait, so there *was* a baby after all?" Theresa scratched her head. "What about the tumor?"

"It's like she didn't even want to kill her," Racky whispered.

"What?"

"When Lenci ran into the Assistant Vice of the WCE, that hellion of a lady started monologuing, even though she could have killed Lenci on the spot. But maybe the plan wasn't originally to kill her," Racky said. "Maybe she wanted to take Lenci but later decided the baby was just as valuable, or more!"

Blair nodded. "And the murder attempt at the hospital was obviously made in spite. Since Lenci survived, though, we have to assume she's still a target—either for murder or experimentation. I mean, surviving a nanobot assassination attempt is unheard of. I could imagine there being some real value in experimenting on Lenci as well."

She stood up and continued as she headed for the door, "Now that Ms. Chang has cut herself off from her family, that baby is the only flesh and blood she has left. We've got to find that kid. And wherever the kid is, the mother won't be far behind."

"Oh, come on, guys!" Theresa exclaimed. "SSI doesn't even exist anymore. What do we care if it's the real Lenci or if the WCE has her kid?"

Blair turned around in the doorway. "The WCE has the best technology and the most advanced weaponry in the world, and they are making a *massive* move to extinguish any last resistance all over the States and abroad. So, if they're interested in Valencia Chang and her child, then the Cooperative FBI is, too. This is not about friendship, Theresa. This is war."

"But—"

"No 'buts,' or I'll send you to prison." She winked. "Now, make sure to ask Dr. Bourghin for whatever notes and materials are in Agent Bourghin's study. And Racky—"

Racky stood at attention, but she could not contain herself.

"I have a suggestion for another team member!" she burst out.

Blair sighed. "Who?"

"Someone who knows Lenci better than anyone, even better than Agent Bourghin did. His mom was just admitted to hospice care, and he's the primary caregiver. But I know that he will want to get in on this whenever he's back to work."

"Racky, this is the Cooperative FBI. We can't just recruit random people."

"No, no, he's not random!" Racky insisted. "He is an experienced law enforcement officer as well as a very intelligent person, and he grew up with Lenci. He told me he was able to use his knowledge of Lenci's preferences and tendencies to predict her movement within the Forsythe district down to the exact street she was on!"

"Well," Blair replied. "This hunt has an area much larger than the district of Forsythe. But I guess it wouldn't hurt to interview him."

"Ey!" Racky squawked gleefully. "In that case, you should know: it's Lieutenant K. Ethan-James Wilson."

Blair grinned. "Great. Call him and say everything necessary to convince him that he'll be serving his country by helping us to track down Ms. Chang."

When the door shut behind her, Theresa groaned. "At this rate, we'll never be rid of Lenci!"

Racky nodded excitedly. "Let's go get our Circus!"

CPSIA information can be obtained
at www.ICGtesting.com
Printed in the USA
BVHW082213051221
623306BV00005B/84